DARWEN ARKWRIGHT

WRITTEN
BY

A. J. HARTLEY

ILLUSTRATED BY
EMILY OSBORNE

AND

THE

PEREGRINE PACT

Darwen Arkwright and the Peregrine Pact

RAZORBILL

Published by the Penguin Group

Penguin Young Readers Group

345 Hudson Street, New York, New York 10014, U.S.A.

Penguin Group (USA) Inc., 375 Hudson Street, New York, New York 10014, U.S.A.

Penguin Group (Canada), 90 Eglinton Avenue East, Suite 700, Toronto,
Ontario, Canada M4P 2Y3 (a division of Pearson Penguin Canada Inc.)

Penguin Books Ltd, 80 Strand, London WC2R 0RL, England

Penguin Ireland, 25 St Stephen's Green, Dublin 2, Ireland (a division of Penguin Books Ltd)

Penguin Group (Australia), 250 Camberwell Road, Camberwell, Victoria 3124, Australia
(a division of Pearson Australia Group Pty Ltd)

Penguin Books India Pvt Ltd, 11 Community Centre, Panchsheel Park,
New Delhi – 110 017, India

Penguin Group (NZ), 67 Apollo Drive, Mairangi Bay, Auckland 1311, New Zealand
(a division of Pearson New Zealand Ltd)

Penguin Books (South Africa) (Pty) Ltd, 24 Sturdee Avenue, Rosebank,

Johannesburg 2196, South Africa

Penguin Books Ltd, Registered Offices: 80 Strand, London WC2R 0RL, England

10 9 8 7 6 5 4 3 2 1

ISBN: 978-1-59514-409-6

Library of Congress Cataloging-in-Publication Data is available

Printed in the United States of America

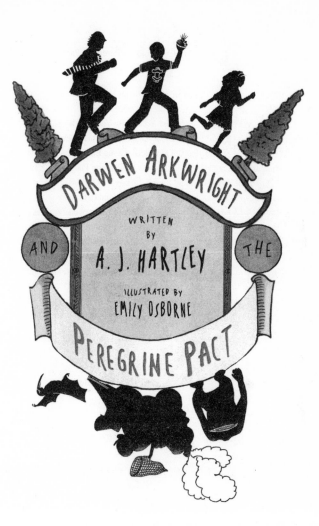

DARWEN ARKWRIGHT

WRITTEN
BY
A. J. HARTLEY

AND

THE

ILLUSTRATED BY
EMILY OSBORNE

PEREGRINE PACT

razOr
bill

an Imprint of
Penguin Group (USA) Inc.

CONTENTS

DEDICATION

To Finie and Sebastian,

with whom I discover wonders.

FLITTERCRAKE

At first Darwen Arkwright thought the twittering he heard was part of a cheesy soundtrack piped through speakers—*Woodland Sounds* or something similar— designed to make the mall feel less like a concrete box in the middle of a city. But when he looked up through the plastic branches above him, he glimpsed a tiny bird fluttering between boughs of fake foliage. *A sparrow or some kind of finch*, he thought, as it disappeared from view. He stood up and tried to follow its call.

"There you are," he muttered. The bird was perched right on top of a potted palm tree and was tweeting so madly that it was amazing nobody other than Darwen was paying it any attention. Darwen had seen birds trapped in malls before, and he supposed they survived pretty well—lots of scraps to eat from the food court, no cars to hit them, no hawks or owls to pick them off—so long as they didn't try to fly through a window. They didn't belong inside, he thought. They were outsiders—like him—but still, they did okay.

The bird's song went up an octave and grew louder and shriller. Something big and dark shot across the mall's glass domed roof, silhouetted against the sky. The bigger bird—if that's what it was—slammed into the smaller one in a puff of feathers, and the sparrow fell completely silent. Darwen stared as the survivor adjusted its grip on the branch and began to eat.

Darwen had always been fascinated by birds of prey, so a part of him thought it was pretty cool that he had seen the attack, even though he felt sorry for the sparrow. He moved to get a better look at the bigger bird and saw that its head was quite bald.

No way!

It shifted, gulping down more of its dinner, and turned to scan the scene below, spreading its wings as it did so. It looked right into Darwen's face. Instantly he knew that this bird belonged here even less than he did—even less than the sparrow—knew, in fact, that it wasn't a bird at all. Its wings were leathery, like a bat's, and there were what looked like arms underneath: arms with hands that ended in tiny little claws. At least part of the body was furry but the face belonged to neither bird nor bat.

It was a man's face, or very nearly: a man's face with a long, cruel-looking beak to which sparrow feathers now stuck. Darwen stared with his mouth open, and in that instant, the creature—he couldn't call it a bird anymore—took flight. It leapt out of the tree with a beat of its leathery wings, swooping across the dome and off down one of the mall's many corridors of stores. Darwen ran after it.

He made it about twenty yards before he slammed into a woman loaded with shopping bags.

"Watch where you're going!" said the woman.

"Sorry," muttered Darwen, still looking up to the ceiling where the winged creature was soaring unnoticed by the people below.

"You know," said a girl emerging from behind the shopping bags, "it's polite to look at people when you are talking to them."

Darwen looked down and blushed.

"Right," he said. "Sorry."

"You really shouldn't go tearing around in here," said the woman. "You'll break something."

"Right," said Darwen again, looking up to where the bird-bat-thing had been. "Sorry. I have to . . ."

He pushed past them, face up to the ceiling, and the girl exclaimed, "How rude!" loudly as he went.

It was a fancy mall. No dollar stores or book shops—the only ones Darwen ever found interesting—nothing but high-end clothing and jewelry. He ran on, desperately scanning the roof beams, window ledges, and potted foliage for signs of the flying creature. Nothing. He had lost it.

He paused for breath, turned all the way around and . . . there it was, high up on the sign of a store which sold handmade chocolates. The creature wasn't so much perching now, as lounging, sucking what Darwen assumed to be sparrow blood off its long fingers. For a second Darwen just stared, and then the creature turned to look at him, grinned maliciously, and stuck its long pink tongue out.

Darwen gasped.

What was this thing?

Then it was moving once more, flapping in long even strokes over the heads of the crowd who—astonishingly—were too taken with themselves and the shop windows to notice the strange whatever-it-was flashing over their heads. Darwen began to run again, determined not to lose it this time.

He had gotten halfway down the next grand corridor of stores—this one filled with brand-name handbags and electronic gadgets—when he collided with a fat man in uniform who sent him sprawling.

"Sorry," said Darwen, still running.

"Get back here," said the man, getting to his feet.

He was a policeman.

Darwen had never been a troublemaker, and if he had been back in England, there was no way he would have run from a cop. But the winged creature had a hold of his imagination and he wanted—*needed*—to see where it went. Darwen shouted "Sorry!" again and kept running, his eyes never leaving the flying beast, which had done a little loop in the air so that it could make a rude face at him. Then it was off again, diving and soaring, feinting right and left, then zooming down a different walkway. Darwen didn't risk a glance back to see if the policeman was following.

This end of the mall was quieter than the rest. Darwen ran past a large department store smelling strongly of perfume, then a furniture shop with a sign advertising massive discounts, and then there was nothing, just a broad open walkway flanked by empty store fronts.

Well, almost nothing. There was one more shop, right at the end of the corridor beside the exit sign, a tiny ramshackle place that looked like it had been lifted out of an entirely different location and dropped in. Even at this unfashionable and largely ignored end of the mall, it was out of place. The exterior was made of chipped brick and ancient wood—the varnish stained and peeling—and little windows crisscrossed with lead. It looked like a shop from another age. Above its door, suspended from two chains, was a faded wooden sign with gold lettering:

Mr. Octavius Peregrine's Reflectory Emporium: Mirrors Priceless and Perilous

Clinging bat-like to the sign, its head cocked in Darwen's direction, was the little winged beast. It blew a raspberry at him, then hopped onto the wall of the shop and through a half-broken diamond of leaded window glass.

Darwen ran to the door but hesitated as he put his hand on the tarnished brass handle. There was something odd about this place. He could feel it. The window displays were dusty, full of antique mirrors in ornate frames, many of them faded, speckled, and scratched, some with obvious cracks.

And how, he wondered, *could mirrors be "priceless and perilous"?*

He peered at the hand-lettered price tags and his mouth dropped open. The store might not look like it belonged in the mall, but its merchandise was not cheap. There was nothing in the window selling for less than a thousand dollars, and that would only buy you a tiny, old-fashioned hand mirror, not much bigger than the compact his aunt carried in her purse. The larger one next to it had a corner missing, but the spidery writing on the yellowing paper tag said that it sold for $4,600.

They have to be kidding, thought Darwen. It was no wonder the place looked deserted.

But he had to know what that bird-thing was. He just didn't have a choice. So he pressed the worn brass latch and, as a little bell tinkled, pushed the door open.

There was nothing particularly remarkable about Darwen Sebastian Arkwright, so it was hard to say why he always seemed to stand out, even when he wasn't chasing after strange winged creatures. He was, after all, about as ordinary as they came.

Well, almost. To be accurate he was ordinary where he came *from*, but that, unfortunately for him, was not where he lived. Darwen was from a town in northwest England, a town of little houses all squashed together and empty factories with tall brick chimneys. His mother was black and his father was white, and Darwen was something in between the two, his skin the color of polished oak, his hair short and tight to his head, his eyes almost hazel but bright with a rim of gold. He was eleven, had a northern accent, and had never been to London. In fact, until three weeks ago, he had never been much of anywhere.

But now he was living in an apartment in Atlanta, Georgia, with his aunt Honoria, and he wasn't sure which of them was more uncomfortable with the situation. Though he had started to get used to the sprawling city with its massive highways and equally massive office blocks, it was going to be a long time before he got used to living with his aunt.

Honoria Vanderstay was his mother's sister. She was tall and slim, with a mouth so thin it might have been drawn on with a pencil. She wore black business suits, even on weekends, and always had her briefcase and BlackBerry in reach "in case of emergencies." She checked her watch every few minutes like she was late for a bus, and walked briskly even indoors, swinging her arms like a soldier on parade. She was a senior executive at a major financial institution, responsible, she had told him, for portfolio diversification and risk management. She talked about this often, and Darwen understood none of it. Once, after she had been going on for about a half an hour, he said,

"So you work in a bank." She had given him the kind of look you might imagine a computer gets inside when someone tries to use the disk tray as a cup holder.

She was at work a lot, though she assured him that would not be a problem, particularly after tomorrow, when he was supposed to start school.

"And there are plenty of wonderful babysitters in Atlanta," she remarked.

That may well have been true. Unfortunately, the one assigned to Darwen was anything but wonderful. Her name was Eileen, a skinny seventeen-year-old, whose only qualification—so far as Darwen could see—was that she was old enough to drive. She didn't much like kids, she had announced the first time they were alone together, so he should find ways to amuse himself when she was around. She had important things to do. It quickly became apparent that these things largely involved watching TV while talking on the phone, though she would take a break from this to go shopping, usually for shoes. Darwen didn't much care. He liked his privacy, and so long as she kept the volume on the TV down, he was content to be ignored. At least that way he could hole up in his room and read.

Darwen and his aunt quickly established a routine. When she got home, she asked him about his day and what he would like for dinner, which usually meant what he would like to have delivered. Aunt Honoria, she had told him, didn't cook, though she could whip up what she called a "mean green salad." His first night there Darwen asked for chips and she produced a tiny bag of baked crisps, telling him that he was going to need to start eating healthier in the future. Darwen remembered, too late, that he would have to start calling chips "french fries." Twice he had asked for tea and got glasses of some brown, sweet stuff with ice in it. The next night he asked for meat and potato pies, but she didn't know what they were, and took him to a Lebanese restaurant as a treat instead. It was good, Darwen admitted to himself, just not really what he wanted.

She meant well, Darwen decided, but she wasn't what you might call maternal, and when she hugged him good night, it was like embracing an unusually slim and well-dressed refrigerator. He knew that it was hard for her to have her nephew dropped on her like this, knew that she had a life, a career, and that he was an inconvenience she was dealing with as well—and as kindly—as she could, but it all made him desperately homesick. Knowing that this unfamiliar apartment in this baffling city where no one walked was now what he had to call home only made it worse.

Tonight their routine had changed. Eileen had banged on his door and yelled, "She's waiting for you in the lobby!

Get your shoes on."

They rode down in the elevator together, Eileen studying the screen of her cell phone and humming to the music blaring from her ear buds until the doors opened. Then she snapped on her professional smile, pocketed the phone, and put a protective arm around Darwen as if he was her very best little pal. When he got into his aunt's car, Eileen bent over and waved with both hands. It was quite a show.

"Such a sweet girl," Aunt Honoria mused aloud. "Okay, Darwen. Let's get you measured for that school uniform!"

She was trying to make it seem fun, all this preparation for his first day at Hillside Academy, but Darwen sensed an anxiety underneath her enthusiasm, so he smiled encouragingly, as if clothes shops were a sort of theme park and he couldn't wait to get there.

The store was in a mall, and as they pulled into the parking lot, his aunt nodded over her shoulder.

"Hillside is just over there," she said. "Just through those trees."

Everything in Atlanta was "just through those trees." Interstate Highways 75 and 85 merged in the middle of the city—his aunt called that section simply "the connector"—but come off that massive tangle of concrete, away from the glass towers of offices, and you could be anywhere: little neighborhoods of mazy roads cut off from the rest of the town by screens of massive trees. How anyone ever got to really know this place, Darwen couldn't imagine. He turned in time to glimpse an old and impressive-looking clock tower and his eyes widened.

"That's a school?" he said, thinking of the shabby little classrooms he had been used to in England. "It looks like the Houses of Parliament."

"I guess it does," said his aunt, pleased.

Darwen sank low in his seat.

Inside the mall his aunt led him to Sanderson's, the kids' clothes shop, or—as the sign over the door read— "suppliers of fine clothing for young ladies and gentlemen." There were a couple of girls inside with their parents but they looked like store mannequins and Darwen avoided their eyes. He was measured and poked while his aunt looked at the green blazers with the gold Hillside crest, talking admiringly to the staff about what a great school it was and how they produced captains of industry and CEOs. Darwen wasn't sure what those were, but didn't like the sound of it. He turned when he was told to turn, lifted his arms, and stood up straight, all the while watching his blank face in one of the dressing room mirrors.

"The uniform will be ready for you tomorrow," said the assistant, smiling like she was awarding a trophy. "You'll have to wait one more day. Think you can manage that?"

Darwen thought he could.

When they were done, his aunt asked him if he would mind giving her an hour to do some shopping "since we're here." Darwen, in no great hurry to get back to his lonely little room, agreed.

"Have an ice cream while you're waiting," said his aunt, thrusting a five-dollar bill into his hand and ruffling his hair like he was four years old.

Darwen had spent ten minutes wandering around, looking at things he couldn't afford and didn't really want anyway, then found a place to sit and just waited, watching people as they passed. A lot of them were black—or African American, as his aunt had told him to say. That should have made him feel more comfortable, he thought, but somehow the more they looked like him, the more he was reminded of the ways he was different. No one had his accent. Many people wore sports jerseys of teams he had never heard of until a few weeks ago: the Hawks, the Braves, the Falcons. Atlanta teams. He sat there, wondering if he would still remember the names of all the Manchester United and Blackburn Rovers players a week from now, wondering if he would ever understand whatever sport the Falcons played, as he stared up at the glass dome of the mall ceiling. . . .

That was when he had seen the bird—and the thing that had it for a meal. That was when he had started running through the mall, knocking people over, and fleeing from the police. That was when it had all started.

Darwen's mind was on none of that now, as he stood at the entrance of the old mirror shop. He stepped within, closed the door behind him, and looked cautiously around.

The inside matched the outside. It was dusty and cluttered, not so much old-fashioned as antique and uncared for. Partition walls hung with old mirrors made a series of narrow corridors through which only one customer at a time could walk—not that the shop would ever attract more than one customer at a time. In the center of the shop was a high desk with a massive and ancient-looking cash register. There was no sign of either the shopkeeper or the winged creature.

Darwen realized he had been holding his breath and released it. He took a step into one of the narrow aisles of mirrors, some square, some round, some oval, some shapes he couldn't describe. Some were as small as his fist, others several feet across, but there was no organizing pattern that he could see. It was as if they had simply been left there, and in spite of the outrageous price tags, the place looked more like a storage space than a shop.

A clock was ticking loudly somewhere, but otherwise the shop was completely silent. Darwen stood very still, his eyes sweeping the walls for signs of the creature, but he could see nothing. Very carefully he took two more silent steps down the little corridor toward the desk with the register and then, faintly but clearly, he heard it: a skittering of clawed hands and feet, and the rustle of folded wings in the next aisle over. Darwen bolted around the corner in time to see a small mirror with a frame swinging on a nail. Darwen raced up to it looking wildly around, but there was no sign of the animal, if animal it was. He cursed under his breath. His eyes, finding nothing else worthy of his attention, fell on the mirror.

He stepped back in astonishment. The reflection, which should have shown his own bewildered face looking back at him, showed a tiny figure with a beak and furious little red eyes, and a look of mean-spirited triumph on its face as it stared back at him.

Darwen gasped.

"Could I help you with something?" said a voice.

Darwen whirled round to find an elderly man wearing a very slim-fitting and old-fashioned suit standing beside him. He wore half-moon glasses perched on the end of his nose, and his face was keen. His eyes, which were a bright, unnerving green, were steady, and his whole posture suggested he had been standing there for some time, though Darwen would have sworn the shop had been empty when he came in.

"This mirror," Darwen managed. "There's something inside it."

The old man's face creased into the cartoon of a frown.

"Something in the mirror?" he repeated, eyes narrow. "What do you mean?"

He snatched the mirror from Darwen's hand and studied it, first the front, then the back, then the sides. He tapped it sharply with the flat of his hand like someone trying to stabilize the picture on an unreliable television.

"Looks like a regular mirror to me," he said, considering it as if he had never seen it before.

"No," said Darwen, speaking quickly. "There was a . . . *thing*, like a bird but not. It was out in the mall but I followed it back here, and I think it went, well, *into* the mirror."

"Into the mirror?" said the old man, eyebrows arching. "And how would it do that?"

"I don't know, sir," said Darwen, "but it did."

"Preposterous," said the shopkeeper, sterner now. "You come into my shop accusing me of housing bird-things in my mirrors. Absurd. I ought to report you to the police. I should call your parents."

"You can't," said Darwen blankly. He opened his mouth to say more, but stopped.

"Indeed?" said the man as if Darwen had remarked on the weather. "Then it will have to be the police. Unless you want to take back the ridiculous things you said about my mirrors."

"I don't understand it either," said Darwen, "but

I know what I saw."

"You aren't from around here, are you?"

"No," said Darwen, suspecting that this would be considered evidence of his untrustworthiness. "I'm from England."

"England, eh?"

"Northwest," said Darwen. "Near Manchester."

"And this bird-thing, was it like anything you have seen in northwest-England-near-Manchester?"

"No, sir. It had a beak, but it was more like a little man with leathery wings, and it attacked a sparrow and ate it and . . ."

"Ah," said the man, tapping his nose and smiling as if all had become clear. "I know what that was. A horn-billed Mexican bird-eating bat."

"A what?"

"A *horn-billed Mexican bird-eating bat*," the man repeated, slower this time.

Darwen pulled a skeptical face.

"Never heard of it," he said.

"Nevertheless," said the old man. "They're migrants, you see. You know what it is to migrate?"

"To go somewhere else, usually flying north or south to avoid really hot or cold weather," said Darwen.

"Exactly so," said the old man leaning in so close that his nose was almost touching Darwen's. "They are quite common around here at this time of year, especially if they can get inside a covered building like the mall."

"But what about the mirror?" Darwen persisted.

"That," said the man, straightening up, "was simply your imagination. You have an imagination don't you, boy?"

"Yes, sir," said Darwen, still unsure.

"Of course you do," said the old man, "and it is probably your best friend, is it not?"

Darwen thought for a moment and then shrugged.

"I suppose so," he said, wishing it wasn't true.

"Very well. But imagination is not always to be trusted," the old man continued, giving the mirror back to Darwen. "Here for instance. Take a good look. What do you see?"

Darwen peered intently into the mirror but saw only his own quizzical face staring back at him.

"Nothing," he said. "Just me."

"Which is more than enough for a small mirror, wouldn't you say?"

"I suppose so," said Darwen.

"So now you can take out your bird-spotting chart— you have a bird-spotting chart, do you not?"

"Yes, sir. How did you know?"

"You can take out your chart and check off the horn-billed Mexican bird-eating bat."

"If it's a bat," said Darwen, "I don't think it will be on my bird chart."

"Then write it in," said the old man. "Birds and bats. The difference is negligible."

He gestured dismissively, and at the same moment, the little bell over the door rang.

"Gracious," said the old man, under his breath. "Two customers in one day." Then, in a low whisper he said to Darwen, "Stay here."

Darwen nodded and the man stepped lightly to the front of the shop, saying, "Can I help you?"

"Yeah," said a gruff and breathless voice that Darwen immediately recognized. "I'm looking for a kid. A boy who came running down here."

Darwen peered through a gap in the shelves to his left and saw the overweight cop standing only a few feet away.

"A boy?" said the shopkeeper.

"Yeah," drawled the cop. "There've been some purse snatchings in the mall and he's probably the culprit. Brown hair, about yea big. Might have been carrying stuff—stolen stuff. He ran down this way. You seen him?"

Darwen held his breath.

"A boy?" said the shopkeeper. "No. I've been here all day and I'm very sorry to say that you are the first person to come in since I opened up."

"You sure?" said the cop. "Kid knocked me on the

floor. Kicked me too. When I find him, he's going to be in serious trouble."

"Quite so," said the shopkeeper. "Kids these days. No discipline."

"But he hasn't been in here?"

"I'm afraid not," said the shopkeeper. "Maybe he slipped into the department store down the way. You might still catch him. And if you do," he added with relish, "you teach him the kind of lesson he won't forget in a hurry. Children today need beating, hard and often."

"Yeah," said the cop, less certainly. "Okay. Well, thanks."

He took a step toward the door, but then stopped.

"You mind if I take a look around to be sure?" he said.

"Be my guest," said the shopkeeper. "In fact, I'd be glad of the company, particularly if you cast an eye over the merchandise. Finest mirrors in town."

"Oh," said the cop. "Yeah, I'm not really looking to buy . . ."

"Take this one for example. Beautiful, isn't it?"

"It's kind of chipped."

"Hence the discount," said the shopkeeper.

"The tag says five thousand dollars," said the cop.

"Reduced from eight."

"You know, I really think I should be going," said the policeman. "See if I can catch up with that kid."

"If you insist," said the shopkeeper. "Come back soon, and tell your friends."

The door opened with a jingle of the bell, then thudded shut.

Darwen took a breath, but before he could walk round to the desk, the shopkeeper was beside him again and his green eyes were bright with mirth.

"Thank you," said Darwen, torn between bafflement and relief. He struggled to remember the name on the sign outside. "Thank you, Mr. Peregrine."

The shopkeeper raised an eyebrow and smiled his secret, thoughtful smile.

"So," he said, "courteous and observant. Interesting."

Darwen flushed and looked down.

"And, as I said, imaginative," said Octavius Peregrine, "or you would never have spotted the flittercrake."

"The what?"

"The creature you saw flying into the shop. It's called a flittercrake."

"But you said it were a bat!" said Darwen, outrage awaking his Lancashire dialect.

"A bat?" exclaimed Mr. Peregrine. "Preposterous!"

"You did," said Darwen, not sure what to believe from this odd old man. "You called it a migrating horn-billed Mexican bird-eating bat."

"A Mexican *what*?" said Mr. Peregrine. "Bird-eating bats in Atlanta? Don't be absurd."

"But you said . . ."

"Don't tell me what I said, young man," said Octavius Peregrine sternly, "or I shall quite revise my opinion of you."

Darwen opened his mouth to say something, but hesitated, sensing something watchful in the old man's eyes, as if arguing now might cost him somehow. He closed his mouth, and the shadow of a smile flashed across the old man's lips, though it did not reach his eyes.

"So the animal I followed," Darwen began, "the bird thingy you said was a . . ."

"Flittercrake."

"Right," said Darwen, "the flittercrake. What's that then?"

The shopkeeper considered him shrewdly for a second, then said, "Some tea, I think, yes?"

"Aye, all right," said Darwen.

"I grow it in my own garden," said Mr. Peregrine, bustling behind the desk and fishing out a tin tea caddy. "Clip and dry it myself."

He shook a little into a strainer, which he dropped into a cast-iron teapot. Then he pushed through a curtain into what looked like a stock room and was gone.

Darwen was alone in the strange little shop. He looked up and around, seeing his own face reflected in dozens of mirrors. He thought about his aunt and wondered if she had noticed he was missing. It was probably time for him to be meeting her by the McDonalds. He checked the long case clock that was ticking so loudly but was amazed to see that it had no numbers and only one hand. The hand moved between two symbols, a sun in the nine o'clock position, and a moon in the three o'clock position. It was getting close to the moon.

Darwen was still staring at the clock when Mr. Peregrine returned with a kettle of boiling water, which he poured into the iron teapot.

"You want to know why it has no numbers," said the shopkeeper, "and what the symbols mean."

"I was guessing it was set to mark day and night," said Darwen.

"Excellent boy," said Mr. Peregrine, beaming. "To be precise, sunrise and sunset. It's a surprisingly complicated mechanism. Has to adjust to the seasons, you know. Never more than twenty seconds off, which is, I think, close enough, don't you?"

"I'm sure it is," said Darwen.

"Sure?" said the shopkeeper, leaning in suddenly. His smile had vanished and his eyes had an urgent, hunted look. "Never be sure about such things," he said. "A lot can happen in twenty seconds, Mr. Arkwright."

The hairs on the back of Darwen's neck stood up. He couldn't recall telling the old man his name.

"Now," said Mr. Peregrine. "Tea?"

"Actually," said Darwen, "I should probably be going."

"Of course," said Mr. Peregrine, pouring the tea into two cups and pushing one toward him.

"I'm sorry," said Darwen, "but I really should . . ."

"Go, yes," said Mr. Peregrine, sipping his tea and smiling. "But perhaps you would like to take something with you. A souvenir, as it were."

As the old man reached up to one of the many mirrors hanging on the wall behind the desk with its huge cash register, Darwen tried his tea absently. It was excellent. He watched Mr. Peregrine lift one of the mirrors down. It was a little over a foot square, tarnished like all the mirrors in the store, and framed with age-darkened wood, which was intricately carved and looked like it had once been covered with gold paint, though most of it had chipped off over the years. It was, in its way, quite beautiful.

"There," said the old man. "Find a nice place for it at home."

"You mean, take it with me?" said Darwen. "I couldn't. I mean, it's very kind of you to offer, sir, and it's a lovely mirror but . . ."

"I don't offer," said Mr. Peregrine, smiling impishly as he pushed the mirror across the counter to Darwen, "I insist."

"But I don't have any money," said Darwen.

"Did I ask for any?"

"I really shouldn't accept gifts from strangers," said Darwen, blushing, sure Mr. Peregrine would be offended by his rudeness.

"Strangers, eh?" said the shopkeeper. "You think I'm strange?"

Darwen did not know what to say. "I have never met anyone like you," he said, at last.

"Which is to say, yes, you think me strange," said Mr. Peregrine, as if this was to be expected. "But you know who I am. My name is, after all, written on the sign outside. And if you do not like the mirror, you can bring it back. If it helps, consider it a loan. Or a test."

"A test?"

"I just mean that, one day, you will return it. Like turning in a completed exam."

Darwen wasn't sure what the old man meant by that, but he looked at the mirror, and though he couldn't explain why, he *did* want it. It felt ancient, like it had been used by people for hundreds of years, and though it made no sense, he thought that the mirror remembered them somehow. He had no idea where this ridiculous notion came from, but for a moment he felt the passage of time and the presence of the people who had used it, coming off the mirror like heat. It was like when he used to visit

Clitheroe castle back home; he could stand on the castle walls and almost feel the knights and servants, the lords and ladies who had been there over the centuries. It was like the little photo album he had brought from home, a window on the past—but unlike the album, he felt no pain, no sense of loss when he looked at it. It was strange. He looked from the beautiful mirror to the old man's smiling face and relaxed.

"Okay," he said. "Thanks."

"I only ask that you keep it in your own room, and that you take special care that it should not get broken. Not even cracked. That is most important."

"Seven years bad luck," said Darwen, grinning.

The shopkeeper's smile vanished and his eyes narrowed.

"What do you mean by that?" he demanded.

"Just, you know . . ." said Darwen, taken aback. "It's a saying, or at least it is in England. A superstition. If you break a mirror, you get seven years of bad luck. That's all. I didn't mean anything. . . ."

"Quite so," said Mr. Peregrine, relaxing again. "Superstition. Quite so. Let me wrap this for you."

"Thank you," said Darwen.

The shopkeeper pulled out a roll of thick brown paper, which he cut to size with large, old-fashioned shears, then bound the package with twine.

"Thank you," said Darwen again.

"Not at all, Mr. Arkwright," said the shopkeeper, turning back to the wall again, "not at all."

Darwen hesitated, but the shopkeeper started humming tunelessly to himself, so he turned and left. As the bell over the door jangled, Darwen turned and, for a split second, thought he saw Mr. Peregrine's reflection in one of the mirrors hanging on the back wall, watching him leave.

THE MIRROR

Aunt Honoria didn't seem to notice that Darwen was late. She was talking on her cell phone about deadlines and meetings, a conversation that took her all the way to the car and most of the way home. Darwen didn't listen. He was thinking about the strange little shop, and Mr. Peregrine's mirrors, one of which he had bundled up on the seat next to him.

Darwen mixed the brown paper parcel in with the large shopping bags, and was able to get it into the house without comment. He took it to his room and, as soon as he heard the TV snap on (a twenty-four-hour business news station), unwrapped it. He found a hammer and a single nail in the kitchen drawer, returned to his room unnoticed by his aunt, who was now sitting with her laptop (making an entirely different phone call about meetings and deadlines), and tacked it up on the inside of his closet door. For a few moments he just sat looking at his reflection in it and, though he couldn't say why, he was glad he had it. He shut the closet door carefully, and returned the hammer to the kitchen drawer just as his aunt closed the laptop and began asking about his day.

Darwen wolfed down his dinner—stir-fried snow peas with tofu—so quickly that his aunt thought he needed more, though he really just wanted to get back to his room. He could almost feel the mirror's presence back there and couldn't wait to return to it. It made no sense, but it was special and it was his. With the exception of what he had been able to fit into two suitcases—clothes, a few toys, and the books he couldn't be without—everything from his old house in England had gone into storage. His aunt had bought him more clothes, more toys and books, but it felt like he had moved into a library or a museum. He could look, he could even touch, but it wasn't his stuff. Not really. For some reason he couldn't pinpoint, the mirror felt different, even though Mr. Peregrine had said that this too was a kind of loan.

Of course, when he finally made it back to his room after three helpings of tofu and snow peas, he began to wonder why he had bothered. Yes, the mirror was nice and old, and he liked the idea of having something special, something secret . . . but after a couple of minutes looking at himself in it, he got bored. He chose a book and settled on his bed to read while the sun went down, sipping from a cup of "tea" his aunt had made; it wasn't iced this time, but she had made it by putting a tea bag into a cup of barely warm water, so it hadn't brewed properly. The tea was thin and flavorless, and every time the tea bag bumped his lip, it felt like there was a dead mouse floating in the cup.

After a few minutes, it had grown too dark to read without a light and as he reached for his bedside lamp, his gaze fell on his old cricket bat. He didn't know why he had bothered lugging it all the way from England. No one here played so he'd probably never use it again. A memory leapt into his head, stark and clear like it was lit by floodlights: He was playing in their little square of garden. His dad was running up to bowl to him and his mum was keeping the wicket behind where he stood with the bat poised to swing. He felt a rush of joy, which turned instantly into a desperate, empty sadness. . . .

Darwen cleared his throat and shoved the cricket bat

forcefully under the bed and out of sight. Then he turned to look through the window at the city. The sky was still a little pink where the sun had gone down, but elsewhere the blue was deep and purplish. The streetlights were on and the roads glowed a soft amber as the traffic snaked through the city with its towers of shining windows. It was all so strange to Darwen but he did like it, and it helped to keep his mind off things he had decided not to think about.

The last pink in the sky faded to nothing and Darwen began getting ready for bed. He took out his pajamas, noticing that there was something in the jacket pocket: a little embroidered Manchester United badge. He took it out and looked at it, wondering how long it had been since he'd put it there. Weeks, he thought. Maybe months. It had probably gone through the wash several times. He was about to stuff it under the bed with the cricket bat, but changed his mind, and put it carefully back into his pajama pocket, resting his hand on it for a moment till he could feel his heartbeat through it.

He only remembered the mirror when he opened the closet to get his clothes ready for tomorrow, and it took him a moment to realize what had happened. When he did realize, he just stood there, his mouth open and his heart hammering in his chest. He blinked deliberately, then looked again, closer this time, and it was impossible to deny.

What had been a mirror was now a window.

There was no longer an image of his own face reflecting back at him. Instead, the faded old frame now showed a moonlit forest with a long straight path stretching away toward a fountain. For a moment he thought it was a trick, some sort of picture you could only see in the dark, like the plastic things you got in cereal boxes with images that seemed to move when you tilted them, or a mirror you could only see through from one side, like the kind they always had in police stations on TV. Then the trees moved. They moved as if they were being blown by a soft breeze, and as his brain tried to make sense of what he was seeing, he felt it on his face: a cool rush of air coming straight out of the mirror.

Darwen took a step back.

No way, he thought. *This isn't happening.* But he couldn't tear his eyes away, and as he looked he saw a rabbit emerge from the bushes and take a few hopping steps along the path. He peered at it and saw that it wasn't a rabbit—not exactly. It was *like* a rabbit, and moved like a rabbit but its ears were short and it had a tail like a squirrel.

What on earth is that? thought Darwen, and he put a hand to the mirror surface, as if by adjusting it he could get a better look. But there was no mirror surface to touch. The image rippled, like he was reaching into water, but there was only air. Cautiously he extended his arm, pushing his hand slowly inside the frame and, when nothing happened to stop him, found that he could reach all the way inside.

This is nuts, he thought. *I must be cracking up.*

He snatched his arm back out and flung the closet door closed so that he could see what was on the other side, as if there might be a hole. But there was nothing. The closet door looked as solid as it ever had and when he tapped on it experimentally, the sound was exactly as he would have expected if he had not just reached right through it.

"Darwen?" called his aunt's voice. "Is that you knocking? You ready for bed?"

Panicking, Darwen leapt into bed and pulled up the covers before shouting, "Yes."

For a moment he lay there in the dark, eyes on the closet door sure there would be some tell-tale sign that he had done . . . something, but when his aunt came in to kiss him good night, her eyes never strayed from the bed.

"You okay, Darwen?" she said. "You feel hot."

No problem, Darwen thought wildly, *I can take a nice cooling stroll through the forest in my closet.*

"I'm fine," he said.

"Hmm. We'll see how you are in the morning. If you have a temperature, you'll have to start school another day."

An hour ago that would have been like announcing

that Christmas was being brought forward a few months, but Darwen could only nod and grin like an idiot. "Oh," he said. "Right."

"You sure you're okay?" his aunt asked. "You don't seem yourself."

Just leave, thought Darwen, *just leave and whatever you do don't look in . . .*

"Let me get your clothes for the morning. . . ."

"No!" shouted Darwen. "I mean, I can do it. . . ."

But it was too late. Aunt Honoria threw open the closet doors and Darwen closed his eyes, waiting for her scream.

"I can't find anything in here," she grumbled.

Darwen opened his eyes with something like relief. He must have imagined the whole thing. Maybe he *was* sick. He had hallucinated because of his fever. . . .

But there it was, big as life, hanging on the back of the closet door for all to see: a framed window onto a dark woodland path.

"Here we go," said his aunt. "You can wear this till your uniform is ready. I'll just set it here."

How could she not see it?

"And if you're not well," she continued, "I'll keep you home. Wait a minute. Where did this come from?"

Darwen just stared at her.

"Darwen?" she said. "Where did this mirror come from?"

"Mirror?" he echoed.

"This mirror on the closet door. It's not mine."

"I er . . . bought it," said Darwen. "At the mall. Today."

"I hope you didn't pay too much for it," said his aunt. "It looks rather shabby to me. If you wanted a mirror, why didn't you say so? I could have gotten you a nice one. This is your home now, Darwen, remember that."

"Right," said Darwen. "Yes."

He sounded calm, but inside his head he was shouting, *Look at it! Why can't you see that it's not a mirror? It's a hole. On one side is my bedroom, and on the other is a forest. Doesn't that strike you as just a little bit strange . . . ?*

"See you in the morning then, Darwen," said Honoria. "Get some rest."

And with one more firm peck on his forehead, she was gone.

Darwen waited till he heard her bedroom door close, and then—very quietly—he returned to the closet, opened it, and took a breath.

Maybe it will be a regular mirror again, he thought, though while he knew that the universe would make a little more sense if it was, he would also be disappointed.

But it was not a regular mirror. It was still a window onto the same forest path, the same fountain, the same rabbit-like creature nibbling ferns in the moonlight. For at least five minutes, he just watched, entranced by it all, feeling the cool, pine-scented air on his face. Then he caught movement up in one of the trees. First he thought it might just be the wind. Next he thought it was a bird. Then the creature crept out along the branch and Darwen knew it for what it was, though it took a moment for Mr. Peregrine's word to come to him: flittercrake. The thing he had seen in the mall, the same one, for all he knew: leathery wings, furry body, long thin limbs with clawed hands and feet, and a mean little face with a hooked beak which somehow did not stop the thing from looking strangely human.

The flittercrake's attention was entirely on the rabbit-animal, and having seen what it did to the sparrow in the mall, Darwen was suddenly overwhelmed with a desire to stop the winged beast before it attacked. But how? Perhaps if he shouted the animals would both run away, but who knew if they would hear him? His aunt would, and that would bring her running.

You were able to reach in, he thought. *Maybe you could climb through. . . .*

He tested the width of the frame against his shoulders. It would be tight, but he would just fit. The flittercrake was inching out over the path and its wings were beginning to unfurl. It was almost ready to drop. Darwen took one more look at those long blade-like claws and the cruel beak, and decided he had no choice. He grasped the lower part of the frame with both hands and boosted himself through headfirst.

MOTH

He felt the rippling air around him like he was diving into a chill pool, and then he was tumbling out onto cold, damp earth. The flittercrake flapped upward, uttered a high-pitched shriek, and, with a malevolent look back at Darwen, flew off into the night. Spooked, the rabbit creature took three long, loping hops and was gone.

Darwen stood up and turned. Behind him the forest continued, but—suspended in midair, exactly at the height he had hung it on the back of the door—was the empty mirror frame, and through it he could see the shelves and coat hangers in his bedroom closet. For a moment, all the strangeness fell away and a single word came to mind.

"Cool," he said into the night.

He tried reaching back through the mirror frame and found he could just about touch the blue shirt hanging inside. He wondered what it would look like to his aunt if she happened to go into his bedroom: an arm sticking out of the closet door! He grinned and took a step away from the mirror frame. So long as he knew he could get back through it, he may as well explore a little.

But where to go? The forest path stretched on as far as he could see in both directions and on either side was nothing but trees, though the ground seemed to slope upward to his right, like the path ran along the side of a hill. Darwen began to walk toward the fountain, scanning the woodland and the sky above for signs of movement. Who knew what strange birds he might see in this place?

As to where he was and how he had gotten here, he had no idea. Maybe it was all some sort of dream. Maybe he really was lying in his bed with a fever of 104, but he didn't care. The real world—the world in which he didn't seem to belong anywhere—fell further away with each step. For the first time in what seemed like months, he felt content, even happy.

The fountain was a large stone bowl shaped like a flower seated on a pedestal. It was twined with bronze vines and green with age. The vines came up over the lip of the bowl, bloomed outward and came together again in a cage-like structure containing a dozen birdhouses, all covered with intricately shaped metal leaves. Water bubbled up in the center of the pool, but it also ran down the bronze vines from the top, so that looking into the cage was like peering through a waterfall. It was a beautiful thing, and it filled Darwen with a sense of peace.

He listened to the sound of the burbling water and watched the reflection of the moon above the trees, but he wanted more. He was—for all he knew—in an entirely different world. He set off along the path.

Darwen had left his watch behind so he had no clear sense of how much time had passed, but it seemed like he had been walking for a half hour or more. He thought the path curved slightly to the right, but it was hard to be sure since the scenery never altered. The forest spread out on all sides, and though he occasionally heard the skittering of small creatures in the underbrush, he could see nothing that suggested he was really going anywhere. He considered turning around and going back.

Five more minutes, he thought and began to count slowly aloud as he walked. He had reached forty-nine when he became sure that there was something on the path up ahead, something that shimmered vaguely in the moonlight. He picked up his pace but as he got closer he slowed again.

It couldn't be.

It was a stained and cracked mirror frame, the same mirror frame he had come through, and when he got close enough to peer in, he saw his own bedroom closet inside. Up ahead was the fountain with the cage of bird-houses. He turned around and looked back at the path and realized that he had been right: the path *did* curve slightly, and he had just completed a full circle. He was right back where he started. He walked slowly back to the fountain and leant on the stone rim of the basin, frowning into the water.

"Not easy to find your way around here, is it?"

The voice was in his left ear, somehow both faraway and strangely close so that he jumped and spun to his left. At first he could see nothing at all, but then his eyes found what he took to be a firefly hanging in the air only a couple of feet from his head. He looked around again and, seeing nothing else, returned his gaze to the insect.

Darwen had never seen a firefly up close before, but he knew there was something about this one that didn't look quite right. For one thing, it was too big: its body about two inches long and its wings broad and filmy like a drag-onfly's. As his eyes adjusted he could see that it looked less like a bug and more like a tiny person—a girl, he thought, at least in the face. In fact, there was nothing insect-like about the girl at all. The flickering wings seemed attached to her back by a system of small straps. They were part of a tiny mechanism that she was wearing, made of little brass cogs and wheels like the workings of a watch. It was this that produced the glowworm light.

"I'm sorry," said Darwen, "but did you speak?"

"Of course," said the miniscule girl, in a voice so small that it sounded like he was hearing it over a bad telephone connection. "You looked lost."

"Not really," said Darwen. "But . . . I'm sorry if this is rude, but what are you?"

The insect girl swerved in the air then returned to her steady hover. Her wings were of the finest metal, etched with copper-colored lines like veins.

"My name is Moth," she said. "I am a dellfey."

"Is that like a fairy?" said Darwen.

"Very like," said Moth. "And what are you?"

"I'm a boy, I suppose. A human. My name is Darwen. Darwen Arkwright. I came through that."

He nodded at the mirror frame.

"Really?" said the dellfey, who seemed as fascinated by him as he was by her.

"Yeah," said Darwen, like it was something he did every so often to relieve the boredom.

The dellfey gave a little clap of delight and did a loop in the air.

"So," said Darwen. "What else is there to see here?

I've walked the path all the way round but it just brought me back to the same spot."

"That is what this locus is, a forest," said Moth.

"Locus?"

"The space you came to through your portula," she said, pointing to the mirror frame hanging in the air over the forest path.

"Portula?" said Darwen. "You mean the mirror."

"That thing you came through, yes," she said, as if this was obvious. "The portula: a small gate between Silbrica and your world."

"Silbrica?"

"This place."

"Wait," said Darwen, "you mean I'm really in another world?"

The dellfey inclined her head seriously.

"You are," she said.

"Chuffin' 'eck!" exclaimed Darwen. "So what else is there? I mean, one circular path can't be the whole world, right?"

"This is only one locus of many," agreed Moth. "But to reach the others we would have to go to a janus."

"What's a janus?"

"All the different parts of Silbrica are connected through doorways."

"Like my mirror?" said Darwen, "the—whatchacallit: *portula*?"

"Kind of," said Moth. "Your portula goes between worlds. A janus is a gate which connects places *inside* our world. The janus can take you all over Silbrica."

"And there's one of these janus gates here in the forest?"

"In the center," said Moth, pointing off through the trees and up to the crown of the hill.

"Your wings," he said, unable to help himself. "I don't want to be rude or anything, but are they . . . *mechanical*?"

"Naturally," said the dellfey.

"How do you . . . ? Where do you . . . ? They're great!" said Darwen, staring as the dellfey did another slow loop so that he could admire them.

"Making them is an ancient skill," she said, "and some of our kind devote their lives to—"

"There are more of you?" Darwen exclaimed.

"Aren't there more of *you*?" Moth returned.

"Well, yes," said Darwen. "But I'm ordinary, not special, like you."

"You are special here," said the dellfey. "I am ordinary. Look."

And so saying she reached round to something on the tiny mechanism strapped to her back and Darwen heard a thin note, high and clear like the sound you get when you run a moist finger around the rim of a wine glass. At first it seemed to come from the little clockwork machine, and the greenish light grew stronger as it did so, but then

Darwen realized it was growing, and it was coming from all around him. The single note was joined by others, slightly different, but all in perfect harmony. Then he saw that the woods were full of lights, and the bronze vines that made up the cage around the fountain were rotating and opening to the night air. From the exquisite little birdhouses, other dellfeys emerged, each one producing a clear, high note of its own. They flew up above the fountain and circled it, moving as one, so that Darwen thought first of a squadron of aircraft and then of a ballet his parents had taken him to a long time ago.

He gazed, eyes and mouth open, as the dellfeys moved around him, some settling lightly on his outstretched hands like birds, others hovering close to his head so they could study him. Each one was different, some male and some female, though they all seemed young. There were tiny differences also in their elegantly fashioned wings and the contraptions that powered them. Darwen raised one with brass-colored wings to his face, gazing at the microscopic device with its dials and levers, and he was amazed that something so mechanical could be so lovely.

After no more than a minute or two, the dellfeys dispersed, some into the woods, some back to their houses inside the fountain, and the cage-vines returned smoothly to their original position. Only Moth remained.

"And what do you do here?" asked Darwen after a long moment.

"Do?"

"Do," Darwen repeated. "Like, do you have a job . . . or schoolwork?" he added, realizing he had no idea how old the tiny creature was.

"Not really," said Moth, unoffended. "We don't really *do*: we just *are*."

"That sounds brilliant!" said Darwen. "You just . . . hang out here?"

The dellfey frowned at his phrase but then nodded.

"We eat what the forest provides, we play, and we watch."

"For what?"

"Things that don't belong here," said the dellfey.

She looked over her shoulder in a way, Darwen thought, that was supposed to look casual but wasn't.

"Such as?" he said.

"Nothing important," said Moth. "Can you run?"

"Of course," said Darwen.

"Then try to catch me!" she exclaimed.

"Easy," said Darwen, cupping his hands and snatching at her.

But it wasn't easy. She slid through his fingers with a flutter of her coppery wings and was off, flashing greenish into the trees. Darwen laughed and gave chase.

For ten minutes the dellfey led him running through the forest, zipping round tree trunks, diving into the foliage, doubling back. . . . From time to time he would lose her completely, but then her green light would wink on, and he would go plunging through the underbrush after her. Once he thought he had her, only to hear her tinkling giggle in his ear as she shot past his head.

He felt huge and clumsy, a lumbering giant trying to catch a hummingbird, but the forest air was so fresh and cool and the dellfey's delight so infectious, that Darwen forgot about all the things that had been weighing on his mind. When he finally gave up and lay panting and laughing on the pine-needled floor of the forest, Moth settled lightly on his chest. He lay there, gazing up at the night sky through the trees.

"Will you be here tomorrow night?" he asked, sitting up.

"Of course," said Moth. "Always. This is my home."

Home. The word touched Darwen like a sad tune, but he just nodded.

"I'll see you again tomorrow," he said.

He didn't want to leave, and though he knew he should be asking himself all sorts of questions about how any of this was possible, he felt only the comfort of the place, the sense that it was his and that no one could take it from him.

But as he walked back through the forest to the mirror, he caught a flicker of movement off beneath the trees.

Darwen turned to look directly at it but could see nothing but shadows.

A trick of the moonlight, he thought, though he glanced back, scanning the forest by the fountain for the telltale glow of the dellfeys. There was no sign of them, and Darwen was uneasy.

He took a breath, turned back toward the mirror and began to walk forward, but then he saw it again. Something dark and large, but no more than a shadow cast— he supposed—by branches. He stopped, staring into the undergrowth of the forest and there was nothing there. Or nearly nothing. And he felt . . . like he was being watched.

It moved again, slowly this time and he was sure now. It was just a shadow, but a shadow of what? There was nothing in front of it, nothing above it that might cast so clear a silhouette. It shifted slightly and he saw it clearly as it moved over the trunk of a tree: a man-sized hole in the night. Once more it moved, vanishing briefly then appearing again as it passed over another tree and a bank of ivy. It drifted sideways, then flashed across the path with a surge of surprising speed. Unnerved, Darwen spun round, turning his back on the mirror, suddenly unwilling to take his eyes off the shadow, sure that it was getting closer. And as it moved, its shape changed a little, exactly as you would expect a shadow to, so why did he find himself looking for its eyes?

The hair on the back of his neck had prickled upright, and he could feel sweat breaking out cool all over his body. He had forgotten the joy and peace he had felt only moments before. Darwen was afraid.

He took a step toward the mirror and the shadow echoed it like a watchful lion. It leaped suddenly across the path in front of him, flashing blackly and covering thirty feet in no more than a second. It was circling him.

Breathing heavily, Darwen took two more steps. The shadow arced round behind him, closer still. Whatever it was going to do, it was going to do it soon, and Darwen was suddenly sure it must not get any closer. He didn't know what it was, had no idea what a mere shadow could do to him, but he sensed danger like a scent in the air. He had to get out of here.

He took a false step to the right, and as the shadow copied it, he surged forward and in three strides had the mirror frame in his grasp. He glimpsed the shadow closing fast in the corner of his eye, felt a rearing terror in his chest, but he stared doggedly into the closet, dragged himself up and in. Panting on the floor of his bedroom, he risked a look back at the mirror, but saw only the serene moonlit forest. In a few minutes he had almost convinced himself that it really had been no more than a shadow.

The next morning Darwen's aunt sent him for a shower as soon as he came to breakfast.

"You must have been feverish," she said. "You smell like a marathon runner."

When he had finished, he removed the shirt he had hung over the mirror. His own reflection looked back at him. It was just a mirror again. He tested its surface with his fingers, gingerly.

Solid.

He thought he should be wondering if it had all been a dream, but he knew in his heart that it hadn't been, and the day ahead looked all the brighter for it. Even the dead-mouse tea bag that his aunt served him in a cup of lukewarm water couldn't dash his spirits, and he thanked her, smiling. The smile clearly surprised and pleased her, and Darwen made a note to be a little more cheerful in the hope that she wouldn't worry about him so much.

Hillside Academy was a little north of the downtown area, and the city's towers of offices were screened out by massive cedars, which surrounded the school like a great green wall. Beyond them, only a few hundred yards away, was the mall with the mirror shop. Darwen tried to spot it through the trees, but his aunt said, "Here we are," in a significant voice, like she was presenting a particularly impressive birthday present.

Impressive was the word.

There was a long, impressive driveway and a parking lot surrounded by immaculate lawns studded with impressive statues, and a similarly impressive flight of broad stone steps that went up to the main entrance. The school was big—huge considering there were only about ninety students between grades six, seven, and eight—and to Darwen it looked like a palace or stately home. It had elegant white columns on either side of the main doors, and the whole place was about as far from the grubby little school he had come from as he could imagine.

His aunt watched his face, biting her lower lip.

"It's great," he managed. "Very . . . nice."

This seemed to be the right thing to say and she laughed with relief. Darwen didn't say that it terrified him, that he would probably fit in at Hillside about as well as a toad in a dentist's office, or that he wanted nothing more than for her to turn the car around and break all possible speed limits getting out of there. As his aunt checked her reflection in her compact, Darwen gazed at the school—old-fashioned but somehow shiny and polished as old things in England never were—and wondered how on earth he was going to fit in here.

They walked up the stairs and into a broad and dimly lit lobby with a marble statue of two kids gazing up at some old guy with a book and a sappy look on his face. The plaque on it was inscribed LEARNING. A bell rang, a great booming bell that sounded like it had been designed to announce the end of the world. Two sets of doors at the west end of the foyer flew open and Darwen was able to see lines of students walking out of their classrooms in perfect silence. They were all wearing the green blazers, white shirts, and green ties trimmed with gold, the boys in gray pants, the girls in matching knee-length skirts. As Darwen watched he realized that they weren't so much walking as *marching*. Somewhere at the back someone was calling "left, right, left, right" to keep them in step.

You have got to be kidding me, thought Darwen.

He shot his aunt a quick look, but she was gazing at the student army as it stalked past like it was the single greatest thing she had ever seen. Darwen looked back at the kids, but no one made eye contact with him, each entirely focused on the back of the head in front of them. All except one, a girl about his age, the only one not in step, who gave him a considering look as she danced past, eyes widening in recognition. It was the girl from the mall the day before, the one who had said he was rude for almost flattening her mother.

"They're so grown-up!" his aunt cooed as the last of them filed through the lobby and into the assembly hall.

"They look like they are about to invade a small country," Darwen muttered.

His aunt nodded, smiling.

"So disciplined," she said. "Oh, Darwen, this is going to be just what you need: a perfect base on which you can build your future."

Suspecting the line came from Hillside's brochure, Darwen gave her a disbelieving stare, hoping she was joking, that she was about to say, "Quick Darwen, let's get out of here before it's too late." No such luck. Her eyes were misty and she had one hand clasped to her heart like he had seen the U.S. team do at the World Cup when they were singing the national anthem.

She steered him into the hall after the students who had formed perfect parade-ground lines. At the end of each line stood a teacher and on the stage at the front was an old man in a tweed jacket, standing so stiff and upright that it looked like he might be fastened to an invisible pole. When everyone else stopped moving he shouted, "Good morning, Hillside," and to Darwen's amazement everyone in the hall (except for him and Aunt Honoria) roared back, "Good morning, Principal Thompson," in perfect unison.

"I have called this assembly to welcome someone to our academic community," the principal announced. "We have a new student entering Miss Harvey's sixth grade class. Raise your hand, Mr. Arkwright."

It took a moment for Darwen to realize that the principal meant him. He put his hand up cautiously and every head in the room swiveled in his direction. They looked, they clapped for three seconds, then they looked away.

"I am sure that you will give him any help he requires," the principal continued, "as he adjusts to the special conditions of our environment."

Adjust? Fat chance, thought Darwen grimly.

"I also want to announce that the eighth grade debate team took first place in the state this past weekend. That is three years in a row. Please congratulate the team and their coach, Mr. Sumners."

Another three second burst of applause.

"And let us not forget," the principal went on, "that the continued success of the debate team, the exam results of last year's graduating class, our study trips to Paris and Guadalajara, indeed everything we do here at Hillside grows out of the three great principles of education. Say them with me, please."

And as one the school shouted back, "Memorization, organization, and logic."

"Chuffin' 'eck!" muttered Darwen.

His aunt noticed and, not being familiar with the exclamation, whispered excitedly, "Just think, Darwen, these are going to be your friends!"

She made it sound like he'd won the lottery.

Darwen opened his mouth but couldn't think of anything to say that wouldn't seem rude or ungrateful so he just stood there, gaping like a fish flopping on the beach. His aunt gave him an encouraging smile and patted his shoulder awkwardly. Once again Darwen was struck by the number of different races represented by the students—but just as he had at the mall, he still felt like he stuck out.

The assembly broke up and the students came marching out past them, eyes front, back to their homerooms. All except for the girl from the mall, who waved as she skipped by. Darwen half raised his hand in response, but then the principal was standing over him and he thought better of it.

"Miss Harvey will send someone to collect you in a moment," he pronounced.

"I can take him down," said his aunt. "It's no trouble. Which classroom . . . ?"

"No," said the principal. "We don't let parents—guardians, in your case—into the classroom. It confuses the students. We need a clean break from home when they come to school in the morning. They come through that door as children, but once inside they are students. You can have them back at the end of the day and they can play with their toys and their video games," he said, with distaste, "but while they are here, they put away childish things and their business—yes, *business*—is to learn. That takes structure and discipline. I'm sure you understand."

With that, he put a firm hand on Darwen's shoulder and gave Aunt Honoria a look that said, quite plainly, that she should leave.

"Oh," she said, looking uncertain for the first time since they had arrived. "Right."

No, thought Darwen, and it was his turn to give her an encouraging look. *It's not right. Say you've changed your mind. Don't go. Don't leave me in this place!*

"Right," said his aunt again. She still looked unsure but

she was almost as out of her depth as Darwen. Faced by the principal's blank face, his certainty, she could think of nothing to say. Eventually she sighed and said, "I'll be here to get you this afternoon, Darwen. Enjoy your first day." Then she was walking back through the main doors and down to the car.

Enjoy your first day? Was she nuts? Darwen took a half-step after her, but the principal increased his pressure on Darwen's shoulder like he was restraining a poorly trained dog. Darwen watched his aunt drive away and turned at the sound of footsteps. One of the students had come back for him.

"Ready to escort Mr. Arkwright to Classroom One, sir," said the boy.

He didn't actually salute, but it was a near thing. The boy was tall, black, and confident-looking, his uniform crisp. His eyes flicked over Darwen, who was wearing jeans and a T-shirt with a dinosaur on it, and his lip shifted slightly toward a sneer.

"As he is, sir?" he said, with a look at the principal.

"Ah," said the principal. "Quite. I take it you don't have your uniform with you, Mr. Arkwright?"

"It wasn't ready," said Darwen. "My aunt hasn't had time . . ."

"Quite so," said the principal, "but you can't go to class as you are. Jacket and tie are considered minimum dress standard. Get a blazer and tie from the supply closet for Mr. Arkwright, please Mr. Whittley."

The boy nodded and marched down the hall and round a corner.

"Standards must be maintained, Mr. Arkwright," said the principal. "Wait for Mr. Whittley here, Mr. Ark-wright," he said. "And remember: this is the first day of the rest of your life. Make good choices."

Darwen, who could think of nothing to say to such baffling remarks, watched the principal walk stiffly to the staircase and up out of sight. He felt momentarily lost and drifted back to the main doors so he could look out into the sunlit parking lot and the grounds, half hoping that his aunt had decided to come back.

There was no one there, just the pale statues, one of which had a bird perched on its head. And then the bird shifted oddly, reaching with its wing like it was going to grab hold of the statue's arm, almost as if it had *hands*, and Darwen could see that what he had taken to be feathers was actually more like dark, rubbery skin.

"A flittercrake!" he gasped aloud. But what was it doing here . . . ?

"Put this on."

"What?" said Darwen, turning suddenly. The boy who had been sent to take him to class was back, and he was holding out a green blazer and matching tie. Darwen blinked, then turned back to the grounds but the creature had disappeared. The statue stood white against the deep green of the grass and there was no sign of the flittercrake.

"Come on," said the boy, thrusting the tie at him. "We don't have all day."

"I can't fasten a tie," said Darwen, his face hot, eyes swiveling back to the empty lawns outside.

Whittley smirked minutely, then his face set like a mask. He put the tie around Darwen's neck and set to work. His fingers moved quickly, efficiently, but Darwen didn't like being dressed like he was a baby. No matter how well tied it was, he thought, the tie would still look stupid because he was wearing a T-shirt without a collar. A T-shirt with a triceratops on it. When the boy started to put the jacket on him, Darwen snatched it from him.

"I can do it," he said.

Darwen was not a big boy and the jacket was at least two sizes too large. The cuffs almost covered his hands and the whole thing hung about him like he was wearing a blanket.

"That'll have to do," said Whittley. "Okay, come on. Quick march."

Darwen hesitated, casting a last look out into the grounds but the boy walked briskly away, and Darwen had to jog to catch up.

The corridor they entered had classrooms on the right

and windows facing onto a grassy central courtyard on the left. Like everything else he had seen so far, the hallway was big and imposing, as if the architect's goal had been to make people—especially children—feel small. Darwen hurried after the boy and came up beside him.

"I saw this bird in the grounds," said Darwen. "Big, but with leathery-looking wings. Maybe you see them all the time but I have never . . . "

It was supposed to be a polite way to get Whittley talking. Instead the boy just said, "We don't talk in the hallways. And walk behind me. Single file."

Darwen dropped back, head down.

The homeroom class was completely quiet, but everyone turned to get a good look at the new boy, and there was a sudden rush of whispering so that it felt like stepping into a room full of snakes.

"Silence, class," said the teacher. The boy who had escorted Darwen from the lobby took his seat at the back and Darwen was left to hover by the door, trying not to make eye contact with anyone. "This is Mr. Darwen Arkwright who is joining us from England," said the teacher, a pale woman with large oval glasses and dark hair cut in a bob. She wore a cream blouse, a straight skirt, and flat shoes, all of which were, to Darwen's mind, rather old-fashioned for someone who looked quite young for a teacher.

"Welcome, Mr. Arkwright," said the class in unison.

"Er, all right?" said Darwen, embarrassed. The class giggled.

"I am Miss Harvey," said the teacher. "Please take a seat there until the bell sounds for the first session."

There were three rows of desks, five desks to a row, all perfectly spaced. Darwen took his place at the only open seat by the window, watched unashamedly by the girl from the mall. It wasn't a critical look exactly, just frank curiosity, but it made him self-conscious and he looked away. Through the window he could see the trees that surrounded the school grounds and the roof of a building that might have been the mall. He had barely sat down when the great booming gong of a bell sounded and everyone got to their feet in a single fluid motion. Everyone except Darwen, who was the last to stand behind his chair, the last to join the line forming by the door, the last to get in step as they marched out. It was going to be a long day, thought Darwen.

And he was right. It started with world studies, taught by a large, tough-looking teacher called Miss Murray who wore a tight blue suit with gold buttons which stood out against her dark skin, and who began the class by saying, "Good morning, children. Ready to work?"

Darwen wasn't. He had never heard of world studies, and though it turned out to be something like history and geography, it involved places and periods he had never studied. When he left his old school, they had been studying life under the Tudor kings and queens of England. The class at Hillside had been working on Polynesia for two weeks. Darwen wasn't sure where Polynesia was, and when he asked, the students laughed.

Miss Murray scolded the class, but the way she answered his question—pointing to the map and intoning "Hawaii, New Zealand, *Polynesia*"—suggested she thought Darwen might be a bit slow, and several of the students snickered behind their hands. Darwen took the old-fashioned fountain pen he had brought from England out of his pocket and wrote his name on the cover of his exercise book, head lowered so that no one would see how red his face was.

After world studies, he had English, which he assumed would be a welcome relief in comparison, but the teacher—Mrs. Frumpelstein—told him he had to stop spelling *color* with a *u* and start working on "something closer to standard spoken English" if he was to make himself understood in the States.

"Most Americans find the English accent appealing," she said, "but the dialect you speak . . . Not so much."

They spent the rest of the class diagramming sentences, using words like *participles* and *gerunds*. The book they were reading was a boring description of the school system in Burundi—wherever that was—and there were no monsters, sword fights, or spaceships in it. Darwen flicked through the pages unhappily, and the boy who had brought him to homeroom—Lawrence Whittley, though Darwen had heard some of the other boys call him Chip—leaned over and whispered, "Looking for the pictures, Arkwright?" He snickered, a high-pitched laugh that sounded like a woodpecker or a tiny machine gun.

Then came lunch.

All three grades ate together at the same time, which meant that there were about ninety people in the cafeteria when Darwen went in. His old school cafeteria had been a huge aircraft-hangar of a building with a linoleum floor, Formica-topped tables, and plastic trays of almost comically bad food. Chicken, chips and beans, mystery meat pie, terrible pizza, all cheerfully wolfed down by kids who had made an art out of making fun of how bad it was. The cafeteria at Hillside was another planet entirely. The students sat at oak tables with green tablecloths and linen napkins. There was classical music playing in the background, menus on the tables (*menus!*), and they ordered through attentive staff in white aprons. Half the stuff on the menu was in French and it all came out beautifully arranged on china plates. One look and Darwen knew that it would be both excellent and healthy, so he couldn't explain why he found himself craving mystery meat pie and chips—er, french fries.

The one thing this cafeteria had in common with his

old school was that you sat where you liked and with whom you liked, but since Darwen knew no one, this wasn't much of an advantage. He looked around the room feeling ignored and unwanted, till he saw one face turned toward him. It was the girl from his homeroom. She waved to him as if he were miles away. With an inward shrug, Darwen headed over, noting at the last moment that she was alone, though the other tables looked overcrowded.

The girl was tall, black, with large, unblinking eyes and arched eyebrows that gave her a frank, considering look. She wore her hair in braids pulled into a ponytail at the back and held in place with a pink plastic clip, and looked supremely confident, as if everything in sight belonged to her.

"All right?" said Darwen. "Can I, you know, sit down?"

"Knock yourself out," said the girl.

"I'm sorry?" said Darwen, who had no idea what that meant. "I thought you were waving to me. I'll go."

"You're from England aren't you?" said the girl.

"Aye," said Darwen. "I mean, yes," he added, thinking of the English teacher's advice to speak more "standard" English.

"Huh," said the girl. "You gonna sit down or what?"

Darwen did, feeling confused.

"I went to England once," said the girl. "Tower of London, Tower Bridge, Madame Tussauds, and Buckingham

Palace. I didn't see the Queen or nothing though."

"Oh," said Darwen, who had just noticed that her uniform was dressed up with huge earrings which were actually glow-in-the-dark skulls wearing goofy-looking grins. "I 'aven't seen any of those things," he said.

"But you *are* from England?" said the girl, skeptical.

"Yeah," said Darwen. "From the north."

"You mean, like, Scotland?"

"No. Northern England. Near Manchester and Liverpool."

"Huh," she said, clearly unsure of what she thought of him. "Is that why you sound like that?"

"Like wha'?" said Darwen.

"Like *that*," said the girl. "Your accent. I didn't hear anyone who sounded like you in London. Or in movies. They don't sound like you in *Mary Poppins*."

"No," said Darwen. "I suppose they don't."

"*Ah spawse thih dawwnt*," the girl repeated carefully, mimicking his accent. Darwen flushed. "You about near killed my mom last night, tearing through the mall like it was on fire. What was all *that* about?"

"Oh, said Darwen, looking away, "I was just . . . in a hurry."

"Next time you're in a hurry, you might want to go somewhere with less people," said the girl. "You know, save on the hospital bills."

Darwen nodded vaguely, saying nothing.

Okay, he thought, *next time I'm chasing an impossible creature toward a shop full of magic mirrors I'll be extra careful. . . .*

"Well," said the girl, sticking out her hand as if deciding to make the best of a bad situation. "I'm Alexandra O'Connor. Alexandra means 'defender of the people.' My friends call me Alex."

"Darwen Arkwright," said Darwen. "You can call me Darwen. And I think I'll call you Alexandra, if you don't mind."

"Do you like Shakespeare?" she said, in a businesslike way. "I saw *A Midsummer Night's Dream* in Piedmont Park last year. Fairies and stuff. Kind of dumb, but pretty funny. I about wet myself at one part."

"Never read any," Darwen said.

"You sure you're English?" asked the girl, cocking her head. "I thought all you people knew Shakespeare."

"Apparently not," said Darwen, who was getting irritated. "But I do like books."

"Like comic books and stuff? Sport books?" said the girl, unimpressed. "That's all the boys here read."

"No, actually," said Darwen. *Who is this girl?* "I read all sorts of stuff. Good books. Real books."

"Just not Shakespeare," she said. "You should read some," she added, her eyes still fixed and unsmiling. "Great literature is good for you."

"Oh," said Darwen, who didn't much like the sound of that. "I just like stories."

"Mmm," said the girl, frowning as she looked him up and down, unimpressed. "Well, maybe you'll be ready for it one day. Did you order your lunch yet?"

"No," said Darwen.

"Most people preorder but since you're new you'll just have to go *à la carte*," she said, handing him the menu.

"À la what?"

"Just choose what you want," she said.

Darwen studied the creamy white card with the food items printed in elegant cursive like it was a wedding invitation.

"What's *au gratin*?" he said.

"Just means cheesy," she said. "Not cheesy like, you know, *bad*," she added as an afterthought. "Not cheesy like a cheesy movie or a cheesy song. Just, you know, with cheese."

"I think I get it," he said.

"It's French," she said, helpfully. "I guess you don't speak French, huh?"

"No," said Darwen.

"Even though it's in Europe and you come from Europe," the girl mused as if this was a fascinating paradox.

"There are lots of countries in Europe," said Darwen.

"Lots of languages."

"Which ones do you speak?" said the girl.

"None," said Darwen. "I mean, one. English."

"In a manner of speaking," she said.

"I told you," said Darwen. "I'm from Lancashire. That's 'ow we talk in Lancashire, all right?"

"Okay, okay," said the girl, "don't get your panties in a pickle."

"My what?" said Darwen. He was beginning to understand why the girl had been sitting alone.

"So why did you move here?" asked Alexandra. "Chip Whittley said he heard the principal talking on the phone and he said that your parents . . ."

"They had to go away," Darwen blurted. "For work. They're scientists and are doing special research. At the North Pole."

"The North Pole?" she repeated.

"Yeah," he said, his face flushed.

"On what?"

"What do you mean?"

"What are they researching?"

Darwen hesitated.

"Polar bears," he said. "And shrinking icebergs. But it's kind of secret so I'm not supposed to talk about it."

"Huh," said the girl, watchful.

Darwen looked down feeling stupid and transparent,

wondering why he had said any of that and wishing he hadn't.

"So what do you think of Hillside Academy?" she said. Darwen knew she had changed the subject on purpose, knew she suspected he was lying. What had Chip overheard?

"Hello?" said Alexandra. "I asked what you thought of Hillside."

"Well, I've only just arrived," said Darwen, cautiously. "It's pretty different from my old school."

"In England?"

"Aye," said Darwen, giving her a pointed look. "In England. My school wasn't so . . ." He looked for the word. She supplied one.

"Awful?" she tried. "Appalling? Abysmal?"

"Well, I wouldn't say that exactly," Darwen began.

"What about nightmarish?" said Alexandra. "Ooh," she added with relish. "That's a good one. *Nightmarish.* Yeah, I like that."

Darwen stared at her as she got out a little notepad and wrote the word down.

"This is going in my next report," she said. "Today I went to my nightmarish school. What a nightmare! I had several nightmarish classes and . . ."

"Yeah, I get it," said Darwen. This was a very strange girl.

She scribbled furiously but her pen had obviously run out of ink.

"You got a pen?" she asked.

Darwen produced his fountain pen and handed it to her. She started to write then paused and considered it critically.

"Where'd you get this, a museum?" she asked.

"Forget it," said Darwen, snatching it back.

"Touchy, aren't you?" she said. "So come on: what do you think of Hillside Academy?"

"Well, it seems very organized and the teachers obviously know their subjects and . . ."

He was interrupted by Alexandra giving a single shout of derisive laughter.

"The teachers here are *aliens*, man!" she said. "I bet a million dollars, they're from, like, Alpha Centauri or something."

Darwen grinned in spite of himself.

"I'm serious," she said. "That Mrs. Frumpelstein, the English teacher?"

"What about her?"

"Well for one thing: *Frumpelstein*? What kind of a name is that?" said Alexandra laying her knife and fork down. "*Ada Frumpelstein.* Come on! That's totally a made-up name. Some alien from the Crab Nebula landed on Earth and said, 'Hmm, what can I call myself? I know, I'll be

Ada Frumpelstein and I'll teach English and I'll mark down that beautiful Alexandra O'Connor girl because she says things like *ain't*.'"

"She seems pretty tough," Darwen said.

"That's right," said Alexandra, as if he had just agreed with the whole Crab Nebula scenario.

"I guess it's a good school though," said Darwen. "I mean, it's really expensive, isn't it? And they take all those trips abroad. And the students do really well on exams."

"Exams!" the girl exclaimed with a dismissive wave of her hand.

"Check out Alexandra making friends," said a voice behind him.

Darwen turned to see a tall boy with brilliant white teeth who had been sitting next to Chip Whittley. He was smiling, but it was more of a sneer. "Starting a club for the pathetic and unwanted, Alex?"

"When I want to talk to you, Nathan Cloten," the girl answered, losing none of her confidence, "I'll let you know. You got me?"

"Whatever, Alex," said the boy, still sneering. "So this is the new kid."

He looked Darwen up and down, managing to look both slightly amused and contemptuous.

"Darwen," said Darwen. "Darwen Arkwright."

"*Darwen?*" said the boy. "What kind of name is that?"

"It's a place," said Darwen. "Back where I come from."

The boy was taller than Darwen by at least two inches, fair-haired and tanned, and his eyes were a bright and icy blue. "You're from England," he said.

"Not from London though," said Darwen, quick to get that out of the way.

"What about your parents?" said the boy.

"What about them?" said Darwen, wary.

"Where are they from?"

"England," Darwen shrugged. "Why?"

The boy's eyes narrowed as he considered Darwen's face, then looked at Alexandra.

"If you're going to take in strays, O'Connor," he said, "you should have the vet check them over first, in case they have fleas or something."

He grinned, then turned away as if bored. For a moment Darwen sat there waiting to speak, but then the boy was laughing at something he had seen at another table.

"Good job, Usually," he called to a boy who had just spilled his drink all over the floor.

Then he was walking toward the boy he had called "Usually" as if he had forgotten Darwen entirely.

"*That* is Nathan Cloten," said Alexandra. "His father's a senator, and he's very popular, but if you ask me, he's not very nice. In fact, I'd suggest you keep out of his way."

"Why?" said Darwen. "What did I do?"

But the girl just shrugged and got up.

"I gotta pee before science," she said, matter-of-factly.

"Bye. See you in class."

Darwen smiled weakly and nodded.

The afternoon began better, with an hour's science, but ended worse, with Spanish, which the other students had been doing for at least a year, and several of them for longer. Darwen knew a few words of German but that didn't help. Worst of all was the two hours of math.

Darwen had never been any good at math beyond basic arithmetic, and the Hillside class was already doing what they called pre-algebra. After ten minutes in which the teacher threw out words like *factorization*, *associative operations*, and *exponentiation*, Darwen began to wonder if this was also a foreign language class. The teacher was Mr. Sumners, a bald, pink-faced man with small, deep-set eyes and a habit of tipping his head back and going "ahhh" in the middle of every sentence. It made him sound like a donkey.

"So that would be six to the power of three, ahhh, and four to the power of two," he said. "Care to take a stab at the next one, Mr. ahhh, Arkwright?"

"No, sir," said Darwen.

The teacher peered at him, brows furrowed.

"I'd like an answer, boy," he said.

"I gave you one, sir," said Darwen. "I said no."

"Not an answer to that," said Sumners, getting pinker. "That was what we call a rhetorical question. Know what a rhetorical question is, boy?"

"No sir."

"Ask your English teacher," Mr. Sumners replied, with a flat grin that made his little eyes sparkle like hard candy. "But in the meantime, ahhh, you can give me an answer to this problem."

He rapped the white board with its numbers and squiggles and Darwen stared at it, trying to make sense of it all.

"Come on, boy," the teacher said. "We haven't got all day."

"I can't do it, sir," said Darwen. "I don't understand the question."

"Can't do it?" said Mr. Sumners with mock astonishment, though Darwen felt sure that he was quite pleased.

"No, sir," said Darwen.

"Ah the great British education system," the teacher said, grinning his cold grin, "perhaps one of the, ahhh, Hillside regulars could help out?"

The boy who had spoken to him at lunch raised his hand casually.

"Nathan," said the teacher. "Enlighten our transatlantic friend."

"Fourteen," said Nathan.

"Exactly," said Mr. Sumners. "Fourteen. Now let's try another."

As he started to scribble on the board, Nathan turned fractionally toward Darwen and smirked at him.

Darwen got through the rest of the day by keeping his head down and waiting for it all to be over. As the other kids went off to after-school clubs, he headed outside and sat on the steps where he would be able to see his aunt's car the moment she pulled up. He couldn't wait to get away from this place and back to the mirror in his bedroom, back to Silbrica, to Moth and the moonlit forest. It was a measure of how desperately he wanted to feel the peace of the woods that he was able to push aside the memory of the strange and unnerving shadow that had stalked him there. He was thinking about this when he realized someone had sat next to him. For a moment he didn't look round, sure that this would be either someone who wanted to make fun of him for being new or Alexandra, the annoying girl from lunch. But when he turned he found it was neither.

It was a boy from his class who Darwen had noticed both because he had gotten all the answers right in science and because his uniform fit almost as badly as the borrowed blazer Darwen had been drowning in all day. But this kid's problem was the opposite. The boy was huge—not fat, just big—with broad shoulders and a thick neck. He had hands like goalie gloves and his shoes looked like canoes. His skin was pink from the sun and he had close-cropped hair so that he looked a little like a smart and friendly pig.

"Hey," he said.

"All right?" said Darwen.

"How was your first day?" said the boy. He had an accent Darwen guessed to be Southern but rougher than most and slow as molasses. He looked and sounded, Darwen decided, like he worked on a farm.

"Okay," Darwen lied.

"Yeah?" said the boy.

"No," said Darwen. "It was rubbish."

The boy's face split into a grin so broad and honest that Darwen couldn't help but return it.

"I'm Rich," said the boy, offering one of his massive hands.

"I'm not," said Darwen, "but my aunt is pretty well off, I think."

"No," said the boy, laughing. "That's my name. Rich. Richard Haggerty."

"Oh," said Darwen. "I'm Darwen."

"Like the scientist?" said Rich, excited.

"What?"

"Charles Darwin," said Rich. "*On the Origin of Species.* You know, evolution and stuff."

"No," said Darwen, almost wishing it was. "It's Darwen with an *e*. I was named after a little town where my parents met."

"Oh," said the boy. "That's cool. *Rubbish*. That's British for trash, right?"

"I suppose," said Darwen.

"I like that," said Rich. "What a load of rubbish!" he added in a terrible British accent. He grinned then reverted to his slow Southern drawl. "It will get better. School, I mean."

"Not sure I'm coming back," said Darwen, admitting the idea aloud for the first time, and immediately wondering how he would convince his aunt to take him somewhere else.

"No, man, you should totally come back," said Rich, flicking a stone down the steps. "It's not so bad so long as you don't take all the marching about too seriously. Some of the teachers are sort of . . ."

He fumbled for the word.

"Aliens?" Darwen tried. "That's what Alexandra says."

"She would," grinned the boy. "Heck, maybe she's right. Some of them . . ." He shook his head and whistled.

"That math teacher doesn't like me," said Darwen.

"Sumners is a dag gum freak," said Rich. "But some of them aren't so bad. Mr. Iverson is cool."

"The science teacher?"

"Yep. Runs the archaeology club. I'm the president,"

he added, proudly. He rooted through his book back and produced a well-thumbed paperback. "Check this out," he said.

It had once been glossy but was now cracked and grubby. Its title proclaimed it *An Introduction to Field Archaeology*. Rich's face positively glowed with pride as Darwen looked at it.

"That's mine," he said. "Best book ever. Didn't think I'd be into archaeology, did you?" said Rich

"Well, I don't know you . . ." Darwen said.

"It's okay," said Rich. "I'm used to people thinking I'm dumb. If I'm not talking about stock cars and barbecue, people get that look."

"What look?"

"The one you got when I said 'archaeology club.'"

"Sorry," said Darwen.

"It's cool," said Rich. "Archaeology is awesome 'cause it's history and science at the same time. What about you? Got any hobbies? You a Braves fan?"

Darwen shrugged.

"I like reading," he said. "And bird-watching."

"Yeah?" said Rich.

"Back home I knew the name of every bird I saw, but here . . ." Darwen sighed. "No idea."

"That's a mockingbird," said Rich, pointing to a gray-and-white bird. "They're all over the place. And that over there is the state bird: a brown thrasher. You know, like the hockey team."

"Hockey?"

"The Atlanta Thrashers," said Rich. "I'm more a Falcons fan, myself."

"The bird?" said Darwen. "Or is that another hockey team?"

"Football, man," Rich grinned.

Darwen sighed again.

"School's not so bad," Rich said, "and we need more regular kids."

"Regular?" said Darwen.

"Yeah," said Rich. "I mean, you don't want to let Nathan and Chip run the place, do you?"

"Do they?"

"They think so," he said, shaking his head with amusement and wonder. "But there's stuff here they don't know about. Stuff that will blow your mind, Darwen. Trust me. You don't want to miss it."

"What kind of stuff?" said Darwen, cautious, thinking immediately of the flittercrake.

"Nothing to do with classes or study," he said. "Other stuff. Stuff you won't see at any other school, I guarantee that."

Darwen smiled, liking the boy as much for the sound of his lilting voice as for what he said. Plus, he sensed

Rich had sought him out to try and make him feel better.

"Give us a hint," said Darwen.

"Tell you what," said the boy. "Come back tomorrow and I'll give you more than a hint. But I'll say this: there's something deeply weird about this place and it goes way beyond that freak-show Sumners."

"What do you mean?" asked Darwen, thinking of the mirror shop. Deeply weird indeed.

But Rich was standing up. A battered pickup truck with the windows open was coming down the drive. It was making so much noise and spewing so much smoke that for a moment Darwen thought it was on fire.

"That's my dad," said Rich. "I'll catch you tomorrow, Darwen with an *e*. Tell your . . . your aunt or whoever, not to pick you up till six thirty. Archaeology club! And bring some old clothes. Expect deep weirdness!"

And then he was trotting down the steps, tossing his book bag into the back of the truck and climbing into the passenger seat. The rust-eaten vehicle gave a perilous shudder like it might stall, then shot a puff of black smoke out the tail pipe and roared off through the trees.

"Aunt Honoria," said Darwen as they drove home ten minutes later. "This school. It's very expensive, isn't it?"

"Don't you worry about that, Darwen. It's paid for."

"Already?" said Darwen.

"The whole first year, and there are no refunds," said

his aunt, laughing. "So don't go failing out. I'm doing okay, but I can't afford to flush that kind of money down the drain!"

She laughed again and Darwen slumped in his seat.

"You're going to be there for a long time, Darwen," she said.

"Right," said Darwen, trying not to sound miserable. "Great."

He thought about Rich's hints about something "deeply weird" going on at Hillside and wondered if it could possibly be as strange as what was waiting for him in his bedroom closet.

GATES

As soon as they got home, Aunt Honoria unveiled the plastic wrapped blazer she had picked up at lunchtime.

"Won't you look handsome in it!" she exclaimed.

Darwen eyed the green jacket warily.

"Go put it on while I warm up dinner," she said, giddy with anticipation.

Darwen grabbed it and ran to his room, flinging the closet open the moment he got his bedroom door closed.

The mirror was just a mirror.

Darwen pressed and poked at it, tried shifting the angle from which he looked, even tried turning suddenly to catch it out, but it remained an ordinary mirror. Miserably, he tried on the blazer, returned to the living room and endured his aunt's rapture. He had spent all day thinking about Moth and the forest. It had never occurred to him that he might never see them again.

He ate his dinner (black bean and orange soup with anchovy and olive salad picked up from what Aunt Honoria called "a darling local bistro," whatever *that* was), then said he wanted an early night.

"Good idea," said his aunt. "Got to be bright-eyed and bushy-tailed for school."

He wondered if that was something her parents had said to her when she was a kid and whether it had made any more sense in those days.

School, he thought, as he closed the bedroom door. *Bright-eyed and bushy . . . ?*

He stopped dead. The closet door still hung open, and inside it hung the mirror. But it was no longer a mirror. It was the window onto the Silbrican forest through which he had passed the night before.

He forgot about school, and stared at the trees through the battered mirror frame, feeling light and happy, as if he had discarded heavy luggage he had been dragging around for hours.

But why? he wondered. *Why was it only a portal some of the time?*

He looked out of the window onto the lights of the city, and thought about Mr. Peregrine's shop with its curious clock that showed only sunrise and sunset.

The mirror changes after dark, he thought. It made no sense, not really, but he was positive it was true.

He changed into his pajamas and had just called his aunt when he realized that the little embroidered Manchester United badge was no longer in the breast pocket. He must have dropped it in the forest. Well, he would be able to look for it soon.

After his aunt had tucked him in, in that over-efficient way of hers, which left him pinned under the sheets, Darwen waited for the sound of the television in the other room, then wriggled out of bed, put on his socks and sneakers and opened the closet door. He remembered the strange shadow in the trees, but shrugged the memory off. He was going to see Moth. He was going to walk in the secret forest. It was a good place. Even if the shadow had been something real, not just the work of his imagination, there was no reason to believe it would have harmed him. Not really . . .

He hoisted himself onto the frame—which took his weight despite the fact that it had been tacked to the closet door with a single nail—and boosted himself through.

It was as wonderful as before, maybe better this time because he wasn't surprised. This time there was no shock and he could enjoy it, drink it all in. . . .

He walked around the fountain for a few moments, scanning the ground for his lost badge, then lay down in the grass, and gazed up at the starlit sky. No more than a minute later, a familiar greenish light showed small in the air above him.

"Hello, Moth," he said, getting to his feet. "You haven't seen a little red-and-gold badge have you? I think I dropped it last time . . ."

"You should not stay, Darwen," said the dellfey, her mechanical wings whirring.

"Why?" said Darwen. "I like it here."

"It is not safe. There are dangerous things about."

"Like the whatdoyoucallit?" said Darwen. "The flittercrake? I'm not afraid of that."

"There are mightier beasts than flittercrakes, Darwen Arkwright. Mightier and more terrible."

"Such as?" said Darwen, ready to shrug it all off. The dellfey was so small that he felt big and powerful.

"There are gnashers and scrobblers and drifters," said the dellfey, "not to mention the hobstrils or the Insidious Bleck."

"Since when?" said Darwen.

"Some say a Shade was seen in these very woods late

last night," said Moth. "Usually the forest is safe, but lately . . ."

"What's a Shade?" asked Darwen, as if he was just curious, but watching the dellfey carefully.

Moth looked haunted.

"I would prefer not to speak of it," she whispered.

"Well I still like it here, gnashers, scrobblers and Shades included," said Darwen, defiant. "And if I see one and it so much as looks at me the wrong way, I'll give it a punch on the nose. I like it here and I'm staying." And then, just to make the point, he shouted again into the darkness of the woods. "I'M STAYING. AS LONG AS I LIKE!"

The dellfey's tiny eyes widened, and though she said nothing, Darwen thought she was impressed. He decided to press his advantage.

"I want to see one of those janus gates you told me about," he said. "The ones up on the hilltop. I want to see where they lead."

"You can't go through," said Moth. "It is not safe."

"I just want to look at them," said Darwen. "There's no harm in that, right? Come on, Moth. Just show me."

The dellfey hesitated for a moment, then nodded. The next thing Darwen knew she was darting up the hill, and it was all he could do to keep pace with the green spark that flitted through the trees. He pounded up the slope, straining to see the pinprick of green light ahead and then, quite suddenly, the trees stopped. They had reached the crown of the hill. Darwen was on the edge of a clearing, bright in the moonlight, and in the center of it was one of the strangest things he had ever seen.

It was, he supposed, a series of gateways made out of the living trunks of trees, but standing in a circle like Stonehenge or one of those Greek temples he had seen in books. Branches formed a canopy over the top so that the whole thing looked like an oversized gazebo somehow growing right out of the forest floor, and lit from the center by a gas lantern. But the tree trunks were also studded with strange controls, like you might see on very old machinery: large brass dials and gauges set into the bark, metal levers sticking out of knots in the wood, copper pipes and tubing that snaked around the branches, and little yellow lights with antique switches and knobs set in wooden panels lacquered to a high shine. It had none of the clean lines of the computers and phones he was used to, but it looked functional and had a grand, old-fashioned elegance.

"Cool," he said.

"This is the Janus Regionalis," said Moth. "Through here you can reach other loci in this regional network or you could go to the Janus Cardinalis which would take you to . . ."

"Other regions entirely," Darwen completed for her. He gazed at the great gateways with their weird little controls and wondered where they might lead.

"We should not be here, Darwen Arkwright," said Moth. "Please. You have seen what you came for. Let us go back down to your portula."

Darwen studied the tiny creature and saw real fear in her face.

"I just want a quick look through," said Darwen.

"This is a bad idea, Darwen Arkwright," said Moth, perching briefly on his shoulder. "What if a flittercrake reported that you were here?"

"Reported to who?" Darwen asked.

"I don't know," she said.

Darwen peered at her. She looked uncomfortable.

"Who would want to know I was here?" he asked carefully.

The dellfey shifted, turning from side to side.

"Moth?" Darwen pressed.

"We have been told to watch out for children," she said, after another long hesitation. "Children, *human* children, are suddenly much prized here."

"Prized?" said Darwen. "What does that mean?"

"It means that if it becomes known that you are here, there are some who would try hard to catch you."

"Catch me? What for?"

"I think you should go," she said.

"But I want to see what's in there," he said, pointing at the circle of tree-trunk doorways.

And as he pointed, something started to happen. The little yellow lights around one gate began to flash. The needles crept across the dials, moving from the white toward the red. There was a rumble of sound that Darwen could feel through the forest floor, and then a jet of steam hissed out of a valve in one of the copper pipes.

"What did I do?" Darwen shouted. "I just pointed!"

"It's not you," said Moth. "Something is coming."

She drifted back, away from the doors, and Darwen did the same, his eyes still on the opening between the tree trunks. Then there was another, even more impressive rush of steam and smoke, and Darwen saw the brass cogs and gears start to turn. One of the levers jolted slightly as something latched home, then came down with a long pneumatic hiss. It clunked into place and there was a momentary silence before a great wall of steam erupted from the sides of the tree trunks, till the nearest gate was a foggy gray wall.

Then there was a roar of noise and something came out in a blaze of light. Something big.

"Scrobblers!" shouted Moth. "Run!"

SCROBBLERS

Darwen only got a glimpse of what came through the gate, but he saw enough to set him racing through the trees after the dellfey. It was some kind of huge motorbike and sidecar, but much larger, and it sprouted pipes from its heavy body. It had what looked like a great boiler covered with wooden planks and bound with riveted leather straps, and hanging over its massive front wheel was a V-shaped plough like on some old steam locomotives. It had a single massive headlight. But the machine itself wasn't the worst of it.

Sitting astride the motorbike and in its sidecar were what Moth had called scrobblers—two huge men with leather helmets, goggles, and heavy lower jaws. Their arms were long and apelike and the one in the sidecar brandished a net on a pole.

They've come to catch me.

There was no doubt in his mind. He didn't know why, he didn't know who they were or what they wanted, but he was sure that he had to get away. So he ran faster than he had ever run in his life, despite the darkness and the tree roots, despite the tangles of vines underfoot and the pounding in his chest, he ran. His mouth was dry, his eyes wide and streaming, and it was all he could do to keep the green light of Moth in sight.

Don't look back, he thought, as the machine behind him came charging after. *Whatever you do, don't look back.*

The scrobblers' vehicle sounded more like a tank than a motorbike, and Darwen could hear its great plough shearing off the smaller trees as it forced its way through the woods. He started picking out the trees with the thickest trunks and running closer to them, hoping it might slow his pursuers, but if anything they were getting closer. Darwen was tearing down the hill, almost out of control now, gathering speed as he ran clumsily to where he hoped he would find the path. The light of the machine's headlamp was all around him, raking up and down the trees as it jolted down the hill.

Up ahead, Moth paused to look back and he thought he could see her waving frantically, though if she was calling, he couldn't hear it over the roar of the engine. He took two more scrambling steps and then heard something different, something new: the swish of the net. They almost had him. He dodged suddenly to the left, went round the biggest tree he could see, and then weaved right. There was an almighty crash as the great bike slammed into the tree, and Darwen risked a look back.

The collision had almost ripped the sidecar off the bike. The scrobbler with the net was climbing out, looking dazed, while the other had snatched a massive two-handed hammer and was pounding at the joint which held the two parts of the vehicle together. Darwen grinned, but looking back had been a mistake. He was running too fast, carried by his own momentum as he descended the hill, and by the time he was facing the right way again, it was too late. His foot caught on a fallen branch and he went sprawling in the bracken, rolling and crashing into a tree trunk.

For a moment, everything went dark, and then he was awake again, his head hurting, his right arm scraped and bleeding from the fall. He was half-covered with the long, heavy ferns that grew at the base of the tree, but not well enough to stay hidden. He heard another heavy, metallic blow back up the hill: the scrobbler with the hammer. But where was the one with the net? He shifted slightly and peered out into the night.

There.

The scrobbler was standing quite still, in his pale boiler suit and leather helmet, his back turned to Darwen, not five yards away. He was sweeping the underbrush carefully with the net. There was another ringing blow from higher up the hill and it sounded like something broke. The one with the net turned to look in the direction of the sound and Darwen got a fleeting look at him, his huge hands in leather gauntlets, his massive lower jaw lolling so that he could see oversized teeth—almost tusks—protruding beyond his lips. The skin around his mouth was thick and greenish. They might look like men, these scrobblers, but they weren't.

The creature turned, still sweeping the net over the ground. It was coming.

Darwen thought wildly but he was too terrified to move, and he knew that if he tried to run, that thing would spot him and net him before he had taken two strides. The scrobbler took another step. One more and it would see him.

Then it grunted, straightened up and started batting the air with its free hand. A tiny green light was flitting round its head.

Moth!

The scrobbler swung at the dellfey but she shot nimbly away, then back again, right into its face. It swung again, this time with the net, and the dellfey was only just quick enough. She hung back, but looked uncertain and the scrobbler swung once more. She reacted just in time, swooping sideways out of the reach of the net, her mechanical wings whirring, but she looked tired. It couldn't go on much longer.

Darwen knew what he had to do. He moved silently into a crouch, took a breath, and bolted up and out of the undergrowth, running hard as he could, down the hill. There was no Moth to follow now so he just had to hope he found the path quickly. He ran, not bothering to be quiet, knowing it wouldn't make any difference except, perhaps, to Moth who might get away if the scrobbler turned his attention back to Darwen.

His head still throbbed and his arm stung where he had scraped it, though he barely felt anything beyond the terror and desperation that kept his exhausted legs moving. He heard the cannon sound of the great motorbike restarting, but this time he didn't look back. Instead he scanned the trees for the path, grateful for the slope of the ground, which—though treacherous—at least told him he was going in the right direction. The scrobbler with the net was coming after him on foot. He could hear its great lunging strides and animal grunting. He hoped Moth had escaped.

He hit the path before he saw it, and it was all he could do to stop himself running right across. He turned sharply to the left, conscious of the scrobbler crashing out of the undergrowth behind him. He ran no more than ten strides before spotting the mirror, winking in the darkness not fifty yards away.

Now it was a race.

Darwen reached inside for his last reserves of determination and sprinted down the path. He could hear the bike, but it seemed far away. It took him a moment to realize that the rider had taken it down the hill by a different route. It had reached the path a little ways past the mirror, and was now turning toward him. Darwen had one scrobbler at his back with the net, and the other directly ahead of him on the massive motorbike. His only chance now was to reach the mirror before either of them.

He ran harder than ever toward the mirror frame, though that also meant running toward the headlight of that monstrous machine and the creature astride it. He heard the one behind him lunge with the net, felt the air of it as it swept behind his shoulders. He saw the bike with its hulking rider steaming toward him. And he saw the mirror between them: Five more strides. Two.

Then he was grasping the frame and diving in, pulling

himself with all his might. He felt the scrobbler with the net clawing at his feet, and heard the smash of the motorbike as it ran into the mirror, though Darwen felt no impact at all. Then he was tumbling into the closet of his own room.

He sat up and turned in time to see one of the scrobblers—beady red eyes behind its heavy brass goggles—pounding at the surface of the mirror, trying to shove its gauntleted fist inside. But for whatever reason, the portula was sealed and Darwen instinctively knew that the scrobbler may as well try to reach through concrete.

He was safe.

"Everything all right in there?" called his aunt's voice through the closed bedroom door.

"Yes," said Darwen. "Sorry. Just . . . fell out of bed. I'm fine."

"You be careful," said his aunt. "And get some rest."

"I will," said Darwen.

He had never felt so exhausted in his life. His arms trembled, though that might have been fear as much as exertion. He snatched the blue shirt that was hanging in the closet and hung it over the mirror. He wouldn't be able to sleep with those things looking in at him.

DEEP WEIRDNESS

The next day Darwen checked the mirror more cautiously than usual, and though it was solid and ordinary looking, he was wary of it. He worried, though not so much for himself as for Moth and her world. What did it all mean? The dellfey had said that the forest was a safe place, that the dreadful things she and her kind watched for generally did not enter, but she had also said that human children were suddenly much prized there. *Suddenly*. That meant that something had changed, though he had no idea what. He did know that Moth—along with all her kind and the woods they called home—were in danger. Darwen had to do something about it. In his mind, the forest had become almost as much a home to him as it was to her, and Moth—tiny, fragile, defenseless Moth—needed him to look after her.

All of which led to one thing: he had to get back to the mirror shop. The old man would have answers. He must.

How he was going to get to the mall occupied his mind for much of the morning. He wasn't allowed to leave school at lunchtime, and he was supposed to go to archaeology club before his aunt came for him that evening— but it was maddening to do nothing. Who knew what had happened after he had left the forest? The monstrous scrobblers might still be there, chasing Moth through the trees. He did not dare to think what would happen if they caught her.

There was no assembly at school so Darwen began the day in homeroom thinking furiously. Perhaps he could cut out of archaeology club early, run over to the mall to see Mr. Peregrine, and still be back in time for his aunt to collect him? It wouldn't give him long, but he couldn't wait a whole day. He just couldn't.

He felt odd in the green-and-gold uniform, but at least it fit and he no longer stood out. He sat between two girls, one small and spindly whom the others called

Mad (he couldn't figure out whether it was supposed to be an insult), the other a blonde girl called Princess who brushed her hair till Miss Harvey told her to stop.

"You know who she is, right?" said Alexandra O'Connor, appearing at Darwen's elbow and nodding at the blonde girl as the students selected books to read from a cart. "Her mom is Gloria Clarkson."

"The actress?" said Darwen, amazed.

"I don't know about *actress*," said Alexandra pointedly. "Let's go with movie star, shall we?"

"Chuffin' 'eck," said Darwen, considering Princess with new respect. "Anyone else have famous parents?"

"Naia Petrakis's dad is some kind of tycoon," said Alexandra, nodding toward a black-haired girl, fiddling with a silver bracelet with little charms on it.

"What about Rich?" said Darwen.

"Rich Haggerty?" said Alexandra, eyebrows raised so high they looked like they were going to fly off her head. "His daddy was a cotton farmer. My mom says they sold off some land by the Chattahoochee but their necks are still redder than a Kentucky turkey's, and Rich is on scholarship."

Darwen, who had no idea what that meant, just shrugged and said, "I like him."

"Yeah?" said Alexandra, clearly surprised. "Good for you. He's smart too. Science smart," she qualified, as if that didn't really count. "But still. Nathan Cloten, you already know, tragically. There's Bobby Park, his parents are Korean, but I don't know what they do," she said. "I think he cuts his own hair. Bad decision."

She pointed around the room: "That's Simon Agu—the cute boy there—he's from Nigeria. Jennifer Taylor-Berry's family is Old South money, but I think her dad is a lawyer. There's Carlos Garcia who's from Mexico. Barry Fails—he isn't too bright if you ask me—and then Melissa Young and Genevieve Reddock. Those two are, like, joined at the hip. Genevieve is the one with that dumb plastic kitty keychain that she's always playing with like she's eight years old. It's computerized and you have to 'feed it' and stuff else it dies, supposedly. *Oh no!*" she exclaimed in a fake whine of despair. "*My little plastic cat has died! Whatever will I do? I shall have to go to the little plastic pet shop and buy another little plastic cat till I kill that one too and have to start over, again and again till I have a little plastic grave yard all full of . . .*"

"Alexandra?" Darwen prompted.

"Anyway," she said, in her normal voice, "those three, Barry, Melissa, and Genevieve all hang out with Nathan and Chip Whittley: the cool kids."

She shrugged, and though her face was blank, the point was clear: she wasn't cool and knew it. Figuring he should at least know who he was in class with, Darwen jotted the kids' names down in the back of his workbook with his fountain pen. Alexandra regarded it with her face wrinkled up in confusion and distaste till Darwen put the cap back on and said, "Yes?"

"You can buy pens from the twenty-first century, you know," said Alexandra. "The stores are full of them."

"This works fine," said Darwen, dabbing at the smudged ink with his finger and making it worse.

Alexandra shrugged and looked away.

"Hey, man," said Rich, lumbering over to Darwen and thumping him amiably on the shoulder. "You came back. Cool. Looking forward to archaeology club this afternoon?"

"Oh you are *not* dragging him along to that?" Alexandra cut in. She turned to Darwen. "You know what the 'archaeology club' is? It's Rich and Mr. Iverson digging in the field out there with a bucket. That's it. The entire operation. Trust me, you don't want to get involved. Take drama with me. Or chorus. Yeah, chorus! It's awesome. I'm going to be a soloist."

"Archaeology club sounds brilliant," said Darwen, deliberately. Rich beamed with delight and gratitude.

"Okay," said Alexandra, with an it's-your-funeral eye roll. "Maybe you'll dig up something older than your pen, but I wouldn't hold your breath."

Darwen had lunch with Rich, wishing he could go to the mall instead, but knowing that breaking a major school rule on his second day would be a very bad idea. Alexandra sat with the girl they called Mad, apparently punishing Darwen for his choice of after-school activity. That suited him just fine. All through lunch Rich talked about what he had found on the school grounds and on the land his father owned. He had an extensive collection of arrowheads and a few bits and pieces from the Civil War including a bullet he had found with his metal detector.

"It's a basic one, kinda cheap, but it works pretty good," said Rich. "I want to use it in our dig area behind the gym, but Dad won't let me bring it to school. The grounds round here are pretty special. I'm sure there's all kinds of stuff to find."

"Special? How?" asked Darwen, sensing something important was coming.

"You saw those trees round the school grounds?" said Rich, leaning in like he was going to confide a secret. "They're eastern red cypress trees. They aren't real cypresses, more like junipers really, and they grow all over the place here, but most of them are small. Those trees round the school are old, like three hundred years old. Maybe more. And they are in a ring, right? *Planted.* This whole area was Muskogee land—Creek Indians— and the cypress was one of their sacred trees. So this area was important. Part of the ring was cleared when they built the mall, so the ring was originally bigger, but the school is pretty much right in the middle. So what is it about this land that made it special, huh?"

"I don't know," said Darwen, prompting, but Rich's response was disappointing.

"Me neither," he said. "But I'll bet it was something big, and if we can do more digging, maybe we'll find out."

"Oh," said Darwen. "Wait, that's it? That's the secret you promised to tell me yesterday?"

"Yep," said Rich, looking pleased. "Pretty cool, huh?"

"I suppose so," said Darwen, feeling deflated.

That's it? he thought. *That's the deep weirdness? Try being chased by subhuman monsters through the forest in your bedroom closet. . . .*

Three hundred years might be old in Georgia, but where Darwen came from, he knew houses, churches, and castles that were three times that age, and after last night's hellish adventure, a little local history wasn't going to get his blood pumping.

"And today the principal is coming to look at the site," Rich continued. "He wants to see what we're doing before deciding whether to approve a budget for the club."

"For what?"

"Tools, mainly," said Rich. "Right now we're borrowing spades and stuff from the janitor, Mr. Jasinski," he said, nodding to a big man in stained overalls who was eating a sandwich from a plastic box, "but I want to get some real equipment: measuring rods and storage units, maybe even a microscope. . . ."

"Hey Haggerty," called a voice at the next table. It was Barry Fails, the kid Alexandra had said wasn't that bright. "You gonna come try out for lacrosse this afternoon?"

"He can't," said Chip Whittley. "Busy collecting Coke cans, right Haggerty?"

Chip gave his machine-gun snicker and the table laughed along. Rich studied his plate, his face flushed.

"Hey, remember when he thought he'd found a Civil War bullet," said Nathan, loudly, "and it turned out to be a bottle cap."

"Shut up, Cloten," said Rich.

The other boys laughed again.

"You recruiting the new boy?" asked Chip, grinning. "Told him you found Tutankhamen's gold under the baseball diamond?"

"Or Blackbeard's treasure in the girl's locker room?" added Nathan.

"Yeah, or . . . I don't know, something really *old* in, like, the parking lot?" added Barry.

"Good one, Barry," said Darwen, very dry.

"Nice choice of friends there, English boy," said Nathan. "Redneck Rich and wacko Alex? So far even

Usually here has you beat."

The others laughed and marched out, dumping their used plates on Darwen's table as they did so. When they had gone, Darwen turned back to Rich who was poking at his food disconsolately.

"What is this stuff, anyway?" said Rich, eyeing a forkful, his face red. "No one here can rustle up a decent pulled pork sandwich and slaw?"

"What's pulled pork?" asked Darwen.

"Barbecue," said Rich, bitterly. "Redneck food."

"*Usually*?" Darwen said, keen to change the subject. "Why do they call Barry 'Usually'?"

"His last name is Fails," said Rich. "Barry Fails. Usually. Kind of harsh, but pretty much true. I wouldn't call him that if I were you, though. Only Chip and Nathan get to do that."

"The cool kids," said Darwen, nodding but feeling a little inadequate. Still, he thought, how many of the cool kids have portals to other worlds in their bedrooms?

He grinned to himself, but then he remembered running from the scrobblers, the sweating, screaming, eye-widening horror of it, and his smile faded.

Mr. Iverson, the science teacher, was the oldest member of staff Darwen had met so far. He was a small man with oversized silvery eyebrows that stood up like tufts and—with his round glasses—made him look like an owl. He wore a shabby lab coat, patched at the elbows, and stained with chemicals, and he had a habit of putting pens behind his ear and then forgetting about them. Some of the students thought he was a bit of a joke, but the man loved his subject, and his classroom was full of colored—and foul smelling—liquids bubbling over Bunsen burners. On the first day he had shown them how brightly a ribbon of magnesium burned "just for fun" and then had taken Darwen through the textbook page by page, suggesting makeup reading for everything he had missed. During their next class, he asked how Darwen was progressing.

"Okay," said Darwen. "Rich is helping me."

"Excellent," said Mr. Iverson. "Sometimes the greatest wisdom is in asking for help. Now," he added, raising his voice so that he got the attention of the whole class, "project time!"

Nathan and his pals groaned, but Rich perked up like a gopher popping out of his hole.

"Form groups of three, then design and build a device that can throw a baseball," said Mr. Iverson.

"A catapult?" exclaimed Rich, delighted.

"Exactly so, Mr. Haggerty," said the teacher. "Bring them to class October 31. Your grade will be calculated according to how well you can talk the class through the physics of your device and, of course, how far it throws."

More groans, mainly from the girls. Rich looked liked he couldn't wait to get started. Mr. Iverson began to assign groups and Darwen sidled up to Rich.

"Who's your third?" asked Mr. Iverson.

"We can manage by ourselves," said Rich. "Right, Darwen?"

"Er . . . sure," said Darwen, who was in the middle of filling his fountain pen.

"Alex!" called Mr. Iverson. "You're with Rich and Darwen."

"Are you kidding?" said Rich. "She'll make it look like a unicorn or something."

"Part of the work on class projects is learning to make group decisions," said Mr. Iverson, with a smile.

Rich sulked all the way through Mr. Sumners's class, but Darwen had other things to worry about. The math teacher seemed to go out of his way to find things he knew Darwen couldn't do before dragging him up to the whiteboard. After three trips up there and no right answers, Darwen could sense waves of contempt from Nathan and his pals, and sympathy, mainly from the girls. In between trips, Darwen gazed out of the window and thought about talking to Mr. Peregrine, until Mr. Sumners—who was proud of his wit—asked Darwen if he might board the next available transport ship back to earth. Most of the boys laughed, which said more about what they thought of Darwen than what they thought of Sumners's joke.

So Darwen did what he always did when upset or under pressure, and read, this time from a copy of *Treasure Island* he had concealed inside the covers of his math book. He had read it twice before, but there were bits that he went back to over and over again. Right now he was reading the part in which blind Pew brought the mark of the black spot to the Admiral Benbow Inn. . . .

"It seems," said Mr. Sumners in his lazy drawl, "that our visitor from overseas has, ahhh, something better to do with his time than study pre-algebra."

The class went quiet and Darwen felt their eyes upon him.

"What are you reading, Mr. Arkwright?" asked the teacher.

"Nowt, sir," said Darwen, closing the book.

"What?"

"*Nothing*, sir," said Darwen, translating the dialect word.

"It's a very big nothing," said Sumners. "A lot of pages for a nothing, wouldn't you say? Ahhh. Perhaps you would share your nothing with the class."

Darwen slowly lifted the book and opened it so that the teacher could see inside the cover to a picture of pirates and distant galleons.

"Stand up, Mr. Arkwright," he said. "Show everyone the wonderful new math textbook you have brought to class."

Darwen turned to his right and left, holding the book up, but his eyes were fixed on the desk.

"Perhaps you would like to read to us from the chapter on long division," said the teacher.

Darwen muttered that there wasn't a chapter on long division.

"What did you say, boy?"

"I said there isn't a chapter on long division, sir," said Darwen.

"What about a chapter on multiplication?"

"No, sir. It's a novel."

"Fractions? Geometry? Trigonometry?" said Sumners rolling the words off his tongue with pleasure. "No? What about, ahhh, pre-algebra, since that is what we are currently studying?"

"No," said Darwen, checking to be sure. "Still a novel."

Alexandra laughed.

"No, what?" said Mr. Sumners.

"No, *sir*," said Darwen.

"Gnaw, sur?" repeated Mr. Sumners maliciously. "What is 'gnaw'?"

"I meant *no*," said Darwen, rounding out the sound as clearly as he could.

"So the Englishman can speak English after all, ahhh," said Mr. Sumners. "And why do you have a novel in my math class?"

"I prefer reading," said Darwen simply.

He hadn't meant to be rude, but Sumners was making him uncomfortable and he said the first thing that came into his head. It wouldn't have been so bad if Alexandra hadn't laughed again, but she did, a single bark of delight, after which she muttered what sounded like, "That's right."

Mr. Sumners looked like someone had slapped him. His face went red from his neck to the top of his bald head and his eyes bulged.

"*You prefer reading?*" he parroted back, snatching the book out of Darwen's hands. "Pirates and treasure!" he announced, holding the book in the air. "How are you going to get a decent job with a head full of pirates and treasure? How do you plan to get into college, sail there?" The class giggled, but there was something about Sumners's anger that unsettled them. "You think you can, ahhh, shin up the mainmast to the crow's nest or hoist the Jolly Roger and that will get you through your SATs?"

"I don't know what SATs are," said Darwen. "But I don't need to do that stuff yet. I'm a kid."

The class didn't actually gasp, but there was a new tension in the air, as if they were waiting to see what would happen next.

"You might be a kid, boy, but in my classroom you are preparing for, ahhh, life, for high school, and college, for law school or business school. Or . . ." said Sumners putting his hands on Darwen's desk and looming over him, "do you plan to become a pirate?"

The class laughed uneasily.

"I'd rather be a pirate," said Darwen, "than a lawyer or a businessman. Or," he added made bold by his anger, "a math teacher."

This time the class did gasp.

Sumners straightened up and walked slowly and silently toward the door. He opened it and held it open, until Darwen couldn't ignore the implication anymore and got up from his desk. He crossed the room, avoiding the eyes of the other kids, and out the door.

"Please, sir," he said. "Can I have my book?"

"At the end of the school year," said Sumners with a nasty grin. "Now stand there and don't move a muscle till I, ahhh, call you back in. And you might spend the time thinking about pre-algebra, because when you get back in, there will be some problems on the board for you to, ahhh, solve in front of the class."

"But, sir," Darwen said, "I left my pre-algebra book at my desk and I can't prepare . . ."

"*Ah left mi algibra boook at mi desk,*" parodied Sumners, in a low mocking voice. "Should have thought of that before, shouldn't you? The principal will be hearing about this, boy. There'll be a letter to your aunt. I would have thought she had enough on her mind without you failing out of school, wouldn't you?"

He closed the door. Rage flared inside Darwen as he watched the teacher walk away through the glass, until

Barry Fails started making faces at him and he pulled back.

His second day in school and he was already in trouble. He should feel terrible, he thought, but beyond the anger and tiredness he found he didn't care that much.

Because there's no one to be disappointed in you, he thought.

There was Aunt Honoria, and he didn't want her to worry about him, but he hardly knew her. People who loved him, people he wanted to make happy? There was no one. And right now a part of him wanted nothing more than to have Mr. Sumners come back and make some more smart remarks about how stupid he was, just so Darwen could tell him to boil his bald head and shut his stupid cake-hole.

"It's not right, the way he's singling you out," said the wiry little girl they called Mad in end-of-day homeroom. "You should complain. Or kick him."

Neither of those strategies seemed likely to help that much, and though Darwen was glad that she felt for him, he didn't like being pitied.

"She's a pistol," said Alexandra, nodding at the girl. "You wouldn't think it to look at her, but she is. First week here, she ordered a vegetarian lunch and it had ham in it. You should have seen her! I thought she was going to explode. The following day they said they had nothing for her, and the day after that they lost all power to the kitchens. I don't know how she did it, but since then she's had her vegetarian stuff every day, no problem."

"Her name's Mad?" said Darwen.

"Madhulika," said Alexandra.

After end-of-day homeroom, the class broke up for after-school activities, and Darwen followed Rich to the changing rooms, where he put on some old jeans, a T-shirt, and a pair of old sneakers. Rich talked about watching the Falcons at the Georgia Dome and how his dad had taken him to Krispy Kreme afterward where they had eaten glazed donuts hot off the conveyor belt. As he talked, he led the way back into the central quadrangle, opened a door onto the grassy square, and then another at the base of the clock tower. Darwen checked the clock. He would stay with Rich just long enough to show interest—a half hour at the most—and then he needed to get to the mall.

It was dark and musty inside the tower and there was a small flight of stairs into a kind of basement.

"Is it okay that we're here?" asked Darwen. He didn't want to get into more trouble.

"Mr. Jasinski lets me come in to get tools and stuff," said Rich. "For the dig. He probably isn't supposed to, but so long as the teachers don't see, it's fine."

He pulled a string and the room was lit by a naked light-bulb hanging from the ceiling. There was a workbench against one wall, a pair of large toolboxes, and a set of cabinets beside an ancient iron stove. The whole place smelled of damp sawdust.

"About our science project," said Rich. "The baseball thrower. How about I draw up some designs?"

"Fine by me," said Darwen, whose mind was elsewhere. "Is that okay with Alexandra?"

Rich gave a dismissive wave.

"She won't care what I do so long as she gets to decide what color it is," he said. "Hey, check this out." He pulled a box of matches and a three-inch strip of the magnesium ribbon from his pocket. "Mr. Iverson said I could take it. Wanna light it?"

"Did you ever see anything that made no sense at all?" said Darwen suddenly. "Something you couldn't explain, couldn't talk about because everyone would think you were nuts?"

"Everything makes sense. If you look at it the right way, I mean. Reality is scientific."

"I suppose," said Darwen, wondering if Rich would think that if his closet opened onto a forest full of monsters.

"Why?" said Rich, handing Darwen a spade. "What did you see?"

"Oh," said Darwen with a shrug that was supposed to look casual. "Nowt. I mean, nothing."

Mr. Iverson was waiting for them out behind the gym where, under a bright blue tarp, a square of the lush grass had been taped off and the top surface scooped out. Beneath the dark topsoil the ground was bright orange.

"Georgia clay," said Rich, pulling out his *Introduction to Field Archaeology*. "Good for making bricks, but not much else."

"Delighted to have a new member!" said Mr. Iverson to Darwen. "Richard has a fascinating theory about this land as a Muskogee ritual space. Of course, if we find signs that this is a burial ground, we will have to stop. We don't want to disturb graves. If you find bone, you contact me immediately, okay?"

Darwen felt a little thrill of excitement and nodded. After Nathan's scorn, it was good to hear someone like Mr. Iverson taking Rich's ideas seriously.

Rich had brought a wheelbarrow from the janitor's shed, which he had filled with tools, and now he climbed carefully into the square with a spade that looked best suited for making sandcastles.

"Can't we use something bigger?" said Darwen, checking his watch. "It'll take ages."

"We might miss something," said Rich, "or confuse what strata it came from."

"Strata?" said Darwen.

"The layers of dirt," said Rich. "Each layer is a different

age. The deeper we dig, the older the find. If you see anything, use this."

He brandished a tiny digital camera.

Darwen looked up at the sound of distant voices jeering. The lacrosse teams were making their way onto the playing fields behind the gym. He could see Nathan and Chip, dressed in white and carrying sticks and helmets, waving at them, though he couldn't hear what they were saying.

Mr. Iverson took a couple of steps in their direction and shouted, "Cloten! Whittley! One more sound out of you and I'll be speaking to Mr. Stuggs!"

The boys laughed and drifted away to join the rest of the team. Darwen, who had never seen lacrosse, watched as they started tossing balls to one another from the nets at the end of their sticks.

"Come on, Darwen," said Rich. "Let's get to work."

Darwen was turning back to the square when he saw the principal coming from the main building. Rich saw too and his eyes were bright with anticipation.

"Hard at work, boys?" said the principal as he wheezed into range. "Showing initiative: always good to see. Not sure Mr. Jasinski will be quite so enthusiastic about you digging up the grounds," he joked, "but let's see what you've got."

"Well, Principal Thompson," said Mr. Iverson, "as

you can see the boys are proceeding in a careful, scientific manner. Their goal is to determine what special function, if any, this land had before the Civil War, while it was still Creek Indian land."

"Ah, the Creek Indians," said the principal, sagely. "Quite. Not here anymore. Moved on."

"Well, forced on," said Rich. "Pushed off the land and sent to Oklahoma."

"Indeed," said the principal. "Long ago."

"In history," said Rich.

"Exactly," said the principal, smiling as if he was making a particularly clever point. "Which I'm sure is interesting if not terribly relevant."

"Relevant?" said Mr. Iverson. "To what?"

"To the school," said the principal. "To life. To now."

"I'm not sure I follow," said Mr. Iverson.

"We're a forward-looking community here at Hillside, boys," said the principal. "We don't want to get too bogged down in the past. We're all about the present and the future. Your future. Ours. Everyone's."

"I'm sorry, sir," said Rich. "But don't we learn about our present by understanding the past?"

"You'd think so, wouldn't you?" said the principal. "But the truth is, Mr. Haggerty, that the future doesn't much care about the past. What's that old saying: 'History will teach us nothing'? There's a lot of truth to that, boys.

You need to know your history—dates and facts and the like—because you have to pass exams, and exams are the route to success. But I'd be wary of spending too much time on what has already happened. Put your energies into the future."

"And the budget proposal I turned in?" said Mr. Iverson, whose eyes had cooled.

"Money's very tight just now, Frank," said the principal, confidingly, "and the lacrosse team needs new equipment if they are going to maintain their winning record. You know how it is."

"Yes, sir," said Mr. Iverson. "I think I do."

"Well then," said the principal, turning toward the lacrosse game that had started up on the neighboring field. "I'll leave you to it. I wouldn't stay out long," he said, looking up at the sky. "Looks like we'll get some rain."

And with that, he started in the direction of the lacrosse field, shouting "Oh, well done, Smithson!" as he walked away.

Rich sat in the dirt square, his face drained of all the hope that had been there moments before.

"I'm sorry," said Darwen.

"No," said Rich, shrugging like he didn't care. "It's fine. I'm sure he's right and all."

"Excuse me, boys," said Mr. Iverson. "I'm going to have a few words with our beloved principal."

Darwen wanted to feel bad, to share in Rich's disappointment, but he had other things on his mind. He checked his watch surreptitiously.

"Come on," said Darwen, squatting down in the square. "So we don't have fancy tools. We can still dig, right? And Mr. Iverson has a lab. So if we find anything, we can analyze it there, yeah? Come on, Rich: hand me that spade."

Rich nodded and smiled gratefully. Together they started scraping the dirt out of the square, inch by careful inch.

"History will teach us nothing," Rich muttered. "Which idiot said that?"

They worked for another ten minutes in almost complete silence, picking at the ground but finding nothing, and when the rain started, even Rich seemed glad to finish early.

"Archaeology is like that sometimes," he said wisely as they walked back toward the school carrying their tools. "Sometimes there's nothing there. Maybe the principal is right."

"No," said Darwen, thinking of the mirror in his closet. "You never know when you are going to find something you couldn't possibly imagine."

"You want to wait in the library?" asked Rich.

"Not tonight," said Darwen, trying to sound casual. "There's something I have to do."

THE
REFLECTORY
EMPORIUM

The rain was falling harder now, though it was still warm. Darwen put his head down, and then ran across the school grounds and through the ring of cedars toward the mall. Rich was right. The trees that had been planted to screen the school from the shops below were much younger. The original circle of cedars would have enclosed part of the mall: the part where Mr. Peregrine's shop was.

Maybe there is a connection. Something about this place . . .

Darwen entered the mall through one of the side doors, dripping, but as he rounded the first corner, he saw the policeman he'd run into last time. He was giving directions to an old lady, one pudgy hand on his broad hips, the other pointing like he was shooting a gun. Darwen stepped into a sports shop, moving just far enough inside that he could watch the cop unseen.

"Hey," said a voice behind him. "If it isn't the transatlantic freako."

Darwen turned and found himself face to face with Nathan, Chip, and two of their older lacrosse buddies, their practice apparently rained out. Both the older boys were big and good-looking, tanned and with brilliant white teeth. They were dressed in the latest jeans and Darwen felt small and shoddy by comparison.

Great.

"Er. All right?" said Darwen.

"Er. All right?" parroted Nathan. The other boys grinned. "No books in here, Arkwright. Or should that be Lord Arkwright? But then that's not your kind of England is it?"

"Not really," said Darwen, trying to play along, conscious of the policeman out there in the mall behind him.

"No," said Nathan, his smile more clearly a sneer. "That's what I thought."

"You've got weird eyes," said one of the older boys, an

athletic-looking kid with blond hair shaped with mousse. "Sort of brown but with yellow round the edge. You wear colored contact lenses or something?"

"No," said Darwen, attempting another smile. "They came with the rest of me."

"Weird," said the boy again.

"So what are you doing in here?" said Nathan. "Come to pick up a Braves shirt?"

"Maybe," Darwen shrugged.

"Yeah?" said Nathan. "Which player?"

Darwen looked away.

"You don't know any, do you, English boy?" said Chip.

"Course I do," said Darwen.

"Name one," said Nathan.

There was a heavy silence; then they started laughing.

"Man, that's so lame," said one of the older boys. "He doesn't even know Chipper Jones. Or Hank Aaron. That's gotta be, like, offensive or something, right Chip?"

Chip Whittley scowled at Darwen.

"That's right," he said. "You ought to know your heritage."

Darwen had no idea what they were talking about.

"You should probably get out," said Nathan. "This is our place."

"Looks like a shop to me," said Darwen, stung. "I thought this was a free country."

"Free and best in the world," said Nathan. "Right boys?"

His buddies nodded and Chip said, "Absolutely," and though they were grinning, it was supposed to be a challenge.

In case he had missed it, Nathan made the point clear. "So what do you think, English boy? Is this the greatest country in the world or what?"

"It seems very nice," said Darwen, dodging. He didn't have time for this. He had to get to the mirror shop.

"*Nice?*" scoffed Nathan. "You hear that, guys? He thinks the United States of America is nice. I didn't ask if he thought it was nice though, did I? I asked him if it was the best country in the world. So, English boy, what do you say?"

"My name's Darwen," said Darwen, stalling but defiant.

"And my name," said Nathan, "is Paul Revere. Answer my question."

"Or what?" said Darwen, whose fists were balled with frustration.

"Ooo!" said the other boys together. "Tough guy," said one.

"Yeah?" said Nathan, taking a step toward Darwen so that he loomed over him a little. "That right, English boy? You think you're tough?"

He poked Darwen in the chest with a finger so hard

that Darwen took a step back.

"I didn't say I was tough," said Darwen. "But I'd like you not to do that."

Nathan grinned and reached to prod Darwen's chest again, but this time Darwen was ready. He reached up, grabbed the finger firmly and lifted it a little. Nathan's eyes widened with surprise and pain.

"Let go," he spluttered.

The other boys took a step toward him, but Darwen tightened his grip on Nathan's finger making him gasp and shake his head at the others.

"I don't want any trouble," said Darwen.

"I don't care whether you *want* trouble," Nathan managed, his face red. "You've found it. You can't hold me like this forever, English boy, and when you let go . . ."

"I told you," said Darwen. "My name is Darwen. Darwen Arkwright. It's not polite of you to keep forgetting it."

"You're dead, English boy," hissed Nathan. "You wait."

Though he had the advantage, Darwen felt trapped. Nathan was pushing with his finger so hard that if Darwen pressed back he might break it. The idea made him feel sick. For a moment he just stood there, still holding Nathan's finger, feeling his hand getting sweaty, unsure what to do. Then the athletic-looking boy was looking over Darwen's shoulder and Darwen knew something was happening. Nathan grinned then started to whine noisily.

"Ah!" he moaned. "Let go! Why are you doing this?"

Darwen let go like the finger was red hot but he knew it was too late. He turned and saw the fat policeman walking quickly toward them, his eyes locked on Darwen.

"You!" exclaimed the cop. "Stay right where you are."

Darwen wanted to run but knew that he wouldn't.

Nathan Cloten had pulled away and now stood there holding his finger out like a bird with an injured wing.

"I think he broke it!" he moaned, though as soon as the policeman stooped to examine it, Darwen saw him grin at his friends.

"I did not," said Darwen. "He was poking me and stuff," he said, lamely.

"You're coming with me," said the cop, whose eyes were small and mean-looking. "First bag snatching, now bullying. What's your name?"

"Bullying?" Darwen exclaimed, unable to believe his ears.

"Bag snatching!" one of the boys repeated, surprised and delighted at just how much trouble Darwen was in.

"I said, *what's your name?*" said the cop, staring down at him as he drew a radio from his belt. His badge said Officer Perkins.

Darwen gaped at him, turning to the others as Nathan, in a pleased voice, said, "His name's Darwen Arkwright.

He's English."

He said it like you might say, "He's a leper," or "He's half goat."

"You here with your mother?" said the cop.

Darwen shook his head.

"He lives with his aunt," supplied Chip, as if this was also a bad sign.

"She here in the mall?" asked Officer Perkins.

"No," said Darwen. "I walked over from school."

"You can start by apologizing to your friends," said Officer Perkins, eyeing Darwen.

Darwen hesitated, then, barely raising his eyes, he muttered, "Sorry."

"Thank you for your assistance, officer," said Nathan, now apparently fully recovered. "But, for the record, he's not our friend."

He said this coolly, his eyes on Darwen, and Darwen knew that, as far as the other boy was concerned, this was far from over.

The cop led Darwen away, wheezing as he walked.

"What's your aunt's phone number?" he said, once they reached his desk at the information center.

Darwen stared at him. They were going to call his aunt? Drag her out of some crucial meeting about millions of dollars or . . . whatever it was she did, to scold him for standing up to Nathan Cloten? It was crazy! And unfair.

"I don't have her number," he said. "Look, I haven't stolen anything and I wasn't bullying that kid. *He* was bullying *me*! He just saw you coming and . . ."

"Your aunt's number, please," said the cop. "I won't ask again."

Darwen thought quickly.

"There is someone else you can talk to," he said. "He's a sort of friend of the family. A kind of great-uncle. Mr. Peregrine. He works here."

"Where?" asked Perkins, skeptical.

"At the mirror shop down there."

"Is that right?" said the cop, putting his pen down and pursing his lips. "That's where you went the other day, right? Yes. I think I would like to have a word with Mr. Peregrine."

Darwen winced. He had forgotten that the policeman had already met the old shopkeeper, forgotten that Mr. Peregrine had covered for him once already.

Well, thought Darwen, *he owes me. After what happened to me in that forest, he definitely owes me.*

But as they walked the length of the mall the policeman's strides got longer and more purposeful. He wanted to give the shopkeeper a piece of his mind.

This, Darwen thought, *could go very badly.*

The shop looked the same—rickety and out of place—though Darwen was relieved to see no snarling flittercrake clinging to its sign. The policeman opened the door, the bell tinkled, and they stepped into the dusty and cluttered interior. Mr. Peregrine was at the desk wearing a curious pair of gold-rimmed spectacles that had multiple round lenses like an old-fashioned microscope. The glasses made his sharp green eyes big so that Darwen saw them narrow thoughtfully from across the room as they came in.

"Hi, Uncle Octavius!" Darwen blurted. "This officer wanted to talk to you about a misunderstanding we had . . ."

"I'll do the talking," said the cop. "Now see here," he said, approaching the shopkeeper and raising his forefinger. "I came in here the other day looking for a boy and you said no one had been in. But that wasn't true, was it? This is your nephew, and you've been hiding him. For all I know, you're selling whatever he steals. What is this anyway, some kind of pawnshop?"

Darwen opened his mouth to protest but the shopkeeper gave him a tiny, silencing look, and smiled at the policeman.

"I thought you were looking for someone thievish, or fiendish," said Mr. Peregrine, apparently unoffended, "some ragamuffin who would sneak in, his coat bulging with ill-gotten gains. Clearly not my nephew."

The policeman's brow furrowed but he said nothing.

"You are more than welcome to look around," said the shopkeeper.

"I plan to," said Perkins. "I'll stay here all day if I have to."

"I doubt that will be necessary," said Mr. Peregrine. "But be aware that we close earlier than the rest of the mall. We're never open after sundown. Wouldn't be wise. Isn't that right, Darwen?"

So his guess had been on target after all.

"That's right," said Darwen. He stared at the shopkeeper in silence, and the old man's eyes sparkled with what Darwen first thought was mischievous amusement before realizing it was something more. It was excitement.

A thought struck Darwen as he gazed around the shop, its walls, partitions, shelves, and tables all covered with mirrors: they were all . . . *special*. It wasn't just the one he had in his closet. It was all of them! That was why the shop closed before sundown. Every mirror in here became a gateway into another world. Darwen's eyes got wide, and the shopkeeper, who was still watching him closely, smiled secretly as he saw the realization dawn.

"I'm gonna start in the back," said the policeman, stepping past Mr. Peregrine.

"Certainly," said the shopkeeper pleasantly, his bright eyes still on Darwen.

As Officer Perkins strode into the back room, muttering

to himself about getting to the bottom of this, Darwen just stared at the old man with his funny glasses. He had wanted to come in shouting, to appeal on behalf of Moth and her forest, but now, surrounded by all those other mirrors, those portulas to other worlds, he felt only wonder and amazement.

"How is this possible?" he mouthed.

Mr. Peregrine smiled.

"*How* is less important than you might think," he said. "It is possible. It is here. That is as much as you need to know to begin with. Now, Mr. Darwen Arkwright, it seems we need to get to know each other properly."

He held out his hand. Darwen hesitated then, feeling a rush of embarrassment, shook it.

"An honor," said Mr. Peregrine, staring at Darwen, and grinning from ear to ear. "A real honor."

"Unlikely," said Darwen, getting uncomfortable under the old man's gaze.

"Beyond unlikely," said the shopkeeper, unabashed. "Beyond rare. You are a most singular person."

"Singular?" Darwen repeated. "You mean, unusual?"

"Oh, much more than unusual," said the old man. "Unique, I suspect. The only one of your kind."

"My kind? What do you mean?"

"Surely you have realized by now?"

"No idea what you're talking about," said Darwen, feeling stupid.

"You have a most remarkable talent: a gift. You are what is sometimes called a Squint, though your proper title, Mr. Arkwright, is a *mirroculist*."

The word hung in the air between them.

"A what?"

"A mirroculist," said Mr. Peregrine, and now his smile was gone and his voice was low. "One who sees through mirrors. Certain mirrors, at any rate. Darkling mirrors, whose true nature is only revealed after sundown. Mirrors like these." He made a sweeping gesture with his hand taking in the contents of the shop.

He was about to say more when the policeman returned with a sour look on his face. He clearly hadn't found what he was looking for and was unimpressed by the state of the shop.

"You need to join the twenty-first century," said Perkins. "There are no lights back there. I had to use my flashlight just to move around without killing myself. That's a health and safety issue, that is. It's no wonder you don't have any customers. Open the register, please."

Mr. Peregrine reached over to the massive, antique till, but his hand hesitated over the bank of keys.

"You know," he said, "I don't believe I will."

"Excuse me?" said the cop, drawing himself up.

"I am always willing to assist law enforcement," said Mr. Peregrine, smiling, "but you have absolutely no evidence for your accusations against this boy, and I find you rude to the point of barbarism."

"I said, *open the register*," the cop repeated.

"I may be old-fashioned," said Mr. Peregrine, still beaming benevolently, "but I know the law. Innocent until proved guilty, I believe. Which is why you will need what they call 'probable cause' before getting the search warrant necessary to get me to open the register. You and I both know that you will not get said warrant, so, unless you would be interested in purchasing one of my excellent mirrors, I will bid you good day."

The policeman stared at him open-mouthed, then turned on his heel and stomped to the door.

"You haven't heard the last of this," he said, as he stepped out of the door, which he then slammed, setting the bell ringing crazily.

"An unhappy man," said Mr. Peregrine, his face serious. "And a bully. I don't care for bullies, do you?"

"No, sir," said Darwen.

"Now, where were we?" said Mr. Peregrine. "Oh yes, my mirrors."

"But . . ." Darwen said, groping for the words. "This is a mall!"

"Perfect camouflage," said Mr. Peregrine, taking out a cloth and starting to polish the little hand mirror in which Darwen had seen the flittercrake. "There's nothing of interest in a mall, Mr. Arkwright. This one doesn't even have a bookstore. But my little shop is most interesting, wouldn't you say? In fact, if the people who come to this mall knew the things that went on in my shop—strange and wonderful and terrible things—they would find it all rather too *interesting* to get on with their rather less interesting lives."

"But I'm not special," said Darwen. "I'm just an ordinary kid. I'm not even from this country. How can I be a . . ." He sought for the word.

"A mirroculist?" the shopkeeper provided.

"Right," said Darwen. "That. Maybe loads of people can see through the mirrors and you just haven't tested them. Maybe the one I took home was broken and anyone could see into it . . ."

"Did they?"

"What, see in?" asked Darwen. "No, but there was no one else around . . . except . . ."

"Yes?"

"My aunt," said Darwen, a weight settling in his chest. "After sundown when the mirror changed, I could see the forest inside but . . ."

"Your aunt could not," said Mr. Peregrine. "Which, I think, confirms it. The mirror worked as it was supposed to. You, my young friend, are a Squint."

"But how?" said Darwen. "Why? Did I get it from

my parents or something?"

Mr. Peregrine heard the hope in his voice and considered him closely, so that Darwen blushed and looked down.

"In truth," said the shop keeper, "I don't know, though I have never heard of the gift being passed from parent to child."

Darwen sat down slowly and stared at the dusty countertop.

"Oh, Mr. Arkwright," said Mr. Peregrine, taking out a rectangle of paper and a pen with a nib that was even more old-fashioned than Darwen's, "if you could see some of the wonders on the other side, you might never want to come back to this world."

Darwen looked up, a wave of competing emotions rushing through him, fear and hope, pride and excitement: to step out of the world, to leave Hillside and his lonely life behind forever and live in a land beyond the mirrors . . .

Mr. Peregrine smiled, dipped his pen into an inkwell, and began writing a note in spidery letters. When he was done, he rolled it up, popped it inside a brass cylinder that seemed made for the purpose and screwed on the top. He raised a little corrugated wooden door in the wall behind the register, slid open a curved metal plate, and slotted the cylinder into the recess behind. He closed it, pumped a handle several times, set a dial, and pushed a button. There was a bluish flash from the edges of the wooden door, a soft pop and a whoosh, then nothing. He flipped open the door and checked inside. There was no sign of the cylinder.

"But . . . Listen," Darwen blurted, refusing to be distracted. "The scrobblers are going to hurt Moth!"

The old man spun around.

"Where did you hear that word?" he demanded, and his manner was quite different now, urgent, even alarmed.

"*Scrobblers?*" said Darwen.

"Yes. Where on earth did you hear . . . ?"

"From her," said Darwen. "Moth."

"Moth?"

"She's a dellfey," whispered Darwen. "She warned me about them right before they came through the gate."

"Do you mean to say," said the shopkeeper, very still, "that you went *through* the mirror? That you crossed over into Silbrica?"

"Of course," said Darwen, as if this was obvious. "Twice. And last time the scrobblers came and chased me and I just made it back to the mirror in time. . . ."

"You were able to climb through that little mirror?" said Mr. Peregrine. "I had not anticipated this. I thought it would be too small. I thought your shoulders would be . . ." he began, considering Darwen critically. "I see I miscalculated."

"I suppose so," said Darwen, a bit put out. He had lost a little weight over the last couple of months but it wasn't like he was the size of a rat.

"But this is extraordinary!" exclaimed Mr. Peregrine. "Tell me everything about your adventure, and quickly!"

"You have to help Moth," said Darwen, insistent.

"Tell me what happened," said the shopkeeper, patiently.

So Darwen did—the whole thing—start to finish. Mr. Peregrine was the perfect audience. He gasped, he laughed and at the end, he clapped his hands together with delight.

"A true Squint—sorry, *mirroculist*," he exclaimed, "right here in my shop!"

"I nearly got flattened by a massive motorbike and a scrobbler with a net," Darwen reminded him.

"Yes, that is unfortunate," said the shopkeeper, though he was unable to keep the smile from his face. "Terrible. Really, very bad indeed. You have my heartfelt apologies. But, as they say, no harm no foul. You returned to what you consider reality and none the worse for wear. Well, this is excellent."

"Excellent?" Darwen repeated. "I almost got killed!"

"*Almost* is such a wonderful word, don't you think?" said the shopkeeper with a wink. "So full of wiggle room and loopholes, so not-absolutely-anything. Almost killed means still very much alive, which, I'm sure you will agree, makes all the difference. So, the only remaining question is, when are you going back?"

"Back through the mirror?" hissed Darwen. "Into the forest with those . . . things?"

"Precisely," said Mr. Peregrine. "Exactly. You have hit the nail on the proverbial head."

"Never!" said Darwen. "I'm not going back in there. No chance. In fact, when I get home I'm going to smash the mirror. I just came here to tell you that so that you can save Moth."

"Smash the mirror?" said Mr. Peregrine. "Oh, I wouldn't do that if I were you. And I think you know why."

"Seven years bad luck?" said Darwen with a laugh. "That's just superstition. An old wives' tale."

"Have you spent much time with old wives?" said Mr. Peregrine. "They can be surprisingly insightful."

"So you're saying that breaking mirrors really does bring seven years of bad luck?" demanded Darwen, mockingly.

"Not all mirrors," said Mr. Peregrine. "But this one might. You recall, Mr. Arkwright, that the scrobblers were unable to follow you into your world. The portula sealed after you went through it. That is because the power of the gateway is bound into the mirror and, at present, only someone with your special talents can go through it. You have, as it were, a kind of key. To the creatures on the other side, the gate is always locked. But break the mirror, and the mechanism jams. Sometimes it jams closed and cannot be reopened. Other times it jams open and cannot be closed. Then it is not so much a gate to which one needs a key, but rather an open door through which all manner of things can come and go as they please."

Darwen swallowed and his eyes grew big.

"The scrobblers could get through?" he asked. "Right into my room?"

"Perhaps not scrobblers which are," said Mr. Peregrine, "quite large, as you observed. But other things that are just as unpleasant, certainly."

"For how long?" said Darwen, fearing he already knew the answer.

"It varies depending on the size of the mirror and the power required by the mechanism to keep it open," said Mr. Peregrine. "Sometimes the gate may stay open only a few minutes before failing, but other times it can stay open much longer."

"Seven years?" said Darwen.

"That is generally considered the maximum, yes," said the shopkeeper, considering the little hand mirror carefully. "Superstitions, you see, often grow out of truth, even if it's a truth no one remembers properly anymore.

After seven years the mirror would cease to be a gateway, but until then, it's wide open. You will notice that many of the mirrors in my little emporium are damaged. Some with broken corners, some just chipped or tarnished, some with major cracks. Did you not wonder how the flittercrake was able to get in here from the other side, or why you were able to see through it when the sun was still up? See?" he added, tapping a mirror with his hand as he had the last time Darwen had been in the shop.

The reflection flickered and behind it he could see a different place entirely, a day-lit valley with heavy trees. Darwen stared, his mouth open, but a moment later, the image flashed, then vanished, and the mirror was itself again.

"The shop is sealed from the mall, more or less," said Mr. Peregrine, glancing at the tiny fractured pane of leaded glass above the sign, "but believe me when I say that you would not wish to be trapped in here after sundown. So, Mr. Arkwright, I speak from considerable experience when I caution you against breaking the mirror."

Darwen nodded quickly but said nothing for a moment. He was scared, but there was a part of him that knew he'd had no intention of breaking the mirror. However dangerous it was, he loved it. It was like living inside one of his books, a story where anything could happen, and he would take that—with all its perils—over the gray world he lived in. Mr. Peregrine, who was watching him closely, seemed to sense this, and smiled.

"But what about Moth?" demanded Darwen, suddenly. "You have to help her."

"Yes, your story of scrobblers on the hunt troubles me," said the shopkeeper. "And your dellfey friend is correct. I chose that particular mirror because the locus to which it connects has always been a serene and peaceful place. Scrobblers and their allies avoid it. If they are hunting there, then I fear something dreadful is afoot."

"What kind of something?"

"Scrobblers do not act alone, Mr. Arkwright," said the shopkeeper. "They go where they are sent."

"By who?" asked Darwen, "and why?"

"Excellent questions, both," said the shopkeeper. "Answering them might be a matter for the council. They will already know of these incidents, of course, but they are sometimes slow to act. We will have to give them a little push."

"What council?" asked Darwen.

"The world beyond the mirrors is governed by an ancient order known as the Council of Guardians, twelve of our kind who maintain the stability of Silbrica. The council sits in permanent session, their minds linked. As Guardians they are law and reason and a force for right. They also govern the gateways and portulas, controlling the energy that makes them work. They sit in a great stone chamber at the heart of our world and their minds reach out across it. It is strange that they have let things go so far," he mused. "Well, I shall speak to them, but I cannot do so without your help."

"My help? Why?"

"Because you, Darwen Arkwright, can do what no one else can. Even me."

"What do you mean?" asked Darwen.

"I am a gatekeeper," said Mr. Peregrine. "While there is much in my world that is fair and wondrous, so is there that which—as in your world—is destructive and determined to bend all to its will. The struggle between those two forces can easily spill into your world with terrible consequences. My role is to keep the portals between worlds closed. It is an important task and I am honored to fulfill it, but it carries a price. I cannot move back and forth between the two worlds. The mirrors I store are, alas, sealed to me as if they were slabs of steel. In the direst of emergencies, there is one way that will open to me, but once I go through there, I cannot return. Until then, I can communicate with Silbrica through the vacuum system, but I cannot, alas, cross over myself."

Darwen considered this in silence for a long moment.

"So you can't go home?" he said.

The old man smiled and Darwen thought that the

shopkeeper was pleased by the question, even if the answer he had to give saddened him.

"As you say," he answered. "I cannot go home."

"I'm sorry," said Darwen. "I know what that's like. But . . ." Darwen shook his head. The memory of the scrobblers coming through the gate on that vast motorbike wouldn't go away.

"I have something that will help," said Mr. Peregrine. He ducked suddenly behind the counter, opened a cabinet, and yanked open a drawer. For a moment he stayed down there, his head out of sight, muttering to himself as he tossed out papers and clutter.

"Aha!" he exclaimed from below. He emerged slowly, carrying a tiny and intricate machine unlike anything Darwen had seen before. It was about the size of an apple, a mass of wheels and cogs, like the eccentric motion of a very strange clock, made entirely out of brass, save for a glass-fronted display that showed a gauge with a needle.

"What is it?" asked Darwen.

"It is a kind of screen," said the shopkeeper. "Or rather, it makes one. You wind it here, and it gives you almost two hours: more than enough time for the little fact-finding mission I have in mind."

"The screen gives me two hours of what?"

"Did you notice the scrobblers' eyes?" said Mr. Peregrine.

"They wore goggles," said Darwen, shuddering at the memory of the one that had pressed its face to the mirror. "But their eyes were red."

"Quite so," said the shopkeeper. "Their vision is different from ours, and though their goggles allow them to function, they still have certain deficiencies. This little device exploits one of them. Carry this with you and, till it winds down, the scrobblers cannot see you. Other creatures can—the dellfeys, for instance—but those who pose a danger to you cannot. You will be able to ensure that your friend Moth is well while learning what we need to know if we are to protect her and her forest."

"Okay," said Darwen, deciding suddenly.

"You are sure?" said the shopkeeper, peering at him intently. "The screen will protect you, but there are still dangers."

"Moth needs me," said Darwen.

"And you would take such a risk to protect her?" said Mr. Peregrine, still considering him very seriously and with something like wonder in his bright eyes.

"I'm a . . . whatchacallit."

"A mirroculist," said Mr. Peregrine. "So far as I know, the only one."

"Right," said Darwen, taking a deep breath. "Well then. Have to go in, won't I? She doesn't have anyone else," said Darwen, simply.

Mr. Peregrine's smile was thoughtful, even admiring. Darwen flushed and looked away.

"What's a Shade?" he asked suddenly. This was the only part of the story he hadn't told the shopkeeper.

Mr. Peregrine's smile vanished.

"Who said anything about Shades?" he said.

"Moth," said Darwen. "She said a Shade had been seen in the forest . . ."

"Nonsense," said Mr. Peregrine. "Dellfey gossip and paranoia. They are wonderful little creatures, but I swear they are only happy when they are scaring one another right out of their wings. Ghost stories and bogeymen: think no more of them."

"But the scrobblers are real."

"True," nodded Mr. Peregrine. "But Shades are . . . folklore. Myth. Terrible things out of Silbrican legend. We will not waste our time on them."

"But . . ."

"Darwen," said Mr. Peregrine seriously. "We have real dangers to deal with. Let us not invent any more."

Darwen shrugged, frowning, then took out his pen, unscrewed the barrel, dipped the nib into Mr. Peregrine's inkwell, and pulled the plunger on the pen to fill it. "Okay," he said, when he was ready to write. "What do you need me to do?"

"Tonight?" said Mr. Peregrine. "Nothing. Do not go

back in through the mirror and tell no one about it. I need time to alert a friend that you will be coming. I want you to go through tomorrow evening, and there's something I want you to do. Write this down. It's complicated and any mistake could put you in grave danger."

AN UNINTENDED ALLIANCE

Darwen left the shop at a brisk walk, the clockwork screening device held tightly inside his pocket. He scanned the mall for signs of the cop and for Nathan and his friends but saw none, which was all to the good. But then a voice from behind stopped him in his tracks.

"You're in serious trouble," said Alexandra O'Connor.

"What are you talking about?" said Darwen. "And what are you doing spying on me anyway?"

"I'm not spying," said the girl. "I just watched you go

in that weird little store with the cop and figured I'd wait for you. And Jennifer Taylor-Berry told me that you got into trouble with Nathan Cloten who I *told* you to avoid. What do you have ears for if you don't use 'em, boy?"

Darwen stared at her.

"I have to go," he said, starting to walk away.

"Yeah?" said the girl, coming after him. "What's so important? Huh? What's the big hurry? And what have you got in your pocket?"

Darwen turned, shocked, then took his hand out of his pocket so it would look less like he was holding something.

"Nowt," he said.

"What?"

"Nothing, okay?"

"You're a bad liar," said the girl. "Let me see."

"It's private," said Darwen, picking up the pace.

"Oooh," Alexandra mocked. "You got the crown jewels in there? Diamonds and stuff?" Then a thought struck her and she stopped. "Hey, you been stealing again?"

"Stealing?" Darwen shot back. "No, I haven't been stealing. Ever."

"You didn't steal Naia Petrakis's silver bracelet?"

"What are you talking about?" said Darwen.

"That silver bracelet with the owls she always wears," said Alexandra. "She left it in her locker when she went out to play lacrosse, but when she came back: gone. She was real unhappy. If you took it, you should give it back."

"I don't have it!" exclaimed Darwen. She really was the most maddening girl.

"You already sold it?" said Alexandra.

"No!" retorted Darwen. "Now listen very carefully. I am not a thief. I have never stolen anything. Got it?"

"Okay, man," said the girl, holding her hands up like he was pointing a gun at her. "Whatever you say. You didn't steal nothing. And you've got nothing in your pocket. And you didn't go into that freaky store with a cop dragging your butt like he was gonna trade you in for a barbecue dinner."

Darwen stopped and considered the girl.

"I didn't say I didn't have anything in my pocket," he said. "I just said that it wasn't stolen and it wasn't any of your business."

"Come on, lemme see!" she said, and—without further warning—she got hold of him and shoved her hand into his pocket. Darwen grabbed her hand but she was stronger than she looked. Moments later she had the device, with its brass cogs and wheels, in her hand, and she had gone quite still.

"What the heck is that?" she asked. "Is it for the catapult thing? Looks like part of a clock."

"That's right," Darwen improvised. "I like clocks. I repair them."

"You're lyin'," said the girl. "Come on, Darwen. What is it? I won't tell no one."

"Yes, it's for the catapult."

"No, it's not," the girl answered. "You think I'm stupid?"

"Yes," said Darwen. "Give it back."

She held it away from him, shielding it with her body.

"You tell me what it is, and I'll give it back," she said. "Come on, man. I'm just *curious*."

She said the last word slowly, dragging out each syllable like she was in pain. Darwen felt how badly she wanted to know, but he also felt an unexpected desire to tell her. He was tired of being alone. He wanted to share his secret with someone, anyone. Even this annoying girl.

But that was ridiculous. She wouldn't believe him if he told her, and if he was to confide in anyone it would be Rich.

"So come on," said Alexandra. "What is it?"

"It's part of a toy," said Darwen.

"You're still lying," said the girl, "but here." She flipped the mechanism back to him and Darwen pocketed it. "You owe me one. Actually you owe me two, since you all but flattened my mom the other day. Running through the mall and looking at the roof. What's up with that? No wonder you were knocking people flying all over the place. You were fixin' to kill somebody. You remember?"

"I remember," said Darwen.

"I said you were rude."

"I remember that too," said Darwen.

"So you owe me," said Alexandra as if that settled it. "You're still not going to tell me what it is?"

"I told you. It's just a toy."

He started to walk and she started to sing. Loudly. And dance, so that people had to lurch out of the way to give her room.

"*Darwen has a toy—or so he says.*

But he's a liar! Such a liar!"

Darwen stared at her.

"What are you doing?" he demanded, but she just kept hopping along, singing at the top of her lungs as the pass-ersby stared.

"*Situation's dire,*

His pants are on fire . . . "

"Will you shut up?" said Darwen.

An elderly couple were staring at Alexandra as she danced around, holding an imaginary microphone like she was on stage in front of thousands of screaming fans.

"I don't know her," said Darwen. "Never met her before."

"*He's even lying now,*" she sang.

"*Says he doesn't know me,*

Though anyone can see,

Even if they're ADD,
That I'm quite friendly
When absolutely
No one else is."

Darwen gave her a sharp look at that.

"What's that supposed to mean?" he said.

"Just what I said," she answered, stopping her dance as quickly as it had begun. "I got no friends at school. Apart from Rich Haggerty the science geek, you got no friends at school. So we may as well be friends to each other, right?"

"I don't know," said Darwen, still glancing around at the shoppers who were flowing around them as if they were unexpected rocks in a stream.

"I'm not suggesting we get married," said Alexandra. "Just, you know. Hang out some. Keep an eye out for each other. School, man, sometimes it's brutal."

Darwen considered this and found himself nodding.

"'Kay," said Alexandra, beaming so that her white teeth flashed. "Put it there, partner."

She shook his hand vigorously.

"What are we gonna do now?" she asked.

"I don't know about you," said Darwen, "but I have to go home."

"Where's home?"

"I live with my aunt."

"Oh, that's right," she said. "'Cause your parents are doing research at the North Pole."

Darwen remembered his lie but couldn't think of anything to say.

"What's her name?" said Alexandra. "Your aunt?"

"Why do you want to know?" asked Darwen, still walking.

"What? It's a state secret or something? My mom's name is Janine. Janine O'Connor. See? Not so hard. And your aunt's name is . . . ?"

"Honoria Vanderstay, okay?" said Darwen.

"Honoria Vanderstay," said Alexandra, trying out the words in her mouth. "Fancy."

"And that's where I'm going now," said Darwen. "To her house."

"Right," said Alexandra, knowingly. "To play with your toy that isn't really a toy."

"Bye," said Darwen.

"See you soooon, buddy," crooned Alexandra. She turned and started waltzing through the mall like she was on stage.

"Crazy," muttered Darwen to himself.

Darwen was almost twenty minutes late getting back to school. When he realized how much time had passed, he ran hard up through the trees and across the wet grounds, but his aunt's car was already parked and empty at the foot of the entrance steps. He burst into the cool lobby and found her with the principal.

"Where on earth have you been?" she exclaimed in a high, unsteady voice. "I was about to call the police! You have no idea how worried I've been. And you're soaked! Your nice new blazer . . ."

"Sorry," said Darwen. "I was with a friend. I kind of lost track of time."

"There," said the principal in a smug, soothing voice directed at Aunt Honoria. "What did I tell you? No need for alarm. But it's as I was saying. Discipline. Organization. Things you need to master if you are going to succeed at Hillside and precisely what I was explaining to Mr. Iverson. Losing track of time. That's what happens when you bury your head in the past."

Sorry though he was for worrying his aunt, a part of Darwen still found the principal's words annoying. He opened his mouth to say something, caught his aunt's angry stare, and closed it again.

The car ride home was quiet, though Honoria (like all the other drivers) did her customary eighty miles an hour whenever the traffic wasn't at a dead crawl. Darwen could feel her watching him even if she never seemed to take her eyes off the road, and busied himself with studying the downtown map she kept in the glove compartment, counting the different roads with "Peachtree" in the name.

Peachtree Street Northeast, Peachtree Street Southwest, Peachtree Place . . .

"So where did you go?" she said. "After archaeology club, I mean."

Peachtree Road, Peachtree Circle . . .

"To the mall," said Darwen. "Some of the kids from school hang out there."

Peachtree Avenue, Peachtree Way, Peachtree Industrial Boulevard . . . What was it with this town and peachtrees?

"So you're making friends!" said Aunt Honoria. "That is good news, I guess. I was worried that you might not, you know . . ."

"Fit in?" said Darwen, putting the map down. "No. It's fine."

"And these friends," she persisted. "Are they nice? Do they work hard? What are their names?"

"Rich," said Darwen and, because he had said *friends*—plural—added, "and Alexandra."

"Well that's good," she said, "so long as they don't distract you from your studies. I believe there was an incident in math class today?"

Here it comes, thought Darwen.

He waited but she seemed to want him to finish the story for her, so he just said, "It wasn't a big deal. Sumners . . . Mr. Sumners . . . caught me reading a book in class. That was it."

"Okay," she said. "But you need to focus on your schoolwork. I don't want you falling behind. You're on my watch now."

Darwen shot her a quick look but said nothing.

"No need to look so worried," she said. "As soon as we're home, I'll make you a cup of tea, English style, no ice!"

Ah, a nice warmish cup of floating mouse . . .

"Thanks," said Darwen. "That will be great."

DIGGING

The next day Darwen did his best to stay out of trouble, and spent his idle moments considering what he might run into when he went through the mirror that night. Some of these moments occurred during the "voluntary" elocution lesson that Mrs. Frumpelstein had decided he needed to get rid of his Lancashire accent. He had been late arriving, and as he ran into her office, Mrs. Frumpelstein checked her watch and frowned.

"I'm sorry, miss," he sputtered. "I were right busy and

it just went right out mi 'ead."

"There's enough material in that sentence to keep us busy till Christmas," she said, with a sigh.

"Sorry," said Darwen. "Mi accent gets strongest when I'm worked up."

"*Worked up?*"

"Flustered," Darwen explained. "Excited."

"This is Hillside Academy," said the teacher, drawing herself up to her full height. "You should never," she said, seriously, "be excited here."

Darwen looked down so she wouldn't see his grin.

"Ten minutes before lunch with me every other day and a little practice," she said, "and we'll have you sounding like a U.S. native in no time. And when you aren't actively practicing your own pronunciation, listen to the other children—not Richard Haggerty or Alexandra O'Connor, mind. I mean the ones who speak a good, standard American English. Nathan Cloten for instance."

Lunchtime itself was spent down in the janitor's basement with Rich and Alexandra devising their baseball-throwing catapult, and sharing rumors about what the other groups were building. Chip Whittley, Alexandra reported, had gotten hold of some heavyweight elastic from his father's factory, and whatever he was building with Nathan was going to shoot over fifty feet.

"That's not fair," Darwen said. "We should all have to

use the same materials."

"It don't matter," said Rich, unrolling a large sheet of graph paper. "It's all about the design."

Darwen peered at Rich's carefully drawn diagram.

"Looks like a can opener," he said. "What is it?"

"That, my friend," said Rich, clearly pleased with himself, "is science and history working hand in hand. It's a trebuchet."

"A what?"

"A medieval catapult that used a counterweight to convert potential gravitational energy into kinetic energy."

"It does kind of look like a can opener," said Alexandra. "Or a mechanical giraffe."

"Trust me," said Rich. "It will work. And we don't need fancy materials: wood, rope, stones for the counterweight, and hardware to hold it together. That's about it."

"It should be purple," said Alexandra, seriously. "With silver accents."

"If we let you paint it any way you like," said Rich, "will you leave us alone while we build it?"

"Deal," said Alexandra, getting up and marching out.

"Okay," said Rich, watching her leave. "Now we can get some work done. Hand me that piece of wood, will you?"

Darwen picked up a heavy wooden beam that was propped in the corner.

"Hey there, boys," said Mr. Jasinski, appearing in the doorway. "What are you working on, a catapult?"

"Trebuchet," said Rich.

"My mistake," said Mr. Jasinski, shooting Darwen a wink. The janitor was a big man in stained overalls. He had a rugged but friendly face and a casual manner that separated him from the teachers. "You need a hand?" he asked.

"I tried to use my utility tool to drill through this," said Rich, showing a complicated-looking penknife with dozens of different implements on it. "But I can't keep it steady."

"Here," said Mr. Jasinski. "Put it in the vice and you can use my power drill."

Rich's face lit up.

"Quite the complicated piece of machinery, eh, boys?" said the janitor, considering Rich's plans.

"It's all about the design," said Rich.

"When I was a kid," said Mr. Jasinski, positioning the drill and squeezing the trigger till the bit came whining out the other side, "it was soapbox derby. We used to race them down the street. I had this one—fire-engine red, it was—man, that thing was fast! Nobody could beat me in that."

Darwen nodded smiling, but he wasn't really listening. He was thinking about his journey through the mirror tonight.

He was still thinking about it in his afternoon classes—which Mrs. Frumpelstein noted with mounting irritation—and after school as he began the poking around in the dirt that Rich found so fascinating and everyone else thought was a joke. He was thinking about it as he lifted a spadeful of earth and saw something pale in the clay beneath.

He paused, then emptied the spade outside the square, and used it to scrape away a little more earth. He cut some more out, then became very still, barely aware of Rich, who was talking about the geological structure of Stone Mountain.

"People think it's granite," he was saying, "but it's actually a quartz monazite . . ."

"Rich?" said Darwen.

"What?"

"You might want to see this."

Darwen knew it was the tone of his voice that silenced Rich and brought him clambering over the string marker lines. Rich started to speak, but then he saw and became as still and quiet as Darwen.

Lying in the red clay, like it was staring up at them, was something like a face, though a face that made no sense. Most of it was bone pale, stained russet from the earth, but it was clearly a skull.

But the skull of what?

It was man-sized, maybe a little larger, and it had a roughly human shape, though the jaw was heavy, ape-like, and marked by huge, curving teeth which slotted together, the lower set coming up and out almost as high as the nose, the upper ones curving down toward the chin. All of which would have been fine—strange, but basically fine—if it weren't for the eye sockets. Because across the skull were the remains of leather straps with broad glass lenses rimmed with brass: goggles.

"I'll get Mr. Iverson," said Rich, vaulting out of the square. The science teacher was standing on the sidelines of the lacrosse field again, talking to the principal.

"Wait," said Darwen. He was still staring at the skull but his mind was racing. "Just hold on a second."

"Mr. Iverson said that if we found bones . . ." Rich began.

"Human bones," said Darwen. "If we found an Indian burial ground, we should stop. These aren't the bones of a man."

"But," said Rich, stooping to get a better look and lowering his voice, "it's wearing *clothes*."

"It's not a man, Rich," said Darwen emphatically. "It's too big, and look at the shape of the head. Look at the teeth."

"Kinda like a gorilla," Rich mused. "You think it could

be from a zoo or circus?"

Darwen said nothing.

A single word was burning in his mind: *scrobbler*. He didn't understand how it could be possible, but he was in no doubt, and he could not explain all *that* to Mr. Iverson.

"Take some pictures," said Darwen, "and we'll see if we can clear some more of the dirt before Mr. Iverson comes back."

"Why don't we just get him?" said Rich. "He's right there."

"I think Mr. Iverson has enough on his plate with the principal," said Darwen, stalling. "If the school finds out about this, they might shut us down completely."

"But this is just what we need!" said Rich. "They'll see that we're doing something important and we'll get the equipment we want."

"For digging up a dead circus animal?" said Darwen. "Let's get a better look at it. Then we'll think what to do next."

He wanted to be honest with Rich, but how could he announce that he knew what the skull belonged to because he had been chased by one two nights before? No one could be expected to swallow that, least of all Rich who had a very tight definition of reality, and Darwen needed to hold on to the few friends he had.

Reluctantly, Rich reached into a bag and produced a

small brush. He crouched over the skull, took a breath, and started carefully sweeping the dirt from the bones. Where the clay stuck, Darwen worked it free with the tip of a trowel. It was slow, painstaking work, but in twenty minutes they had uncovered the whole head, chest, and left arm.

It was big—even bigger than they had first thought—and some of those teeth were three inches long. The shoulders were broad, and the arms long and heavy. Rich's comparison to a gorilla was not far off, but it wasn't just the goggles that made it clear this was no ape. Though it was badly decayed, the creature was clearly wearing a leather coat with a belt and brass buttons, and when Darwen probed into the clay lower down, he found more leather: boots with laces and metal studs in the soles. Rich bent over the bones to photograph one of the buttons and said, "Check this out."

Part of the leather jacket had a clean hole in it that did not look like decay. Rich carefully lifted the flap of leather to expose the pale ribs beneath, then took a pair of long tweezers and poked into the dirt.

"What is it?' said Darwen.

"Hold on," said Rich, grimacing as he worked the tweezers back and forth. Carefully he pulled out a metal ball, which shone as he smeared away the clay.

"That," he said, confidently. "Is an eighteenth-century

musket ball—the kind they had before pointed bullets. Whatever this thing is," he said, peering at the skull, "someone shot it. A long time ago."

They worked for ten more minutes and Rich extracted two more musket balls. They took pictures, and then, at Darwen's insistence, sprinkled the skeleton with a light dusting of dried clay, just enough to hide it from a casual glance, and re-covered the square with the blue tarp, fastening it to the ground with wooden pegs. When Mr. Iverson came over to tell them it was time to pack up, they were already done.

"All right, boys?" he said. "Anything to report today?"

"No," muttered Rich, looking at the ground. "What about the principal?"

"Did he change his mind, you mean?" said Mr. Iverson, his smile evaporating. "I'm afraid that doesn't happen very often. We'll have to manage with what we have. Perhaps one day . . ." He smiled but it wasn't what you would call a hopeful smile.

"You think if we found something interesting or important," said Rich, carefully not looking at Darwen, "he might reconsider?"

"That would depend," said Mr. Iverson, "on what it was. Principal Thompson has very particular ideas about what Hillside is all about. If he thought a find on school property would attract positive attention to the school, he might reconsider, but if he thought the find might make things difficult for the school . . ." His voice trailed off. "Why do you ask?"

Darwen watched Rich out of the corner of his eye. The big boy shrugged, looked away to the old cedars that circled round to the mall. "No reason," he said at last.

Rich wasn't happy about misleading Mr. Iverson, but he knew what boys always know: that if they revealed something important to adults, the adults would take over. Rich didn't want to give his dig over to the teachers or to experts, though Darwen didn't know how long they would be able to keep it secret. A day? Two? Darwen had bought himself a little time to think, but he feared he had damaged his friendship with Rich in the process. One thing was clear: he had been right. There was a connection between Silbrica and the school. Perhaps before the night was over, he would know more.

OUTMANEUVERED

While his aunt prepared dinner, Darwen sat in his room studying the little clockwork device that Mr. Peregrine had given him, and went over his notes. He lifted the shirt hanging over the mirror, but the sun wouldn't be down for another hour, and he saw only his own reflection. He looked up *scrobblers* and *dellfey* in his dictionary, but they weren't in it. He read for a while but couldn't concentrate, so he started his homework. Sumners had given him two extra pages of problems, to help him "catch up," though it felt more like spite.

Fine, he thought. *I'll do them so he won't have an excuse to complain.*

But that was easier said than done. Darwen just didn't get pre-algebra. He could count, add, subtract, multiply, and divide, but add letters and he quickly got lost. What was the point of letters if they didn't make words? Why should he care what *x* equaled if it didn't turn out to be buried treasure? Or a magic mirror.

He checked the sun again. Still shining.

He put the math problems aside and thought about the skeleton he had found with Rich and whether it had been a mistake to hide the find from Mr. Iverson. He checked the mirror one last time, and then—finally—his aunt was calling him to dinner.

But a rather unsettling surprise awaited him in the other room. Two extra places were laid at the table, and his aunt had opened a bottle of white wine.

"Is someone coming?" asked Darwen, thinking about how this might delay his mission.

His aunt gave him a funny, sideways look, then returned her attention to her BlackBerry.

"Of course they are, Darwen," she said. "Your friend's mom called me, said you'd arranged a playdate to work on a project. You should have said, but I'm glad to meet your friends."

"A friend?" said Darwen, stupidly. "Who?"

"Alexandra," said Aunt Honoria. "You didn't know it was tonight?"

"I didn't know it was *ever*," said Darwen. "You're kidding? Alexandra's coming here?"

"I'm confused," said his aunt. "You didn't give her my name and tell her mom to call me?"

"I gave her your name," said Darwen, the full horror of it dawning on him, "but I didn't think . . ."

"You don't like her?" said his aunt, suddenly frantic. "I thought you liked her. You said she was your friend. I can stall. Call her mom and say . . . you're sick. Or I'm sick. Something . . ."

Aunt Honoria's panic—and the disappointment he sensed under it—made Darwen speak.

"It's fine," he said. "*She's* fine. Annoying, but fine." Then, with an effort, because he saw his aunt needed to hear it, he added, "Thanks for arranging it."

A wan smile shaped her lips and she rested her head on one hand.

"I just thought, you know, making friends is good . . ." she said. "I'm sorry, Darwen. I'm not good at this stuff."

"It's okay," said Darwen, not quite meeting her eyes. "And you are. It's just . . ."

"I'm not your mom," she said, "I know."

"No, that's not it," said Darwen, so quickly and with

such force that his aunt blinked and sat back. "I mean, it's just . . . It's Alexandra. She's so . . ." But he couldn't find the words, and when the door buzzer went, he concluded simply, "You'll see."

And she did.

Alexandra's mother was perfectly nice and normal. She greeted Aunt Honoria and they set to comparing notes about the school and the cost of babysitters, before moving on to restaurants in Buckhead and the fancy malls close by. That took about ten minutes, but by the end it was getting difficult to ignore Alexandra, who had an opinion on everything. She had switched out her little skull earrings for some plastic spangly things that pulsed with tiny colored pinpricks of light, first blue, then green, then yellow, then back to blue. They were very distracting.

"And I think that the school buses should be purple with flashing pink lights," she was saying, "because that would be pretty and would make the kids happier about going to school. And I think the books should be colored better too. Everything is so boooorrring at school. It's like they hired some kind of expert on boring, to make sure that nothing would be interesting at all ever. *No*," she said in a clipped voice, "you can't do that. It's too interesting. Everything here has to be boring. Tedious. Dull. Absolutely without interest or value of any kind. In fact if anyone looks like their brain is being stimulated, that they are actually starting to have thoughts, you know, *ideas*, then we'll shut the whole place down . . ."

This went on all through dinner. Alexandra had opinions about the food, the weather, the fountains in Centennial Olympic Park, the political situation in various African nations, Christmas, her favorite exhibits at the Georgia Aquarium, and which fast food restaurants gave you the best value for money. Darwen kept his face to his plate except to steal a look at his aunt's astonished face. By dessert Aunt Honoria was starting to look like she had brought home a stray puppy only to find that once in the door it had grown considerably and eaten her furniture. The only time Alexandra stopped talking was when her mother produced photographs of Alexandra's baby sister, Kaitlin. As the adults cooed, she sat very still and said nothing for ten whole seconds, before launching suddenly into a loud and rapid consideration of why the Falcons would win next year's Super Bowl based entirely on the "coolness" of their end-zone celebrations. When Alexandra laid down her silverware and asked if "the kids" could be excused, both women said "yes" very quickly.

"Come on, Darwen," said Alexandra. "You can show me your room."

Darwen gave his aunt a wide-eyed look of protest, but his aunt was clearly ready for a little adult-time.

"Sure," she said. "Go ahead, hon."

"Don't break anything," called Mrs. O'Connor to Alexandra's stampeding back.

Darwen hesitated just long enough to see the relief on the grown-ups' faces and then gave chase. By the time he reached his room, Alexandra was already in, opening drawers, picking things out, and putting them back.

"What's this?" she was saying, pulling something from under the bed.

"It's a cricket bat," Darwen began. "It's a bit like baseball but . . ." But Alexandra had already put it down and was studying a book.

"Is this a story?" she demanded. "What's it about?"

"Well, it's kind of a . . ."

"What about this?" she said, holding up a plastic dinosaur model. "Is it supposed to be this color?"

"Will you cut it out!" Darwen said suddenly.

"What? I'm just looking. You don't have much stuff, do you? Is this it or have you got more some place else?"

"Some is still in England," Darwen said, forcing himself to sit on the bed.

"Right," she said, wisely. "England. I see. What's in your closet?"

"So you have a little sister," said Darwen, hurriedly. "That must be nice."

"You'd think so, wouldn't you?" said Alexandra. "But that's because you don't have one. I asked what was in your closet?"

"Nothing," said Darwen, leaping to his feet and trying to block the closet door with his body. "Just clothes."

"Let me see," Alexandra said.

"Why?

"Why?" Alexandra repeated, like she had never heard the word before. "'Cause I'm curious. What's the big deal? You got, like, secret stuff in there or something? That where you're keeping that thing from the shop? The thing with the wheels and stuff?"

"It's just . . ." Darwen fought for the word. "Private."

"Private? What's up with that? Private. I'm your guest. I'm your friend, remember?"

"Kind of," muttered Darwen. "Only 'cause you said so."

"You agreed," said the girl, unoffended. "Hey, what's that?"

She was looking out the window and down to the street and her eyes had grown wide with amazement.

"What?" said Darwen. He turned and took a step toward the window but couldn't see anything unusual. "I don't see . . ."

He half turned, realizing he had been tricked. Alexandra had slipped past him and yanked open the closet.

"So," she was saying. "What's the English boy hiding?"

Darwen forgot his politeness. He threw himself past her, slamming the closet door closed so that she had to snatch her hand out for fear of losing a finger, but all he succeeded in doing was knocking the shirt off the mirror. The door swung open again, and there it was, the mirror frame showing a moonlit forest with a path to a fountain.

For a moment Darwen just stared at it. Then Alexandra spoke.

"So you have a mirror in your closet," she said. "Big deal. It's sort of huge. You must really want to look good for school . . ."

"Right," said Darwen, trying to laugh. "Okay. I have a mirror. Not illegal, is it?"

"I guess not," said Alexandra. "Kind of lame for a secret, but I won't tell no one if you don't want me to."

"Okay," said Darwen, intensely relieved. "Sure."

Alexandra put her hand out.

"Shake," she said.

Darwen rolled his eyes, then took her hand in his and shook it once.

"Whoa," she said.

"What?" said Darwen.

He had let go of her hand, but she grabbed it again and held on, vicelike. She was staring at the mirror.

Instantly he knew what had happened. He didn't know why or how, didn't know why Mr. Peregrine hadn't bothered to warn him, but there was no doubt. Alexandra—like his aunt—had not been able to see through the mirror. But while she was touching him, she could. Darwen said nothing and, for a whole minute—which must have been some kind of record—neither did Alexandra. She just stared at the mirror frame and the forest beyond it, holding his hand.

"Okay," he said, at last. "You can't tell anyone about this."

Still mute, Alexandra shook her head in quick agreement, her wide eyes never leaving the woodland scene which showed so impossibly through the closet door. Darwen waited for the questions—*Where'd you get that? How does it work? What is it, some kind of flat screen TV?*—but Alexandra just stared and he knew she understood. For a long time the two of them did nothing but watch the darkened forest, and all was still, save when the breeze stirred the trees into gentle movement.

Darwen heard adult laughter from the other room and he picked up the shirt to throw it over the mirror again.

"Wait," said Alexandra suddenly, returning to her old self like someone had thrown a switch, "I'm not done. Give me your hand."

"It's not safe," said Darwen, trying in vain to wriggle out of her grip. "My aunt might come in."

"It's fine," said the girl, as if she'd had a portal to another world in *her* closet for years.

"No," said Darwen, arranging the shirt.

Alexandra reached for it, lost her balance, and put her hand flat on the mirror surface to stabilize herself.

Except, of course, that there was no surface to hold. She fell through up to her armpit, then snatched herself free, took a step away from the closet, and her eyes were wide again.

"You can go *through*?" she said. "I mean, it isn't just like a picture? You can reach inside? You could climb into it?"

"Yes," Darwen said, nodding gravely. "But it's not safe."

She looked from the mirror frame back to him, and her eyes got that knowing look of hers.

"You been through already!" she announced. "Yeah?"

"Yeah, but I told you: it's not safe," he replied. "There's scrobblers and all kinds of . . ."

But she wasn't listening. She was letting go of his hand, elbowing past him, and reaching for the mirror.

She stopped as if the lights had suddenly gone out.

"Darn," she said. "It's gone again. Take my hand."

"No way," said Darwen, backing off.

"What's wrong with you, boy? Don't you want to *share*?"

She lunged for him, grabbed him by the wrist, and yanked him hard toward the closet, her eyes fixed on the mirror. Then she was hoisting herself up and in, dragging him afterward. Darwen grabbed at her bare legs to stop her going through, but he was just embarrassed enough about doing so to hesitate, and that split second cost him any chance of stopping her. The surface of the window rippled, and then he was looking in at her, standing in the moonlit forest and gazing about her entranced.

There was nothing else to do. He started to climb through, remembered to take the little clockwork device from his bedside drawer, then clambered into the mirror frame.

He dropped softly onto the pine needle floor and looked about him. There was no sign of Moth, no trace of scrobblers. There was only the forest with the burbling fountain and Alexandra. Talking.

"Check this out!" she was saying. "It's—like—*real*. A forest right here in the city. Smell those trees, man! Cool. I *got* to get me one of these mirror things. And it's chilly, you know? Not cold. Just nice. Not Atlanta early October, that's for darn sure. Where does this path lead?"

"It goes round in a circle."

"No way. Really? Looks straight to me."

"It's a circle."

"Check out that fountain! Neat."

"Alexandra, we should really . . ."

"What kinds of trees are these?"

"I don't know," said Darwen. "Pines. That's an oak."

"Not like any oak *I* ever saw. You sure?"

"Pretty sure."

"Hey," said Alexandra. "I know my trees. I know red

oaks and white oaks, pin oaks, willow oaks, and water oaks, and that, my friend, is none of them, so if you think . . ."

"I'm sorry," said Darwen, "but would you shut up for a moment?"

Alexandra stared at him for a moment as if no one had ever said this to her before, then she cocked her head to one side, put her hands on her hips, and said, "Yes, Sir. Certainly, sir. Whatever you want, sir. What are you now, the king of the forest?"

And with that she began to launch into a song from *The Wizard of Oz* about being king of the forest, singing so loudly that strange birds squawked out of their roosting places and went flapping through the treetops.

"Shhh," said Darwen. And this time he reached over and clamped a hand over her mouth. She fought, but he held firm and whispered urgently into her ear. "This is not our world, Alexandra, and there are things here that will try to capture us. I don't know exactly what they'll do to us, but it won't be fun, I can tell you that. So we have to keep a low profile, you understand? Quiet."

Slowly he took his hand away from her mouth, waiting for her to shout. She didn't, but she leaned very close and whispered, "Next time you put your hand on my mouth, I'm gonna bite your fingers off. Just so you know."

Darwen held his hands up and mouthed, "Okay." Then

in a hushed tone, he said, "You should go back through."

"Just me?"

Darwen hesitated a moment too long before saying "No, I'll come back with you."

"You want to stay here," she whispered accusingly. "You want to get me out then you can come back. Why? What are you going to do?"

"I have a job to do," he said. "But only me. Like I said: it's dangerous, and your mom will be looking for you."

"Yeah, right," Alexandra scoffed. "With an adult to talk to and pictures of Kaitlin to look at? She'll miss me at graduation. Maybe. Besides, they have a bottle of wine. In about a half hour, she'll be on the table singing 'I Will Survive.'"

"You have to go," said Darwen. "This is something I have to do by myself."

"No way," said Alexandra. "I'm coming with you. You can be dang sure I'm not going back through there by myself," she said, nodding toward the mirror frame which now showed the inside of Darwen's closet. "And if you come back in here without me, I'll tell my mom. And your aunt."

"That's not fair," Darwen protested.

"Fair?" said Alexandra. "What are you, five years old? I've got shelves full of plastic ponies in my closet. You got a secret door into a magical world. What's fair about that?

Hey!" she added, as an afterthought. "Have you told Rich about this?"

Darwen, feeling oddly guilty, shook his head.

"Probably smart," said Alexandra wisely. "He'd think you were whacked out. Better keep this between us."

Darwen didn't know what to do. He wanted to proceed alone, but Alexandra wasn't going to leave willingly, and the longer it took to get her out, the more danger they would be in. There could be scrobblers coming through the gate at the top of the hill even as they stood here arguing.

He took out the mass of wheels and cogs and considered it.

"Mr. Peregrine said this would screen me from the scrobblers," he whispered as he wound it. He looked at Alexandra and sighed. "Let's hope it covers two of us," he said.

Darwen wound the device till it wouldn't go any more, then slid a little switch into the on position. There was a faint whirring sound as the mechanism awoke, and from somewhere inside came a soft bluish radiance. At the same instant a brighter light pulsed outward like a bubble being suddenly inflated. It ballooned until it contained an area about five feet around the device in all directions, shimmered, and vanished.

"I hope that means it's working," said Darwen. "You'll

need to stay close to me."

Darwen looked for Moth but he couldn't see her, and the little metal birdhouses were quiet. It worried him. He said her name, not daring to shout, but nothing happened and Alexandra gave him a look.

With a sigh Darwen left the path and led the way up the hill toward the circle of gates. As he looked about for the dellfey and listened to the tiny ticking of the little brass screen mechanism. Alexandra asked questions, not loudly, but constantly. What were scrobblers? Why could he see through the mirrors? Were they in the real world but on another planet or was it some kind of parallel dimension thing? Who lived here? Did the mirror work by magic, or was it some kind of science they didn't understand? And why should the scrobblers ("and you still haven't told me what they are") want to catch them anyway?

And so it went on as they trudged through the ferns and vines between the trees, and Darwen realized that he could answer none of Alexandra's questions, and though she was annoying him, he kicked himself for not having gotten more information from Mr. Peregrine. Moth might have answered Alexandra's questions, but there was still no sign of the dellfey. Maybe she was hiding, scared off by the sight of this strange girl talking a mile a minute. Darwen was suddenly struck by the possibility that bringing Alexandra had been a grave mistake, something that would make it impossible for him to help Moth or fix the terrible things Mr. Peregrine thought were happening.

At the top of the hill, the light shifted and there was a great whoosh of steam followed by a heavy clanking sound. He turned quickly to Alexandra and laid his finger on his lips. She faltered for a second, but then broke into a jog toward the crown of the hill. Darwen hurried to keep up.

Other sounds were coming from the top now, grunting and labored breathing like big men moving furniture. Darwen and Alexandra edged closer, pausing behind a tree on the rim of the clearing. There in the bluish light of the gas lamp was the henge-like ring of doorways, wreathed in steam. One of them had just closed and its lights were still on. Beside it were the creatures that had come through, hulking shapes with long, powerful arms and short legs. There were three of them. They seemed to be stooped over a massive tractor with a great boiler covered in pipes and dials. It was towing a trailer laden with equipment, iron girders, and coils of steel cable.

"They're building something," Darwen muttered half to himself. He turned to see what Alexandra made of this and saw she was staring in horror.

"What?" he said.

"Scrobblers?" she managed.

"I don't think so," whispered Darwen. "These are different."

"Why don't they have heads?" she asked.

"What do you mean . . . ?" said Darwen turning toward the creatures lugging the equipment, but the words died on his lips. She was right. He had thought the figures were simply bending over so that he could not see their faces, but as he watched one of them stood up and turned toward them. It was all he could do not to cry out.

The creature was roughly man-shaped, if bigger and heavier, with long apelike arms and short bowlegs, but where the head should have been there were only shoulders. In the center of its bare chest was a dark red gash—a mouth—but there were no eyes. The beast grunted, the mouth in its chest opening wide to show row upon row of sharklike pointed teeth, and he remembered a word Moth had used: gnashers.

At first Darwen thought they must have eyes somewhere else, but then he saw the way they worked, their fingers feeling around like insects, sensing by touch. And from time to time, they rocked back, opened those terrible mouths in their chests, and stuck out long wormlike tongues with flat tips. Then they became quite still, as if tasting the air, before going back to work.

Would the screen device protect them from whatever the gnashers' tongues could do? He had no idea. It certainly wouldn't protect them from those teeth. But then the monsters were moving away, oblivious to Darwen and

Alexandra, rolling the great tractor-thing and its trailer down the hill in the direction of the mirror.

It was a long moment after the gnashers had gone before Darwen dared to speak, and when he tried, he found his mouth was dry. He swallowed, and took a breath.

"Okay," he said, taking a sheet of paper from his pocket and unfolding it. He peered at the notes he had taken as Mr. Peregrine had talked him through his mission.

"We have to go through one of these gates," said Darwen. "They should all be numbered 423, plus one number which will be different for each gate. Help me find number four."

Alexandra, eyes still wide as searchlights, nodded and said nothing, her attention on the gnashers in the distance.

"Alexandra?" he said.

She snapped back as if just woken up. "Right," she said. "Number four. On it."

She began to circle the stand of trees studying the brass plates set into their barks and murmuring "4232, 4233, 4234. This one."

Darwen checked his notes. "Now I have to set this dial."

He turned a knob till the dial read 7.

"Now pull this lever," he said aloud, concentrating as he leaned his weight on it. It came down slowly and latched with a heavy thunk. "Now these," he said as he threw a series of four switches. "And this."

He pushed one last button, and the gateway hummed with energy. An arc of electricity coursed between the trees like purple lightning and then a jet of steam burst from each side. The space between the trees shimmered with a pearly light and Darwen took a breath.

"Okay," he said. "Now we go in."

He swallowed. Alexandra took his hand, and together they stepped into the wall of light.

For a moment the world went white, and there was a smell that reminded Darwen of his old model train layout in England. Then they were through, and standing on what was unmistakably a railway platform.

"Whoa," said Alexandra again. "This is better than Six Flags. Where are we? No, *when* are we?"

She had a point.

The station didn't belong in the present. There were no brightly lit vending machines, no cigarette butts, or trash cans full of fast food wrappers. There were no computerized displays, no recordings warning you not to stand close to the edge, no commuters with laptops and iPods. There was no plastic, no chrome, no concrete. In their place were brick and stone, wood, brass and iron.

There were two platforms separated by a pair of tracks. Each platform had a canopy and a central building that served as ticket office, waiting room, and shop. The platforms were connected by a wrought-iron footbridge and there were old-fashioned signals on posts. The station was lit by pearly gas lamps on ornate iron stands, and it was dark and smoky, but Darwen could make out the brick mouth of a tunnel at one end of the station and what seemed to be fields and trees at the other.

There was a single, silent steam engine parked beside their platform, a primitive looking black thing covered with pipes, brass rails, and a tall smoke stack. It was unlike the sleek locomotives you saw in movies, and looked like it had been cobbled randomly together from spare parts by someone's nineteenth-century eccentric uncle. Behind the whimsical engine were two wooden coaches painted a dark, glossy green. There were no other people around.

"You got a ticket?" asked Alexandra.

Darwen shrugged.

"Don't think we need one," he said.

Together they boarded the train and took seats opposite each other. The coaches were as old-fashioned as the engine, wood and iron with little glass windows and buttoned cloth seats. There were no lights inside so they sat in the dim glow of the platform's gas lamps and looked out of the windows.

"This is weird," said Alexandra.

"The part about the forest in my closet or the part about the deserted railway station?" Darwen remarked.

"The deserted part," said Alexandra. "I mean, how do we know this is even going to go someplace?"

"Mr. Peregrine told me to take the train to the first stop," said Darwen. "I have to find the house of a friend of his. Mrs. Jenkins. I have to ask her some questions."

"What if she's out?"

"She'll be waiting," said Darwen, hoping it was true. "Mr. Peregrine sent her a message."

"So why doesn't she just send him the answers?" Alexandra demanded. "Why do you have to come?"

"She hasn't been responding," said Darwen. "I have to find out why and see if anything looks unusual."

"Unusual?" repeated Alexandra. "How you gonna know what's unusual here? We're on a steam train driven by nobody on a railway line that winds up in the back of your closet. If a talking teddy bear served us meringues and ketchup, how would you know if that was usual or not? This whole place is plum whacked out."

Darwen didn't know what she meant by that, though he got the gist, but before he could respond the coach rocked forward.

"We're moving," he said. He slid down one of the windows and leaned out. The train was creeping forward, belching smoke and steam through the deserted station. As it picked up speed, he checked the screening device and smiled. They'd used less than a quarter of their time.

"Why do you keep checking that thing?" said Alexandra.

"It's clockwork," said Darwen. "If it runs down, it stops working."

"Can't you just wind it up again?"

"No," said Darwen. "It has to recharge. It uses two kinds of power; there's the mechanical part, which is clockwork and has to be wound up, but there's something else, another power which produces the . . . er . . ."

"Magic?"

"No," said Darwen. "Yes. I don't know."

"Oh, you're really on top of things, aren't you?" said Alexandra. "Awesome."

"It's a different kind of energy, all right?" said Darwen. "The screen needs both the mechanical and the . . . other kind . . . to work."

The train entered the tunnel and everything went black. Darwen was glad to have a moment of darkness for his blush to fade.

"Ooh. Scary," said Alexandra, and Darwen could hear her grin.

"You are really odd," he said into the darkness.

"So they say," she answered. "But so are you, fountain-pen-boy, so I guess we're cool."

"I suppose," said Darwen, glad it was too dark for her to see his smile.

"So tell me all of it," said Alexandra. "Right from the start."

The start, thought Darwen. What was that? Following the flittercrake into Mr. Peregrine's shop? Or had it begun earlier than that, on a day in his old school when the headmaster had come to see him . . . ?

Don't think about that, he thought furiously.

"It started in the mall," he said into the darkness. "I looked up and saw this bird up in the dome . . ."

He told her everything, and then the darkness seemed to soften and they caught sight of lights ahead.

"It's a station," said Alexandra. "This us?"

Darwen craned his neck to read the painted sign on the platform as the engine slowed with a great whoosh of steam.

Woodvine.

"Yes," he said. "Come on."

They got down onto the deserted platform and as the train fell still and quiet Darwen noticed something very strange.

"What do you see up the tracks?" he asked Alexandra.

She peered through the steam but shook her head.

"Too much smoke," she said. "I can't see nothing."

"You sure it's just the smoke?" said Darwen. "It looks like fog."

"Yeah," said the girl. "But, not quite. It's more like . . . I don't know. *Nothing*."

Darwen stared and he felt strangely cold and anxious.

Alexandra was right. Behind them, back the way they had come, the railway lines stretched on till they reached the tunnel into a dark, steep hill; but ahead, only yards beyond the station platform, there was nothing but a featureless gray mist. Darwen walked toward it till he was standing beside the curious locomotive, then he stooped and picked up a stone chipping. He aimed and lobbed it, hard as he could, straight down the railroad tracks and into the mist. It vanished and there was no sound of its fall. He shivered.

"How about we find that path?" said Alexandra. "I'm not crazy about this place."

"Me neither," said Darwen. "It's like . . . I don't know: like the world ends right there. Like if you walked a few yards that way, you would just be . . . *nowhere*. You'd disappear."

He had no idea why he thought that, didn't know how such a thing could be true, but Alexandra said nothing, and he guessed she felt the same.

"Here's the ticket office," she said. "What a surprise: there's no one there. You ever been to a ghost town, Darwen?"

"I don't believe in ghosts," said Darwen, walking after her.

"No, not ghosts like spooks and specters," she said. "I mean a town that people abandoned."

"No," said Darwen. "You?"

"I went out to this place called St. Elmo, out in Colorado when I was visiting my dad," she said. "He lives out west now. I don't see him much but he's cool. He's not Kaitlin's dad. That's *Uncle* Bob. *Uncle* Bob hasn't moved in yet because my mom knows I don't want him to. Kaitlin, though, she's moved in. Boy howdy, has she. It used to be just me and mom, but now . . . It's Kaitlin this and Kaitlin that. *Don't bother me now, Alex: Kaitlin has to be fed. Hey Alex, change Kaitlin's diapers for me while I get ready to go out with Uncle Bob . . .*"

"You were saying about the ghost town," Darwen inserted.

"Oh, right," said Alexandra. "St. Elmo. Yeah. Seriously weird place. It was a gold mining town but it shut down and everyone moved away. There are houses and a saloon and stuff, but no people. It feels like this."

Darwen just nodded.

"There's supposed to be a path," he said. "The sooner we see some people, the better."

Alexandra had her face pressed up to the window of the ticket office and store.

"You see any candy?" she said. "I could go for some chocolate right about now. Not that there's anyone here to sell us anything anyway. You think maybe we're the only people in this whole world, except for those . . . *things* we saw back in the woods. I could go a long time without seeing them again. You see their mouths? They had mouths in their chests, man. That ain't right. And those teeth. Like half man, half shark. I hate sharks. I don't ever go in the ocean. No way, Jose. Swim where something could take a chunk out of me? I don't *think* so. One time, there was this kid in Florida . . ."

"Here's the path," said Darwen.

It was paved, but weeds were poking through between the flagstones. As they walked, trees appeared on either side and the path started to wind. In moments the faint glow of the station platform was gone and the moon was lost to them. Darwen was aware that Alexandra had gone quiet and was close enough that he could hear her breathing. He lifted the screen device up close to his face so he could see the dial: a third gone. They wouldn't have much time before they would need to head back.

It got darker still, and colder. They pressed on, both spreading their hands out in front of them to clear branches and cobwebs. Neither spoke. Darwen was beginning to wonder why he had come. It had seemed like a great adventure, but out here in the darkness of the forest, having seen the gnashers, he began to wonder if Mr. Peregrine knew what he was talking about, or maybe—and much worse—if he had sent them into danger on purpose. Maybe he was working with the scrobblers.

Maybe he wanted them caught. . . .

Them?

Mr. Peregrine hadn't intended *them* to come at all. He had sent Darwen alone. If anything happened to Alexandra, it would be Darwen's fault.

"We should go back," he said. "This is taking too long."

"Wait," said Alexandra suddenly taking a step ahead. "What's that through the trees? I see lights."

She was right. There, settled in the forest was a cozy-looking cottage with bright, glowing windows. There was a tang of wood smoke in the air, and Darwen's heart leapt. All of a sudden, with the darkness and danger all around, he wanted nothing more than to go inside and sit by a warm fire. Maybe Mr. Peregrine's friend would have a homemade apple pie all ready for them. . . .

The house was brick and had a heavy thatched roof, which hung over the eaves. The windows were leaded and shuttered, and the door was a cheery red that matched the roses growing on the trellis. It was a cottage out of a painting, and Darwen found himself grinning at Alexandra as they rapped the heavy brass knocker. They had made it.

THE JENKINSES

The old lady who opened the door had to be someone's grandmother. She was plump and smiling, her apron floury, her silver hair pinned back in a bun.

"Mrs. Jenkins?" said Darwen.

"Why, you must be Darwen," she said, peering at him through spectacles whose lenses looked like the bottoms of soda bottles. "Come in, come in. Mr. Peregrine has told us so much about you." Then she called into the back. "He's here, dad! Get the kettle on."

She stepped aside and Darwen and Alexandra stepped in, muttering their hellos. The old lady closed the door behind them and called in again.

"Dad! Did you hear me? I said Darwen is here."

"I heard you," came a voice, and an elderly man lumbered into view. He was bald, brandished a brass cylinder, and was smiling as broadly as his wife. "Hold your horses there, Mother, I'm just sending this note to Mr. Peregrine to let him know you made it all right."

Darwen was shown the way down a tiled hallway into a kitchen bright with firelight. It was warm inside and the table was laid with china plates, and cups and saucers with little roses on them.

"Sit down, dear," said the old lady, "and have some tea. How do you take it? Milk? Sugar? And I made a cake specially. Where's that cake tin, Dad?"

The old man who was fiddling with the message cylinder wagged a delaying hand while he opened a vacuum chute almost exactly like the one at the mirror shop. There was a bluish flash and a soft pop. Once he had the cylinder whooshing on its way, he turned, beaming to the room.

"Right," he said. "Cake. We get so few visitors these days . . ."

"It's very kind of you," said Darwen, who had taken one of the three seats at the kitchen table.

"Yes, thank you," said Alexandra who was still hovering by the door. "I'm sorry to crash and all . . ."

The old woman started and turned.

"I'm sorry, dear," she said. "I didn't see you there. Come in, come in. Let's fetch another chair. Any more of you outside?"

"No," said Darwen. "It's just the two of us."

"Probably as well," said Mrs. Jenkins with her grand-motherly air, moving her rolling pin out of the way. "It might get a bit cramped in here with more. And what's your name, dear?"

"Alexandra."

"What a nice name," said Mrs. Jenkins, busying herself with another cup and saucer.

"It means defender of the people," said Alexandra.

"Oh my!" said Mrs. Jenkins.

The house was as cozy on the inside as it had looked outside and Darwen felt an immense sense of relief.

"We can't stay long," he said, putting the screening device on the table. "And it's very dark outside."

"Not to worry about that," said Mrs. Jenkins. "We'll get you back to the station in plenty of time. Dad can take the car, can't you Dad?"

"What?" said the old man.

"You can get the car out when it's time for them to go back," shouted Mrs. Jenkins. Her husband was obviously a bit deaf.

"Right. Certainly," said the old man.

"And you can save yourself some time by turning that off while you're here," said Mrs. Jenkins. "You're safe enough inside."

"Right," said Darwen. He switched the device to the off position and its barely audible ticking stopped so that the only sound was the hissing of the kettle on the hob.

"That's better," said Mrs. Jenkins, considering them both smilingly.

"We shouldn't stay too long anyway," said Darwen. "Our parents will be worried about us."

He wasn't sure why he said 'parents.' It just made things easier. Less to explain.

"So how is Mr. Peregrine?" said Mrs. Jenkins. "Still worrying about everything, I see."

"He's fine, I think," said Darwen. "But he wanted me to ask you a few questions about what was happening here."

"Happening?" said the old lady. "What do you mean?"

"Anything unusual?" said Alexandra.

"Unusual?" repeated Mrs. Jenkins. "I don't think so. Dad, what do you think? Has there been anything unusual lately?"

"Unusual?" shouted her husband. "Like what?"

Darwen shifted in his chair. The cottage was really very warm and he was starting to sweat.

"I don't know," roared Mrs. Jenkins back at him. "Unusual. Mr. Peregrine is asking if there has been anything unusual happening."

"No," yelled Mr. Jenkins with an expansive shrug.

"And get that tea, would you, Dad?"

"What?" he shouted back. "Hold on: I'll just get the tea."

"And the cake," said Mrs. Jenkins, leaning over and screaming it into his ear.

"No need to shout, woman," bellowed her husband. "I'm not deaf."

"He was worried," said Darwen, trying to redirect the conversation, "because he hadn't heard from you for a while."

"Oh that," said Mrs. Jenkins, waving the thought away with a little laugh. "The vacuum pump was broken. Dad tried to fix it and that made it worse. We just got it mended." She nodded to where her husband had just sent the message, and Darwen noticed that the floor beside it was littered with dusty old cylinders.

"Could we maybe open a window?" asked Alexandra, pulling at the neck of her shirt.

Mr. Jenkins passed the cake tin to his wife and she set it on the table.

"Now," she said to herself. "Where's that cake knife?"

She turned to a drawer by the sink and took out a long

knife. She tested the blade against her thumb and beamed.

"Good," she said. "You need a sharp knife to cut cake or it all breaks up."

"Mrs. Jenkins!" exclaimed Darwen. "You cut yourself."

The old lady looked at her thumb where a thin trickle of red was running onto her wrist.

"So I did," she said.

Her voice was quiet, thoughtful as she looked at the blood, and then—to Darwen's amazement—she licked her lips, and her tongue was long, and thick and brown. Darwen stared, but then her husband was pouring their tea and Alexandra's gasp redirected his attention. He looked at her, but she was staring at her teacup with a hand over her mouth.

The liquid in the cup was black, thick, and dotted with mold and fungus. There were lumps in it, and one of them looked like it might once have been a mouse.

"Drink up," said Mr. Jenkins. "It'll do you good."

Darwen stared at Mr. Jenkins but in leaning over to pour the tea, something had slipped and his face looked twisted, like one side had been pushed out of position.

"I'm not that thirsty, actually," said Darwen, getting quickly to his feet.

"Nonsense," said Mrs. Jenkins. The skin where she had cut herself had peeled completely away, and the hand was hanging like a rubber glove from the end of the arm.

In its place was something long and black with a clawlike hook on the end.

"Alexandra," said Darwen taking a step toward the door. "I think we ought to . . ."

"You can't go yet," said the thing that had been Mr. Jenkins, his face splitting completely now to reveal something slick and dark beneath it. "We've not had supper."

"I don't think we're hungry," said Alexandra, rising.

"No, dear," said Mrs. Jenkins, advancing with the cake knife. "But we are."

"Run!" shouted Darwen.

"The screen!" Alexandra answered. "Turn it on."

Darwen grabbed at it, but it slid out of his sweaty grip, and fell off the table. He dropped to the tiled floor just as "Mr. Jenkins" issued a bellow of rage quite unlike the voice he had used so far, and reached across the table after him. Something tore as he stretched, and Darwen was horrified to see the entire body of the old man falling away like a discarded costume. Beneath it was something smaller, with spindly limbs ending in claws and a body covered in stiff, bristly black hair coated with slime. The head was a mass of red eyes and a gaping beak-like mouth surrounded by feelers that moved by themselves.

For a second he was too scared to move, but then Alexandra yelled "Darwen!" and he snatched at the brass mechanism. The creature which had been Mrs. Jenkins slid out of the old woman's body like some nightmare butterfly emerging from its chrysalis, still brandishing the cake knife in one front claw, then his finger found the switch and he turned the machine on.

Both creatures froze with surprise and confusion; then Darwen was rolling away as "Mr. Jenkins" slashed with its talon at where he had been. Alexandra stepped quietly to the side as "Mrs. Jenkins" lunged blindly with the cake knife, then she picked up the rolling pin, hefted it, and whacked the creature upside the head. The monster—whatever it was—slumped, momentarily stunned, but it was alert again before Alexandra could slip past it. It was now guarding the door, knife still clutched at the end of one branch-like arm.

"Get out!" shouted Darwen.

The monster closest to him turned quickly toward his voice and stabbed with one claw that caught him in the shoulder. Darwen felt a cut open under his shirt, but he couldn't let it slow him down. He picked up the nearest chair and threw it at the beast, then took a step toward the door.

"Stop," said the one that had been Mrs. Jenkins. "Listen."

There was a sudden and unnerving silence as the two monsters tried to hone in on the sounds of Darwen and Alexandra.

The one that had spoken was standing in the hall, trying to block the way out, spindly limbs groping blindly, legs spread. Alexandra gave Darwen a wild what-do-we-do-now? look and Darwen pointed down between the creature's legs. Without uttering a sound he mouthed the word "crawl." Alexandra shook her head but Darwen nodded. Slowly, very slowly, and looking like she might burst into tears, Alexandra dropped to her knees. She started crawling silently toward the insect-monster.

Darwen, hardly daring to breathe, did not move, but the other creature was coming toward him with its thin arms spread wide. He thought furiously. He reached for the table at the same moment that Alexandra started to slide headfirst between the insect-legs of the thing by the door. He grasped the handle of his teacup with its rancid contents, and threw it at one of the windows by the stove.

The creature closest to him spun in the direction of the noise and Darwen made a dash for the door, throwing himself headfirst through the legs of the other right after Alexandra. It wasn't a clean slide, and he caught "Mrs. Jenkins"'s left leg, sending her spinning, but he was up on his feet before she could turn, and a moment later they were through the front door and dashing into the night.

As he ran, Darwen felt a shrill keening in his head, like his brain was screaming in horror.

"What were those things?" shrieked Alexandra.

"Don't talk," said Darwen. "Run! Back to the station. And stay close to me. Whoever they sent that message to, I'll bet it wasn't Mr. Peregrine."

"You mean they called for back up?" said the girl as she ran. "There might be more of them out here?"

"Let's just get to the train," said Darwen. "Stay on the path."

"What kind of place is this?" yelled Alexandra, grabbing hold of his arm. "You think this is fun? I can't believe you brought me here!"

"Can we discuss this later?" said Darwen, wrenching himself free and trying to run faster.

From back at the house they heard a bang followed by the rumbling growl of an engine.

The car, thought Darwen. *They said they had a car.*

"Faster!" he shouted.

If they hadn't walked the path only minutes before, they never would have found their way in the darkness. The paving slabs wound their way down through the forest, and suddenly—flashing between the trees—Darwen could see the lights of the railway station. At the same moment he heard voices some ways behind him and the crunching sound of a heavy vehicle shoving its way through the undergrowth.

Alexandra could run. Darwen was going as fast as he could, but she was still ahead of him. He knew that she was probably outside the screen device's bubble, but he just couldn't go any faster. His legs were unsteady with the effort and the fear of what was behind him, but he pushed himself as hard as he could. Moments later he was leaving the trees and pounding down the path to the platform, where Alexandra was waiting for him, breathing hard. Darwen arrived at full speed, but he missed his footing on the platform step and tripped, falling heavily on his left side.

He put out his hand to break his fall, realizing too late that it was the hand holding the screening device. There was a pop and a flicker in the air around them, and the mechanism stopped.

"Now what?" said Alexandra.

"Get on the train," Darwen panted.

"And just sit there? We don't know when it will leave! The Jenkinses will be here any moment."

It was so strange hearing her use their human names that Darwen almost laughed, but he knew she was right. He looked down the platform but there was only the track into the tunnel in one direction and the strange gray nothingness in the other.

"We could hide," he said, not liking the idea. "Get to the other side of the track and, I don't know . . ."

Darwen realized that the sound of the Jenkinses' car had been joined by something else, another engine with a higher pitch. He spun round in time to see something emerging from the tunnel in the blaze of a headlight.

Scrobblers.

It wasn't the same motorbike and sidecar, but it was similar, and there were two of the heavyset creatures sitting on it. One of them was holding a net, and the back of the bike was fitted with a cage just big enough to hold a couple of children.

"This way," said Darwen, running down the platform toward the locomotive, toward the strange gray fog. But then there was a flash of light, like one of the portals opening, and something came drifting out of the fog toward them. It was almost the same color gray as the pearly fog behind it, but he had seen it silhouetted in that flash of light, and it had looked like a man in long pale robes with a hood. Darwen tried to tell himself he had imagined it, that it was just steam from the railway engine, that it wasn't really there.

But it *was* there, and now it was on the platform, not flitting over surfaces as that strange shadow had done on his first trip to the forest, but gliding slowly toward them as if moving on invisible wheels. This was something he had not seen before. For the briefest moment, Darwen thought the pale figure might have come to help, but then with a certainty he couldn't explain, he knew that whatever this was, it was worse than scrobblers and gnashers, worse even than the hellish things Alexandra had laughably called the Jenkinses. This was their leader.

Darwen and Alexandra turned back the way they had come, back toward the bike still barreling down the track from the tunnel, back to where an oversized vintage car covered in copper tubing roared down the path and onto the platform. Doors flew open and the spindly insect legs of what had been Mrs. Jenkins—still clutching her cake knife—emerged.

Darwen just stared. There was nowhere to go. They were trapped.

He had barely processed the thought when Alexandra seized his hand and dragged him to the train carriage.

"Get in!" she yelled.

"It's not going anywhere!"

"Then jump out the other side and run!" she roared back.

Darwen clambered into the first coach and unlatched the door on the other side with fumbling fingers. He was out and down on the other side when he saw the coach lurch into motion. There was a rush of steam from the engine and a deafening whistle blast, and the whole train was suddenly shunting back toward the tunnel, gathering speed.

No!

Darwen got to his feet and started to run after the

train. Alexandra was half in, half out of the coach door. She fought to control her balance, and then reached for Darwen who was sprinting hard. His fingers brushed hers once, twice, then caught. She pulled as he jumped and Darwen found himself sailing into the coach doorway.

"Thanks," said Darwen.

There was a smashing sound as the train hit the bike coming down the track, and Alexandra leaned out the passenger side window to see.

A long insect claw swiped at her, snagging her hair. Mrs. Jenkins, now more like some monstrous praying mantis, was clinging to the side of the coach, fighting with the door latch to get in.

Alexandra shrieked, and Darwen grabbed her round the waist. The creature was trying to pull her out of the window headfirst. He tugged, and when that didn't seem to help, took to bashing at the revolting insect arm with his fist. Alexandra drew her head back into the carriage as far as she could, but the terrible crimson insect eyes seemed to fill the window and those mouthparts were groping to gather her into its beak-like jaws, and then there was a crash, a scream, and darkness.

The train had reached the dark hillside and Mrs. Jenkins had been swept off the window by the wall of the tunnel. Alexandra rubbed wildly at her head till she had plucked the remaining length of a sticklike insect leg from her hair, and it fell to the floor. She kicked it away, and for a long moment she just stared at it, saying nothing.

Then she started.

"Nice trip, Darwen," she said. "Let's take a little jaunt into the woods. That'll be nice, won't it? Oh, and then we'll go visit some massive carnivorous bugs that will try to tear our heads off. Your Mr. Peregrine is one heck of a travel agent."

Darwen's heart was pounding and he was gasping for air.

"I broke the screen," he said, miserably. "How will we get back to the mirror in the forest without it?"

"Let me see," said Alexandra.

Darwen handed her the device and she studied it. She raised it to her ear and rattled it gently like she was trying to guess the contents of a Christmas parcel.

"Sounds okay," she said. "Maybe you didn't break it. Maybe it just needs resetting."

She turned the machine off, wound it a little more, and turned it back on. The device pulsed with energy and the air rippled.

"Fixed," she said.

"That was brilliant!" said Darwen, the small victory briefly eclipsing all the evening's horrors.

There was no sign of life at the station—something they checked carefully before disembarking—and the portal behind it opened without difficulty. When they came through to the forest, however, they were astonished to hear the sound of heavy machinery. They traced their way back down toward the mirror frame and saw a mass of gnashers at work on an elaborate frame of girders. There were two large pieces of mechanical equipment in addition to the steam tractor they had already seen, but what they were building Darwen couldn't imagine. It was big though, as big as a house, and the work made so much noise that Darwen figured they could have made their way down to the mirror frame undetected even without the screen device. But as he watched those loping, headless figures and the way they bounded on their knuckles like gorillas, he was glad that his adventures for the night were finally over. He helped Alexandra into the portula and then swung himself through and into his own closet with a greater sense of relief than he had ever felt in his life.

As Alexandra put her hand on his bedroom door handle, Darwen spoke. He hadn't really planned to. It just came out.

"My parents," he said.

"What about them?" said Alexandra, turning.

"They aren't doing research at the North Pole," said Darwen. "They were killed in a road accident. They were driving and a furniture truck coming in the opposite direction crossed over the center line."

There was a long moment of silence.

"I know," said Alexandra. "Everyone knows."

"I'm sorry," said Darwen. "For lying, I mean. I just don't want to talk . . ."

"It's cool," said Alexandra. "And besides," she added with a glance at the mirror, "we have other things to talk about now."

RAVEN'S WATCH

School the next day began with an unexpected assembly. It turned out that Naia Petrakis's bracelet was not the only thing to have gone missing from the gym lockers. An eighth grade boy had lost a stack of baseball cards and Princess Clarkson had lost her hairbrush. This last caused some private grins and eye-rolling, but the principal hinted at other cases for which he didn't supply details.

"This must stop immediately," he said.

The thief was instructed to bring all stolen property

to a box outside the staff room by the end of the day with a note of apology. "If that does not happen, drastic measures will be taken." The teachers exchanged serious looks and the students whispered furtively.

"In better news," said the principal, "I am pleased to announce that Hillside will host its first ever Halloween Hop at the end of the month . . ."

As the assembly ended, the students speculated about what the teachers might consider "drastic measures."

"They could order searches," Melissa Young was saying to a teary-looking Naia.

"Who would steal from kids?" said Alexandra.

Genevieve Reddock looked up from her plastic kitten and shot a glance in Darwen's direction.

"Never been a problem before this week," she said with a meaningful look at Melissa. Her keychain cat started mewing in its tinny digitized voice.

"Aw . . ." she cooed. "It's time for his milk. Isn't that adorable?"

Darwen marveled at Alexandra's ability to think about anything other than what they had been through the night before, but was not surprised: Alexandra bounced from subject to subject like a pinball machine. She could be standing in a burning building and still let you know exactly what she thought about her teachers, the best music downloads, and the chance of the Halloween Hop being "deeply lame." Darwen, by contrast, couldn't think about a little petty theft now. The world looked different because he had glimpsed the horror of what was just beyond it. He had to see Mr. Peregrine immediately.

But classes came first, and in PE Darwen found himself playing American football. He had no idea what he was doing, though it seemed that the unofficial aim of the game was for Nathan and Chip to take every opportunity they could to flatten him. This seemed to amuse the fat gym teacher, Mr. Stuggs, who was refereeing from a folding chair on the sidelines.

"Get up, Arkwright," he bellowed. "What, this game too tough for you? Let's see a little backbone!"

Darwen got to his feet wearily and rejoined the game, thinking that if they kept this up for long, they'd see more than his backbone. He got steamrolled twice in the next five minutes, and when Mr. Stuggs complimented Nathan on "a nice hit," Darwen became furious.

"I don't know what I'm doing!" he protested. "Will someone please explain the rules of this stupid game before I get killed?"

Nathan and Chip thought this was hilarious but Mr. Stuggs rounded on him.

"You think this game is stupid?" he said, getting slowly out of his chair and rolling toward Darwen like a tank. "You think you're too good for *American* football?"

Darwen didn't like the way he emphasized "American." He saw right away that Nathan and Chip had stopped snickering and were exchanging dark looks.

"No, sir," said Darwen. "But I don't know how to play."

"So it's not the *game* that's stupid," said Mr. Stuggs. His fat face creased into a smile so that his eyes almost disappeared.

"How am I supposed to play if I don't know the rules?" Darwen demanded. "It's not fair."

"Don't whine," said Mr. Stuggs. "I can't stand whiners. Chip! Give him the ball."

Chip exchanged a grin with Nathan and tossed Darwen the ball. Darwen caught it reluctantly, and stood there wondering what to do next. He turned to Mr. Stuggs in time to see him blow his whistle. Instantly Chip and Nathan came at him.

Darwen dodged instinctively and started to run. He weaved right and Chip missed him. He cut left, blood roaring in his ears, and began sprinting for the end zone, the ball clutched to his chest. Someone came at him but he sidestepped and ran on. Then he saw Rich coming for him.

Rich was on *his* team. Darwen hesitated, then kept going, sure the other boy would stop. Perhaps this was an elaborate trick to protect him so he could score. . . .

Rich slammed into him and the ball went flying.

Darwen hit the ground hard and rolled onto his back.

"Fumble!" roared Mr. Stuggs, delighted. "Recovered by Mr. Cloten!"

"What do you think you are doing?" Darwen demanded, struggling to his feet and glaring at Rich. "I was going to score!"

"For them," said Rich. "You were going the wrong way."

Darwen could hear the other team laughing now. Chip was doubled up on the ground, crying with mirth. Darwen stood there, anger and humiliation pouring out of him.

"Thanks," he said to Rich. "Thanks a lot."

"Would have been worse if you'd scored," said the other boy.

"Nice try, Arkwright," said Chip, sneering. "Too bad you have your mom's sense of direction."

Darwen was walking away, determined to ignore them, so it took a moment for him to realize what Chip had just said.

Your mom's sense of direction . . . ?

The road accident.

It took fully two seconds for Darwen to understand the joke but less than half of that to turn and run at Chip Whittley, head lowered, blinded by fury. Whittley was half turned away, snickering, and Darwen hit him before he even knew he was there. A moment later, Chip was on his back, his hands up to protect his face from Darwen's wild punches.

It was over in no time.

A meaty hand grabbed Darwen by the scruff of the neck and hauled him off. It was Mr. Stuggs, and his face was scarlet.

"Get off this field," roared the teacher. "You're a disgrace. Haggerty! Escort him to the locker rooms."

Darwen began stalking across the field to the school, not waiting for Rich. He clenched his eyes shut to hold back the tears and walked blindly. It was all he could do not to run, but Rich somehow kept up with him.

"What did he say?" said Rich. "Chip, I mean. What did he do?"

"Nothing," Darwen answered, staring ahead.

"Something about your parents, right?"

Darwen shot him a look but he remembered what Alexandra had said: they all knew, even Rich.

"I said it was nothing, okay?" he said.

"Listen, Darwen," Rich said, urgently, his voice low. "We need to talk."

"Not now," said Darwen.

"What, because of the game?" said Rich.

"Oh, that was a game, was it?" said Darwen. "Didn't feel like a game to me."

"Oh come on, man," said Rich. "It's over. Everyone will have forgotten about it by lunchtime. We need to talk about . . ."

"Not now," said Darwen, picking up speed.

Rich slowed, and Darwen returned to the empty locker room alone.

He didn't speak to anyone all the way through English, but as the bell rang for lunch, Rich cornered him again.

"Look," he said. "I'm sorry about the game. You should have said you didn't know the rules. I would have explained."

"It's fine," said Darwen, in a voice that said plainly that it wasn't fine at all.

"I've been thinking about you-know-what," said Rich, who either didn't hear Darwen's tone or decided to ignore it. "I have to show you something."

"Now?" said Darwen, stopping so that a seventh grader marched into him.

"Single file!" bellowed Miss. Murray.

"In private," said Rich. "We can use the janitor's workshop. Mr. Jasinski is at lunch."

"Haggerty! Arkwright!" yelled Miss Murray. "You are blocking the hallway!"

Darwen considered Rich's serious face then nodded. They walked quickly down the corridor and into the quadrangle, then out to the clock tower and down to the basement.

Rich perched on a stool but he suddenly seemed very uncomfortable.

"Right," asked Darwen. "What's the big deal?"

"Okay," said Rich. "I'm not going to try to explain anything, I'm just going to show you this."

He swung his book bag up onto his knee and opened it. He lifted out his *Introduction to Field Archaeology* (which he seemed to keep with him at all times) and then produced an even older and more battered book, its spine marked with the code numbers of the Hillside library.

"I got it out last night," he said, opening it to a page he had marked with a piece of paper. "I think we have to talk to Mr. Iverson."

He turned the open book toward Darwen.

The print was small and the paper faded so that Darwen had to lean in close. The section was entitled "Massacre at Raven's Watch, 1813: a colonial settlement attacked by Red Stick rebels." He frowned and began to read:

The assault began shortly after midnight, and caught the fort militia off guard. The Lower Creek Indians under Chief McIntosh fought shoulder to shoulder with the white men, but the Red Sticks appeared out of nowhere riding great engines of war, the like of which no one had ever seen. The Red Stick warriors were of huge and barbaric appearance, quite unlike the Lower Creek men so that some said they were not true Indians but some monstrous species which had allied with them. Nor were they dressed like usual Red Stick warriors, but wore protective eyeglasses, and were armed with strange and terrible weapons. The soldiers who survived testified that it took many musket shots to even slow the brutes down, and they appeared out of the night with no warning, so that soon the settlement was in total confusion. The settlers and their Creek allies fled the scene and returned the following day to remove their dead, but such was the brutality of the assault that no attempt was made to rebuild the village or the fort, and—in accordance with Creek superstition, which had long said that the place was evil—the settlers withdrew from the area and did not return. Of the monstrous Red Sticks who had attacked, nothing more was seen and the invaders seemed to have vanished as completely and silently as they had come.

Darwen stared at the page then looked up into Rich's eager face.

"Where is Raven's Watch?" he said.

"You're sitting on it," said Rich. "You don't think they'd name a fancy school after a famous massacre, do you? Hillside is so much nicer."

"It was here?" said Darwen, forgetting his frustration.

"Yep," said Rich. "And historians have been arguing

about it ever since. See, there was a feud between the Upper and Lower Creek Indians, or the Muskogee as they were called. The Lower Creek and their representative, Chief McIntosh, wanted the Native Americans to live according to the whites' brand of civilization. In the process, he signed a lot of Indian land away. The Upper Creeks rebelled and there was a war between the two parts of the Creek nation, with the U.S. government supporting the Lower Creeks. It only lasted a couple of years and ended badly for the Upper Creeks, but not before they had killed McIntosh.

"But here's the thing. The fighting was generally west of here, around the Alabama border. The Raven's Watch massacre was the exception, and no one has ever been able to explain how or why it happened as it did. The strange description of the attackers has led some to believe that the massacre had nothing to do with the Creek Indian war and was really orchestrated by the Spanish or other settlers who wanted the land. It never made any sense. Till now."

"What do you mean?"

"I mean that thing we found was killed during the massacre," he said. "The musket balls prove it. But the clothes don't fit the period. Then there's the skull. The attackers at Raven's Watch—I don't know what they were—but they weren't Red Stick warriors. Darwen, I can't explain it, but that thing isn't human."

Darwen looked from the book to his friend's troubled face and realized that he no longer had a choice.

"I know what they were," said Darwen.

"What do you mean?"

Darwen considered Rich carefully.

"My turn to tell you something," said Darwen. "Something big. And if you laugh at me, or talk about 'scientific reality' we won't be friends anymore, okay?"

Rich nodded once.

"Swear?"

"Swear," said Rich, gripping the stool. "What is it?"

Darwen swallowed.

"The bones we found," he said. "It's not a gorilla. It's not a man. It's a . . . a scrobbler."

"A what?"

"A scrobbler," said Darwen.

"Which is . . . ?"

"A kind of monster from another world," Darwen blurted. "And yes, I know how stupid that sounds. But I've been there and I can prove it."

"What?" said Rich. His face was blank, like he was working hard to show no emotion. "Are you making fun of me? 'Cause if you are . . ."

"I'm serious," said Darwen. "I went through a mirror. It has . . . I don't know. Powers, I suppose. Anyway, I went through one and I saw the world on the other side, including the scrobblers. They came after me. I nearly got killed. Twice."

"O . . . kay . . ." said Rich, his voice still toneless. "And you can prove this?"

"Yes," said Darwen. "Last time, I took someone with me. You can ask her."

"*Her*?" said Rich. "Who?"

"Alexandra," said Darwen.

For a long moment, Rich said nothing, though once his mouth moved as if he had started to say something and thought better of it. Darwen suddenly wished his witness was someone—anyone—other than Alexandra.

"I have another witness," he said at last. "A grown-up who will tell you that what I'm saying is right. Come with me to the mall, and I'll introduce you to the man who gave me the mirror."

"Okay," said Rich.

"It's not magic exactly," said Darwen. "It's just . . . I don't know. A different kind of science. Only I can see through the mirror, unless I'm touching someone else, then they can see through too. I'm what they call a mirroculist."

"Okay," said Rich, still noncommittal.

"And on the other side are monsters," said Darwen, matter-of-factly. "You've already seen the bones of one of them."

"Let me get this straight," said Rich, carefully. "You found a magic mirror that leads to another world, and you took *Alex* in there with you?"

"That's right," said Darwen, just as carefully.

"What were you trying to do, lose her in there?" said Rich.

And suddenly they were both laughing. The situation was absurd and the tension had grown unbearable, and they both howled with laughter till their eyes swam. Darwen had no idea what Rich believed, but after all he had been through it was good to laugh.

"So when can we go to the mall?" asked Rich.

Darwen checked his watch.

"How about now?" he said.

"We're not allowed off school property at lunchtime, remember?" said Rich. "And you're supposed to have elocution lessons with Mrs. Frumpelstein."

"You want to know the truth?" said Darwen, who was feeling mutinous. "Then now's your chance."

Rich bit his lower lip, then looked down at his book about the Raven's Watch massacre.

"Okay," he said. "Let's make it quick."

They left the basement at a brisk walk, bolted across the quadrangle and into the corridor, forcing themselves to march in single file as they steamed toward the main entrance. As they reached the steps down to the lawn, a shrill voice stopped them in their tracks.

"Hey!"

Darwen turned and saw Alexandra standing with her hands on her hips, glaring at him. "I heard about you fighting during PE! You're just determined to get thrown out, aren't you? And where do you think y'all are going now?"

"Just, you know, for a walk," he said.

Alexandra came toward them, her face like thunder, and actually marching for what was probably the first time in her career at Hillside.

"I've said it before and I'll say it again," she remarked. "You're a bad liar, Darwen Arkwright. I know where you're going and I'm coming with you."

Darwen turned to Rich, who looked like he was going to protest, but Alexandra was already stomping down the steps and turning toward the mall.

"Great," Darwen muttered. "Just great."

MR. PEREGRINE'S LIE

"**Y**ou've got some explaining to do, mister," said Alexandra as she stormed into the mirror shop.

Mr. Peregrine looked from her to Darwen and then to Rich and, very politely, said, "I'm sorry, do I know you?"

"You sent Darwen through that mirror and your so-called friends tried to kill us," she answered, taking up her most dangerous pose, hands on hips and head cocked sideways.

"I'm sorry," said Mr. Peregrine. "I'm not sure I understand."

"It was my fault, Mr. Peregrine," said Darwen. "I didn't mean for her to come, but she saw the mirror and . . . Anyway, it's a good thing she did. I wouldn't have made it back alive without her."

Alexandra gave him a glance, but she didn't drop her attitude to the shopkeeper.

"The woods were full of gnashers and Lord knows what else," she said. "And the *Jenkinses* are such nice welcoming people! They served us tea and everything before climbing their insect-selves out of their people-suits and trying to eat us."

Mr. Peregrine's eyes tightened, but then he shook his head.

"I'm afraid I don't know what you mean," he said.

"We went through the mirror together," said Darwen, spelling it out.

"Through the mirror?" said Mr. Peregrine, apparently quite baffled. "What do you mean *through* the mirror? How would you go through a mirror?"

Rich shot Darwen a look.

"No," Darwen said, "you can tell them. It's okay. I mean, Alexandra has already been through, and Rich has seen a scrobbler skeleton. We found one."

"Scrobbler?" said Mr. Peregrine. "I don't think I'm familiar with that term. What is a scrobbler?"

Darwen felt his head spinning.

"Scrobblers," he said, fighting to stay calm. "Like the ones destroying Moth's forest!"

"I'm sorry," said Mr. Peregrine, "I really don't know what you're talking about."

Darwen couldn't believe what he was hearing. A wave of emotion, the kind of emotion he had been trying to keep locked away for months now, rose up inside him: sadness, despair, and—on top of it all—anger.

"You know!" he shouted. "Don't lie to us. You *know*."

"I'm sorry," said Mr. Peregrine, "but I don't."

"Now you listen . . ." Alexandra spluttered.

"No, young lady, *you* listen," said Mr. Peregrine in a voice suddenly filled with seriousness and authority so that Alexandra went still and silent. "This is my shop. And if you are going to come in here making wild and unfounded accusations, then I shall have to ask you to leave."

"But I did it for *you*!" exclaimed Darwen, a desperate fury overtaking him. "I went through because you asked me to."

"I'm sorry," said the shopkeeper, "but there seems to have been some kind of misunderstanding. I think you should leave, and I would appreciate the return of my mirror immediately. Today please, before we close."

"But . . . !" Darwen sputtered.

"Before we close," the shopkeeper repeated. "Good day."

"We aren't done with this," said Alexandra, as she marched toward the door.

"I believe," said Mr. Peregrine, "that we are."

There was nothing else to do, so Darwen led the others out. He could not speak. He was filled by a raging sense of injustice. He could not look at Rich and dared not open his mouth in case he started to cry.

"Come on," said Alexandra. "We're going to be late for math."

They were, but Darwen didn't care. Rich and Alexandra ran but Darwen—almost glad of not having to explain what had just happened—walked miserably back across the parking lot and up to school alone. He reached the classroom no more than two minutes behind the others, but Sumners was waiting for him at the door, his eyes shining with vicious glee.

"Late for class," he pronounced, "and seen leaving Hillside grounds during school hours. Fighting in gym class too, I hear. And all that on top of your usual, ahhh, incompetence and insolence. My, my . . ." he mused. "The principal will be having a very interesting chat with you, followed, I suspect, by another with your aunt."

Sumners scribbled a note and Darwen stood there, feeling the class watching him over their textbooks.

"Take this to the principal's office," said the teacher. "And be sure you get back in time to collect your, ahhh, homework. *Extra* homework."

He gave Darwen a dangerous smile and pressed the note into his hand.

"Off with you to the principal's office," he said. "And don't dawdle."

Darwen turned to the door and a paper airplane hit him in the back of the head. He turned in time to see Nathan high-fiving Chip Whittley, but he felt nothing. He slid out of the classroom door and into the massive hallway, which seemed even bleaker and more imposing than usual. In the lobby by the statue of the two dopey kids inspired by "Learning," he took one of the half-spiral staircases and trudged up to the unfamiliar second story. There, hardwood floors were covered with oriental rugs and the air was filled by the steady ticking of a grandfather clock. The classrooms felt miles away. The walls were hung with age-darkened paintings, so that he might have been in the unvisited wing of a minor museum.

Darwen checked the polished brass nameplate on the first door he saw. "Principal J. Thompson," it said. The door was made of such heavy wood that when Darwen first knocked, there was almost no sound, like he was rapping on concrete. He tried a second time, harder, and a voice from within said, "Come."

Darwen grasped the handle—feeling it slide in his sweaty palm—and pushed the great door open. Facing him was a massive desk in the same dark, heavy-looking wood, and looming over it was the principal.

"Sit," he said.

Without looking up from the book on his desk, he reached out a long, thin hand, palm open. Darwen, who was climbing into the equally massive leather chair, offered the note he had been clutching as he walked. The paper was limp and smudged.

"Sorry," he muttered.

The principal said nothing, but took the note, spread it on the desk, and read it, before looking up.

"Mr. Arkwright," said the principal.

"Yes, sir?" said Darwen.

But the principal said no more, and for a long moment they stared at each other across the huge desk until Darwen, feeling uncomfortable, looked down. He could hear the clock in the hall ticking slowly away: ten seconds. Fifteen.

"Not the best of starts to your time here, is it?" said the principal.

"No, sir."

He wanted to say more, to protest his innocence, but his heart wasn't in it.

"There have been a number of items stolen from students," said the principal.

"Yes, sir," said Darwen.

"And would you have any knowledge of where those things are?"

"No, sir," said Darwen. "Why should I?"

"The thefts—which are unheard of at Hillside—began the day you arrived," said the principal. "Coincidence, perhaps, but the timing is . . . unfortunate."

Darwen kept very still and said nothing, but his eyes were hard and level, fixed on the principal's.

"As to this other business," said the principal, glancing back at Sumners's note. "Leaving campus during the day. Fighting. Missing your elocution meeting with Mrs. Frumpelstein, which she is giving out of the goodness of her heart . . ."

Darwen frowned.

"She has requested me to say," the principal confided, "that she will not be offering you more such meetings unless she receives a full apology."

"Oh," said Darwen, suddenly seeing a bright side to the situation. "Right. Well, I appreciate her offer and all, but she needn't bother."

"Wasn't she trying to help you blend in, accent-wise?"

"Aye, I suppose," said Darwen, "but it's all right. I don't mind not completely fitting in."

"Not completely," echoed the principal, with a look that said that Darwen didn't fit in at all. "I'm sure you have things on your mind, but . . ."

Darwen thought of the mirror, the scrobbler skeleton, and Mr. Peregrine's denial of everything.

"Yes, sir," said Darwen.

"And that is to be expected," said the principal. "Perhaps we should arrange some counseling sessions . . ."

"Oh," said Darwen, suddenly realizing what they were talking about. "No. I'm fine."

For a moment, he was back in his old school in England, sitting in class when the headmaster's face had appeared in the window of the classroom door. The class always took notice when the headmaster showed up, figuring someone was in trouble, and everyone watched closely as he stooped to whisper into Mrs. Arden's ear the name of the poor kid who was going to get it. . . .

Darwen Arkwright.

Darwen had stared, mystified. He hadn't done anything. Why was he in trouble? The other kids were staring at him, eyes wide, some horrified, some grinning and pointing. But there was something about the teacher's face, something also about the kindly way the headmaster put his hand gently on Darwen's shoulder as he led him to the door, that filled him with panic. Something had happened. Something bad.

That was when they had told him about the accident. Darwen hadn't really heard the details, hadn't wanted to be able to imagine it. Instead he had started checking off the birds he had noted down in his book for that week: blackbird, song thrush, starling . . . The headmaster had kept talking and Darwen had nodded from time to time to show he understood. But sitting there he had begun to take his memories from the place where his parents had been and hide them away inside, like he was burying something dangerous in the deepest shaft of an abandoned mine, a place so remote and treacherous that he would not even think of going back there to find them . . .

"Mr. Arkwright?" said Principal Thompson, carefully.

Darwen came back to the present with a jolt. He didn't want to be rude, but he also didn't want to discuss . . . anything. He certainly didn't want pity. He looked out of the window but could feel the principal's eyes on him, willing him to speak. There was a long silence but Darwen stared out to the grounds where he had seen the flittercrake.

At last Principal Thompson said simply, "Very well. It is our policy to address detention promptly. Your aunt will be notified that you will be kept in school this evening until seven o'clock. A suitable task will be assigned to you."

"Today?" said Darwen. How would he return the mirror to Mr. Peregrine?

"Today, Mr. Arkwright."

"But, sir . . ."

"But nothing, Mr. Arkwright," said the principal,

returning his gaze to the papers on the desk. "Good day."

Darwen left the office, closing the heavy door behind him and, for a moment, he considered just leaving: going downstairs and walking out of the gloomy lobby into the brilliant sunshine and not coming back. It was suddenly very tempting and, for almost as long as he had been in the office, he couldn't think of a good reason why he shouldn't.

But Rich and Alexandra had been right about this place. There was something odd about the school and Darwen needed to find out what. Forces from Silbrica had broken through to this very spot at least once before when it had been called Raven's Watch, and people had died. Whatever Mr. Peregrine might say now, it was clear that terrible things were happening in Moth's world, and remembering her words about how human children were suddenly "prized," he wondered if those terrible things might again spill over into his world. He needed to learn more, and to do that he would need to stay at Hillside, at least for a while.

Darwen returned to classes and was generally ignored by everyone except Mad who gave him an encouraging thumbs-up. Rich and Alexandra had been separated and neither of them made eye contact with Darwen all the way through art, in which Darwen painted something very like a flittercrake without really thinking about it. From time to time he would glance over to Rich in the hope of getting some kind of sign that they were still friends, but Rich never looked up. To Darwen, this was almost as depressing as his upcoming detention and the conversation he would have to have with his aunt afterward.

Knowing that he couldn't get the mirror back to the shop before nightfall filled Darwen with a savage pleasure. He was furious with the shopkeeper for almost sending him to his death and then refusing to admit he had done so. Somewhere under his anger was a doubt, a question, that asked if there was more to Mr. Peregrine's lie than met the eye, but Darwen didn't have the patience to think about that. He made his flittercrake extra mean-looking and then added tiny people running from it. One for Mr. Peregrine, one for the principal, one for Sumners . . . He considered adding Rich to the picture but decided he would wait on that.

In end-of-day homeroom, as Darwen was filling his pen with ink, an eighth grade boy arrived with a note for Miss Harvey which she, in turn, gave him.

Darwen read it twice.

"Why do I have to go to Miss Murray's office?" he asked, thinking of the stern world studies teacher who seemed to think Darwen was a bit slow.

"For your detention," said Miss Harvey, in a serves-you-right-too sort of tone. "I believe you will be helping her prepare for a class project. Your aunt has already been informed."

Great, thought Darwen.

Miss Murray was fearsome and had a tendency to snap if she thought you weren't listening, thinking, walking, or sitting in the correct way. Rich called her Miss Moray— like the eel with the beady eyes and scary teeth. Darwen grinned ruefully, then remembered that Rich might not be his friend anymore, and stopped.

Miss Murray was waiting for him. She was a big, powerful woman with a no-nonsense manner and eyes that could get very hard. Her hair had been rigidly straightened and shaped so that it looked like a helmet, and she wore suits made of stiff, bright fabric used for covering sofas, all with large gold buttons and matching shoes. She wore tortoiseshell glasses—Rich said she probably caught the tortoise herself—and heavy gold jewelry with diamonds the size of pennies. She smiled a lot but it never seemed quite real. That, Darwen guessed, was unlikely to change now.

"Good afternoon, child," said Miss Murray. "Ready to work?"

"Yes, miss."

"Mr. Arkwright," she said. "Not the best beginning to your time at Hillside."

"So everyone tells me, miss," said Darwen.

"You will address me as *ma'am*," said Miss Murray.

"Right miss," said Darwen. "I mean *ma'am*. Sorry miss. Ma'am."

Miss Murray gave him a long flat look, and Darwen could almost hear her wondering at his stupidity.

"No one says that in England, ma'am," he explained. "We say 'miss.' Or 'sir.' If the teacher is, you know, a man."

The more he talked, the thicker he sounded.

"Where in England are you from?" she asked, her gaze still level.

"Northwest," he said. "Near Manchester. Not really near London. That's further south . . ."

"I'm a world studies teacher, Mr. Arkwright," said Miss Murray, her eyes flashing over the maps that covered every inch of wall space. "I know where London is."

"Right," said Darwen. "Course you do. Sorry miss. I mean, ma'am."

Miss Murray blinked.

"Do you have pictures from home?" she asked. "An album, perhaps?"

"Yes, ma'am," he said.

"You should bring them in to show the class," she said.

"Oh," said Darwen. "Right. They're not very good. Just family stuff: places I used to go and things."

"I'm sure they'll be fascinating," said Miss Murray,

smiling and nodding. "Did you pick them out yourself?"

"Yes ma'am," said Darwen. "I couldn't bring much with me, so I just got one book and filled it with pictures before I flew out."

"They must mean a great deal to you," said the teacher sympathetically.

"I guess," said Darwen. "Not really."

The admission surprised him. They *were* precious to him and he was glad that he had them, but the album was in a box in his bedside cabinet and he hadn't looked at it since he'd arrived in Atlanta. He had almost forgotten that he had them.

"Curious," she said, her head tilting to one side. "But you must miss England very much," she said.

She was still smiling that understanding smile, but there was something different in her eyes, something that was merely curious, like she had posed a math problem. Perhaps it was that odd look but Darwen found himself considering the question seriously and was surprised to find that the answer was *no*. He had been sad to leave England but he had not thought about it much after he had left. This place certainly felt strange and unfamiliar, but if his aunt arrived and offered to take him back to Lancashire right now, he didn't think he would go. After all, home was where his family had been, and they were gone. Did he miss England? In some ways, sure, but without his parents, what was there to miss?

He had lowered his eyes as these unexpected thoughts chased through his head.

"No," he said. "They're just pictures. I've moved on now."

He looked up again and found Miss Murray watching him intently, and her smile—though still there—had shed some of its sympathy and become fixed, watchful. Darwen blinked, and in that instant the teacher's face changed, became as stern and professional as usual.

"Well," she said. "We aren't here to chat. You have work to do."

She got up and crossed the room to a row of cupboards whose doors didn't close completely because they were so packed with stuff.

"Our class will be working on the Maori of New Zealand," she said, indicating three boxes. "I need these files alphabetized. Each card needs to be categorized by subject, labeled, and filed in the cabinet. There are tape and scissors there. Questions?"

"No, ma'am," said Darwen.

"I have other jobs to do but I will be back in an hour. You stay till it's done," she added. "So don't dawdle."

It was slow going. He read every sheet, figured out where it should go, wrote out a suitable tag with his fountain pen (being careful not to smudge the ink), taped it on, and filed it away in the cabinet. He considered a photograph of a man with tattoos all over his face and filed it under "culture."

He was lifting the second box from the cupboard when something on the shelf caught his eye. It was a basket half-covered by a pale cloth. Moving the boxes had dislodged one corner of the fabric and Darwen caught a glimpse of something shiny inside. He gave the cloth a nudge with one finger and lifted it just enough to peer in.

There was a plastic bag containing a stack of cards bound with an elastic band, a book with a spaceship on the cover, and a hairbrush. The shiny thing he had spotted turned out to be a silver bracelet adorned with tiny owls.

Darwen snatched his hand away as if the basket might burn him. Why did Miss Murray have all the stolen student property? Being caught even looking at that stuff would be sure to make more trouble. He carefully repositioned the cloth over the top of the basket and stepped away.

He turned his back on the cupboard deliberately and got back to work, labeling and filing for what felt like hours. The light outside was getting low. If the sun wasn't actually down, it would be soon. Mr. Peregrine would not be getting his mirror back this evening.

"Almost done, Mr. Arkwright?"

Miss Murray was back, blocking the doorway and looming over him. He got to his feet quickly and said, "Almost, miss—I mean, ma'am."

She peered at him through her tortoiseshell glasses then stalked over to the filing cabinet and opened it. Darwen stood in silence while she considered what he had done.

"Tattoos are culture?" she said. "I suppose so. Looks like you have a few yourself. You should get a new pen."

"What?" he said.

She nodded at his ink-stained fingers.

"Oh," he said looking at them. "Yes, ma'am. If that's all, ma'am . . ." he said, looking up to find the teacher already seated behind her desk and watching him.

Darwen colored, but she just said, "Very well. Off you go."

His aunt said little to him on the ride home, and Darwen got the feeling that she didn't know what tone to take.

"I'm sorry," he said simply. "I'm sure it was inconvenient for you . . ."

She waved the apology away, but said nothing.

She was still quiet when they sat down to a stir-fried dinner for which she had laid out the obligatory cup of warm water with the teabag in it and chopsticks. Darwen had never used chopsticks in his life, and after ten minutes he thought there was a good chance he would starve. He fished at a piece of water chestnut, conscious that his aunt was watching him sideways.

"So," she said at last. "What happened?"

"I went to the mall at lunchtime . . ." Darwen began, sipping the flavorless "tea" so he wouldn't have to look at her.

"I know what you did," his aunt interrupted. "I'm asking why?"

Darwen continued to poke at his food experimentally, eventually managing to lift the water chestnut halfway to his mouth.

"Dunno," he said. "I guess I just needed a break."

"Mr. Sumners says you are behind and not trying," said his aunt.

He squeezed the two chopsticks a little hard and the slice of water chestnut fired out across the room and landed on one of his aunt's treasured Persian rugs.

"He said your attitude needed improvement," said Aunt Honoria, ignoring the way Darwen was redecorating the apartment with his dinner. Darwen wanted to tell her exactly what he thought of Mr. Sumners, but he glanced at her face and knew that she wasn't angry so much as concerned.

"I'll try harder," he said, then smiled in a determined sort of way.

His aunt put her chopsticks down and reached across the table and touched his ink-stained hand. For a moment, it looked like there were tears in her eyes.

"If there's anything I can do to help, Darwen." she said. "Anything you need . . ." She hesitated.

"Can I have a fork, please?" he said.

Before going to bed that night, Darwen took a peek into the mirror. He wasn't sure what to expect given his last meeting with Mr. Peregrine. Maybe it would just be a regular mirror now, its powers somehow blocked by the shopkeeper in retaliation for his indiscretion. That was how he had come to understand Mr. Peregrine's curious lie: Darwen had broken a rule by telling other people about the mirror, so he was being cut off from the world on the other side.

But all such thoughts went out of Darwen's head when he opened the closet and looked into the mirror. It still worked. There was the Silbrican forest, the pine-scented air breathing through into his room. But it wasn't the same.

Some of the trees had gone. Darwen could see their stumps, smell the sawdust. And that wasn't all. He could smell oil and smoke. He could hear movement close to the mirror, the grunting labor—he guessed—of gnashers and scrobblers, coupled with mechanical clanking and hammering. He did not dare to go through again, even with the screen device, but he was sure of one thing: the scrobblers were building something. He had no idea what it was, but Darwen felt a surge of dread at the thought of what they might be able to do when it was finished.

He was peering through the mirror thinking about this, when he caught a flicker of darkness like black water moving rapidly over the remaining underbrush: a shadow cast by nothing. It shifted, surged suddenly close, and passed over the surface of the mirror itself. For a moment it was like the light was sucked out of the forest. It wasn't just that Silbrica vanished. It was a black emptiness like the vacuum of space, as if—for a moment—whatever the shadow touched just ceased to exist. Darwen flinched away, and then it was gone, and the shattered forest was there again.

But there was one other thing that Darwen hadn't noticed before. The elegant fountain where the dellfeys lived had been roughly pushed over and lay at the foot of a tree, the intricate bars of the cage bent and twisted aside.

Thursday classes were suspended that week for a field trip to the Atlanta zoo. The teachers did their best to make the outing joylessly educational, but for Darwen it would have been a thrill to be out of school even without the animals. Better still, and before they even got off the bus, Rich told him that he believed him.

"Alex might have a vivid imagination," he said, "but even she couldn't have made up that stuff about the Jenkinses."

"So you believe me because of what Alexandra said?" Darwen snapped. "Thanks."

"Well, not just that," said Rich, uncertain.

"I thought we were mates," said Darwen, giving him a hard stare.

"What's that, like, buds?" said Rich. "Yeah. Sure. But, dude, I'm supposed to believe that you climbed through your bathroom mirror—defying all laws of physics—and into another world just because you said so?"

He had a point.

"It's not in my bathroom," said Darwen. "The mirror. It's in my closet."

"Ah," said Rich, grinning. "That changes everything. Much more plausible now."

Darwen shrugged and grinned and said, "Fair enough." Then, as Alexandra rolled her eyes and muttered "boys" in a knowing sort of way, they shook hands and went to look at the orangutans.

It turned out to be a wonderful day, good enough to almost silence Darwen's various anxieties. The sky was a clear blue but the air was cool, and all the animals were out enjoying the weather. Darwen loved high-quality zoos, the kinds that didn't make you worry about whether the animals had enough room or the right kind of food. He remembered going to a little zoo in England where a solitary brown bear had paced the same tiny circle constantly, like it was a recording stuck in an endless loop. It had depressed him for days and he had written an angry letter to the zoo, to which he got a form reply thanking him for his interest.

Darwen leaned over the wooden rail and watched the gorillas roaming around their enclosure, the young ones swinging playfully around the climbing apparatus and the big silverbacks sitting meditatively, watching the crowds in a way that made you wonder who was entertaining whom.

"Looking for your relatives, Arkwright?" said Nathan Cloten, who had showed up behind them with Chip and Barry.

"Get lost, Nathan," said Darwen, without bothering to look at him.

"Hey Nate," said Barry "Usually" Fails. "Check that one out. It's scratching its butt!"

He roared with laughter and then started imitating it.

"Suits you," said Alexandra. "It's about time you dropped the whole *human* act."

"You should talk, O'Connor," sneered Nathan, his eyes blank. Chip gave him a quick look, but he didn't say anything.

"Why don't you go and share your dizzying repartee with someone else," said Darwen.

"Hey, you know what?" said Barry, grabbing him by

the elbow suddenly, and snickering. "You should go in. Family reunion, right?"

Nathan laughed and grabbed Darwen under his other arm. He and Barry pushed upward and Darwen suddenly felt his feet clear the ground. He clutched at the rail to try and stop himself going over, but Barry and Nathan were much stronger than he was. Alexandra seized Nathan from behind and he turned, snarling.

"Chip!" he spat. "Little help?"

Chip seemed to hesitate, but he pulled Alexandra away and pushed her clear of the struggle. Darwen felt himself hoisted up against the bar. Another second and he would tip over and in.

Then Rich laid a big hand on Barry's shoulder and squeezed.

"I wouldn't do that, if I were you," he said.

Barry started to squirm and his face flushed.

"Let go," he said, releasing Darwen. "I didn't do anything."

Rich squeezed a little more, then pushed him away.

"You ought to watch yourself, Haggerty," said Nathan, pointing at Rich, though Darwen was amused to see how the other boys kept their distance from Rich, who was bigger than all three of them. "You're not on your daddy's farm now, cracker."

Rich's face clouded and he took a step toward Nathan,

who skipped backward, his eyes cautious. Alexandra laughed, but Nathan's confident sneer was back in a moment.

"Enjoy the apes," he said, and then they were walking away, Barry casually flicking a candy wrapper in their direction.

"Litterbug," Alexandra called after them.

They ate fat hot dogs and nachos for lunch, then lounged in the sun, absently watching the kangaroos hopping languidly about. Alexandra imitated them, leaping around with her hands stuck out in front of her so that Rich and Darwen found themselves giggling uncontrollably.

"She's crazy," said Rich.

"Bonkers," said Darwen.

"I can hear you, you know," said Alexandra, hopping.

"We know," they answered.

Darwen sipped from a can of soda while Rich and Alexandra discussed what still had to be done to their trebuchet and realized that—in spite of all the trouble he had been in, in spite of all the madness and mystery, the worry about Moth and everything that was happening to her world—he was, for the moment, happy. He even joined in when they discussed whether or not they would attend the Halloween Hop and what they might go as.

"We could all pick an animal," suggested Rich.

"Nah," said Alexandra. "We should go as something

no one else would think of, like . . . an Atlanta traffic jam."

"What?" said Rich.

"Yeah," said Alexandra. "We all have cardboard cars that we wear on straps, and we walk around in a line blowing our horns at each other . . ."

But Rich and Darwen were laughing too hard to pay her any more attention.

"So when do I get to go through the mirror?" said Rich, later, looking up from the *Introduction to Field Archaeology* he had produced from his bag during lunch.

"You don't," said Darwen. "None of us do. It's too dangerous."

"You got that right," called Alexandra, who was watching the elephants. "Anyway, he's too big. He'd never fit."

"But you can still look in, right?" said Rich, who had insisted upon a full account of the mirror and how it worked. "So at least let me see it."

"You could come over after the trip," said Darwen, "if your dad wouldn't mind. You'll have to stay till sundown."

Rich fished in his bag and pulled out his cell phone.

"You clear it with your aunt and I'm there, man," he said.

"Just no going through," said Alexandra. "Not without me. Okay?"

Aunt Honoria was polite to Rich but Darwen got the

distinct feeling that she was checking him out, making sure he wasn't what she would call "a bad influence." She asked a lot of questions about what his parents did and what his interests were, and Rich's remarks about growing up on a farm seemed to confirm her fears.

"But your father's in business now?" she said, hopeful.

"Yes, ma'am," said Rich. "Runs a yard care business up in Villa Rica."

"Oh," said aunt Honoria, obviously disappointed.

"And Rich is in the archaeology club," Darwen supplied, trying to stay upbeat.

"Yes, the principal told me about the archaeology club," she said, in a way that was supposed to be neutral but was clearly disapproving.

"Ah well," said Rich, as soon as they were alone, "you can't win them all."

It was still light outside when they first looked at the mirror and there was nothing to see, but by the end of dinner (steamed asparagus with tofu, rice, and artichoke hearts flavored with hot peppers, all of which Rich pushed around his plate warily), the sun had been down for at least twenty minutes.

"Ready?" said Darwen, his hand on the shirt he kept hanging over the mirror. Rich swallowed and nodded, but said nothing. His eyes were fixed on the mirror like he was looking for a fastball.

Darwen cocked his head, listening to his aunt's familiar bustle in the kitchen, then whipped the shirt aside. Darwen didn't look at the mirror but at Rich who looked confused.

"I don't see anything . . ." he began.

"We have to hold hands," said Darwen, shuffling over to him, embarrassed.

Rich shrugged, they did so, and Darwen turned toward the mirror.

Both boys gasped.

Rich was amazed because it was true. He had believed Darwen, but that was nothing compared to actually seeing with his own eyes. But Darwen was amazed too, and while Rich kept muttering about how "totally cool" it was, Darwen was alarmed, even afraid.

Because the mirror was bigger. He didn't know how that was possible, but there was no doubting it. The frame looked exactly as it had before, except that what had been about a foot and a half square was now at least six inches bigger all round.

"I thought you said I wouldn't fit through," said Rich, slightly accusingly, as if Darwen had been trying to keep the portula to himself.

"You wouldn't have yesterday," said Darwen. "It got bigger."

"How? Why?"

"No idea," said Darwen.

"We should totally go through," said Rich. "Just for a moment. You still have that screen thing, right?"

"It's too dangerous," said Darwen, but his eyes flashed to the drawer beside his bed where he kept the little brass contraption.

"Just for a quick look," said Rich. "Come on, man. It's just too cool."

"Listen," said Darwen. "There are scrobblers on the other side. I can hear them."

Rich listened too. Mechanical noises and muffled grunting drifted from the mirror.

"They don't sound too close," he said. "I bet we could just get in and look without being spotted."

Darwen wanted to tell him that he didn't know what he was talking about, that one look at those gnashers and scrobblers and he'd wish he had never even seen the mirror, let alone gone through it, but he was gripped by a sudden curiosity.

Why was the mirror bigger now? What did it mean? Was this something to do with Mr. Peregrine, or was it connected to whatever work was going on in the forest?

He was still shaking his head at Rich, but even as he did so he drew the screen device from its drawer and considered it.

"Just for a minute," said Rich.

"Okay," said Darwen, winding the screen. "Just for a minute."

He went through first, and the act of doing so scared him even more. What had been a tight squeeze was now easy, too easy, and he dropped softly onto the forest floor already turning to see what else was different.

Behind the mirror a huge area had been cleared of trees, and in their place was a vast metal machine with copper pipes and a great smokestack. From one end of the mechanism grew a kind of beam, like you'd see extended from a crane, and from that was suspended a great iron square at least twenty feet across with pulleys. Steel cables ran from the pulleys like the strands of a spiderweb, all ending in hooks that were attached to the sides of the mirror frame. Darwen could immediately see what the machine was designed to do.

They're stretching the mirror! he thought. *They're making it bigger.*

He was still thinking about this as he reached back inside to pull Rich through, and was too late with his "Shhh!" as Rich exclaimed, "Wow!"

From behind the machine came a scrobbler, brandishing a massive pipe wrench and staring in their direction.

Rich's eyes went wide, but Darwen held up the screening device to remind him, then put his finger on his lips.

Don't move, he thought.

Rich looked stricken with panic, and Darwen couldn't blame him. The scrobbler was huge, bigger than the ones he had seen before. It was wearing a coarse boiler suit stained with grease, and the usual brass-rimmed goggles, but there was no way anyone could have taken this creature for human. The gorillas in the zoo looked more like people than did this hulking monster, with its yellow, tusklike teeth and its massive clawed, greenish hands. It looked at them—or rather it looked in their direction—then turned back to the machine and shouted something.

A gnasher appeared pushing a wheelbarrow of what looked like coal. Like the others Darwen had seen, it had a thick body with long formidable limbs but no head, and its chest was marked with slit-like nostrils and a broad gash full of shark teeth. It tipped the barrow out and got to work with a shovel, spading coal into the iron contraption, its long tongue flicking out as if to taste the air. The creature was brushed with a bright orange light and Darwen realized it was feeding a furnace in the heart of the machine.

When it was done it turned away, taking the barrow with it, and the scrobbler slammed the firebox door with a clang that rang through the forest. Darwen took a step off the path to get a better look, pulling Rich after him. Underfoot, a twig snapped loud in the night.

The scrobbler wheeled in their direction. The gnasher

turned, tongue lolling. The two boys froze where they stood. Slowly, carefully, the scrobbler took one long stride toward them, raising its huge pipe wrench. The gnasher stooped, sniffing the ground, its tongue hovering and feinting like a dancing cobra. Rich had gone very pale. Neither of them was breathing. The scrobbler took another step. It was almost within arm's reach. They could smell the oil and sweat on its clothes.

The machine hooked up to the mirror frame groaned and steam gushed out in a thick jet. The gnasher and scrobbler turned toward it in time to see the cables inside the great square web begin to tighten. This seemed to be some kind of signal to the creatures that the machine was about to do something. With one last look around, the scrobbler hastened to the machine's controls, the gnasher loping in its wake. As Rich sagged with relief, the scrobbler flipped switches, turned a great crank, then pulled a lever as long as Darwen was tall. There was a metallic screech and then, to Darwen's horror, he saw the mirror frame start to stretch slowly and evenly apart: one inch, two inches, four. Then there was another gasp of steam, and the scrobbler wrenched the lever back into its original position. The cables relaxed and the entire machine seemed to sag slightly. The mirror was now well over double its original size.

It made no sense. Why would the scrobblers bother

to expand the mirror? Unless . . . ?

Darwen suddenly felt very cold. He looked away from the mirror and his eyes fell on the overturned fountain. He had to get a closer look, but when he turned to Rich, he saw that he was pointing through the woods. Off in the distance, in another area where the trees had been felled, was an even bigger machine. It was surrounded by scrobblers and gnashers—perhaps five or six of each—which seemed to be working on it. He saw flashes of a very bright light—some kind of blowtorch scattering sparks—and heard the ringing of heavy hammers.

Darwen beckoned to Rich and together they moved quietly through the ferns. When they were in between the two machines—about a hundred yards from each—Darwen risked a whisper.

"These are new," he said. "They weren't here last time I came. Looks like that one is still being built."

"What is it?" asked Rich. "It's huge!"

It wasn't just the whispering that made his voice so breathy and uncertain. He was scared. Darwen couldn't blame him, but he needed to know what the contraption was. He forced himself to move carefully toward it and Rich followed reluctantly. As they got closer, they circled it to get a better look, though Darwen was careful to stay downwind of the laboring gnashers with their overactive tongues.

The machine spread through the clearing like some immense, metal insect, an ugly mass of sharp angled girders, tubes, and wires. At its heart sat a great engine—still and silent for now—sprouting smoke stacks and studded with dials, levers, and the kinds of stops you'd find on an old church organ. Around the edge of the central engine were large rectangular frames of riveted iron all joined to the engine by spider-leg tubes and cables. They cast long, dreadful shadows in the moonlight, and with the smell of oil and the clanging of hammers came something else, something almost as distinct as scent or sound but not quite, something that Darwen felt in his gut, something cold, like dread.

"What is it?" Rich hissed again.

"I don't know," said Darwen. "It looks a little like . . ." He hesitated.

"Gates," said a small voice in his ear.

Darwen turned startled to see a tiny oil-spattered figure with a green firefly light in her chest.

"Moth!" he exclaimed. "Thank goodness! When I saw the fountain, I was afraid that . . ."

"Quiet," said the dellfey. "Come away."

Her light flashed out, and she vanished, only to reappear ten yards away, moving back toward the mirror and the structure that had been erected around it. The two boys followed as quickly as they dared and Darwen felt a sense of relief as they moved away from the other machine.

"I was so worried about you!" he said as soon as they caught up to her.

"Shh . . ." said Moth. "The Guardian council controls all the gates in our world. They can stop you from using a particular gate or can shut it down completely. That is why it was so surprising when the scrobblers came here. They have never been permitted inside the forest."

"But they are here and they're building . . . ?" Darwen began.

"Gates of their own!" exclaimed the dellfey with something close to terror. "Gates *they* control, gates powered by their own engines, which they can use whenever they like. Once the gates are working, we do not know where they will be able to go. The Guardians will not be able to stop them. Nowhere will be safe. *No one* will be safe."

"Can't you do anything?" whispered Rich.

The dellfey shook her head.

"My people have scattered and are hiding," she said. "Our only hope is that it will take more than steam to power the gates."

"What do you mean?" asked Darwen.

"Portals require a special kind of energy directed by the Guardians, and drawn from the life force of Silbrica. I do not think the scrobblers can use such energy, and certainly the Guardians would not let them."

"But why build something they know can't work?" asked Darwen. "They must have some other power source in mind."

"There is no other power," said Moth in her tiny voice. "None I know of, anyway. But there is something else. Follow me."

And she was moving again, but this time she went straight down the hill beyond the path. Darwen and Rich gave chase but they quickly began to slow, their faces peering uncertainly ahead.

"What is that, fog?" asked Rich.

Just beyond the trees in front of them was a curtain of pale gray mist like a bank of clouds that had drifted to earth and been blown into a wall. Darwen had seen it before, or something very like it at the railway station on the night he and Alexandra had met the "Jenkinses."

"Not fog," said Moth. "Not anything. One of my kind flew in to bring word of what was beyond the mist, but did not come back. This has never been seen in my world before. Two days ago it was not here. Now it circles the forest. And it is moving. Each hour it tightens a little. In a week, only the hill will remain. After that . . ."

Her voice trailed off. Darwen nodded absently, but his eyes were fixed on the strange gray air. There was nothing behind it, no sign of trees fading into the distance, just the curtain of fog, then . . . absence. It was, he realized, somehow worse than the scrobblers and their machines.

"And the stories are true," she added, the fear in her voice building. "Whatever is at work here has brought a Shade to the forest. I have seen it myself."

"A Shade?" said Rich. "What's that, a kind of scrobbler?"

The dellfey shook her head emphatically.

"Worse," she said. "Much worse. A terrible thing that can kill with its touch alone. A bodiless shadow that moves like lightning and cannot be killed . . ."

"We have to get out of here," said Rich. "And fast."

"Okay," said Darwen. "But I have to see Mr. Peregrine."

"That guy?" said Rich. "Why would you want to talk to him after what he did?"

"It's not about *want*," said Darwen. "I have to because he's the only one who has any idea what is going on."

"What if he won't talk?" said Rich.

"He'll have to," said Darwen, thinking of the machine that was stretching the frame of the mirror in his closet. Maybe they didn't have the right kind of power yet, but the scrobblers wouldn't bother widening the mirror-portal unless they had a reason, unless they thought they would soon be able to get through. Right into his bedroom.

"He just has to," he said.

Darwen, Rich, and Alexandra marched purposefully to the mall as soon as the end-of-school bell chimed. They had no plan, no strategy for dealing with any lies Mr. Peregrine might offer, except stubbornness. They wouldn't leave till he produced some answers. Simple as that.

Darwen felt he had to know what was going on, felt even that he was *supposed* to know. Over the last few days an odd thought had surfaced in his head, something that he hadn't shared with Rich or Alexandra, but which had been nagging at him.

In fact it was two ideas, though they were related. The first was that Darwen was meant to be involved with Silbrica somehow. He was the mirroculist, one out of all the world possessing the ability to go through the darkling mirrors. The second was that since he had learned this right after his parents died, wasn't it at least possible that the two events were linked? Could it be that his parents had known about Silbrica, that they had been working to protect it, and that now they were gone he was supposed to take over for them? And if that was the case, was it not also possible that their deaths had not been some random road accident (*the furniture truck strayed over the center line . . .*), but a cover for something else, something with purpose and meaning? Perhaps they had been assassinated by the scrobblers before they could finish their work. He couldn't say these things to Rich or Alexandra, but he would say them to Mr. Peregrine.

Darwen, Rich, and Alexandra walked in silence, their pace picking up with each turn through the mall's corridors. By the time they reached the near-deserted hall that led to the mirror shop, they were almost running.

The door was—as ever—closed but unlocked, but everything else was different. It looked like a bomb had gone off inside. There was broken glass everywhere, most of it silvered on the back. Twisted fragments of frames were strewn about the shop, and two of the shelf stacks had been pushed over. The antique register had been dashed against the floor and smashed open, and the curious clock that told only the time till sundown was lying on its side, silent, its glass shattered and its workings pulled out and tossed about the store.

Mr. Peregrine lay behind the counter.

Darwen ran to him and squatted by the old man's head. He had a nasty cut above his left eye and a bruise all down the side of his face. His jacket was torn and his broken spectacles were lying on the ground beside him. His eyes were closed and he wasn't moving.

"Mr. Peregrine!" shouted Darwen. "Rich, get help. Quick!"

Rich ran, slipping on the splintering pieces of broken mirror. Darwen heard the tinkle of the bell over the door. Then there was silence. Alexandra stood over him and together they stared at the shopkeeper, looking for signs of life.

"Mr. Peregrine!" shouted Darwen again. "Can you hear me?"

"Darwen," said Alexandra softly, "I think he's . . ."

"No, he's not!" Darwen yelled back, louder than he had meant. "He can't be. Come on! Mr. Peregrine! Wake up. It's Darwen."

The old man's eyelids fluttered and then parted slightly.

"You came back," he managed.

"You're alive!" said Darwen, relief washing over him like a great wave. "Alexandra, get him some water. There's a kitchen through there. Stay with me, Mr. Peregrine," he added. "What happened?"

"I am so sorry, Darwen," said Mr. Peregrine. His mouth barely moved and the words came out in a whisper. "I should never have . . ." He broke off, coughing, but then Alexandra was there with a cup of water and Darwen was helping him to raise his head. He sipped, coughed again, then sipped some more. "I should never have involved you in this," he said. "I tried to make you forget it all. I am sorry for that too, for the lie."

"Huh!" exclaimed Alexandra with triumph, though her face was still serious.

"It doesn't matter," said Darwen. "What happened?"

"They came through, the scrobblers," said Mr. Peregrine, weakly. "I don't know how. The seal on the shop held them, but they should not have been able to get here. When they couldn't get out into the world they were . . ." He smiled slightly. "Upset."

"I think I know how they were able to come through," said Darwen. "They are building gates of their own. Gates they can control without the Guardian council's knowledge."

Mr. Peregrine's eyes opened wide for a moment and

there was real fear in them.

"Then I was right," he said. "They are coming. Trying to get into your world."

"What can we do?" asked Darwen.

"I must address the council," said the shopkeeper. "I must tell them . . . But how can they not know? How . . . ?"

He began coughing again, a long, sputtering fit that rolled him feebly onto his side. He took another drink.

"Even if you could get through, you can't talk to the council like this," said Darwen. "I'll do it."

Alexandra gave Darwen a wide-eyed look, but Mr. Peregrine merely shook his head.

"You can never go through the mirror again," he wheezed. "Not now. It is too dangerous."

"But if the scrobblers are breaking into our world, we can't just sit around and wait!" said Darwen. "We have to do something. Perhaps if we could figure out why they want to cross over . . ."

"Some creatures do not need a reason to invade other than the fact that they can," Mr. Peregrine wheezed. "Though I suspect you are right. They want something. Something important . . ."

"We'll stop them," said Darwen, his eyes shining. "I promise."

Mr. Peregrine tried to shake his head but at that instant

the bell over the shop door rang again and Rich returned. Officer Perkins was with him: the cop who had threatened to return with a court order to search the place. There was no trace of that memory on the policeman's face now, however. He took one look at the state of the shop and he was all business.

"The ambulance is on its way," he said. "Is your uncle conscious?"

"Your uncle?" said Alexandra, raising her eyebrows.

"He's awake but very weak," said Darwen, standing up so he could get out of the policeman's way. "He's been badly beaten."

"Give him some air," said the cop. "The paramedics will be here in a moment. Who did this?"

Rich flashed Alexandra a worried glance but Darwen just shrugged. "He was like this when we arrived," he said.

A silence descended on the shop so that Mr. Peregrine's shallow and ragged breathing seemed to get louder. After what seemed like an hour, the door burst open and the paramedics came in—two men and a woman—with some kind of wheeled stretcher. As they started checking Mr. Peregrine's pulse and giving him oxygen through a mask, one of the men gave the policeman a nod.

"Okay, kids," he said. "Let's clear out."

The policeman led them outside and then moved away, as if giving them some space, taking up a position down the hallway to intercept the shoppers who came to gawk. Darwen stood by the shop door with Rich and Alexandra, waiting. When the paramedics emerged, Mr. Peregrine—masked, blanketed, and trailing IV tubes—was unrecognizable. Darwen pressed close to the gurney but the shopkeeper lay still and did not respond when Darwen called his name.

"Let him rest," said one of the paramedics.

"Is he going to be okay?" said Darwen.

"He's going to get the best care we can provide."

"But is he going to be okay?"

"It's too soon to say," said the paramedic. "You need to let us do our job now, son. We're taking him to Emory University Hospital Midtown. You can check in on his condition there later."

And then they were gone, rushing Mr. Peregrine through the mall to the excitement of the people coming out of the jewelers. The cop locked the little shop and pocketed the key, then gave Darwen an encouraging nod, and went after the paramedics. Darwen sank down into a squat, head lowered.

Alexandra sat beside him and put her arm around his shoulders in a sisterly way, squeezing him hard. Rich hovered looking uncomfortable, but when Darwen glanced up he nodded encouragingly.

"I *hate* those scrobblers," said Darwen. It was a stupid,

pathetic thing to say, but he pronounced it with such venom that his friends looked taken aback.

"There's nothing we can do about it," said Alexandra. "If I were you, I'd get rid of the mirror in your closet before the scrobblers figure out how to get through that one too."

"You could bring it back here," said Rich. "We could put it back inside and then it would be okay. You said the shop has a kind of seal on it, so that if they do come through, they're stuck in the shop."

"And what happens when they break the seal?" said Alexandra, looking alarmed. "Can you imagine what would happen if they started getting out into the city? How many are there? Dozens? Hundreds? Thousands even? They'd have to bring in the army or . . ."

"But the scrobblers couldn't get out, right?" said Rich, sounding a little desperate. "They came through the mirror but they were stuck in the shop. So maybe there's no problem."

"Mr. Peregrine said, 'They're coming,'" Alexandra cautioned. "I don't think it's about 'if'; it's about 'when.' They want something from us, from our world. That skeleton you found was like eighteenth century or something, right?"

"Early nineteenth," said Rich.

"And none of your accounts of the massacre said

anything about big mirrors being dotted around the village, right?" she persisted. Rich was going from pink to white. "I mean," she went on, "you're the historian and all, but I don't recall reading much about early-nineteenth-century sharecroppers investing in mirrors the size of a gorilla, do you?"

"So?" said Rich, stalling. He didn't want to hear her point.

"So in the past they could come through without mirrors," she said. "In fact, I'll bet this shop was built to kind of plug the gap. Maybe there's a hole or something in the barrier between our world and theirs, like when the fabric of an old dress wears real thin. The thin spot is here: Hillside and the area round it. After the massacre, the Guardians or whoever closed the gap—sewed it up, like—and part of that was putting the shop here. But what if these new gates the scrobblers are building don't need mirrors? What if they can just open anywhere?"

"The army would hold them," said Rich, though he didn't sound convinced.

"How?" said Alexandra. "How do you fight monsters who can step out of the wall, or appear inside your tank, then disappear again as soon as you get your guns aimed?"

Rich said nothing.

"We can't fight them in this world," said Darwen, speaking—for the first time—quietly but with certainty so that the others stopped and stared at him. "We have to fight them in theirs. That's where the machines are. We stop them from building their own gates and we stop them from coming through."

"But how?" said Rich.

Darwen shrugged.

"I don't know," he said, getting to his feet. "But I have to try."

Rich nodded solemnly.

"And you did promise," said Alexandra. "For all of us. Hey, we're like a club! The Mirror Defense League. No, that's not quite right. It's not a club. More like a mission. A commitment . . . Wait. I got it. We've made the Peregrine Pact."

Darwen took a bus to the hospital, but was only able to get in at all because Officer Perkins was still at the desk going over paperwork and he waved away the security officer's questions.

"He's the old guy's nephew," he remarked, though his gaze lingered on Darwen. Something knowing passed between the cop and the security guard. They were cutting him some slack because of his "uncle," but outside the hospital he was the kind of kid they should watch like hawks. Darwen bobbed his head in thanks and went into the patient's room.

He took one look at the shopkeeper and his heart sank. Mr. Peregrine was hooked up to various monitors and pieces of equipment and though he was still breathing by himself, he showed no sign of knowing Darwen was there.

"He's in a coma, isn't he?" Darwen said to a nurse. He had heard of people being in comas for days, weeks, even years, though he also knew they sometimes didn't wake up at all.

The nurse nodded. "I'll give you a moment alone with him," she said, "but then you'll have to leave him be, okay?"

She left, and Darwen waited no more than a second before opening the drawer in the cabinet by the bed. There was Mr. Peregrine's wallet, his watch, a handful of change, and a key. Darwen reached in and took the key.

"Sorry," he said, to Mr. Peregrine. "I'll bring it back. Promise."

STOLEN GOODS

INTRODUCTION *to* FIELD ARCHAELOGY

Darwen's frustration built over the next two days. He was no closer to having a plan for stopping the scrobblers, and it didn't help to know that whatever they were building was probably well on its way to completion. He visited Mr. Peregrine in the hospital twice more, once alone, once with Rich and Alexandra, but there was no change in the old man's condition, and Darwen had no new ideas as to what he could do to help. But how could he just move on with his life knowing what was happening in Silbrica, knowing that the only adult who knew about it was lying in a coma?

But life did go on. Darwen spent a whole Saturday working absently with Rich on the trebuchet at his farm northwest of the city, taking breaks from the heat outside to browse through Rich's comic book collection. Rich's favorite was one called *Antimatter Boy*.

"Antimatter is real," Rich said, looking over Darwen's shoulder. "It's not just in stories. If you mix regular matter—like what the universe is mainly made of—with antimatter, they destroy each other. Neat, huh? But there's also a way to collide matter and antimatter so that they produce a massive power surge, like atomic power only bigger. I used to think it was just made up, but there's this lab in Geneva called CERN where they make antimatter. . . ."

Darwen nodded occasionally, grateful for Rich's attempts to distract him from his other thoughts, but not really listening.

Life also went on, unfortunately, at school. That week, Miss Murray's world studies classes began their work on the Maori of New Zealand, and in the Friday class (right after her usual "Good morning, children. Ready to work?"), she announced that the class would be divided into groups to make models of Maori-style art or—as she insisted on calling it—a *taonga* based on traditional carvings.

"Each group will follow the *kaupapa* behind all Maori *wakairo*," she said.

"The what behind the what?" muttered Rich as soon as she stopped talking. "Either I'm going crazy or she's not speaking English."

"She means that whatever we make has to have the same kinds of meaning that the Maori carvings do," said Darwen, who was a step ahead of everyone after his evening organizing Miss Murray's research materials. "That means it should probably say something about who we are or things that have happened, as well as looking nice."

"Okay," said Rich. "Sounds doable. Alex!" he added, "pull your chair over."

But that was not how groups were assigned in Miss Murray's class.

"Mr. Haggerty!" said the teacher, giving Rich a beady stare. "What do you think you are doing?"

"Just forming a group, ma'am," said Rich, going pink. "For the project. The Waikiki toggle thingy."

The groups for the *wakario*-based *taonga*," said Miss Murray, carefully, as the rest of the class snickered, "will be assigned by me, since I am the teacher."

"Right, ma'am," said Rich. "Of course they will. Silly me."

"Take your chair and join Mr. Whittley, Mr. Agu, and Miss Young," said the teacher. "And do so with a good grace, Mr. Haggerty," she added, as Rich gave Chip Whittley a scowl, "or I will see you in detention. When orders are given at Hillside, how do students respond?"

"With spirited resolution," Rich murmured. He was obviously quoting some school saying.

"I beg your pardon?" said Miss Murray.

"With spirited resolution," said Rich, louder this time, and with a forced smile.

"That's better," said Miss Murray. "Mr. Arkwright," she said, turning to Darwen, "you are with Miss Petrakis, Mr. Garcia, Miss O'Connor, and Mr. Cloten."

Nathan, thought Darwen miserably. He shot the other boy a glance and saw his grin of anticipation. Nathan was obviously looking forward to the opportunity to push Darwen around some more.

"We could make masks," suggested Naia. "One for each of us that said something about us."

"Masks?" sneered Nathan. "Why don't we just go back to first grade and play with blocks?"

"You think you're ready for blocks, Nathan?" said Alexandra.

"I should have known you'd like stuff like this," said Nathan. "If I had a face like yours, I'd want a mask too."

"What do you say, Carlos?" said Darwen, ignoring him and turning to the quiet Hispanic boy.

"Sure," shrugged Carlos. "Masks. Okay."

"Great," said Darwen. "Then we're agreed."

"I didn't agree," said Nathan.

"You got a better idea?" said Darwen. "If you have, let's hear it and we'll vote."

"What's the point?" Nathan returned, flicking the pages of the book dismissively. "It's a stupid assignment anyway. Fine. We'll make masks. Whatever."

"We can't carve them," said Naia. "But we could create the same effects with modeling clay."

"I'm not sticking clay to my face," said Nathan.

"No one said you had to *wear* it," said Alexandra. "It's just to look at."

"What's the point of that?"

"It's art," said Alexandra, as if this was obvious. "It doesn't have to have a point."

"Let me know when we do something useful," said Nathan.

"We should grab some art supplies before the other groups have the same idea," said Naia. "Darwen, help me carry the clay."

Darwen went, glad to get away from Nathan, who was leaning back in his chair and pulling faces at Chip Whittley across the room.

"You aren't wearing your bracelet," said Darwen. "The one with the owls."

"It was stolen," said Naia, frowning. "Remember?"

"But it was turned in, wasn't it? Miss Murray had it," said Darwen.

Naia turned to look at him and her dark eyes were big with hope.

"Really? When?"

"I don't know," said Darwen. "Last week. I thought she would have given it back to you by now."

"No," said Naia, shaking her head. She turned to the teacher. "Miss Murray?" she said. "Do you have my bracelet? The one with the owls."

"Your bracelet?" said Miss Murray, her face blank. "I don't have it."

"But Darwen said . . ." Naia faltered and looked at Darwen.

"Yes?" said Miss Murray.

"When I did my detention," he said, "I thought I saw . . . in one of your cupboards . . ."

"You went through my things while I was out of the room?" said Miss Murray.

"No, miss," said Darwen, blushing. "It were right next to the one I were working on. The door were open and I saw a basket with some things in it. Naia's bracelet were in there. I thought someone 'ad perhaps turned it in to you and . . ."

"No," said Miss Murray. "No one turned it in to me. But if it is there, it should certainly be returned to its rightful owner."

"It wasn't the only thing," said Darwen. "There were other things too, things that had gone missing. Maybe they're still there."

Miss Murray reached into the pocket of her fuchsia suit and produced a ring of keys. "Go with Miss Petrakis to my office," she said. "If the basket is there, please bring it to class immediately. And quick march, Mr. Arkwright. Don't run."

Darwen could feel the class watching him with interest as he left the room. Naia was at his heels, almost skipping with anticipation.

"It's from Athens," she said, beaming. "I love it more than anything in the world. When I lost it I cried for two days."

"Let's hope it's still there," said Darwen.

"Why wouldn't it be?" said Naia, with something like suspicion. "You're sure it was there, right? You're sure it was my bracelet."

"I'm sure," said Darwen. "Silver, right? With little owl things hanging off it."

"Charms," said Naia. "It's a charm bracelet. The owl was sacred to the goddess Athena."

"Oh," said Darwen. "Right."

They climbed the stairs to the faculty offices and Darwen unlocked the door. Naia held back, but she was positively hopping with delight when Darwen opened the cabinet, reached in, and pulled out the basket with its fabric cover.

"This is it," he said.

He whipped the square of material off, like a conjurer.

"What?" said Naia. "Is that supposed to be funny? Come on, Darwen, where is it?"

The basket was empty.

Darwen searched the cupboard shelves, then tried the other cupboards and the filing cabinet, but it was gone. As they walked slowly back to the classroom, Naia's eyes welled up with tears.

"You said you'd found it," she shot at him with an accusing stare. "What did you say that for if it wasn't true?"

"It was there," said Darwen. "I swear it was. And the other stuff too. Baseball cards and a book and . . ."

"Whatever, Darwen," said Naia, opening the classroom door. She stepped inside and met Miss Murray's inquiring glance with a single shake of her head. Then she returned to her chair and sat with her head down, refusing to participate in the group work for the rest of the class.

"Nice one," said Nathan to Darwen, grinning. "You really had her going."

"It was true," said Darwen. "I saw it . . ."

"Yeah, sure," said Nathan, smirking.

At lunchtime the other kids seemed to give Darwen

an even wider berth than usual, and their chatter about the costumes they were planning for the Halloween Hop died as he came close.

"They're just confused," said Rich. "You should probably tell Naia that you made a mistake and you're sorry for getting her hopes up."

"But I didn't," said Darwen, poking at the olive oil drizzled artichoke hearts on his plate. "I know what I saw. Someone must have stolen them."

"Again?" said Rich. "That doesn't make much sense, does it? Someone steals a bunch of stuff, turns it in to a teacher's office, then steals it again?"

"Maybe it was a different thief this time," said Darwen.

Rich pulled a face and shook his head, and Darwen knew there was no point arguing. Rich was right. It made no sense.

"Maybe there's a connection," said Alexandra.

"Between what?" asked Darwen.

"The thefts and . . . you know," she whispered, lowering her head. "The scrobblers, Mr. Peregrine, and everything."

Mr. Peregrine, Darwen thought, and his heart sank at the memory of the old man in the hospital bed. He should be doing something to help, but what?

"Nah," Rich said, chewing a wedge of bread. "Totally different."

Alexandra looked at Darwen, but he just shrugged. He couldn't see how something as ordinary as stealing could be linked to what was happening in Silbrica.

"Hurry up and finish your lunch," said Rich. "Got to have time to digest it before PE or you'll be making yourself even more popular by throwing up all over the other players."

PE. Darwen had forgotten. He had come to hate PE with its games that only he didn't know how to play and Mr. Stuggs who was just plain mean.

"Great," said Darwen. "And what are we playing today? Curling? Unicycle hockey? Aztec-rules basketball?"

"Nope," said Rich, enjoying himself. "An obscure and ancient game originating in the British Isles but known over here as . . . soccer."

"You're kidding," said Darwen. "We're playing footie? That's the best news I've had all week."

Darwen had no cleats with him, but the field was dry and—for once—he knew what he was doing. Back in England Darwen had played several times a week for as long as he could remember. He loved it. He had never been a star, but he was good enough to be a fairly regular pick for his school team. At Hillside, he looked like a professional.

They played five on five, each student rotating through each position, and apart from when he was goalkeeper, Darwen scored at least once from each. He ran, dribbled, passed, and shot like he was about to be signed to Manchester United, even nodding one goal in with his head from a throw in. Better still, the team followed his lead, passed to him, and started to work like a well-oiled machine. Carlos—who was as good as Darwen—scored three, Rich one, and Mad (boys and girls played together) got a remarkable four, the last of which she slotted coolly past the opposing keeper—Barry "Usually" Fails—after he had threatened to kill the next person to score on him. Barry gave a bellow of rage, but Mad was safely out of reach, and one stern look from Rich made Barry take his frustration out on the ball. He hoofed it onto the neighboring field and Mr. Stuggs yelled at him for interfering with the other game.

Darwen's team won thirteen to four, and they left the field laughing and reliving key plays. Darwen only wished that Nathan and Chip had been playing.

"I would have loved to see their faces when you ran rings round them," said Rich, grinning. "Next time we have to challenge them in advance, come up with some game tactics, maybe. That would be sweet."

Darwen opened his locker saying nothing. This had been his best hour at Hillside so far, and a part of him would have played all afternoon and well into the evening.

"No!" said Rich suddenly.

"What's up?"

Rich was staring into his open locker, his face pale and his mouth open.

"My book!" he said. "My *Introduction to Field Archaeology*. It's gone."

Rich was beyond miserable. Days passed and he didn't lose his silent, hangdog look. Only Darwen understood why Rich was so upset by the theft. The guide was no mere book to Rich. It was his private passion, his secret world, and what made him just a little bit special. Rich had loved it, and Darwen felt a prickle of anger at whoever had taken it.

The thought stoked an idea that had been smoldering at the back of his mind, and during their next world studies class—their last session on their Maori masks—he found a moment to voice it to Alexandra.

"I want to check Miss Murray's office," he said. "Make sure Rich's book isn't there."

"And if it is?" said Alexandra, wide-eyed.

"I'll take it," he said resolutely. "Last time I left them, thinking they would all go back to their owners, and what happened? Nothing. So this time I take back whatever is there and make sure it finds its way back to the right people."

"What are you now, Robin Hood?" asked Alexandra, trimming clay from her mask with a box cutter.

"Rich loved that book," said Darwen, defensively, lowering his voice since Miss Murray was glaring through her tortoiseshell glasses.

"You're right about that," Alexandra answered. "Weird, huh?"

"Miss O'Connor," said Miss Murray. "Is there something you need to discuss with the class?"

"No ma'am," said Alexandra. She lowered her gaze to the mask and started painting, smearing thick red paint around the eyes. As soon as the teacher turned away, she shot Darwen a nasty look.

"Thanks a lot," she hissed.

"You know what I think?" said Darwen in a forced whisper. "I think that all the things that have gone—Naia's bracelet, Rich's book, even Princess's hairbrush—were really only of value to their owners. They were precious, and they were stolen not because the thief really wanted them, but because he—or, I suppose, she—wants to make their owners miserable."

"Pretty scummy," Alexandra agreed. "And strange. But hey, welcome to Hillside: The Capital of Weirdsland. Center of Bizzarreworld. Hub of All Things Nutso, Wacked, and Bonkers."

"But maybe it's more than that," said Darwen. "Maybe you're right and there is a connection to . . . you know. *Everything else.*"

"Before you agreed with Rich," she said. "What's changed?"

Nothing's changed, Darwen thought. *And that's the problem. Mr. Peregrine is lying in a hospital bed, Moth's forest is being destroyed, the scrobblers are poised to invade, and I am doing nothing about any of it.*

"Are you going to help or not?" said Darwen.

"Help you get into Miss Murray's office?" exclaimed Alexandra. "Uh-uh. No way. I might be crazy but I'm not stupid."

"I just need a diversion," said Darwen.

"And a key," said Alexandra.

"Hmm," said Darwen. "How are we going to get that?"

"There is no *we*," she retorted.

"Come on," said Darwen. "For Rich."

Alexandra gave him a long look and sighed.

"That is the worst, most pathetic attempt at manipulation I've ever heard," she said. "*For Rich*," she repeated, giving him a soulful look. "Like you're trying to save a starving puppy or something. Pathetic."

"Don't you want to get that stuff back?" Darwen demanded.

"I'm not going to get expelled for breaking into a teacher's office . . ."

"You won't," said Darwen. "Come on, Alexandra. Don't you want to know who it is?"

"I thought it was Nathan," said Alexandra, running her box cutter over a bump on her mask, "but Genevieve just lost that dumb computerized kitten thing, and I don't think he would go after her."

"When did she lose it?" asked Darwen.

"Some time this morning," said Alexandra. "Left it in her bag in homeroom. By the time she got back from lunch . . . Poof!" She made a disappearing gesture. "She was sobbing over it worse than my baby sister when you take away her dumb bear."

"Well?" said Darwen, giving her a steady look.

"Okay, okay," said Alexandra, picking up the box cutter again. "I'll help."

"Excellent," said Darwen.

"So what's your plan, Robin?" asked Alexandra. "We head back to Sherwood and round up some merry men?"

"Funny," said Darwen. "Okay, I'll tell you what . . ."

But Darwen never got the chance to announce his plan. Without warning Alexandra began shrieking. She was clutching her left hand, and there was blood running down her wrist.

"What happened?" gasped Darwen.

"Cut myself!" exclaimed Alexandra, tears in her eyes, as she dropped the box cutter.

The class was suddenly on its feet, craning to look and wincing with revulsion.

"Let me see," said Miss Murray. "Someone go for the nurse!"

Darwen stared at Alexandra. How had she managed to cut herself so badly?

"Get the nurse!" hissed Alexandra through her tears. Then, with a pointed look at Darwen, she said, "Please, *someone*, get the nurse."

Darwen blinked, then looked at the pot of crimson paint and stared at Alexandra with amazement and admiration. This was his diversion.

He got up, pushed through the crowd of fascinated students, snatched Miss Murray's keys off her desk, and left the classroom at the closest thing to a run Hillside would permit.

The nurse's office was two doors down from Miss Murray's. He went to the world studies teacher's room first, unlocked it, and made straight for the cabinet where he had seen the basket of stolen property. He tried it, but it was locked. He fumbled through the key ring, his fingers trembling, found the key, and opened the cabinet.

There was no sign of the basket or Rich's book.

He tried the other cabinets, knowing he was running out of time, that at any moment Alexandra's ruse would be discovered and Miss Murray would miss her keys. . . .

The basket was nowhere to be seen.

Cursing under his breath, Darwen had no choice but

to close everything up and get out. He ran to the nurse's office and opened the door.

"Sorry, miss, but Miss Murray needs you in Classroom Four," he blurted. "A student has cut her hand."

The nurse, a slim and severe-looking woman with her hair drawn back, snatched up a first aid kit and marched out. Darwen followed, wondering how he was going to sneak the keys back onto the teacher's desk.

Back in the classroom, Alexandra was still trying to outdo Princess Clarkson's mom in the contest for best actress. She was holding her hand away from anyone who tried to look, wailing about how much it hurt, screaming if Miss Murray so much as reached for it. Darwen walked in, felt all eyes turn his way, then shrunk back as the nurse took over. As Alexandra's shrieks increased, he sidled over to the teacher's chair, pulled the keys from his pocket, and slipped them onto the desk, all the time keeping his eyes on the spectacle of Alexandra's performance.

"I can't help you if you won't let me see it!" exclaimed the nurse to Alexandra.

"It'll be fine," Alexandra, moaned. "I don't need those fingers anyway. Just leave me alone."

But the nurse was not to be fobbed off. She gave Miss Murray a look and the world studies teacher pounced, grabbing Alexandra's arm and gripping it tight. The nurse forced her fingers open one at a time and then straightened up.

"Is this supposed to be funny?" she said. She sniffed the smear of red on her fingers and looked pointedly at Alexandra's paint pot.

Alexandra opened her palm gingerly and peered at it.

"Huh," she said, as if mildly surprised. "Look at that. You know, I always have healed really fast."

"You made it up?" exclaimed Miss Murray, amazed.

"My mom had a new baby—Kaitlin—so I act up to get attention," said Alexandra, brightly. "That's what *Uncle* Bob says."

"Detention, Miss O'Connor," said Miss Murray. "During which you will be able to consider reforming your dreadful sense of humor."

Alexandra shrugged, then gave Darwen a questioning look. When he shook his head apologetically, she glared.

As soon as class was over, she cornered him.

"After all that," she exclaimed, "you found nothing?"

"'Fraid not," said Darwen. "Sorry. I'll buy you an ice cream to make up for it."

"Not tonight you won't," said Alexandra, "because I have detention, remember?"

"Right," said Darwen. "Sorry. Again. Still sorry."

"You're a loon, O'Connor," said Chip, as he walked past.

Alexandra marched away.

Darwen, shrugging, turned to Rich. "Archaeology club?" he asked.

"It's raining," said Rich, who was still miserable over the loss of his book.

"Only a bit," Darwen answered, ignoring the rumble of thunder overhead. "Come on."

"What's the point?" said Rich.

"We don't need your book to do some work outside," said Darwen, determined to cheer his friend up. "Who knows? We might find something important."

"How?" said Rich. "Anything we dig up we have to cover again so that no one finds out. We'll spend half the time uncovering what we already found, ten minutes digging, then another fifteen covering it all up again. It's a waste of time."

"Come on, Rich," said Darwen. "You'll feel better. And we have to do *something*. Maybe we'll find a clue to how to stop the scrobblers or . . ."

Rich gave him a look that said he doubted that very much, but eventually he nodded and they went to report to Mr. Iverson.

The science professor was in his office talking to Miss Harvey over cups of coffee, but he waved the boys in and said he was delighted to hear that they were going to do some digging.

"I thought you'd given up on it," he remarked, heartily. "It's important work, and you really don't need the tools we had been planning to buy."

"It's just disappointing," said Darwen, jumping at a chance to explain their absence. "Not getting the budget and all."

"I know," said Mr. Iverson, seriously. "And I heard about the loss of your book, Rich."

"Theft," said Rich, getting sullen again. "Not loss."

"True," said Mr. Iverson, nodding. "Terrible. I know how much it meant to you or I'd suggest you got a replacement from the library. We have a couple of the Mott's guide. Not as good a book, to be sure, but not too bad."

Darwen gave Mr. Iverson a long, searching look. *I know how much it meant to you. . . .*

"I barely recognize you without it," said Miss Harvey. "You should definitely get a replacement."

Rich nodded noncommittally.

"We'll just get some tools from the janitor's basement and get to work," Darwen said. "There's no need to come out. The weather is not that nice."

Both teachers glanced at the window, which was already rain streaked. The sky beyond looked unusually dark.

"If it starts to rain hard, boys, you come in, you hear?" said Mr. Iverson. "And if there's any lightning . . ."

"We'll stop," said Darwen.

They walked down to the quadrangle and round to the clock tower. Rich opened the door to the janitor's basement and led the way down the steps into the dank-smelling workshop. The janitor in blue overalls was bent over a rectangular metal box and muttering under his breath as he strained with a large pipe wrench.

"Hey, Mr. Jasinski," said Rich.

"Richard, my friend," said the janitor, turning and straightening, one hand on his lower back. "Off to dig up my grounds? What do you need, shovels? Picks?"

"Thanks," said Rich. "I can get them."

"Help yourself," said the janitor, returning to his work. "It's cooling down. If I can't get this furnace working in the next couple of days, the principal will have my head. Brand new heating system last year and it's already acting up," said the janitor. "The building was originally heated by this little beauty here," he said, reaching over and patting the black enameled stove with the kind of little firebox door you might see in a steam engine. "They knew how to build things in those days."

Rich murmured his agreement as he gathered together the spades and picks, but Darwen was staring at the ancient stove. Sitting beside the firebox door was the little wicker basket that had been in Miss Murray's office, the square of pale fabric folded neatly inside. He stooped to the firebox and raised the sliding iron door.

"Keen on anything old, eh?" said Mr. Jasinski. "No wonder you are into the digging thing."

But Darwen barely heard him. He was feeling around

inside the firebox, hoping to find some telltale scrap, some fragment of a book cover or the partly melted remains of a tiny silver owl. . . .

But there was nothing. Not even ash. The stove seemed not to have been used for years and had been thoroughly cleaned.

"Where did this basket come from?" asked Darwen.

The janitor frowned.

"Don't rightly know," he said. "Wasn't there yesterday. I hope you aren't encouraging other students to come down here. I don't mind you guys because I know you'll be careful with my tools, but I don't want anyone getting hurt."

"What was all that about?" asked Rich as soon as they got outside.

"I just wondered if . . ." said Darwen. "I don't know. Nowt, I suppose. Come on. Let's get the tarp up. The rain has eased off."

The two boys dragged the blue sheeting off the square of dirt, spilling the pooled rainwater into the grass beside it. The dirt beneath was still dry. Darwen squatted down with a trowel and started probing the surface for the hard spots where the bones were.

"Wait," said Rich. "This isn't right."

"What?"

"This earth has been turned over," he said.

"It's just been protected by the tarp," said Darwen, shrugging.

"No," said Rich. "I know dirt, Darwen, and not just because I like to dig up Civil War knickknacks. I grew up on a farm, remember? This dirt has been moved around in the last couple of days, and not by us."

Darwen gave him a look, then watched as his friend jumped into the hole and started sifting through the bright clay with his bare hands. He scraped it away till he was several inches down, and then he grabbed a pickax.

"Wait!" shouted Darwen. "You can't use that! You'll damage the skeleton."

But Rich wasn't listening. He swung the pick, tearing at the ground with something between fury and desperation. Darwen stepped back with a sinking heart, conscious that the rain was starting up again. The hole in the center got wider and deeper. Rich's face was spattered with the rain-moistened clay, and his hands were covered with a thick orange slime. At last, he stopped and turned to Darwen, his face streaked with rain and dirt.

"It's gone," he said. "The skeleton. Someone has taken it."

PORTALS
AND
BATTERIES

For a long moment they stood there in the rain, staring at the empty dirt square.

"Now we talk to Iverson," said Rich.

"And say what?" said Darwen. "That we deceived him? That we found a monster and now it's gone? For all we know, he's the one who took it."

"He would have said something," said Rich. "Anyone would. Everyone knows this is our patch. Why hasn't anyone asked us about it?"

"Whoever took it is keeping it quiet," said Darwen. "In fact, that's probably *why* they took it: to keep it secret. Now if we say anything we just look like fools and liars."

Thunder rolled overhead and, as the rain started to sweep in great gusting sheets, lightning flickered over the school.

"But why?" shouted Rich over the swelling storm.

"To protect the school from scandal?" said Darwen.

"Seems a bit extreme, digging the bones up and hiding them."

"Well, there is one other possibility," shouted Darwen, turning his back to the wind. They were both getting very wet but neither felt ready to go inside.

"Which is?"

"That whoever found the bones knows what it is," said Darwen. "Knows that this isn't *just* an archaeological find, knows even that the scrobblers are real and are still around. We have to find out if Mr. Peregrine is awake."

"I'll call the hospital," said Rich. "Let's get out of the rain."

They ran into the half-shelter of one of the massive cedars and Rich pulled out his cell phone. Rich spoke first to directory assistance, then to the hospital operator, and finally to someone at the nurse's station. Darwen was impressed. Rich sounded so composed, adult, and when he got through to a nurse he asked professional-sounding questions about whether there had been "any change in Mr. Peregrine's condition," what his "BP" was and his "rate of respiration."

"He's still breathing by himself but is unresponsive," he sighed as he hung up. "He could wake up in an hour, in a year, or never. If he's still like this in a few days, they'll move him to another facility. They aren't equipped for long-term care."

"How do you know all this medical stuff?" asked Darwen.

"Oh, you know, TV shows," said Rich, but he looked off into the rain. "We'd better pack everything up. We're late."

Darwen checked his watch. Eileen the dreaded baby-sitter was supposed to be collecting him. She was probably already parked out front, yakking on the phone to her boyfriend.

"I'll give you a hand," said Darwen.

Darwen felt like he was trying to juggle four different balls. One was the scrobbler skeleton and where it had gone, another was the state of Silbrica, then there was the spate of thefts in school, and lastly there was Mr. Peregrine and his shop. Could Alexandra be right? Could all these things be linked? Maybe he wasn't juggling four balls at all: maybe there was only one, one single issue that he was glimpsing from different angles. He just couldn't make sense of how it all fit together.

They re-covered the patch of earth with the tarp and rolled the barrow of tools back to the school building. It was almost dark now, and with a muted sense of panic, Darwen realized that the storm had hid the sunset from them. It was effectively night. Eileen was sure to try and make trouble for him with his aunt.

They checked round corners as they walked, in no mood to get yelled at for spattering muddy water all over the place, then slipped down into the janitor's basement. There was no sign of Mr. Jasinski. Darwen propped a shovel up in the corner and was turning to leave when something caught his eye: the empty basket by the old stove's firebox.

He stooped to it, thoughtfully, and as he did, he saw something else, a thin line of bright, bluish light. He saw it only for a moment, and at first he thought it was some weird reflection of the lightning. But there were no windows down here. He paused, frozen in the act of bending down, then carefully straightened a little.

There it was again, and this time he could see where it was coming from. The vertical sliding door to the firebox was cracked very slightly at the bottom. He hadn't closed it properly before. When he got his head at just the right angle, he could see the sliver of light within. He reached out and touched the stove quickly with one finger, half expecting it to be hot, but it was cold as before.

"What?" said Rich. "Come on. You'd better . . ."

"Wait," said Darwen. "Look at this."

And carefully he grasped the handle of the firebox door and dragged it up. The bluish light within splashed out and over the basement room like the flickering glow of a television set.

"What the . . . ?" blurted Rich, shielding his eyes, then turning slowly to look at it directly. "Is that what I think it is?"

"If you think it's a portal," said Darwen, "then yes. A small one, but a portal for sure, and right here at Hillside."

The four balls he was juggling were only one after all.

"Here, let me try this," said Rich. He had picked up one of the pickaxes and was squatting down by the stove. Carefully, he shoved the handle into the little curtain of light. When, after a couple of seconds, nothing happened, he pulled it back out. The pick handle seemed undamaged.

"Huh," he said, and reached into the firebox with his hand.

"What are you doing?" cried Darwen. "Pull it out!"

"It's fine," Rich said, dismissively. "I can't feel anything. Just air."

"I really don't think . . ."

But Darwen didn't get to finish his thought. It was like

Rich was being sucked in. His whole body slammed up against the stove.

"Something's got my arm!" he spluttered.

Darwen grabbed him by the waist and started to pull.

"Ahhh!" Rich moaned. "I can't get out! It's trying to pull me in!"

Darwen tugged harder and Rich tried to use his other arm to brace himself against the stove.

"It's no good!" Rich managed. "I can't get free!"

"What is it?" asked Darwen, frantic now. "Is it like a magnet or . . . ?"

"Something is holding me!" Rich cut in. "A hand."

He cried out again in pain and Darwen had a horrible idea: nothing could pull Rich through a gap that small, but if it was a scrobbler that had hold of him on the other side it might just tear his arm right out of its socket.

"Do something!" Rich begged.

Darwen looked wildly round and saw the pickax. There wasn't room to get the head through, but perhaps if he shoved the handle in hard enough . . . He grabbed it, worked the end of the handle into the opening just under Rich's arm then slammed it through as hard and as far as he could. He felt it hit something on the other side, and in the second that followed, Rich was able to snatch his arm back out of the firebox.

He sat on the floor as far from the stove as he could get,

nursing his strained arm, his eyes wild and frightened.

"Just for the record," said Darwen, "that was a terrible idea."

Eileen complained about how late and wet he was, but Darwen barely heard her. His mind was swirling with possibilities. Rich had promised to call Alexandra and tell her everything. Darwen had plans of his own. As soon as he was home, he left Eileen flopped on the couch, cell phone mashed against the side of her head, and went to his room.

It smelled of oil and smoke, a harsh, bitter scent that burned his nostrils. He opened the window to let some of the smog out, then, stumbling over his cricket bat, which was sticking out from under the bed, and opened the closet door. He gasped.

The shirt he had used to cover the mirror was too small now that the scrobblers had stretched it, and he had resorted to using one of his aunt's discarded raincoats, but even that wasn't big enough any more. The enemy had been busy. The mirror was now as big as the closet door. Big enough to let a scrobbler in.

What had been a small window was now a door that went right to the ground, and Darwen stood there looking in with a sense of dread. There was oil, slick and black, everywhere, and though the bulk of the machinery was outside his line of sight, the forest floor was strewn with cable, discarded rivets, and broken pieces of ironware. As he watched, there was a mechanical roar, and a shower of sparks scattered from the right side of the mirror frame. They were working again.

Darwen set the screen device, holding it tight to his chest, then took a deep, steadying breath and stepped into the mirror. Once through he turned and gazed horror-struck. The green and beautiful forest he had seen when he first brought the mirror home was almost gone. In its place was an industrial wasteland dominated by a wall-like row of hulking black machines that stretched all the way between the two work sites. The place was alive with scrobblers and gnashers, the latter emptying wheelbar-rows of what looked like coal, and shoveling it into fire-boxes, which appeared every few yards along the wall of machines.

It's a generator, thought Darwen.

But it had to be more than that. It couldn't just be pro-ducing steam or electricity, because Moth had said that the energy required to run the gates was different, spe-cial. The Guardians controlled that energy, perhaps even produced it. So how were the scrobblers going to open their gates?

Darwen eased into the remaining trees to keep away from the machines and then walked quickly toward the scrobbler gates. The complex of machines was massive, a vast tangle of dark iron belching smoke and steam. Darwen felt sick, though whether that was just the smoke or some more revolted response to what was happening to the forest and the creatures that lived there, he couldn't say.

There was no sign of Moth.

The wall of machines, it occurred to him, looked oddly familiar, and now that he looked at them from the side, he realized that they looked less like a wall and more like a great pipe, each segment connected like the batteries in a flashlight.

That was it. Batteries. That was what they reminded him of. The whole construction was not just making energy, it was storing it, directing it toward the gates they had built. At the far end, between the battery line, which went back to his own mirror, and the ring of iron-framed gateways, was a bulging mass of the most grotesque and complex machinery he had yet seen. This was the source of the steady humming. It was studded with lights that glowed red, and spewed wire and cable back to the batteries and forward to the gates. This was the heart of the machine.

And then Darwen saw it. In the center of that tangled mass of iron were two small openings not unlike the fire-box in the old stove at school. Both were surrounded by innumerable switches, levers, and dials, and though the one on the right was dark, the other contained a panel of flickering bluish energy that mirrored the one he and Rich had found in the janitor's basement.

So this is where it opens, he thought. *They've built a portal and it goes right to Hillside.*

It was strange that they would go to such trouble for something so small, something the scrobblers and gnashers couldn't hope to pass through themselves, but perhaps this portal was going to be stretched like his mirror. . . .

"Hello Darwen."

He barely heard the dellfey when she spoke, and when he looked at her his delight stalled.

"Moth!" he exclaimed. "What happened?"

The dellfey looked battered and exhausted. One wing was cracked and the green light in her chest that had been so bright was dull and erratic.

"We will not last much longer," said the dellfey. "The air. The trees. The scrobblers are destroying this part of the world and our only hope is that the gray fog takes it soon."

"Don't say that," whispered Darwen. "Can't you go somewhere else?"

"Dellfeys are bound to the land of their birth," said Moth. "We cannot move. We will die with the forest."

"We have to stop them," said Darwen.

"We do not know how," said the dellfey. "Each day we wait for the Guardians to intervene, but they do not come and now . . . "

Her voice trailed off.

"You can't give up," said Darwen. "I'm sure the Guardians will come."

"They have begun to build up the energy to open their gates," said Moth. "We do not know how. But when they have enough, all will be lost."

"This special energy," said Darwen. "What is it?"

The dellfey shook her head wearily.

"It is different from what the Guardians use," she said. "We can feel it. It is very powerful and it is not of our world."

"You mean it comes from *my* world, from the other side of the mirrors?" asked Darwen.

"We do not know," said Moth again. "It has always been said that energy from your world would be dangerous here, that it would be the opposite of what fuelled our portals, like a reflection that is backward. But perhaps the scrobblers have found a way to use it, though how they could have done so alone, I can't imagine. The scrobblers are creatures of hatred and violence. They have no capacity to build, no interest in making. They only destroy. There is some other force at work here, Darwen, and I fear it will kill us all before we know what it is."

Darwen began to speak, but at that moment the drone of the machine shifted into a higher register. Lights began to flash and there was a jet of steam from beside the tiny portal whose bluish light went white for a second. A lamp lit green, and one of the scrobblers that had been working close by hurried over with great loping strides. It reached down and picked up a huge, solid-looking helmet with a plate of thick glass in front and put it over its head. Darwen was reminded of a welder or one of those deep-sea divers who work from oil rigs. The scrobbler then put on chain-mail gauntlets and picked up a pair of long metal tongs. Carefully it pushed the tongs into the tiny curtain of pulsing blue light, opened them, closed them on something inside, and drew them out, holding the object away from its body like it was a bomb that might go off at any second.

The object gripped in the jaws of the tongs was small and brightly colored, and as the scrobbler set it gingerly into the second opening, it emitted a thin, electronic crying sound.

No, thought Darwen. *Not crying. Meowing!*

"That's Genevieve Reddock's toy kitten!" he exclaimed in an astonished whisper.

The scrobbler, just as carefully, closed the metal door upon the plastic cat, muting the sound of its mewing, removed the helmet and gloves, and started flicking switches. Lights came on and needles began to inch across their dials. When all was ready, the scrobbler pulled three levers and pushed a button. A red light, much larger than the others, came on, and a deafening horn blew three warning blasts, at which the other scrobblers seemed to pause in their work and turn toward the machine. The one operating the equipment threw one last switch and then took several quick steps backward.

There was a great rumbling sound and the machine blew steam as lights all over it flashed quickly. The air seemed to shimmer around the container holding the plastic kitten. And then, quite suddenly, everything went back to the way it had been. The scrobbler opened the little door with his tongs, but there was only a wisp of smoke inside, and as that dispersed, they all got back to work.

Darwen turned to Moth again, and there was a new urgency in his voice.

"When we first met," he said, "you told me that I was in danger because human children would be hunted by the scrobblers, that we were precious somehow. What did you mean?"

"Scrobblers despise what they see as their opposites," said Moth simply. "Anything which comes through from your world is alien to them, and anything marked by love, imagination, and trust—things the scrobblers are utterly without—even more so."

Love, imagination, and trust. Their opposites.

Darwen thought furiously, trying to string together bits of things he had learned in science about opposites, about the positive and negative sides of magnets and batteries, protons and electrons. He thought about the comic book he had read at Rich's when they were working on the trebuchet—*Antimatter Boy*—and about the bits of science behind the story that Rich had said were real.

An answer started to glow in his head, and as he thought, he looked at those firebox grates in the great central machine, and he thought of the little wicker basket that sat beside the stove at Hillside. All those stolen things, those *precious* things marked by love and trust and imagination, which weren't just *different* from the scrobblers: they were the opposite of the scrobblers.

Like antimatter.

What had Rich said? That if you mixed regular matter with antimatter, they destroyed each other? But he had also said that there was a way to crash matter and antimatter into each other so that they produced a massive power surge . . .

"What if . . ." he said slowly, piecing it all together. "What if the scrobblers learned—or were taught—not simply to destroy their opposites but to use them, to process them somehow to make power? What if they built a machine that would act like that lab in Geneva? For scrobblers, antimatter is stuff from my world that was treasured by the kids who owned it—the stuff the scrobblers hate, their opposite. That's it. That's what's been happening. The scrobblers—somehow—steal things from my world that were marked by love, put them into a machine that crashes it into "matter" from their world, and the machine produces power which the Guardians can't control: power so massive that it can be used to open up the gaps between our worlds."

Moth just looked at him, hovering weakly, her face drained of color but her tiny eyes bright with a new fear.

"Moth," said Darwen. "I have to see the Guardians! How do I reach them?"

"They sit in perpetual council in a valley far from here and only certain gates will take you there."

"Which ones? Can I go there from the hilltop?"

"Once you could have," said the dellfey. "But the fog has swallowed up whole areas and the portals within them, so that the old network is broken. There are entire regions that can no longer be reached from here. The Guardians' council chamber is one of them."

"Then I'll have to find another way," said Darwen. "Moth I need you to . . ."

But the dellfey wasn't listening. She was staring, white-faced over his shoulder, her mouth open, eyes frozen with horror. Darwen turned and saw it: a shadow, bigger than a man, leaping from tree to tree, flashing black over the ground as it came toward them.

The dellfey began to scream, a high wail of powerless despair that chilled Darwen almost as much as the sight of the Shade. He forced himself to run, aiming at the mirror, ignoring the mass of scrobblers and gnashers, knowing that the Shade was worse, and that it could see him. He caught a dark flash in the corner of his eye as he spun round a massive scrobbler with a wheelbarrow, passing it with only inches to spare, and then everything went black.

The Shade had caught him.

He stopped running. The forest and everything in it vanished and there was nothing. No light. No sound. No air. Darwen could not even see himself. He gasped, but there was nothing to breathe, and his empty lungs tightened. He closed his mouth, his brain screaming silently as the panic took hold like a hand about his throat. He was drowning in darkness.

He tried again to draw breath but failed. The Shade had enveloped him completely, and inside its airless shadow there was only absence. He was getting dizzy. In a few more seconds he would pass out. It wouldn't be long then . . .

A tiny prick of greenish light flashed before his eyes.

The color reminded him of something . . .

Moth.

She had flown into the Shade itself. At first he could see only the light on the tiny device that powered her wings, but then he realized that the light had made a minute hole in the blackness. Through it he could see the forest beyond, as if he was looking through a narrow tube. He fought to clear his head.

The forest was still there. He was trapped inside the Shade but the forest was still there. . . .

He summoned all his strength, focused his mind, and leapt sideways. It didn't matter which way he went. He just had to get out of the darkness for a moment. He took two blind steps and the world was there again, almost dazzlingly bright. He sucked in the air before the Shade could surround him again, spotted the mirror, and was running toward it before the darkness returned.

This time he did not stop moving, blind though he was, nor did he try to breathe. He held the air down in his lungs like he was trying to swim a lap underwater, and kept moving through the darkness and silence. The Shade kept pace with him but Darwen ran on, hoping he wouldn't run into a tree or—worse—a gnasher.

He had been running for almost ten seconds before he realized he couldn't make it without another breath. His throat was contracting like he was going to throw up.

He swallowed it down, but it was no good. He was out of air. With his last ounce of strength, he reversed course, and in two strides, emerged from the back of the Shade, which had gone past him.

Again he took a deep, desperate breath, found the mirror in the blasted forest—only a few yards away now—and turned to meet the Shade's deadly embrace head on. With a surge of speed and defiance Darwen ran right into the shadow, through the blackness and silence, then out the other side and into the mirror frame.

He took his next breath in his own bedroom.

Darwen told them everything, including his desperate battle with the Shade.

"I told you so," said Alexandra. "I knew the thefts were part of it. But no scrobbler could be stealing that stuff. Someone would have seen."

They were walking briskly through the mall, which was crowded with weekend shoppers.

"Maybe they have something like a flittercrake working for them," said Darwen. "I saw one at school and it could have come through that little portal in the basement."

"Or someone at Hillside is helping," said Alexandra.

"They'd have to be pretty small to fit through that portal," said Rich.

"Could be a baby," said Alexandra. When the boys gave her a look, she shrugged. "What? Babies are evil. Trust me, we have one."

"Maybe someone just pushes the stolen stuff through the portal," Rich mused.

"And then stays at the school?" asked Alexandra.

"Maybe," said Rich. "Could be a student."

"Or a teacher," said Alexandra.

Darwen tried the door of Mr. Peregrine's shop but it was still locked. He pulled the key he had taken from the hospital from his pocket, checked no one was watching, and opened the door.

"What are we looking for?" asked Rich.

"I don't know," said Darwen. "A portal that will get us to the Guardians. It might be a mirror, but I doubt it."

"If it's a mirror," said Alexandra, picking her way through the broken glass, "we're in trouble."

The place was still wrecked. Darwen studied a portion of the wall that had four deep scratches gouged into it: claw marks. Whatever had done that, he thought, was bigger than any scrobbler.

He searched the tiny kitchen, but found nothing. He frowned so hard his eyes shut.

Maybe there's nothing here, no way through . . .

He remembered the vacuum communication system, and went to examine it, but the wood around it was splintered and the dial had been shattered. Darwen tried pumping the handle, but it hung limp, disconnected from the mechanism inside.

If only they could talk to the old man. There was so much Darwen needed to know, and not just about how to get to the Guardians. Those questions about his parents still smoldered in his mind. If he could find out that they had somehow been involved in all this, that they had died for a reason, and that he could complete their work for them, it would make all the difference. But Mr. Peregrine was in a coma and Darwen was stuck with his friends, finding no answers, not even sure if they were asking the right questions. . . .

"This is hopeless," he muttered. "There's no portal, or if there was, the scrobblers or whatever put him in the hospital have already destroyed it."

"Did he say he wasn't *allowed* to travel back or that he wasn't *capable* of traveling back?" asked Alexandra.

"Couldn't," said Darwen. "He said the mirrors were like slabs of steel to him. He said he could get across in an extreme emergency, but it would be a one-way trip."

"So if we find this way and use it," said Alexandra, "we might not be able to get back? I don't like the sound of that."

"Maybe that only applies to Mr. Peregrine," said Darwen, "because he is a gatekeeper. We're different."

"You think?" said Alexandra.

"Best I can do, Alexandra," said Darwen. "But since we can't find the portal anyway, it doesn't matter."

"Practically the only things in here which aren't smashed are books," said Rich, hefting an ancient-looking volume thoughtfully.

"I don't think he could climb through a book, do you?" said Darwen, an edge to his voice.

"I wasn't saying he could go *through* the book," said Rich, prickling like a cornered hedgehog. "I was just saying that the books weren't destroyed."

"So how does that help?" said Darwen. He should have known coming to the shop was a dead end.

"Maybe it doesn't," said Rich. "But maybe we could do what the scrobblers didn't bother to."

"Which is?" pressed Darwen.

"*Read* them!" said Rich, who was getting red in the face. "There may be some kind of clue. Maybe there's a manual or something, you know? Rules for gatekeepers or something."

"Yeah, right," said Darwen dismissively.

"You got any better ideas?" Rich snapped. "'Cause if you do, I'm all ears."

"Will you cut it out?" said Alexandra. "We have enough

to worry about without you two going at each other like a pair of rabid Chihuahuas."

"Chihuahuas?" said the boys at the same time.

"That's right," said Alexandra with her trademark don't-make-me-come-over-there stare. "Little yipper dogs. Rats with attitude."

"Okay," Rich muttered.

"Sorry," said Darwen. "It's just so frustrating . . ."

"Er, guys," said Alexandra. "What's that?"

She was pointing at an area of the wall beside a cupboard stacked with books.

"It's a wall," said Rich. "Judging by the nails and the piles of smashed glass, there were mirrors hanging on it, but it's just a wall . . ."

"It's not," said Alexandra, walking over. "Move that frame."

Darwen lifted a huge empty mirror frame and shunted it to one side. Then he could see it too. In between two broken cabinets was what looked like an alcove. The rear wall had—as Rich had pointed out—been hung with mirrors, but it wasn't plaster or sheet rock. It was textured like fabric, but hard, like the cover of a book.

"You've got to be kidding me," said Darwen.

"Clear the floor," said Alexandra, pushing the fragments of wood and glass away from the foot of the wall. Then she stepped into the alcove, worked her fingers into the tiny gap between the wall and the cabinet on the right, and opened it.

"You were right," said Darwen to Rich.

It was a book, three feet wide by seven feet high, a book that could pass as a wall, particularly when hung with mirrors, but a book nonetheless. Inside the cover was a massive sheet of paper with a beautifully etched drawing of a lush valley with distant mountains behind it and a lamp-lined road that ran straight through. In the center of the valley was a marvelous building, round and studded with ornamental turrets that shone in the sunlight. Written above it in sweeping script were the words "The Guardian Council Chambers."

"Turn the page," said Darwen.

Alexandra fingered the edge of the paper and lifted it slowly back till her face flooded with light. The three of them stared into what could only be another portula. Without a word they moved in close together so that the rippling energy of the gate was only inches from their faces, and then, as if they had planned it, they took one another's hands.

"Ready?" said Darwen.

"Ready."

They stepped forward. The world of Mr. Peregrine's shop shimmered and vanished behind them. They were standing in the beautiful valley depicted inside the book, but it took no more than a second to realize that something was very badly wrong.

The road looked as it had in the picture, and the distant mountains were still there, but the valley itself, which should have been a deep green pulsing with life and energy, was brown and blasted as if there had been a long drought. The streambeds were dry, the flowers wilted, and the trees bare of leaves. Over to their left an ominous and familiar wall of gray fog had gathered, blotting out whatever was—or had been—beyond.

"These Guardians," said Alexandra, "need a gardener."

"The Council Hall looks okay," said Rich, nodding.

Directly ahead lay the magnificent stone building, its columns, arches, and elegant spires approached by stone steps. It was somehow welcoming as well as impressive, though Darwen thought it would look better thronging with people.

"I hope you're right," he said.

They set out along the long straight path lined with old-fashioned gas lamps, gazing out over the dying land. Other paths, equally straight, came to the hall from other directions, other gates, so that the roads converged on the structure like it was the center of a compass.

"Everything comes from here," Darwen mused aloud. "This is what holds it all together."

"No birds," said Rich, gazing about. "No rabbits. Nothing."

The path ended in a flight of stone steps. The three of them moved up, but at the top they hesitated and looked at one another and at the valley laid out around them. It was weird: the silence, the sense of isolation.

"Another ghost town," said Alexandra.

Darwen walked through an arch and along a stone corridor with ornamented columns. The walls were set with elegant panels of varnished wood and brass inlay, which might have been controls of some kind, but might also have just been decoration.

"What was that?" asked Rich. He was gazing off down one of the shadowy vaulted hallways.

"What?" said Alexandra. "I didn't see anything."

Rich continued to stare into the dim passage, but he shrugged.

"Nothing, I guess," he said. "Trick of the light."

Darwen passed a circle of stone-framed portals humming dully, then another arch so deep that it was almost a tunnel and then . . .

The floor opened up before him and he was looking into a vast space like a sports stadium or theatre with steps going down to a circular floor surrounded by twelve stone thrones. In the center, was what looked like a pool of purple water covered by a shallow transparent dome like a snow globe. The dome flickered with soft radiance, like a lamp turned low and failing.

Darwen ran down the steps. At the bottom he went straight on up to the great disc with the stone seats, right up to the edge of the dome with the smoldering, liquid light beneath.

The pool flickered and sparked, and with shock he realized that it was somehow alive. It wasn't an animal, he didn't think, but it was an energy, and, though he couldn't say how he knew this, he thought it was aware. It was conscious, perhaps even thinking.

But it was also dying.

Tentatively, Darwen laid one hand on the dome. It felt warm, and where his palm made contact, the pool beneath seemed to pulse with a deep red glow, then faded again. In some places the purplish glow had burned out completely like a blackened candlewick.

"The Guardians," breathed Rich. "Look!"

Darwen followed his gaze to the ring of carved thrones, the rich wood of their arms set with brass and silver controls, and marked with names etched into copper plates. They were occupied by men and women sitting quite still and silent, heads tipped back, eyes closed. Each one was pale, covered with what looked like dust, and cobwebs hung across their ancient, noble faces.

"They're not dead," said Alexandra, who was standing beside a man with long silver hair that broke around his shoulders and over robes that may once have been white but were now yellowed with age. "They're sleeping." She said it with amazement. "I can hear them breathing. Listen!"

But before they could, she leaned close to the throne beside her and shouted: "Hey! Wake up, man! There's some stuff you need to see here."

She shook him, but though the pool pulsed weakly, he did not wake up.

"There's someone missing," Rich said.

It was true. Two thrones over from where Alexandra stood, one was empty. The name engraved into it read "Greyling."

"Sit in it," said Alexandra. "See what happens."

Rich flashed a quick look at the sleeping inhabitants of the other chairs.

"No way," he said.

"Fine," said Alexandra, walking over. "I'll do it."

"No!" said Darwen. "Wait."

"It's fine," said Alexandra. "Don't get your panties in a pickle."

And she sat in the vacant throne.

Immediately, the pool flickered, this time with a deep blue light, and there was a rumble that coursed through the building.

"Get up!" shouted Darwen.

But Alexandra's eyes first went very wide and then began to close.

"Get her out of there!" Darwen roared, scrambling to his feet.

Rich grabbed Alexandra and pulled but nothing happened.

"I can't move her!" he said. "She's stuck! It's like . . . Oh no. Darwen!"

Alexandra's skin was changing, turning gray as if being sprinkled with a fine powder. Her eyes closed completely and her head lolled back, mouth slightly open.

As Darwen reached her he saw that the webs that draped the others were starting to appear around her, spun as if by invisible spiders, so that as he watched she began to look like she had been sitting there for months, years. He swept some of the cobwebs away and grabbed her hand.

"Come on!" he said to Rich.

The pool under the globe was beginning to boil and flash with a dark blue light.

Rich grabbed Alexandra's other hand and they pulled. She moved, but it was like she weighed ten times her normal weight.

"Again!" said Darwen.

They pulled a second time, straining so that Darwen could feel the blood rushing to his face. The rumbling was getting louder. Somewhere Darwen thought he heard stone collapsing.

"She's not moving!" Rich gasped.

"She is," said Darwen. "Again!"

Once more they pulled, and this time Alexandra seemed to shift. Her eyes, though closed, flickered as if she was dreaming, and her mouth tightened in a frown of concentration.

"That's it, Alex," said Darwen. "Fight it. Again Rich. One. Two. THREE!"

They pulled at the girl's arms and, quite suddenly, she shot out of the throne as if falling from a height, and they had to catch her, which sent all three of them sprawling into a heap on the floor. The rumbling stopped and the pool returned to its dull purple glow.

"You okay?" said Darwen, between deep, sucking breaths.

"You called me Alex!" she said, beaming at him.

"What happened?" said Rich.

"He never calls me Alex," said Alexandra.

"What happened?" Darwen echoed.

"It was seriously weird," said Alexandra sitting up. "I could feel them," she said, nodding at the men and women in the other thrones. "I could sense their minds. And the water or whatever it is. That was connected too. And I could sort of see the whole world—their world, I mean—only really far off, but I was so tired, and the rest of them were all just drifting away."

"You shouldn't have sat there," said Rich. "I thought the whole place was going to come down."

"That would have been bad," Alexandra conceded. "Thanks for getting me out."

"It was like you'd put on a thousand pounds!" said Rich. "We couldn't shift you."

"I could sort of feel you trying," she said. "But I just wanted to sleep . . ."

"I think," said Darwen, considering the domed pool, "I'm starting to understand."

"I'm not," said Rich, flatly. "What's going on?"

"When you were in there," Darwen said to Alexandra, "you said you could see the whole world. All of it? Were the Guardians thinking about all of it?"

Alexandra thought.

"Hard to say," she said. "They were so sleepy. It was like they were barely there. Their minds were wandering, but no, I guess they focused on certain places. I could see more, but as soon as my mind touched theirs, parts started to fade away, like I was forgetting them."

"Yes," said Darwen. "That's it. They're forgetting. That's what causes the gray fog. This place, the energy in the dome, it's like the heart and mind of their world, and the Guardians control it, channel it so that the land stays healthy. There's power here too, the same power that makes the gates work. And because the Guardians control that power, they can stop others from using it."

"Like the scrobblers, you mean?" said Rich.

"Right," said Darwen. "That's why the scrobblers are building their own gates and finding other ways to power them."

"They're building generators that are off the grid," said Rich. "They don't tap into the power the Guardians control so the Guardians don't know what's going on."

"And I don't know why," said Darwen, pacing as he thought it through, "but the Guardians are falling asleep on the job, literally. That gives the scrobblers more freedom to operate, but it also means that parts of the world are just fading away. Some of it is dying, like the valley outside, but some of it is just disappearing into that mist we keep seeing. The thoughts of the Guardians keep this whole world alive, and when they forget a part of it, that part dies. Eventually it vanishes completely."

"No wonder the scrobblers are trying to break into our world," said Alexandra. "Theirs is collapsing."

"It's more than that," said Darwen. "They're going to use our world to power theirs."

They had reached the network of circling stone hallways and Darwen paused to get his bearings.

"There it was again," said Rich suddenly.

"What?" asked Alexandra.

"Same as I saw before," Rich answered, without turning

round. "I thought I saw someone, but I guess it was just a shadow."

Darwen felt his blood run cold.

"Where?" he asked.

"It was down there," said Rich, "near the entrance to that passage but now . . . Wait. There."

In the gloom at the end of the hallway, there was a deeper darkness, like a starless patch of night sky, shaped precisely like a man. Darwen stared, feeling his heart starting to thump. The shadow flickered and then it was on the other side of the passage and twenty yards closer.

"Run!" shouted Darwen.

They sprinted down the hall.

"This way!" called Alexandra, as she took a sharp left, never slowing. The others followed, not daring to look back. They took two more turns in the labyrinthine hallways and then Rich stopped, breathing hard.

"I think we lost it," he gasped, peering back the way they had come.

"You think it was that Shade thing, not just a shadow?" Alexandra panted.

"Pretty sure," said Darwen, his voice low and steady, despite his fear. "Pretty sure too that we didn't lose it."

"What?" asked Alexandra. "Why?"

"Because there are three of us," said Darwen.

"So?" said Rich.

"So why," said Darwen, in a whisper, "do we have four shadows?"

There was a heavy silence as they all looked down, and saw it was true. Darwen started to run, but the silence and the darkness changed, became absolute, so that he could see nothing, could not even hear his own screaming. It had caught him. He was inside the Shade.

He was already out of breath from running. He forced himself to hold what air was in his lungs, and try to step out of the Shade's enveloping grasp, but he couldn't find a way out. He took several steps one way, then another, but there was still only blackness and the soundlessness of space. The nausea swelled in his throat and he started to gag silently, dropping to his knees. His stomach tightened and his chest burned. His mouth opened and he tried to pull oxygen in, but there was nothing. He sagged onto his side and rolled slightly, wondering why he could still feel the cool stone of the passage floor when the rest of the world was lost to him. The darkness and silence were unchanging, but Darwen was fading like a guttering candle. His mind wandered and even the terror and pain became fuzzy as he drifted into unconsciousness and death.

Candle . . .

A tiny wavering yellow light wandered into sight. It fluttered like a flame about to go out, then leapt into blue-white brilliance. It opened a hole in the darkness like a canon blast, and as Darwen's dying eyes focused, he thought he could see Rich beneath it, holding the searing white flame above his head like a torch. Darwen had to look away, but he tasted air streaming toward him from where Rich stood, and he gulped it down.

His head cleared and he dragged himself into a crouch, from which he rose unsteadily, then stumbled out into the light. Alexandra had shrunk back against the passage wall, one hand over her mouth, but she reached out to him and pulled him toward her. Rich stood alone beside the writhing shadow-beast, the blazing light held aloft, and the hole in the darkness swelling, as if it was burning up the Shade from the inside.

Darwen and Alexandra watched as Rich took a step toward the flickering blackness, pouring the flare-like radiance into it, eating the darkness, until—with a bellow of rage and pain—the Shade exploded into nothing.

Darwen sat against the wall breathing in the blessed air.

"What the heck was that?" said Alexandra to Rich. "You carrying some kind of nuclear weapon, just in case?"

"Magnesium ribbon," said Rich. "You fight darkness with light, right?"

"I guess," said Alexandra. "Darwen? You okay?"

"Against all odds," said Darwen getting to his feet.

"Thanks, Rich.

"Remind me never to make fun of science again," said Alexandra. "Magnesium, huh? We'd better get us a boatload of that stuff."

"You think?" said Rich.

"Well," Alexandra replied. "What did we learn today? Apart from Rich's Fun Facts for Blowing Up Bogeymen."

"Go on," Darwen prompted.

"We're on our own," she said. "No Mr. Peregrine, no Guardians, no help. It's just us."

"Bound by the Peregrine Pact," said Rich, dryly.

"Next time I start a club," said Alexandra. "I'm sticking to singing and dancing. No monsters, no chairs that won't let you out. Just me with a microphone and an audience."

"Sounds terrifying," said Darwen.

On the last day of October—the day that was to end in Hillside Academy's first ever Halloween Hop—their science projects were tested. Each group moved out onto the sports fields with their equipment, took twenty minutes to set up, then gave five minute presentations on the physics of their device. Nathan, Chip, and Barry talked for no more than thirty seconds, but their catapult—an oversized crossbow construction—was strung with high tensile cables on pulleys and looked very powerful.

"There's no way they built that," said Alexandra.

"It's not fair!"

Mr. Iverson asked questions about the construction process that suggested he also had his doubts, but he didn't disqualify them, and when it came time to shoot, the catapult shot their bright blue baseball low and fast like a canon.

"Wow!" exclaimed Simon Agu. "That must have been fifty yards!"

Simon's group went next. He was with Jennifer and Mad, and their catapult shot a red baseball in a higher arc, so that for a moment it looked like it might go even further, but it wound up dropping ten feet short. Bobby, Genevieve, and Melissa went next, followed by Naia, Princess, and Carlos, and though both groups did better presentations, they didn't fire anywhere near as far.

Rich, Darwen, and Alexandra pushed their trebuchet into position and hoisted the counterweight.

"Only the losers' team left," remarked Nathan. "Look at that thing! Hey, Haggerty, I see the archaeology club finally found something. I didn't know they had purple paint in the Stone Age."

Half the class giggled. The trebuchet did look rather ridiculous. It was twice the size of any of the other catapults and was the most obviously homemade, a great wooden ramshackle construction that Alexandra had painted purple, with silver stars and lightning flashes.

Rich led the presentation, but the class was distracted by Chip and Barry making caveman noises. Mr. Iverson told them to stop but Nathan had joined in.

"Me bang wood together with rock," he was saying, hunching his shoulders like an ape. "Me make noise with sticks."

" . . . highly efficient energy transfer," Rich was saying, still trying to finish his presentation, though the students were now completely ignoring him.

"Just fire the bloody thing," muttered Darwen.

Alexandra dropped her purple baseball into the sling and looked up.

"The conversion of potential gravitational energy into the energy of motion, also called kinetic energy . . ." Rich said.

"Fire in the hole!" shouted Alexandra.

"Wait!" Rich protested.

But she pulled the pin.

The counterweight dropped, the catapult arm swung upright, and the sling with the purple ball in it whirled round and up, shooting the ball out in a long, climbing arc.

"Holy moly!" yelled Alexandra.

The class stared as the ball shot high over the field, over the trees beyond, and out of sight. There was a roar of delighted amazement.

"Whoa!" said Barry.

"Unbelievable!" exclaimed Naia.

"Chuffin' 'eck!" said Darwen.

"That's what I'm talking about," said Rich, quietly. "History and science."

Winning the catapult contest in such dramatic fashion left Darwen, Alexandra, and Rich buzzing.

"Did you see Nathan's face!" said Alexandra. "I thought he was going to throw up."

"I didn't think it would go that far," said Rich.

"You should get all the credit," said Darwen to Rich. "It was your design. All I did was help build it."

"And I was just responsible for making it cool-looking," said Alexandra.

"Oh," said Darwen, shooting her a grin. "That's what you did. I wasn't sure."

"Hey," said Alexandra, nodding at Rich, "he's the science guy. I'm an artist. But that doesn't mean I don't have ideas."

"Yeah?" said Darwen, sensing something coming. "Like what?"

"You're gonna think it's nuts," said Alexandra. "Heck, even I think it's kinda nuts. It probably is. Well not *nuts*, exactly. Just sort of out there, you know? Not crazy but a bit off the wall . . ."

"What's the idea, Alex?" said Rich.

"Okay," said Alex. "Hold onto your hats."

"Go on," said Darwen.

"The Guardians don't know what's going on, right?" said Alexandra. "They're asleep at the wheel and the entire mirror world is getting scrobbled. Hey!" she said, interrupting herself as only she could do. "I like that: *scrobbled*. The world is getting scrobbled! That's awesome. . . ."

"The idea, Alex," said Darwen, rolling his eyes at Rich.

"Okay, so we have to somehow wake them up and let them know what's going on, right?" she persisted as if no one else had spoken. "And we want to get Mr. P out of his coma. Now when I sat in that stone chair . . ."

"Bad things happened," said Rich.

"Yes, but that's because I wasn't part of Silbrica," said Alex. "My thoughts, my energy, or whatever, didn't fit with theirs, so it didn't work."

"But Mr. Peregrine does belong," said Darwen, completing her thought for her in an awed voice. "He could complete the connection between the Guardians, and maybe the energy from the pool and the other Guardians would wake him up. He could tell them what is happening, maybe help them stop it. Alex, that's brilliant!"

"I'm a genius," said Alex. "What can I tell you?"

"Er, guys," said Rich. "I hate to spoil the party, but Mr. Peregrine is lying in a hospital bed while the chair you want to put him in sits in a different world altogether. How do you propose to get him there?"

He gave Alexandra a significant look and, after a long pause, she shrugged.

"I'm the idea girl," she said. "You guys can handle the logistics."

There was a thoughtful silence.

"We're going to need a wheelchair," said Darwen.

That wasn't all they were going to need. They made it to the hospital but still hadn't figured out how they were going to get a sleeping man in a wheelchair to a mall without transport.

"You sure you can't drive, Rich?" asked Alex. "You're big enough."

"No Alex, I can't," said Rich. "What are we going to do? We'll stand out a mile pushing him along the sidewalk."

"Why?" asked Darwen.

"Three kids and a wheelchair?" said Alex. "Please. And how many people have you seen walking in this city? We need to get us some wheels."

"Eileen!" Darwen exclaimed.

"Your babysitter?" Rich said. "Won't she ask a lot of questions about why you have an old guy in a wheelchair?"

Darwen laughed out loud.

"I'll be amazed if she even notices," he said. "Rich,

lend me your phone. I'll text her, say I'm Aunt Honoria and can she pick us up outside the hospital in, say, twenty minutes."

"Let's make it fifteen," said Alexandra. "We're going to have to be fast."

"Will she come?" asked Rich, handing Darwen his phone.

"I'll pay her double," said Darwen, punching in the message. "And she gets to go to the mall. She'll think it's Christmas."

Darwen sent the text.

"Okay," he said. "We need a wheelchair."

"They have to take you out in one when you get discharged," said Rich. "It's a legal thing. There'll be some by the doors over there. Yeah. See?"

"How do you know that?" asked Alexandra gazing in the direction he was pointing.

"Common knowledge," said Rich. "I'll grab one."

A moment later, he was back with a wheelchair.

"Okay," said Darwen. "Ready?"

Their eyes met and there was a pause as they all considered the seriousness of what they were doing. Then, as if their minds were linked like the Guardians in the stone chairs, they nodded in unison, and went inside.

They walked briskly to the elevator and up to Mr. Peregrine's room on the third floor. Darwen signed in as he had done before, and the security guard who had been chatting to Officer Perkins the first day nodded him through without even a glance at the others or the wheelchair Rich was pushing in a would-be casual manner.

"Okay," said Rich as soon as they got inside. "Make sure he's not hooked up to anything crucial before we move him."

"Like what?" asked Alexandra.

"Like a *respirator*," said Rich, as if that was obvious. "No, he's still breathing for himself. Good. We'll take the IV drip with us," he added, nodding at the bag of clear fluid that was being piped into Mr. Peregrine's arm.

"How are we going to get past the nurse at the front?" asked Darwen.

"We need a diversion," said Rich, looking pointedly at Alexandra.

"On it," said Alexandra. She left the room, walking like someone who knew what she was doing.

Rich gave Darwen an inquiring look, but Darwen shrugged and shook his head.

"Don't ask," he said.

"Okay, we've got to get him into the chair," said Rich. "You pull, I'll push. And support his head."

"Have you done this before?" asked Darwen.

"Stolen someone from a hospital? Yeah, right," said Rich. "But I know my way around hospitals and wheelchairs, yeah," he said, shooting Darwen a quick, cautious glance as he manhandled Mr. Peregrine's sleeping body across the bed and lowered his thin legs over the side. "My mom," he said. "She was in hospital a lot before she died."

"Oh," said Darwen, taken aback. "I didn't know. I'm sorry."

"Yeah," said Rich, not meeting his eyes. "You and everybody else. Okay, this is the hard bit. Get your arm under his back and help me lift him into the chair."

The old man was heavier than Darwen had expected, perhaps because he was sleeping.

Dead weight, he thought.

He pushed the words away.

He'll be fine. He has to be.

"Come on, Mr. Peregrine," Darwen whispered. "We're taking you home." And since that last word brought a catch to his throat, he added in a lighter tone, "And we have to be back in time for the Halloween Hop, so don't make this harder than it needs to be."

They strained and shoved and finally Mr. Peregrine was in the chair. Rich was checking the IV tubing and throwing a blanket over the shopkeeper when they heard screaming from down the hall.

"My momma!" yelled a shrill voice. "Not my momma!"

A siren went off and suddenly there were running feet

in the corridor outside. At least two people in scrubs and one in a lab coat ran past.

"Alex," said Darwen and Rich together. They grinned and then started to walk, Rich pushing the chair, Darwen in front to open doors.

Whatever Alexandra had done had emptied the hallway and the nurse's station. Darwen ignored the security cameras and made for the elevators.

"Not too fast," said Rich. "Running in hospitals attracts attention almost as much as it does at Hillside."

Darwen forced himself to slow down. He hit the elevator call button and waited.

"Come on," he muttered. He had started to sweat. Rich was glancing over his shoulder toward the still empty nurses' station. A man in glasses who had come from another part of the floor was standing beside them, and as he waited for the elevator, he gave the boys a curious look.

The elevator pinged and the light went out as the doors slid open. Rich started to push the chair in, but there were people on the elevator who had to get off. One was a doctor. Another was a policeman.

Darwen turned to the man beside him, trying to look like they were with him, that they weren't just two kids with an old man in a wheelchair. The man in glasses turned to Darwen and gave him a curious look.

"In England," said Darwen, saying the first thing that came into his head, "we call elevators lifts."

The man nodded and smiled vaguely, and then the elevator was empty and they could get in. As the doors started to close, a foot stuck through. Someone wanted in. For a second nothing happened, and Darwen felt that rising tide of panic again, but then he saw the tiny skulls on the laces of what was far too small a shoe for a policeman. He hit the button that opened the doors, and Alexandra, looking breathless, stepped in.

"Thanks," she said. Then, when the man in glasses gave her a searching look, she said brightly "How you doin'?" with such confidence that the man nodded and looked away.

They left the elevator, then crossed a hallway and the lobby, picking up speed as they went. For the first time in his life, Darwen was delighted to see Eileen, parked against the sidewalk, blowing pink gum bubbles and talking into her cell phone. She popped the door locks and kept talking without looking round or asking about the curiously restful old man who was being loaded into her car like a sack of potatoes. Rich folded the wheelchair expertly and shoved it into the trunk.

"I'll bring it back," he said to Alexandra's accusing stare.

Darwen kept watch on the hospital doors as they drove

away but there was no sign of pursuit.

The mall, when they reached it, was quiet. Darwen told Eileen they'd be back in an hour and she paused in her phone call long enough to give the man in the wheelchair a long look.

"Him too?" she said.

"I hope not," said Darwen.

They raced through the mall, shoving the wheelchair in front of them so that shoppers scattered out of their way. Darwen unlocked the door to the mirror shop, and they made straight for the huge book in the alcove between the cabinets, broken shards of mirror cracking under the wheelchair's hard tires. Alexandra dragged the book open and there it was, the shimmering portal to Silbrica.

"Here goes," said Rich.

"Hang on," said Darwen. He drew the screen device from his pocket and checked it was ready should they need it.

"You carry that thing around with you now?" asked Alexandra.

"All the time," said Darwen.

He considered Mr. Peregrine's gaunt and lined face, but he was still sleeping soundly.

"Okay," said Darwen, and they stepped through, pushing the chair in front of them.

The Silbrican valley looked worse than ever, the grass parched and brown, the stark trees leafless. As they got close to the council chambers, they could see piles of broken masonry where the elaborate stonework had fallen away.

"We don't have much time," said Rich.

He took three steps and then released the wheelchair and cried out. He fell, clutching his leg.

Darwen had barely seen it: a flashing movement from the scorched undergrowth, like a striking snake. But not a snake. It was more like a pale worm at least three feet long and with a broad flat head whose underside was serrated with tiny hooklike teeth. It had clamped onto Rich's leg just below the knee and the rest of its body was curled tight around it.

"What is it?!" shouted Alexandra.

"I don't know," said Darwen. "But we have to get it off him."

Darwen dug his fingers under the creature's slick, milky body, revolted by it, but its coils tightened and Rich cried out. The worm's head was rasping back and forth over Rich's thigh which was starting to bleed.

"It's trying to dig its way in!" said Alexandra, horrified.

"You have that penknife with you?" asked Darwen.

Rich, his sweaty face tight with pain, reached into his pocket and drew out his utility tool. Darwen snatched it and opened up a blade.

"Hurry!" said Rich.

His leg was bleeding more than ever. The worm was starting to push its spear-shaped head into the wound it was making.

Carefully Darwen slid the flat of the blade between Rich's leg and the worm's body, easing as far as it would go. Then, wincing, he turned the blade edge out and pulled.

The movement cut the worm in half, but the head was still wriggling. Darwen dropped the knife and grabbed the worm before it could tunnel any further. He gripped it tightly, yanked the head free like he was tearing off a Band-Aid, and threw it as far as he could. Rich gasped out a silent cry of pain.

"Some kind of parasite," Darwen said, shuddering. "Like a tapeworm or something."

"I love coming here," Alexandra remarked. "Did I mention that lately? Man-eating bugs, fog that actually eats away at the fabric of reality, and getting attacked by worms. It's awesome. Next year, I say we go to Paris instead."

Rich was staring horror-struck at the wound as Alexandra wrapped it with a handkerchief and the belt off her jeans.

"That should slow the bleeding," she said. "Can you walk?"

"I think so," said Rich, who looked rather green. "For a ways at least. Not sure I'll be doing much Halloween Hopping."

"Oh great," said Alexandra. "I forgot there were stairs."

Rich turned the wheelchair around grimly then started backing up the steps. He looked unsteady but determined. Darwen and Alexandra helped as best they could, each lifting some of the weight off the small front wheels, but Rich was still doing most of the work in spite of his injury, and by the time he got to the top, he looked pale and exhausted.

"I'll take it from here," said Darwen, stretching his aching back. They'd had to make their crab like way up the stairs almost doubled over. "This way."

Ahead, past the circle of stone-framed portals, was a tunnel that took them directly down to the central area with the thrones and the covered pool. Between them they dragged the chair onto the circular platform, and as Rich fought to get his breath back, Darwen considered the liquid under the dome. It was darker now, the flickering light dimmer than it had been.

"I hope this works," he said.

Panting, they scooped Mr. Peregrine out of the chair and into the stone seat. Then they stepped back.

A ripple of light coursed around the circle of thrones, like energy pulsing through a newly completed circuit.

"It's working," said Alexandra.

And for a second, it looked like it was. The Guardians seemed to stir in their sleep and the pool rippled with amber light. But then it darkened again, and before their eyes, the Guardians seemed to age a little more. Cobwebs crept over Mr. Peregrine's face and hands, and a new, terrible pallor came into his skin so that he looked molded from wax.

"Get him out!" cried Darwen. "It's not working!"

But no matter how hard they pulled, the old man would not move. Darwen, Rich and Alexandra, who were already tired, strained till they could barely stand, then settled, defeated, onto the stone steps.

"We made it worse," said Darwen. "Now he'll never wake up. And the rest of the Guardians are deeper asleep than ever."

"Like they caught his coma," said Alexandra, thoughtfully.

"Okay," said Rich. "Think. What can we do to reverse the effect?"

"Nowt," said Darwen. "Nothing. It's over."

"No, it's not," said Rich, rubbing his leg. "The Guardians are connected to their world, right? Especially to the portals. So we have to run some power back into those gates, pump some energy back in, you know? Like recharging a battery."

"But the Guardians control the power," said Alexandra.

"If we can't get it from them, then where?"

"Same place the scrobblers do," said Rich. "They've built their own power source. What we need to do is pipe some of their energy back into one of the gates on the Guardians' grid. That way we send a shock through their system, maybe wake them up . . ."

"But the scrobblers' power is different," said Darwen. "It could make it worse."

"Better ideas welcome," said Alexandra.

For a moment they all sat in silence, then Darwen nodded.

"Okay," he said, considering the sleeping Guardians. "But someone will have to stay here with them."

"Me," said Rich. "I'll slow you down too much. What you'll have to do is find a way of connecting the scrobblers' generator to the gates on the hilltop. Some kind of cable should do it."

"I don't know, Rich," said Darwen. "You're the science guy. Maybe you should . . ."

"You can do it," said Rich. "Alex will help."

Darwen thought for a moment, then reached into his pocket and produced a little note pad and his fountain pen. He wrote two sentences on the paper, then folded it in half and set it on the lip of the platform under a broken fragment of stone.

"If Mr. Peregrine wakes up," he said, "give him that

and see what he says. If he doesn't wake up though . . ." His voice faltered.

"I won't read it," said Rich.

Darwen nodded quickly. "Thanks," he said.

"We'll go through one of the portals back there," said Alexandra.

"You sure you'll be okay, Rich?" said Darwen.

"Safer than going with you, that's for sure," said Rich, managing a smile.

Darwen and Alexandra ran back the way they had come, not speaking, not looking back at Rich who had slumped down onto the stone, almost as still as the figures in the ancient thrones.

"How do we know which gate will get us to the forest?" said Alexandra.

"None of these will," said Darwen. "The forest is a remote, minor locus. All we can do from here is get closer and hope we can find a connecting portal. It may take several gates. We might have to take a train . . ."

"Back to the land of the Jenkinses and their cozy cottage in the woods?" exclaimed Alexandra. "No way, man. I'm not going near those . . ."

"We'll find a way," said Darwen, not sure if he believed it. "We may not have a choice. I don't think these all work."

Of the six gates, two were cold and dark, blackened as

if by fire. One of the others was emitting a small whistling noise like air escaping from a punctured tire.

"Think I'll pass on that one," said Alexandra.

"Me too," said Darwen. "One of these three then."

Darwen studied the dials with their number settings, but none of them showed the forest's combination.

Darwen read aloud: "6000, 7500, 4000. So which one? We could end up further away from the forest."

"What are we looking for?"

"It's 423 something" said Darwen. "It will be four numbers but the last one doesn't matter. If it has those first three digits, it should get us to the hill. It's none of these."

"You said one was 4000, though, right?" said Alexandra. "So let's use that one. The Guardians are smart, so there must be a logic to the numbers. They have to be grouped. So we take the numbers closest to the one we want, and that should take us closer."

"If you say so," said Darwen, shrugging.

"You know," said Alexandra, setting the dial and pulling a lever. "Sumners is right. You suck at math."

"Thanks," said Darwen as the gateway started to hum and flicker.

"You're welcome," said Alexandra, taking his hand. "Three, two, one . . ."

And they stepped through.

THE
FOREST

It took five more gates to get them to the forest, but Alexandra's theory was right. They might have done it in three, but one was faulty, and they had to make a detour through a desert of gray windswept sand where there was nothing to see in any direction beyond the cluster of portals. When they were ready to enter the forest, Alexandra asked Darwen if he had wound the screen device.

"Of course," he answered, but he checked to be sure. He didn't know what would be awaiting them on the other side, but he knew it wouldn't be good. "Keep your eyes open for Moth," he added, then took a deep breath, and stepped through.

For a moment, Darwen just stared.

"No," he whispered. "It can't be."

There was almost nothing left of the forest. Everywhere he looked the trees had been cut down and burned. A great shaft had been carved into the hill and Darwen could hear the ringing and clanking of heavy machinery deep underground. A system of steel cables ran down the shaft, and as he watched in horror, great metal scoops came winching up and out, full of what looked like coal. The scoops traveled through the remains of the forest to a huge machine that belched thick brown smoke from massive brick chimneys. The whole woodland hung with a bitter fog. The leaves and branches that had not been cut down were coated with soot, and there were pools of spilled oil everywhere. In one of them, floating face down was a tiny dellfey, her wings broken, her body smeared black. She had drowned in the filth.

"Oh no," said Alexandra.

Darwen's heart caught. He stooped to the little figure and turned her over with one finger. It wasn't Moth. But as Darwen looked, he lost all hope of seeing her here.

Where before there had been trees as far as the eyes could see, there was now only the hill surrounded by the wall of gray mist, which was almost at the perimeter path. The world was tightening like tidal water closing over a sandcastle. Soon there would be nothing left, though perhaps that was not so terrible, not now that the scrobblers had ravaged the woods.

The hillside was covered in coils of wire, serpentine pipes, and thick cables, so that the forest floor looked like it was awash with huge black snakes. They trailed between the coal plant with its chimneys, the batteries below, and the generator into which the stolen items from the school had been fed. They snaked out not just to Darwen's mirror, but to points all over the forest where new gateways were being constructed.

"We can't stop this," said Alexandra. "It's too much."

"We have to," said Darwen. "Look."

He pointed down to the first of the iron gates and shivered. The place was alive with scrobblers—dozens of them, maybe hundreds—and not just scrobblers. There were gnashers and other creatures for which Darwen had no name, some small like the flittercrake he had followed through the mall, some as big as elephants. And at the center of it all was something that glided through the trees like a man in a long pale robe.

They had seen this being before, at the station the night they had encountered the Jenkinses. Darwen stared at the figure, feeling something cold gathering in his belly, a deep and powerful dread.

"That," he said, quite sure, "is their leader."

Alexandra didn't argue. She looked and she nodded, her eyes wide. A huge gnasher lumbered past, its shark mouth slobbering. Darwen checked the screen device. If it failed them now . . .

"What are the scrobblers carrying?" asked Alexandra.

The scrobblers were different from those they had seen before. They wore crudely shaped armor that made them look even bigger than usual and face-concealing helmets like welders' masks, and many of them were standing quite still.

Soldiers, thought Darwen.

They were all wearing a device like an oversized rucksack on their backs connected by a piece of wire or hose to what looked like a gun, which they held in their hands. The packs were studded with dials and switches like those on the generator.

"They look like flamethrowers," said Darwen. "But I'll bet they shoot . . . I don't know. Power? Electricity?"

"Fantastic," said Alexandra, deadpan. "So where are they going?"

"Good question," said Darwen.

"While you think on that one," said Alexandra, "let's fry that gate."

The scrobblers didn't exactly tidy up after themselves.

The tools and materials of their work were scattered all over the hillside, and it didn't take long for Darwen to find two lengthy coils of wire wrapped with insulating fabric. With Alexandra cradling the screen device, Darwen led the way down to the generator. A whole new podlike structure the size of a small submarine had been added next to the power outlets. Cables sprouted from ports all down a central panel, held in place by screws with milled rims, but not all the ports were occupied. Alexandra stood on her tiptoes and checked the switches.

"I think these are off," she said. "Plug in here."

"You *think* they're off?" said Darwen.

"What am I, an expert on scrobbler technology?" she hissed.

Darwen swallowed, then closed his eyes and stuck two ends of the cable into the empty ports. When nothing happened, he tightened the screws.

"Er . . . Darwen?" said Alexandra. Her voice was odd, uncertain but clearly scared.

"What?" said Darwen, turning.

"What is that?"

She was staring at the new podlike structure attached to the generator. It was iron and riveted, and had a single large hatch with a pane of thick glass. Darwen, still holding the cables, moved closer and peered over her shoulder.

"We don't have time . . ." he began, but his voice dried up.

The pod was dimly lit inside and the heavy glass distorted the view, but he could see the curiously small seats, the restraining straps and the metal headpieces with their cables.

"It looks like an execution chamber," said Darwen.

"Like electric chairs," Alexandra agreed. "This just keeps getting better. Newly refurbished death room: seats ten. No waiting."

She was trying to be flip because she was rattled.

"I don't think it's an execution room," said Darwen. "Or at least, that's not its main function."

"The chairs are so small," said Alexandra. "Come on. We need to hook these cables up."

She turned away and started heading back up the hill.

"Wait!" said Darwen, stumbling after her. She still had the screen device. He hurried up after her.

The wire was heavy but as Darwen spooled it out behind him it got more manageable. In a few minutes they were back at the top and studying the Guardians' gates for somewhere to plug in.

"Come on," said Darwen, who was tiring with the weight of cable coiled over his shoulder. "We don't have much time."

"I'm trying," said Alexandra, "but I can hardly see through this smoke. Wait! Here. I think we have to disconnect one of these . . ."

There was a popping sound and the thin hum coming from the gate stalled and died.

"Okay," she said, "pass me the cable ends."

Darwen did so, reaching into the smog. She took the cables from him and a moment later said simply, "Done. Now to turn it on."

They retraced their steps to the generator with the little pod of tiny seats.

"Hold on," said Darwen grasping the circular handle of the hatch on the side. "I have to see this."

"Darwen, no!" hissed Alexandra. "It's too dangerous."

But Darwen was already half in.

It was even more like a submarine on the inside: all bolted iron and exposed cable. Darwen sat in one of the little seats and looked for controls that would confirm his suspicions. He picked up the metal headpiece with its trailing wires and was studying it when he caught movement through the porthole window. He saw Alex's stricken face, her eyes wide, and her body rigid, and behind her he saw why.

A massive scrobbler, jaws lolling, greenish muscle flexing was standing inches behind her. It was adjusting the controls on the outside of the machine and didn't seem to know she was there, but if it moved a foot to its left, or if she was unable to stifle her sob of terror . . .

Darwen sat up, staring through the oily window,

mouthing silently at Alexandra—"It's okay. Don't move"—as she clenched her eyes shut and prayed for it to be over.

The scrobbler worked for another few seconds then, apparently satisfied, turned to walk away. But as he did so, his red eyes rested on the open hatch and, with casual might, he reached out a long taloned arm and slammed it shut.

Darwen gasped, like he was in the grip of a Shade, and for a second he didn't realize just what was happening. The scrobbler did, however. It paused in its lumbering walk and turned back to the machine.

The chamber had started to hum. Indeed, the entire apparatus seemed to be throbbing with energy. Lights came on outside. A circuit popped with a shower of sparks. The equipment was coming to life.

What was stranger still, though, was that Darwen felt none of the panic he would have expected. Instead he felt weary and miserable. He wanted nothing more than to curl up right where he was and go to sleep. He slumped into his seat as if the very life was draining from him and with it went all joy, all conviction, all hope. So what if the scrobblers got through to his world? It wasn't like he could do anything about it anyway.

His eyelids felt heavy, but as they started to droop, he caught Alexandra's face at the window, heard her fist drumming on the glass, and realized she was pointing at him.

No. Not at him. At his hands.

Darwen looked down and realized he was still holding the metal headpiece with the wires. He wondered vaguely what it was and why it seemed to pulse with electricity. Alex was still pounding on the window, and behind her he could see the scrobbler staring in. Others were coming. Something must be happening . . .

He dropped the headpiece.

Instantly the light faded and the throb of power stopped. His head cleared a little and he realized that the scrobbler was unlatching the door.

Alex's eyes had opened again and they were wider than ever. In the last second he wondered if he was close enough to the screen device Alex was holding, and thrust his back to the window, as the great green fist of the scrobbler reached inside.

Darwen could tell from the way the splayed fingers felt around that the scrobbler couldn't see him, though its huge head was mashed up against the window, goggles chinking and scraping on the glass. Darwen shrank away. The hatch was too small for him to squeeze through undetected. He was trapped. He could hear other scrobblers coming. They wanted to know why the generator had suddenly come to life.

Because Darwen understood it now. He probably wouldn't live long enough to do anything with the knowledge, but he understood the terrible purpose of the submarine-like chamber with its little chairs and its cables. If the scrobblers could get power from things that kids treasured, this was the next logical—and horrible—step: sucking energy from the kids themselves.

The green fist was reaching toward him. Another few inches and it would have him, invisible or not.

And then he saw what was, in comparison, a small dark hand reaching in.

Alex!

Very carefully it opened, and set something down on the metal floor of the pod-chamber, then it snatched itself away. Darwen stared.

Alex had given him the screen device. He could see its little wheels spinning, see its glow. But what was the point of that? The scrobbler was about to touch him. The screen device wouldn't protect him. Unless . . .

He reached out and grabbed it at the same moment that he heard a bellow of recognition from outside. The massive green claw that was sweeping the air in front of his face became still then was yanked out, leaving the hatch open.

Darwen didn't wait. He rolled and scrambled out of the hatch, clutching the screen device, and dropped to the forest floor in time to see Alexandra streaking through the forest with half a dozen scrobblers on her tail.

Darwen knew what he had to do, but it still took all his strength to tear his eyes away. He forced himself to find the controls where they had plugged in the cables, climbed up the outside of the machine, and took hold of the main lever. He took a breath and pulled it.

Instantly there was a pulse of light, a throb of energy from the generator and then an explosion at the top of the hill. Darwen jumped down as the cables surged with life, and glimpsed a blaze of blue light arcing between the gates at the top, before they emitted a single, violent flare of yellow and went dark. All around the woods there came pops and flashes as other pieces of equipment malfunctioned and shut down.

Then Darwen was running, scanning the shattered woods for Alexandra. She was, it seemed, the only other thing still moving. The explosion had stopped the gnashers and scrobblers in their pursuit, and she had taken the opportunity to change course. She was making for the mirror, which was larger than ever before, stretched by a web of metal arms and cables. Between them and the mirror was an army of scrobblers, most of which were coming their way.

But unless Darwen was touching her when she reached it, the portal would be no better than a wall. . . .

He sprinted toward her, holding out the screen so that it would cover her the moment they were close enough, but in doing so he realized that the little device was smoking. It had been overloaded by the explosion. The scrobblers could see him too.

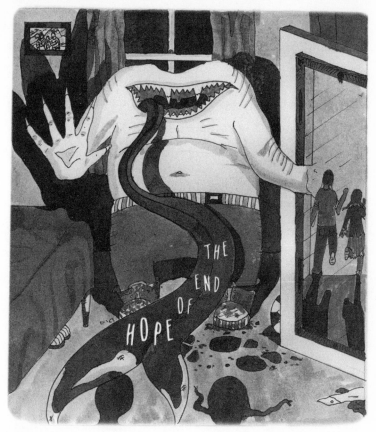

He ran, and the scrobblers came after him. Some had been converging on the generator to see what had gone wrong with it, but then the ghostly drifting figure in the pale, smoky robes pointed at Darwen and emitted a terrible, keening scream. It was an awful sound, high and desperate and full of hatred.

One of the scrobblers turned and aimed the weapon he wore on his back, and there was a sudden white flash. A jet like lightning came forking out of the nozzle and

Darwen threw himself to the ground as the bolt sizzled through the darkness overhead. A tree stump only yards from him exploded in a blue-white flare and Darwen, who was already scrambling to his feet, was showered with fragments of burning wood.

Out of the corner of his eye he saw Alexandra dodging and weaving, leaping over tree stumps like a gazelle and rolling as two then three other scrobblers blasted at her with their weapons. Behind her a tree caught fire, and another kicked backward, dropping huge boughs, one of which caught a scrobbler and pinned it to the ground. Darwen grabbed a rock and flung it hard at the nearest scrobbler, which was resetting its weapon. The stone hit the creature on the side of the head and it stopped, momentarily stunned. In the second or so before it regained its senses, Darwen was past it and sprinting down.

He could see the mirror now, glittering through the smoke. A gnasher was bounding toward him, running on all fours, its knuckles turned back like an ape's, and its headless body gaping with teeth. He tried to sidestep it, but the thing was too fast and strong and it grabbed at him with one clawlike hand and tried to shove him toward its terrible jaws. For a moment Darwen saw the rows of flat, curving teeth and the gaping throat beyond, and then he was kicking his way free. The monster lost its grip and fell awkwardly as Darwen dashed for the mirror.

He was almost there when he realized that the hooded figure was not giving chase. Instead it had drifted to the generator and was doing something. There was a great rattle and a tearing sound and the cables around the mirror flexed.

It was doing something to the mirror, but what? A terrible possibility dawned on Darwen. Perhaps the scrobblers had learned how to seal the mirror, trap him and Alexandra there with them.

He ran harder than ever but Alexandra still beat him to it. She sidestepped a gnasher, then turned back to Darwen, hand outstretched in desperation. Stumbling with exhaustion he reached for her, and as the gnasher bounded after them, they threw themselves at the mirror.

They were through.

And then, even as he was picking himself up from his bedroom floor, meeting Alexandra's wide, terrified eyes, he realized what the hooded figure had done, realized it because at that moment the gnasher that had been chasing him came right through the mirror after them.

For a moment he could do nothing but stare in horror at the monster that thundered into his little room with its books and pictures and scattered clothes. Alexandra screamed, which was so unlike her that it was almost as terrifying as the monster itself, which stood inches from

Darwen's bed. Her cry caught the blind gnasher's attention and it turned on her, its long, flat-tipped tongue probing the air for information. Alexandra flattened herself up against the wall with the window and the monster climbed up onto the bed, poised to spring. Its tongue was reaching toward her, inch by inch. Through the horror of the moment, a single thought struck Darwen to make it worse:

There will be more.

This one had been closest, but others would follow. He had only one choice.

He seized his cricket bat from under the bed and charged the gnasher, head down, and roaring as if he was one of them. He caught the thing off balance and unprepared so that it went sprawling back, toppling off the bed, and backward. For a moment it teetered, ready to fall anywhere, and Darwen charged it, ignoring the flailing claws and the savage red mouth with its rows of teeth. He hit it with his shoulder as Rich had hit him when they were playing American football, and it fell back, rolling through the mirror and into the forest.

Then Darwen, without a second's hesitation, seeing the drifting figure and a half dozen scrobblers only feet away, swung the bat against the mirror frame. He hit first one side and then, when one corner of the frame kicked out of joint with an electric spark, another. The scrobblers were right at the mirror, almost close enough to reach through, when the second part of the frame tore out of place. Darwen swung the bat once more, like he was thwacking a cricket ball over the boundary, and the frame collapsed. There was a rippling of the air between him and the forest, and then the mirror glass was visible as it slipped out of the frame and fell to the floor.

There was a deafening crash and the mirror smashed into a million pieces.

Alexandra stared.

"Isn't that . . . seven years bad luck?" she said.

Darwen thought back over what Mr. Peregrine had said about breaking mirrors, about how sometimes it jammed the portal shut and sometimes it jammed it open.

"I suppose we're about to find out," he said. "Though if it's bad luck, we won't have anything like seven years to put up with it."

Alexandra stood very slowly, and together they stared at the closet door with the twisted, broken remains of the mirror frame. Seconds passed. Then a minute. Then there was a sudden shrill beeping.

They both jumped. It took a second for Alexandra to realize that it was her cell phone. She snatched it up and stared at the display. It was glowing with a greenish radiance that—with a pang of guilt and sorrow—reminded Darwen of Moth. She raised it cautiously to her ear and pushed a button.

"Hello?" she said.

Darwen watched her face as her eyes widened.

"Rich!" she exclaimed. "How are you calling . . . ? But, what happened . . . ? Yes, but we barely made it back."

She listened for a moment then said, "okay," and hung up. Her eyes strayed to the mirror, but there was no sign of joy that the portal was jammed closed.

"Well?" said Darwen, hopeless.

"It worked," said Alexandra. "But only kind of. Mr. Peregrine is awake and they were able to modify their communication system to call me, which is pretty cool when you think about it. . . ."

"But . . . ?" Darwen prompted.

"But . . ." She hesitated and looked down.

"Alex," said Darwen. "Tell me."

"They—the Guardians—can't help," she said in a low, deadened voice quite unlike herself. "It's too late. They can't do anything to disrupt the scrobblers' power supply, so the scrobblers are going to break through into our world. I guess we weren't fast enough," she said, staring blankly at the phone in her hand. "And guess where the gate will open up?"

"Hillside," said Darwen.

"Bingo," said Alexandra. "Oh, and Rich gave Mr. P your note."

Darwen looked up.

"And?"

"He said 'no.'"

Darwen slumped onto the bed, his head lowered. He suddenly felt more tired, more drained than he had ever felt before. After all they had achieved, everything they had done, they had lost after all.

"What was the question?" asked Alexandra, settling beside him cautiously. "What did you write on the note for Mr. Peregrine?"

For a long moment Darwen didn't speak, and when he did his voice was low and unsteady.

"I asked him if this was why my parents died," said Darwen. "If they had been Guardians or gatekeepers or something and a part of all this. I guess not. I guess they just . . . died. No secret. No reason. Just a stupid road accident."

The weight of what he was saying hit him and tears started to his eyes.

"I'm sorry, Darwen," said Alexandra. "Really I am. But you don't have time for this right now. We have to get to school."

"You go," said Darwen, thinking of the blasted forest, of how he had failed Moth, of the sucking despair he had felt inside the generator pod. "I . . . I can't."

Ever since they had stepped into what remained of the

once lovely wooded hill, Darwen had felt a sense of defeat stealing over him. He had been unable to stop the scrobblers from destroying Moth's world, and he would be unable to stop them destroying his. It was only a matter of luck that he hadn't already let them into his own room. Soon they would be pouring through—at Hillside and who knew where else—led by a lethal army that would sweep all resistance away. What could a couple of kids do against that?

And what was the point of trying?

People were going to die, but people always died. That was just how it was. They weren't heroic sacrifices or principled defiance. They didn't mean anything. They were just deaths, random as dice, as car wrecks. People died and they left you.

Darwen took the photo album from under his pillow, threw it hard against the wall, and lay on the bed face down.

"**W**ait," said Alexandra, standing up and giving him a baffled look. "What do you mean you're not coming?"

Darwen lay there, his knees drawn up to his chest.

"I'm talking to you!" shouted Alexandra.

"I heard you," said Darwen.

"So?"

"You saw those things," said Darwen. "The scrobbler soldiers and the rest. What can I do about that?"

"Maybe nothing," said Alexandra. "But that doesn't

mean you don't try."

"It's over, Alex! Remember the forest? That was Moth's world . . ."

"What about *my* world, Darwen?" Alexandra shouted. "*Our* world. Our families and friends! The people we don't even know who have no idea what is about to come walking out of the night. What about them? Heck, what about the kids we hate? They're snotty and snide and full of themselves so we decide we'll do nothing while they get blown to pieces? They make fun of your accent so you're happy to sit by as they get carried off and locked in that pod thing where the scrobblers will suck the life out of them to fuel their machines? That's what it does, right? It drains the energy from kids to power the scrobblers' machines. That's how they plan to power their invasion."

Darwen looked away.

"Oh, you don't like me *saying* it?" Alex bellowed. "Like that's worse than what it's going to do? It's going to kill children. It's going to do it slowly, and when it's done the scrobblers will feed a new set of kids into it and start all over again. You okay with that, Darwen?"

"Of course not," said Darwen sitting up. "But what can I do? I'm just a kid."

"You're a kid," said Alexandra. "There is no *just* about it. Only adults say *just a kid* and what the heck do they know about anything? Have you looked at *their* world lately? And you're not an ordinary kid, Darwen. You're a mirroculist. You saw the flittercrake. You went through the mirror. You saved Mr. Peregrine. Me and Rich helped out, but this is your show, man. We need you."

"I'm not special," said Darwen, with certainty. "I'm not destined to save the planet. I don't believe in any of that stuff."

"Fine," said Alexandra. "But the Halloween Hop is about to get all kinds of scary, and of the three people in the world who know that, *you're* the one who knows more about what is coming through that portal than anyone. You're the only one who can get us through the gates if necessary. So save the pity party for later. You're not only coming, you're going to lead."

For a long moment, Darwen just looked at her, and something in her eyes—her fire, her faith in him—got under his skin and into his heart. He took a long breath. He stood up, and nodded, very small. He stared at the photo album, which had fallen open in the corner.

"Pictures of your family?" said Alexandra.

Darwen nodded, his lips tight.

"Bring it," said Alexandra.

He shook his head.

"They *left* me, Alex," he managed. "They might not have meant to, but they did. I have to forget about them. I already have."

Alex scowled.

"That pen of yours," she said. "The one you have to keep filling up with ink instead of buying a two dollar ballpoint like everyone else."

Darwen's hand reached for his pocket instinctively.

"What about it?" he said, defiant, though he avoided her eyes.

"Come on, Darwen," Alex pressed. "Where did you get it?"

"It was a present, okay?" he said, snatching it out of his pocket as if he was going to throw it as he had thrown the photo album. His eyes were bright again, and his voice came through clenched teeth. "It was my dad's," he said. "He gave it to me for my first day at school. It's old and it doesn't write very well and I have to keep filling it from a bottle, and the ink always smudges and . . ."

"And you love it," said Alex.

Darwen hung his head in silence. His shoulders quivered.

"You can't *not* care about them," she said, picking up the photo album and thrusting it into his hand. "They're a part of you."

Darwen nodded again, eyes still lowered, and at the same instant he heard the front door. His aunt was home.

"Come on," said Alex, leading the way into the kitchen. "And bring the album."

His aunt was shrugging out of her coat and kicking off her pumps. She jumped when she saw Darwen.

"You frightened me half to death!" she exclaimed. "What are you doing here? I thought you were staying at school for the dance. Are you okay? You look . . ."

"Came home for some stuff," he said, snapping on a smile. "Any chance you could give us a ride back over?"

"Well, I just got in," said his aunt, sounding weary and checking her watch. "I can make you a cup of tea if you like . . ."

"We really need to go," Darwen cut in.

"Now?" said his aunt.

"Things are about to start," said Darwen. "We have to be there. Pretty much now."

His aunt started to say something but caught the seriousness in his eyes and stopped herself.

"Okay," she said, as if not quite believing she was agreeing to this. "Let's go."

They didn't say much in the car, and when Darwen's aunt got monosyllables even from Alexandra to her inquiries about the Halloween Hop, she stopped asking. The driveway up to Hillside was almost completely dark, especially under the shadows of the ancient cedars. The parking lot in front of the main building was full of cars and the school windows blazed with inviting yellowish light, but Darwen felt only dread.

Alexandra's phone rang before they had parked. It was Rich, and he was shouting so loudly that his first question—"Where are you?"—was audible to the whole car.

"Someone's excited that you're coming," Aunt Honoria remarked to Darwen with a smile that was supposed to be encouraging but was marked by more uncertainty.

"I think the parents are all having drinks with the staff upstairs," said Darwen.

"The kids have to go outside," said Alexandra, with a significant look at Darwen.

"Not to the gym?" said Darwen's aunt. "I'm sure the e-mail from school said . . ."

"We have to go to the gym later," said Alexandra. "But Rich said we have to go outside first. To where the archaeology club has been working."

She gave Darwen another meaningful stare.

"That's right," said Darwen. "You can drop us here and we'll meet up with you later."

They were out and running before his aunt had a chance to respond.

There were no lights on in the grounds, and the school's erratic roofs and whimsical tower showed black against the night sky. They could see people in classrooms and corridors dressed up for the occasion, but knew they were invisible to those inside. It was a weird feeling, like being in another world, peering at people who didn't know you existed.

"There," said Alexandra.

Up ahead they saw a feeble flashlight: Rich waving frantically. He was standing only yards from the blue tarp that covered their dig site, his bandaged leg still bloody. The tarp drew Darwen's gaze so he didn't see the gate till Rich shone his light on it.

It was vast, at least twelve feet high and wide, made of the same black iron and cables as the scrobbler machines. It looked like it had been bolted together in sections, and its dials and levers were far simpler than anything they had seen anywhere in Silbrica: this gate went to only one place—the ravaged forest where Moth had once lived— and no one in their right mind would ever want to go there.

"Now what?" said Alexandra.

"We smash it," said Darwen.

"You sure?" asked Rich. "Mr. Peregrine said he didn't know how long it would be before the scrobblers got it online. He doesn't understand the power they are using . . ."

"So it's our call," said Darwen. "And I say we smash it, and fast."

Alexandra and Rich looked at each other quickly, then nodded.

"We're going to need tools," said Darwen. "But I don't think we can risk going into the janitor's basement. The scrobblers were using the stove down there and someone might have been working with them on this side. You still have that utility knife on you?"

Rich pulled it from his pocket.

"I usually leave it in my locker," he said, sheepish. "Not really supposed to have it on school grounds."

"Are you serious?" said Alexandra. "We got the hosts of hell about to come marching through this door here and you're worried about breaking school rules?"

"Does it have pliers on it?" asked Darwen.

Rich nodded and snapped them out.

"See if you can loosen those bolts," said Darwen, "while I find a rock to smash those gauges. I don't know if anything we do here will stop them coming through but we have to try. Alex, help me find something heavy."

Darwen bent down, and something whistled over his head and shattered against the edge of the gate, showering dust and grit all over.

"What the . . . ?" Rich shouted.

Darwen straightened up, rubbing fragments of hard clay from his hair and looked around. Over by the gym he saw dancing flashlights flicking over the ground. They were held by three boys.

"Nathan," said Darwen. "And they have our trebuchet."

"Perfect," said Alexandra.

"Just ignore them," said Rich, his voice straining as he tried to unscrew one of the bolts. "This is way more import . . . Ouch!"

A hunk of hard clay caught him on the side of the head and broke apart. As Rich clutched his ear, a howl of laughter came from Nathan and his friends. Darwen didn't need light to know he was with Chip and Barry. He picked up the largest chunk of the clay and thumped it against one of the dials, but it crumbled in his hand.

"Try this," said Alexandra. She had found one of the rocks they had dug out of the square under the tarp.

Darwen gripped it carefully and pounded it against the dial twice. The first hit cracked it. The second shattered the glass. Another clay missile from the catapult whistled overhead but Darwen ignored it. He rammed the rock home twice more till the needle inside broke off and the mechanism buckled, but he had no idea if he was doing any real damage to the gate's workings.

"They're coming over," said Alexandra, gazing off into the darkness by the gym.

"These bolts are too tight," said Rich. "I can't shift them."

"Do you have any wire cutters on that thing?" asked Darwen, refusing to turn toward the approaching boys. "You could cut these cables."

"What if they're live?" asked Rich.

Darwen thought furiously. Any moment now the gate could open and the scrobbler army could start pouring through. . . .

"I don't know," he said. "Can you insulate the handles?"

"I'll try," said Rich.

Alexandra had picked up a branch and was whacking at the lever mechanism. It didn't sound like it was doing much.

"Smashing up school property now, eh, Arkwright?" said Nathan, striding out of the dark. "I can't wait to see what kind of trouble this gets you into."

"Go away, Nathan," said Darwen, barely looking at him. "For your own good: get out of here."

"Is that a threat, English boy?" scoffed Nathan, clearly delighted. He and the other two boys were dressed as vampires, with long black capes, slicked back hair, and white makeup on their faces. They wore plastic fangs and had little dribbles of red at the corners of their mouths. "What do you think, Chip?" he went on. "You think the loser gang just threatened us?"

"Boy," said Chip. "I hope so. It's time we taught these cretins a lesson."

"You need to go," said Alexandra. "Any moment now . . ."

"Our parents are going to get here," Darwen cut in, finally turning to face them, and shooting Alexandra a look. "They're meeting us here. So if I were you . . ."

"Your parents, Arkwright?" sneered Nathan. "That would be a trick."

"My aunt then," said Darwen. His grip on the rock in his hand tightened.

"Ooh," said Barry with mock terror. "His aunt is coming. Whatever will we do?"

Chip snickered his machine-gun laugh, and Barry started making stupid faces that were, Darwen supposed, intended to look like someone's aunt. Nathan smiled, but he was watching Darwen and the others closely.

"What are you doing?" he demanded suddenly. "What is this thing? It wasn't here yesterday. Did you build it? Why are you trying to smash it?"

"You'd never believe us if we told you," said Darwen.

"I got one wire cut," said Rich. He sounded breathless with relief that he hadn't been electrocuted.

"Let me see that," said Nathan, stepping up to the gate.

"I'm telling you," said Darwen sticking out an arm and catching Nathan in the chest. "You don't want to get close . . ."

There was a sudden silence. Barry and Chip were staring with anticipation.

"I told you, Arkwright," said Nathan, turning furious on him, "that if you touched me again . . ."

He pushed Darwen backward.

"I don't have time for this," Darwen muttered. "Go away, Nathan. I'm not kidding. Tomorrow we can . . ."

"Tomorrow?" said Nathan, shoving Darwen again, harder this time, so that he almost lost his balance. "What's wrong with now?"

"I'm telling you," he shouted, getting into Nathan's face and pushing him back, "to get OUT of here . . ."

He should have expected Nathan's punch, but it was so dark and he was so angry and anxious that he missed it. It caught him just above his left eye, a hard, stinging blow that drove all other thoughts out of him. Darwen felt his head kick backward where it hit the metal frame of the gate with a clang. For a moment it was like lightning had struck in his brain, and then the pain shouted in his ear and his blood raged. He threw himself at Nathan, swinging wildly.

He was barely aware of Chip and Barry wading in, of Rich reaching with his big hands and trying to haul them off, of Alexandra flailing madly at Barry so that he yelled out with surprise and pain. But in seconds it was over. Something else happened and they had stopped. Darwen wondered why Nathan's face had started to flash with blue light, and then he heard the brief *woo* of a siren.

A police car had pulled up on the edge of the grass. One cop was climbing out, and the other was strolling toward them, his big bright flashlight picking them out of the darkness.

"Hold it right there," said the cop.

Darwen knew the voice. It was Officer Perkins.

"I said, hold it!" repeated the policeman who had started trotting slowly toward them. Darwen turned to find Nathan, Chip, and Barry bolting away into the darkened grounds.

"You three!" roared the cop. "Stay right there now. Oh . . . " he added, his voice almost amused. "It's you."

The light held Darwen's face.

"You want to tell me what you think you're doing out here?" said Perkins. "The dance is inside. And this looks a lot like criminal damage. You kids are going to have to come with me."

"We can't!" Rich blurted. "We have to stay here. This . . . thing . . . It's not supposed to be here."

"Yeah," said Darwen. "It has to be taken down and moved inside. In pieces. It's . . . er . . . "

"For the dance," said Alexandra. "Part of the scenery. It has to go on the stage."

"That's not what I was told," said the cop. "The principal reported kids out in the grounds."

"Check with the janitor," said Rich. "Mr. Jasinski. He'll tell you."

"You're gonna have to come with me," said Officer Perkins, unmoved. "I'm sorry about your uncle and all," he added to Darwen, "but that's no excuse for . . ."

"I'll take it from here, officer," said a voice behind them.

Out of the darkness came the large, waddling form of Miss Murray. She was dressed in a tight teal-colored suit with a matching purse that seemed to glow in the policeman's flashlight. She was smiling widely.

"Halloween pranks?" she remarked.

"Well, ma'am," Perkins said, "I'm afraid it might be a bit more than that."

"Well," she said, still smiling, "these are my students and this is a school matter."

"There were some others," said the policeman, pointing, "but they made their escape in that direction."

"I'm aware of that," she said, laying an arm on his shoulder and turning him gently back toward his car.

"School matter or not," the cop persisted, "if there's criminal activity, I should really file a report . . ."

"That won't be necessary," Miss Murray countered.

"Ma'am, with all due respect," said the policeman, "that's not your call."

"I appreciate your help," returned the teacher, "but as I said, I will take it from here. If you wish to come back tomorrow to make your report . . ."

"Ma'am," said the cop. "I don't think you understand . . ."

"I understand perfectly," said Miss Murray, and her

smile was now fixed and her eyes hard. "And I don't care. I want you off these grounds immediately."

Darwen, who had been staring at this bizarre exchange risked a glance at Rich and Alexandra. They gave him wide-eyed looks. What was going on?

"Ma'am," said the policeman, lowering his voice slightly, "I realize that you think you are doing the best thing for these kids, but I'm here to tell you that you cannot order an officer of the law off school property if said officer has reason to believe that some sort of crime has been . . ."

She stopped him by raising her hands in surrender.

"Fine," she said, fumbling in her purse. "Don't say I didn't warn you."

And she pulled out a metal box the size of a cell phone on which a tiny red light glowed. She pressed a button and the light went green. Immediately, the gate flashed and shimmered. Darwen, Rich, and Alexandra threw themselves on the ground as a great mechanical roar erupted from the gate.

And suddenly it wasn't just a metal frame standing on the school grounds. It was a doorway onto a familiar stretch of blasted forest, and beyond it—marching purposefully three abreast—was a wall of armored scrobblers with lamps on their helmets.

"What the . . . ?" began the policeman.

"Officer Perkins," said Miss Murray turning with the first real smile they had ever seen on her face toward the scrobblers. "Welcome to Hillside."

And they came through.

the trebuchet

Officer Perkins took a step backward, then reached for his gun without taking his eyes off the gate and what was coming through it. His other hand pulled the radio on his shirtfront closer to his mouth, but as he started to speak the first scrobbler pressed a button on the pack on his back and a wave of energy pulsed out, rippling as far as the school.

All the flashlights went out with a series of pops. The police car's lights burst and other parts of the car snapped like firecrackers. Officer Perkins's radio crackled and died with a puff of smoke. The gun, which was still in its holster, fired into the ground, each round in the clip exploding, so that the policeman unfastened the belt and cast the holster away like it was hot.

Darwen stared. Every electrical circuit in range—as well as the bullets in the policeman's gun—had just blown.

The next scrobbler aimed his weapon at the police car just as the other officer jumped back, and fired. There was a lethal arc of blue-white energy and the vehicle exploded.

The cop started to run toward the school building. Out of the sudden silence came a single serene voice:

"Good evening, children," said Miss Murray, smiling evenly. "Ready to work?"

"Run!" shouted Darwen.

They didn't need telling. Alexandra was sprinting in the direction that Nathan had gone. Rich went the opposite way, limping toward the trees and the mall. One of the scrobblers aimed at his back and fired.

The grounds were lit by the flash, like lightning strobing overhead, and then one of the great cedars burst into flame. Rich kept running.

"Don't shoot the children!" roared Miss Murray. "Catch them!"

As she said it two huge motorbikes came roaring

through the gates, each covered in pipes and steam vents, each with a sidecar holding a burly scrobbler with a net. Behind them came gnashers, some with tools that they put to use on the damaged portal, some dragging wheeled cages. Then came something huge, which had to squeeze itself through the gate, something with rope-like hair that hung over its face and claws a foot long that reminded Darwen of the terrible gouge marks in the walls of Mr. Peregrine's shop. Last of all came a familiar hooded fig-ure, gliding slowly through the gate to survey the chaos.

In a fraction of a second, Darwen took it all in, then ran after Alexandra.

"That way!" shouted Miss Murray behind him.

One of the motorbikes came lurching after them. The other went for Rich. Darwen ran across the grass of the sports fields, but he could see little beyond what showed in the juddering headlamp of the bike pursuing him. So it was with considerable surprise that he realized that Alex-andra was in front of him and no longer running. Instead she was bending over something, straining, working . . .

The trebuchet!

He realized just in time, leaping aside as a huge clod of sun baked clay, hard as a brick, came hurtling toward him. It shot past his head and hit the motorbike rider square in the chest, sending it tumbling backward out of the saddle, the bike veering wildly to the side.

"Nice shot," said Darwen, as the scrobbler with the net leapt from the sidecar.

"You haven't seen anything yet," said Alexandra, cranking the counterweight back into position and fitting another clump of earth in the sling. There was a pile of cut clay chunks beside the catapult. Nathan and his friends had obviously been planning to spend the entire evening shooting at whomever came into range.

"That's too soft," said Darwen, eyeing the clay whose sides were silvery slick. "It won't stop them."

"I know," said Alexandra, unhooking one of her trademark skull earrings and pushing it into the orange earth. "But this will."

She loaded up the clod and squatted down, squinting through the trebuchet like a sniper. The scrobbler from the sidecar was coming, net poised. Alexandra waited for a second. Then another. The monster was almost on top of them. It raised the net.

She fired.

The clay hit the creature wetly in the face. It clawed at the muck, though it kept coming, and for a second that felt like ten, it looked like it was still going to reach them. Then they saw a red burn starting to spread along its jaw. The scrobbler halted, pawing wildly at the spot, which was now blazing white like Rich's magnesium ribbon. A terrible, brutal sound came from it, an unearthly scream full of anger and hatred, but then the creature's whole head was ablaze, its body, its arms and legs. The sound rose to a piercing wail, and then there was a burst of pale light. Then nothing. Where the scrobbler had been was only a smoking patch of scorched grass.

Darwen gaped and turned to Alexandra.

"How . . . ?" he began.

"Like antimatter, right?" said Alexandra. "I loved those earrings."

"Tell me you have about a hundred of them," said Darwen, as one of the scrobblers fired and something exploded.

"'Fraid not," she said, loading up another handful of clay and studding it with her other earring.

Five scrobblers were coming toward them, weapons raised, masks lowered, and moving with alarming speed. With them came the hulking thing with the claws, its massive lumbering strides eating up the ground. Miss Murray was directing them, and behind her hung the hooded figure, which was sliding evenly over the ground.

"I don't think this will work if I can't hit skin," she said. "We should probably run."

"They're too fast," said Darwen.

"So what do we do?"

She gave him a desperate look. Darwen's mind was racing.

"Those packs on their backs aren't generators, right?" he said.

"More like receivers," said Alexandra. "Why? Come on Darwen. They're almost on us."

She fired the trebuchet again catching the massive beast on one bare shoulder.

"That's for Mr. Peregrine!" she shouted.

The creature roared once and vaporized, but the scrobblers came on undaunted.

"If the power is coming from their generator on the other side," Darwen was babbling, "then they must all be linked."

"So?" shouted Alexandra. "Darwen, they are almost . . ."

"So if we could override one, blow its circuits or something, it might blow all of them."

"And how are we going to do that?"

Darwen thought desperately. The five scrobblers were starting to spread out, encircling them. A pair of gnashers was behind them, unfurling a large net of metal cables.

"I don't know," he admitted.

Alexandra turned to him with horror and a sudden, wrenching sadness. Her eyes welled up with tears and she did nothing. She was still standing there just looking at him, when the net was tossed over them.

They were caught.

Two of the scrobblers scooped them up wordlessly and dragged them back toward the gate where the cages had been set up. Rich was already inside, holding his bandaged leg.

Darwen and Alexandra were stuffed roughly in and the door slammed. One of the scrobblers stood over them as the others returned to the hunt. Miss Murray turned from the hooded figure and leered at them.

"Nice of you to join us, children," she said. "We're going to put you to all kinds of good use."

"You are not a good teacher!" exclaimed Alexandra, as the woman strode away.

"You have a gift for understatement," said Rich to Alexandra. He smiled sadly and patted her hand.

"I'll get her with a good one later," she said.

For a moment no one spoke. All around the school grounds, there were distant shouts and explosions, but where the three of them were it was suddenly quiet.

"I'm sorry," said Darwen.

He had cuts on his hands and face and his ribs ached from the way he had been thrust into the cage, but the pain didn't bother him.

"I never meant for any of this to happen," he said. "Maybe if I had never gone through the mirror in the first place . . ."

"They would have come anyway," said Rich.

"Maybe not here," said Darwen.

"Remember the dig?" said Rich. "They were always going to come back here."

"Anyway," said Darwen, brushing all that aside. "I'm sorry."

"We're not done yet," said Alexandra. "Tell Rich your plan."

"Plan?" said Darwen, wearily. "What plan?"

"The one about reversing the current on their backpacks so they'll all blow up," said Alexandra.

"How?" said Rich.

"I don't know," said Darwen. "It was just an idea."

"We'd need power from the Guardians," said Rich. "And it would have to be massive. They won't be able to produce it yet, and I don't know how we'd get it out here anyway . . ."

"It was just an idea," said Darwen. He suddenly felt exhausted and incapable of thought.

"Course, we might not have to reverse their current so much as overload it," said Rich, musingly.

"How?" said Alexandra.

"I'm not sure," said Rich, whispering, though the scrobbler on guard seemed not to be paying attention. "They are fuelled by some kind of reaction between Silbrica and its opposite, our world, right? Matter and antimatter."

"All the things they don't have or value," said Alexandra.

"You should have seen what happened when I stuck one of them with my earring. Could we stick something like that into their backpacks? There are outlets, see?" she said, nodding at the scrobbler guarding their cage.

The scrobbler had turned his back on them and Darwen could see that she was right. At the base of the backpack, which hummed with energy, and surrounded by little red and green lights, were electrical sockets. He could probably just about reach them if he really stretched. . . .

"I think that would just boost their power," said Rich. "We need something that would completely overwhelm their system, a rush of energy that would feed back and blow all their circuits."

"Such as?" said Alexandra.

"No idea," said Rich.

"Antimatter," said Darwen.

"I'll hop over to Geneva," said Rich.

"Not literal antimatter," said Darwen. "Just whatever is the scrobblers' opposite."

"And that is?" said Alexandra, gripping the bars of the cage.

"What did Moth say?" said Darwen. "The scrobblers are destroyers. Haters. They don't trust, they don't imagine, and most of all, they don't love. Give me your knife."

Rich stared at him and Alexandra's eyes widened.

"What?" said Alexandra.

"Love?" said Rich. "That's nuts."

"No," said Darwen. "It's not. That's what the scrobblers don't get. That's their opposite, their antimatter, so that's our weapon. Now give me the knife."

Rich did so, but he looked unconvinced, even annoyed.

"Soooo, we tell the scrobblers we love them?" said Alexandra, looking skeptical. "I don't think I can make that play."

"No," said Darwen, unfolding the longest blade. "Close your eyes. Think about your families. Think about your friends. Think about everything you have ever loved."

"Darwen, this is crazy!" said Rich. "They're going to put us in a microwave that seats ten and you want me to think about *love?*"

"Look at that, Rich," said Darwen, as another arc of lightning went coursing across the school grounds and ended in an explosion. "That power is made from things we touched, things we valued. It's been twisted around, but it's a power that comes from love."

"This isn't science, Darwen!" Rich protested.

"Just do it," hissed Darwen. "You can't rely on science here."

"Science is power!" Rich protested. "Science showed us how to use electricity to blow their system. . . ."

"Yes," agreed Darwen, speaking slowly and with a certainty he couldn't explain. "And it got us this far. But now we need a different kind of power. Trust me. Think about what you love. See it."

"Like my archaeological field guide?" said Rich, cautiously.

"That's a start," said Darwen. "But I mean the real stuff. Even the stuff you don't talk about because it hurts too much. The stuff you can barely even think about. Like your mom, Rich."

Rich gave him an accusing stare and he opened his mouth as if to shout something, but then he paused, and time seemed to stop. A long way off there was an explosion and the sound of someone screaming. Rich blinked, then nodded once.

"You too, Alex," said Darwen. "Think of the people you love. Your mom, your dad, even your baby sister . . ."

"I told you," she snapped, "I hate my . . ."

"You wouldn't see her fastened into that generator, would you?" Darwen said, his voice hard. This was no time for pretending. Alexandra stared at him, then shook her head. "You don't hate your sister, Alex," said Darwen. "You just don't want her to come between you and your mom. That's not about hate. It's about love, even if it's painful."

Alexandra looked away for a moment, her face squeezed tight and her eyes shining; then she blinked her tears away and nodded.

"I just liked it the way it used to be," she said.

"I know," said Darwen. "Me too. Rich?"

Rich avoided his eyes but he nodded in agreement.

"Ready?" said Darwen, setting the knife down in front of him.

"Ready."

They closed their eyes and Darwen reached for their hands. He took them in his and clasped them tight. Rich's hands were large and sweaty, Alexandra's slick with clay and powdered over with dirt.

Darwen thought of home, of England, of his old school, but that wasn't right. It felt too far away, like he was looking at a distant mountain through thick cloud. He thought of his new friends and felt something warmer, but there was still a space, a hollow that he had been ignoring for weeks, hoping that if he didn't look directly at it, it would eventually just fade away.

He looked at it.

He saw his parents' faces. Saw them laughing, heard them calling to him, chasing him round a ruined castle, his dad kicking him a ball and clapping, his mum reading to him, singing to him—though it had been years since she had done that. Tears flowed down his cheeks but suddenly, unexpectedly, he smiled. The memories broke his heart into pieces but they were good memories, and for the first time since his parents had died, he knew that he had to hold on to them.

Without opening his eyes, he put Alexandra's hand on top of Rich's, then reached down for the knife with his free hand. He found it, picked it up and stretched back through the bars of the cage. Fumbling he brushed his fingers over the scrobbler's backpack, found the input port, and, with a surge of decision, thrust the blade in.

A wave of energy coursed through him. For a moment he could feel Alex and Rich, sense their thoughts, their feelings, as clearly as if they were his own. The energy seemed to pause as if unsure which way to go, and then it shot through them up into the scrobbler like water from a fire hose, a jet of undiluted power. He felt the mechanism strapped to the creature's back flood with it, then overflow.

The hum of the backpack rose in pitch and volume, and Darwen knew it was working. He opened his eyes and tried to pull the knife out of the port but it had welded itself in. He let go and pulled his hand back into the cage. Then he thrust Rich and Alex to the ground and turned to look up as the pack started to glow. The scrobbler was trying to wriggle out, but it was no good, and suddenly every scrobbler in sight was doing the same thing, squirming, reaching back, fumbling at controls as the packs turned from amber to red to a pinkish white.

"No!" roared Miss Murray. "Make it stop!"

But it was done.

Darwen looked away, his eyes closed, but he still felt the flash that went coursing through the scrobbler force, heard the explosions of their equipment. There was an almighty bang and the gate collapsed in on itself, and when Darwen opened his eyes, the scrobbler army had been utterly vaporized. Rich's utility knife fell to the ground and Darwen reached for it but it was inches too far away.

Only the hooded figure and Miss Murray remained. As the cloaked man gazed at the remains of the gate, screaming in a high terrible tone, like fingernails on a blackboard, Miss Murray came toward them.

"Open the cage!" hissed Darwen.

"It's jammed," said Rich, pushing at the door with all his strength. "It. Won't Move. Get the knife."

"I can't reach it," hissed Darwen, straining with every joint and muscle from his shoulder to the tips of his fingers. Alexandra joined him, pressing hard against the bars and stretching to where the utility tool lay.

"Nearly got it," she breathed. "Just another inch . . ."

"You three!" snarled Miss Murray, glaring at them and slapping Alexandra's hand away. "In all my years at Hillside, I have never encountered such disagreeable, meddling, impudent, disrespectful children."

As she spoke she leaned toward them and her face split open from forehead to chin. Snaking through it, sloughing off the teacher's body as it came, was something long and thick, something greenish with small beady red eyes and a long wide mouth full of teeth even more dreadful than the gnashers'.

"There is only one thing to do with children like you . . ." the thing that had been Miss Murray said as the body in its vivid suit collapsed empty on the ground. "Eat them."

The eel-monster gaped and pushed its muzzle up against the bars. Its nostrils flared as it inhaled their scent and then its head was pushing its way in. Rich and Alexandra squashed themselves as flat as they could against the rear of the cage, but the monster was already in and there was nowhere to run. Darwen stared, horror stricken.

"Good evening, children," croaked the eel-monster. "Ready to die?"

To Darwen's amazement, Alexandra punched it hard on the snout, knocking it out of the way so she could launch herself hard at the cage wall. She lunged with her arm through the bars and came up with the knife.

"Get it open!" she cried, thrusting the tool into Rich's hand and then squashing herself into the corner, as far from the eel-monster as she could get. It wasn't nearly far enough.

"You first, Miss O'Connor," it said.

Darwen gave Rich a wild look but the other boy, his face pink and damp from straining against the cage door, just shook his head.

"Can't," he managed. "It's stuck."

The eel-monster's face split into a terrible, saw-toothed grin and seemed to sigh with anticipation, but then—quite suddenly—she flinched first to one side, then to the other, as if avoiding a mosquito. She turned backward and as she moved Darwen saw that the night was alive with what looked like fireflies, tiny greenish lights flitting out of the smoking remains of the gate.

No. Not fireflies . . .

"Moth!" he yelled.

The dellfey whirred about the eel-monster's head and the beast thrashed with irritation. More were coming, diving at what had been Miss Murray like a squadron of tiny bombers in a hail of little lights. The monster roared and snapped at them, but the confusion bought Darwen the three seconds he needed to snatch the fountain pen from his pocket, unscrew the barrel with practiced fingers, and point the nib at the monster.

It turned on him and he thought he saw confusion in its face.

"My father gave me this," he said, defiant. "It's a terrible pen, but I love it."

He pushed the plunger as far as it would go and a jet of ink shot out of the tip, hitting the creature in the eye. It reared back with a shriek of pain, and Darwen thought he saw smoke where its right eye had been.

The eel-thing was not done with them, even if it was blind on one side. It lunged again. Darwen aimed the pen and pressed the plunger one more time, but the ink was gone and only a thin trickle issued from the nib. What had been Miss Murray gave a long, rasping gasp, which might have been a laugh, and slid in close enough to strike.

Alex pulled her hands in tight to her body as the monster's terrible teeth snapped at her. Darwen thrust his hand into his pocket.

"You wanted this," he said. "Remember?"

It was his photo album. He thrust it in front of him like a shield just as the monster lunged, and the book brushed its face leaving an angry red welt. The eel recoiled in pain.

"You said that meant nothing to you!" it gasped. "Just pictures, you said. You had moved on."

"Aye," said Darwen. "That was then."

And he swiped at the monster with the book. The creature whipped away again, as if scalded, and now *she* was trying to escape. Darwen pressed his attack, holding the album out in front of him. The creature hissed, then dived headfirst through the bars and out, dragging her scorched body after her.

At almost the same instant, Rich got the cage door open.

"Go!" he shouted.

In seconds they were out. The eel that had been Miss Murray was racing snakelike across the grounds toward the school, the hooded figure drifting along after it.

"What are they doing?" asked Alexandra. "Are they still going to try to take kids from the dance?"

"I don't think so," said Darwen. "Now they are just trying to get back."

"Moth!" said Darwen. "Can they get back through the gate you used?"

"No," she said. "The Guardians supplied their own gates with power and rerouted one to bring us here, but the enemy cannot use it. They will have to find another way back."

"The janitor's basement!" said Rich. "Quick!"

As Rich and Alexandra gave chase, Darwen smiled at the dellfey.

"Thanks," he said.

"You are welcome, Darwen Arkwright," said Moth. "You would have done the same for me. You did. Now go."

Darwen nodded and ran after the others.

The grounds were deserted. The burned-out police car sat smoldering on the edge of the grass, but the policemen themselves were nowhere to be seen. The school was still dark and Rich's flashlight was useless, so they slowed down to avoid tripping over the steps.

"We'll never catch them," said Rich.

"Yes we will," said Darwen, who was burning with a grim new determination. "Keep going."

They made it up to the lobby where a confusion of adult voices drifted down from the darkened halls above and the only thing visible was the pale statue of LEARNING. The corridors were deserted.

"This way!" said Rich.

He led them to the base of the clock tower in the quadrangle, but stuttered to a halt as he reached the steps. Someone was coming up.

Darwen ran to the front, brandishing the photo album.

"Hello there," said a familiar voice. "Looking for someone?"

It was Mr. Jasinski, the janitor, and he was holding an old-fashioned oil lamp.

"Oh," said Darwen, lowering the book. "We were looking for . . ."

"Shouldn't you be at the Hop?" said Mr. Jasinski, grinning. "Too dark for excavating now, Rich."

"Mr. Jasinski," said Rich, carefully. "Did you see two . . . er . . . people come down here?"

"Down here?" said the janitor. "No one but you and I come down here, Rich," he said, his eyes twinkling. "Come and have a look."

He stepped aside, and Rich led the way down. There

was no sign of anyone or—more importantly—*anything* in the basement room. Rich moved directly to the stove at the back and raised the sliding metal door. The room flooded with flickering blue-white light.

"Well I'll be!" exclaimed the janitor. "What is that, some kind of electrical fire?"

"It's a door," said Darwen.

"A door!?" said Mr. Jasinski. "To where?"

"Doesn't matter," said Rich. "We were too late. They got away."

"Well, I'm sorry you didn't find what you were looking for," said the janitor. "I'll get that fire looked at right away. You enjoy the Halloween Hop, you hear."

They nodded, caught between relief and disappointment.

"Well," said Alexandra. "I guess that's it."

"Not quite," said a voice from the shadows in front of them. Someone was blocking the stairs.

Alexandra grasped Darwen's hand and stood quite still. Very slowly, the figure in front of them stepped down into the light of the basement's lamp.

It was Mr. Peregrine and he was frowning.

Darwen had never been so pleased to see anyone in his life. He took a hurried step, ready to embrace the old man, but Mr. Peregrine stayed him with a gesture.

"One moment, please, Darwen," he said. "I have a little

business with your friend here."

Darwen followed his gaze to where the janitor stood. Mr. Jasinski was still holding the lamp high.

"Can I help you, sir?" he said.

"You can show yourself," said Mr. Peregrine.

"I'm sorry?" said the janitor.

"Er, Mr. P?" said Rich. "This is Mr. Jasinski. He's the school janitor."

"He isn't," said Mr. Peregrine, his eyes still fixed on the man with the lamp. "Are you, Greyling?"

"Greyling?" said Rich.

"Greyling was the twelfth member of the Guardian council," said Mr. Peregrine. "A brilliant young man who made the council faster than anyone in history. A man who saw me exiled and who—somehow—left the council some years ago to pursue plans of his own."

"You're mad," said Mr. Jasinski, setting the lamp on a chest of drawers. "I'm the janitor. Tell him, Rich."

"You're not," said Mr. Peregrine, his voice even and level as his eyes. "How long have you been planning this, breeding your army, building your machines, pushing into this world? How long have you been seeking the destruction of your own land and people?"

And suddenly the janitor was not there anymore. In his place was a tall, misty figure in a hooded robe. He didn't come out of Mr. Jasinski as the thing inside Miss Murray had. He just changed. One moment he was the janitor; then there was a shimmer of gray light, and he was there, hanging in the air. His voice changed too, winding out of the hooded robe as if it came from miles away.

"Long enough," he said.

Rich and Alexandra shrank away. Darwen stared.

"You!" he exclaimed. "All this time we thought you were helping us, but it was you working with that thing that called itself Miss Murray. You're the one who created the generator on the other side. You're the one who took the scrobbler bones from our dig."

"Couldn't have people asking questions about my servants, could I?" said the cloaked figure. "You talk of the destruction of my land and people," he said, turning on Mr. Peregrine, his tone thoughtful and cold. "My people? My people lack ambition. They are too content with old ideas, old powers. I see further."

"I hardly think that murder and enslavement is seeing further," said Mr. Peregrine. "And it is thanks to others who value life more than you do that you failed."

"Failed?" said the hooded figure called Greyling. "I think not. A setback, certainly. But all things can be remedied in time. And with regard to your little helpers, it might amuse you to know that were it not for your Squint, none of this would have happened."

Darwen stared at him.

"Me?" he said.

"You," said Greyling, and he reached into his robes and drew out a glass object the size of a matchbox. Inside it was something smaller still, a piece of red fabric embroidered with gold thread.

"That's my Manchester United badge!" Darwen exclaimed. "I dropped it when . . ."

The truth of it stopped him cold.

"Exactly," said Greyling. "You dropped it and my servants found it. It burned them, so they brought it to me for investigation and what did we find? Power. Such extraordinary potency drawn from your sad passions, your nostalgia, your worthless devotions. . . ."

"They are not worthless!" Darwen protested. "My dad gave me that badge."

"Quite," said Greyling, holding up the glass box. "I wanted you to know that if you had not dropped your sentimental trinket in the forest, none of this would have happened. It's all your fault, Darwen Arkwright."

For a second, it was like wrestling with a Shade. The room felt dark, silent and airless.

"Nonsense," said Mr. Peregrine. "The badge provided you with an opportunity, perhaps with an idea, but the responsibility for what followed is entirely yours. That is why you must come back with me and face the council."

Greyling laughed.

"I think not," he said, "and let us not bother to pretend that you could prevent me from killing you and your little friends right now."

"We will do more than pretend," said Mr. Peregrine, and from his pocket he produced a metal disk with a bright blue stone in the center. The disk was a fine filigree of brass wirework and the gem seemed to glow with a shifting light that reminded Darwen of the covered pool around which the Guardians sat.

"You know what this is," said Mr. Peregrine, "and the place to which it will bind you if you refuse to come with me."

Greyling became still, and though Darwen could still see nothing of his face, he sensed uncertainty in the hooded figure, even fear. The movement, when it came was breathtakingly fast. Greyling's pale hand swept from his robes and in it was a long, bright knife. He leaned and swept the tip of the blade precisely and deliberately not at Mr. Peregrine, who was too far away, but at Alexandra.

"No!" shouted Darwen.

The girl's eyes went wide and she clutched at the wound on her neck, but she said nothing as she slumped to the ground. Rich and Darwen stepped toward her, and as Mr. Peregrine reached out to break her fall, Greyling turned into a silvery vapor and shot back toward the stove, vanishing into the tiny portal as if sucked through from the other side.

"**I**'m sorry," said Alexandra.

Darwen felt like he couldn't breathe.

"It was my error," said Mr. Peregrine. "Let me see the wound."

Carefully he lifted her hand. The cut was small but quite deep, and it was bleeding heavily.

"Get help," said Mr. Peregrine.

Rich faltered for a second, then left the room at a run, barreling up the steps and shouting.

Mr. Peregrine looked up and his bright green eyes fell on Darwen's.

"How bad is it?" asked Darwen, taking her hand.

After all they had been through, he could not bear to think that Alexandra might not make it.

"It's a nasty cut, but not, I think, a fatal one," said Mr. Peregrine. "See? No arterial damage. It was a spiteful and selfish way for Greyling to effect his escape. I fear we should attribute her survival more to her luck than his mercy."

"Who is he?" asked Darwen, deliberately looking away from the wound.

"I thought I knew," said Mr. Peregrine. "But it seems I was wrong, as were the Guardians. And I'm afraid that, in one sense at least, Greyling was right. My people have become complacent and trapped in old ways. Their world changed around them and they did not see it until it was too late—did not see it, indeed, until roused by three children from another world, by one in particular. My world owes you a great deal, Darwen Arkwright."

Darwen looked down at Alexandra.

"He said it was all my fault," said Darwen. "I know it's not. Not really. But if I had never gone through the mirror in the first place . . ."

"Things would have been different," Mr. Peregrine said. "That is true. But different is not necessarily better, and you could not possibly have known what would transpire. Nothing which has happened should be near your conscience, and for what you have done since, the world—both our worlds—owes you a great deal."

"I thought you couldn't come back once you returned to Silbrica," he said.

"As a gatekeeper I could not," he said. "But after the destruction of the mirror shop, I was no longer a gatekeeper, and when I visited the chambers, I became briefly—thanks to you—a member of the Guardian council."

"But now you can go home," said Darwen.

"I could, yes," said Mr. Peregrine, thoughtfully. "It's a funny thing though, Darwen. I've been gone so long I'm not sure I really belong there anymore. It has changed too much, though it is possible that I have changed more. Perhaps you understand."

Darwen looked at him and for a moment he felt almost as old as the shopkeeper, as if the last weeks had actually been years, years crammed with experiences good and bad.

"Yes," he said. "I know. So, does that mean you will stay here, in our world?"

"I'm not sure yet," said Mr. Peregrine. "But I believe I might."

"Yeah!" whispered Alexandra, feebly.

"How do you feel?" asked Darwen, taking her hand.

"Like someone stuck a knife in my neck," said Alexandra. "I'll tell you what, I'm not done with that floaty cloak-wearing fool. That's for darn sure."

Mr. Peregrine smiled.

"I think she's going to be fine," he said.

They heard a clatter of footsteps and raised voices in the stairway, and then Rich burst in, leading Miss Harvey and Mr. Sumners.

"An ambulance is on its way," said Miss Harvey. "What happened?"

"An unfortunate accident," said Mr. Peregrine. "Nothing more. I am confident she will make a full recovery."

"And you are?" said Mr. Sumners.

"I am Darwen's uncle," said Mr. Peregrine. "In an adoptive kind of way."

"Are you indeed?" said Sumners, critically eyeing first Mr. Peregrine then Darwen. "I thought you might be, ahhh, involved in some way, Arkwright."

"Oh Darwen has been extraordinarily helpful," said Mr. Peregrine, beaming. "Without him, Hillside Academy would be little more than a smoking crater in the ground!"

Mr. Sumners's mouth fell open and he stared from one to the other, dumbstruck.

"The principal has people from the power company in

his office," said Miss Harvey, "but they aren't sure what caused the outage. Some sort of explosion, they said. It's a wonder people weren't killed. Is that how Alexandra got hurt?"

"More or less," said Mr. Peregrine. He gave Alexandra a reassuring smile. "Can you walk?"

She nodded.

Together, with the teachers trailing baffled in their wake, they made their way back to the quadrangle and through the corridors to the front entrance where they waited for the ambulance.

"Learning," remarked Alexandra, eyeing the sappy statue of the two kids gazing up at the teacher. "I guess this is the place for it after all."

The paramedics arrived and put Alex on a stretcher, and by the time they were wheeling her to the ambulance, her throat and shoulder strapped with a heavy dressing, she was talking like her old self, even though everyone told her not to. Staff and students—many of the latter still in what was left of their Halloween costumes—milled around the parking lot where the faculty had rounded up the few lanterns and flashlights that still worked. Two vans and a truck with flashing yellow lights were surrounded by power company employees, all of whom were trying to act professionally while looking completely bewildered.

"You need to get in," said one of the medics to Rich,

indicating his bandaged leg.

"It's just a flesh wound," said Rich with a stoic look.

"Get in," said the paramedic.

"I'm fine! Really!" said Rich, but the ambulance crew was having none of it. He was hoisted up and sat beside Alexandra, which, for some reason, seemed to amuse her.

Darwen stood next to the ambulance with Mr. Peregrine watching the hubbub of students being loaded hurriedly into cars and driven away. Some of the parents looked as rattled as the students, and though none of them knew even the beginning of what had happened, wild rumors had already started and some of the kids were quite hysterical. Barry Fails was confidently reporting that a bomb had gone off on the grounds.

"Good old Usually," said Alex. "Can always be relied upon to get it completely wrong."

The principal was running around looking anxious and making consoling noises, while one mother in particular—an elegantly dressed blonde with a sour face—was loudly demanding that someone explain "the manner of the evening's activities." Darwen was pleased to notice that when she was finished with her tirade, she turned to her expensive-looking car and gathered a shame-faced boy dressed as a vampire into her arms.

"Come on, Pookie," she said. "Let's leave this horrid place and get some ice cream."

It was Nathan Cloten. As their car pulled forward, Alexandra sat up and waved them off.

"Bye, Pookie," she called. "Don't hurry back."

At the same moment, Alexandra's mother came running down the steps. Darwen had only seen her that one time at dinner, and he would not have recognized her.

"My baby!" she wailed hysterically. "What happened to my baby?"

"Here we go," sighed Alexandra, lying down. "Tell her I'm in a coma or something," she said to the paramedics. "Scrobblers, gnashers, and eel-teachers I can handle. But my hysterical mother . . . ?"

"She's a little stressed out," said Darwen to the confused paramedic.

As her mother, sobbing wildly, clambered into the ambulance, Alexandra could be heard saying, "Why don't you leave me and take her?"

Then the doors were closing and the ambulance, lights splashing red over the cluttered parking lot, rolled off down the driveway and into the night.

"What will happen to Moth and the forest?" said Darwen in the sudden silence.

"The scrobblers have retreated," said Mr. Peregrine. "For now. The Guardians will have to direct vast amounts of energy if the forest is to return to its original state and that will take a long time, perhaps generations. Whether

Moth and her kind will stay there or move, I can't say."

"The forest is her home," said Darwen.

"True," said Mr. Peregrine. "And leaving home is hard, but people survive, even dellfeys."

There was another long silence broken only by the slamming of car doors.

"Was Alexandra right about Greyling?" asked Darwen suddenly. "That we're not done with him?"

"Well, Darwen," said Mr. Peregrine, "that remains to be seen. But it seems unlikely that we have heard the last of him. Hillside has been a point of weakness in the barrier between our worlds for many years, as you know, so we shall have to monitor the area closely. And this is not the only place where Greyling may attempt to open a gate."

"There are other places?"

"Oh, yes," said Mr. Peregrine. "Many. Places of ritual and power, places that the people of your world have known for centuries were somehow special. It may be here—the next attempt—but it may be in any number of other places, some of them far away. It could be that we will need the assistance of brave and capable souls in this world as well as that beyond the mirrors."

"And where will you find those souls?" asked Darwen.

Mr. Peregrine smiled and patted him on his shoulder.

"I believe I already have," he said.

"And Rich, right?"

"Naturally."

"And Alex?" said Darwen.

"I would hardly dare not include her," said Mr. Peregrine. "It is unfortunate," he added with a thoughtful smile, "that you and your friends have seen Silbrica only in crisis. Most of the time it is extraordinarily beautiful. I look forward to sharing it with you."

"So the Peregrine Pact lives on," said Darwen.

"The . . . ?"

"I'll tell you later," said Darwen. He had spotted his aunt bustling out of the main doors behind them.

"There you are, Darwen!" she exclaimed. "I was worried half to death. Such strange stories going around! People in costumes letting off fireworks and someone setting fire to a police car! Then little Alex getting hurt! Principal Thompson says that this is the last time Hillside hosts a Halloween party. He can't imagine what Miss Murray was thinking when she proposed it. Where have you been? Are you all right? Who . . . ?"

"I'm Mr. Octavius Peregrine," said Mr. Peregrine, standing and bowing courteously. "I have been helping Darwen and his friends in a consultancy capacity concerning their archaeological endeavors."

"Oh," said, Aunt Honoria, clearly impressed. "You run the mirror store that was burglarized."

"Tragically so," said Mr. Peregrine, smiling. "Though I fear my days as a shopkeeper are over."

"I'm sorry to hear that," said Darwen's aunt.

"It is no matter," said Mr. Peregrine. As soon as Honoria turned away, he added in a low, amused voice, "I believe there may be some local positions vacant."

There was a pause.

"For a janitor?" said Darwen, hardly daring to believe it.

"Or a teacher of world studies," said Mr. Peregrine with a half shrug. "I'm an expert on more than one world so that should give me an edge over the competition."

On the way home, Darwen's aunt took him to the hospital where Alex and Rich were being kept overnight for observation, though they had both been told they would make full recoveries and—so far as Darwen could tell—already had. While his aunt, who had been away from her e-mail for several hours (almost certainly a record) went to check in on some work issues, the three of them relived every moment of the day's events.

"And I'm not going to say I told you so about the teachers being aliens . . ." said Alex.

"One teacher," said Rich.

"That we know of," said Alex. "Anyway, I'm not going to make a big deal about the fact that I totally called that weeks ago. I'm not saying anything."

"I get the feeling you're not going to say it a lot," said Rich.

Darwen grinned.

"You know what though?" said Alex, suddenly, looking at Darwen. "I knew you'd save us. I just had a feeling. An intuition. Almost a premonition. No, an instinct. Yeah, an *instinct*."

"Alex," said Rich. "One word will do fine."

"Only if it's the right word," said Alex. "Instinct is right. I just knew it. That stuff you said, when we were in the cage, that stuff about love and memory: that was right on the money, man. I won't forget it."

Darwen flushed and looked down, but she took his hand, and Rich's, as they had in their darkest hour, and Darwen knew she was right. You had to remember this stuff, even if you never talked about it.

Darwen drove home with his aunt, silently studying each picture in the slightly scorched photo album by the light of the streetlamps.

"I was wondering if you would ever look at that," said Aunt Honoria. She paused, not looking at him, and finally added, "I miss them too."

Darwen looked at her. She was watching the road, her face tight with worry and focus.

"They would be glad," he said, "knowing that I'm here

with you, I mean: that you're looking after me."

She turned to him with a gasp, which was somehow both a laugh of delight and a sob, and her eyes brimmed with tears.

"Thank you, Darwen," she said.

"When we get home," he replied, "I'll make you a cup of tea: piping hot so it brews properly."

She nodded and wiped her eyes as Darwen's gaze returned to the photo album.

"You should treasure those pictures, Darwen," she said. "Never forget."

Darwen thought of the Guardians who had become trapped by their own past and the scrobblers who thought of nothing but controlling the future and, as he gazed at the faces in the photographs—faces, including his own, which he would never see again—he knew there had to be something in between.

"I won't," he said.

It was a promise, to her, to his parents, to his friends, and to himself.

THE END

ACKNOWLEDGMENTS

Special thanks to Paula Connelly, Mark de Castrique, and Melissa Thomson who read early drafts, to R.L. Stine who generously gave me notes, to Stacey Glick who found the right home for the book, to Brianne Mulligan, Ben Schrank, and Gillian Levinson who guided it into print, and to Emily Osborne who provided the illustrations. Thanks also to my family, always my first readers and my target audience.